Mediterranean Playboys

*They're sexy
They're dangerous
And they want you in their bed!*

from

LYNNE GRAHAM,
MICHELLE REID
& SUSAN STEPHENS

BILLIONAIRE
Heroes

Mediterranean Playboys

featuring

The Greek Tycoon's Convenient Mistress
LYNNE GRAHAM

The Purchased Wife
MICHELLE REID

The Spanish Billionaire's Mistress
SUSAN STEPHENS

| **DID YOU PURCHASE THIS BOOK WITHOUT A COVER?** |
| If you did, you should be aware it is **stolen property** as it was reported *unsold and destroyed* by a retailer. Neither the author nor the publisher has received any payment for this book. |

All the characters in this book have no existence outside the imagination of the author, and have no relation whatsoever to anyone bearing the same name or names. They are not even distantly inspired by any individual known or unknown to the author, and all the incidents are pure invention.

All Rights Reserved including the right of reproduction in whole or in part in any form. This edition is published by arrangement with Harlequin Enterprises II B.V./S.à.r.l. The text of this publication or any part thereof may not be reproduced or transmitted in any form or by any means, electronic or mechanical, including photocopying, recording, storage in an information retrieval system, or otherwise, without the written permission of the publisher.

This book is sold subject to the condition that it shall not, by way of trade or otherwise, be lent, resold, hired out or otherwise circulated without the prior consent of the publisher in any form of binding or cover other than that in which it is published and without a similar condition including this condition being imposed on the subsequent purchaser.

M&B™ and M&B™ with the Rose Device
are trademarks of the publisher.
Harlequin Mills & Boon Limited, Eton House,
18-24 Paradise Road, Richmond, Surrey TW9 1SR

BILLIONAIRE HEROES: MEDITERRANEAN PLAYBOYS
© by Harlequin Books S.A. 2008

The Greek Tycoon's Convenient Mistress, The Purchased Wife and
The Spanish Billionaire's Mistress were first published in
Great Britain in separate, single volumes.

The Greek Tycoon's Convenient Mistress © Lynne Graham 2004
The Purchased Wife © Michelle Reid 2005
The Spanish Billionaire's Mistress © Susan Stephens 2005

ISBN: 978 0 263 86686-5

024-0908

Printed and bound in Spain
by Litografía Rosés S.A., Barcelona

The Greek Tycoon's Convenient Mistress

LYNNE GRAHAM

Lynne Graham was born in Northern Ireland and has been a keen Mills & Boon reader since her teens. She is very happily married with an understanding husband, who has learned to cook since she started to write! Her five children keep her on her toes. She has a very large dog, which knocks everything over, a very small terrier which barks a lot, and two cats. When time allows, Lynne is a keen gardener.

Don't miss Lynne Graham's new novel,
The Greek Tycoon's Disobedient Bride,
**out in December 2008 from
Mills & Boon® Modern™!**

PROLOGUE

ANDREAS NICOLAIDIS kept a powerful grip on the steering wheel as his Ferrari Maranello threatened to skid on the icy, slippery surface of the country lane.

The rural landscape of fields and trees was swathed in a heavy mantle of unblemished white snow. There was no other traffic. On a day when the police were advising people to stay at home and avoid the hazardous conditions, Andreas was relishing the challenge to his driving skills. Although he owned a legendary collection of luxury cars he rarely got the chance to drive himself anywhere. In addition, he might have no idea where he was but he was wholly unconcerned by that reality. He remained confident that he would at any moment strike a route that would intersect with the motorway, which would enable his swift return to London and what he saw as civilisation.

But then, Andreas had always cherished exceptionally high expectations of life. He led an exceedingly smooth and well-organised existence. To date every annoyance and discomfort that had afflicted him had been easily dispelled by a large injection of cash. And money was anything but a problem.

It was true that the Nicolaidis family fortunes, originally founded in shipping, had been suffering from falling profits by the time Andreas had become a teenager. Even so, his conservative relatives had been aghast when he'd refused to follow in his father's and

5

his grandfather's footsteps and had chosen instead to become a financier. In the years that had followed, however, their murmurs of disquiet had swelled to an awed chorus of appreciation as Andreas had soared to meteoric heights of success. Now often asked to advise governments on investment, Andreas was, at the age of thirty-four, not only worshipped like a golden idol by his family, but also staggeringly wealthy and a committed workaholic.

On a more personal front, no woman had held his interest longer than three months and many struggled to reach even that milestone. His powerful libido and emotions were safely in the control of his lethally cold and clever intellect. His father, however, had been on the brink of marrying his fourth wife. His parent's unhappy habit of falling in love with ever more unsuitable women had exasperated Andreas. He did not suffer from the same propensity. Indeed the media had on more than one occasion called Andreas heartless for his brutally cool dealings with the opposite sex. Proud of his rational and self-disciplined mind, Andreas had once made a shortlist of the ten essential qualifications that would have to be met before he would even consider a woman as a potential life partner. No woman had ever met his criteria…no woman had even come close.

Hope curled her frozen hands into the sleeves of her grey raincoat and stamped feet that were already numb.

She was hopelessly lost and there was nobody to ask for the directions that she needed to find the nearest main road. Pessimism was, however, foreign to Hope's nature. Long years of leading a very restricted life had taught her that a negative outlook lowered her spirits and brought no benefits. She was a great believer in looking on the bright side. So, although she was lost, Hope was convinced that a car containing a charitable driver would soon appear and help her to rediscover her bearings. It didn't matter that the day she had already endured would have reduced a less tolerant personality to screaming frustration and despondency. She knew that nothing could be gained from tearing herself up over things that she could not change. Yet it was hard even for her to forget the high hopes with which she had left home earlier that morning to travel to the interview she had been asked to attend.

Now, she felt very naive for having pinned so much importance to that one interview. Hadn't she been looking for a job for months? Wasn't she well aware of just how difficult it was to find employment of any duration or stability? Unfortunately she scored low when it came to the primary attributes demanded by employers. She had no qualifications in a world that seemed obsessed with the importance of exam results. Furthermore, hampered as she was by her lack of working experience, it was a challenge for her to provide even basic references.

Hope was twenty-eight years old and for more than a decade she had been a full-time carer. As far back as she could remember, her mother Susan had been a sick woman. Eventually her parents' marriage had broken down beneath the strain and her father had moved out. After a year or so, all contact had ceased. Her brother, Jonathan, who was ten years older, was an engineer. Having pursued his career abroad, he had only ever managed to make occasional visits home.

Now married and settled in New Zealand, the Jonathan who had flown in to sort out their late mother's estate a few months earlier had seemed almost like a stranger to his younger sister. But when her brother had learned that he was the sole beneficiary in the will, he had been so pleased that he had spoken frankly about his financial problems. In fact he had told Hope that the proceeds from the sale of his mother's small bungalow would be the equivalent of a lifebelt thrown to a drowning man. Conscious that her sibling had three young children to provide for, she had been relieved that their late mother's legacy would be put to such good use. Back then, she had been too ignorant of her own employment prospects to appreciate that it might be very hard for her to find either a job or alternative accommodation without a decent amount of cash in hand.

The silence of a landscape enclosed in snow was infiltrated by the distant throb of a car engine. Fearful that the vehicle might be travelling on some other road, Hope tensed and then brightened as the sound grew into a reassuring throaty roar and the car got audibly closer. Her generous pink mouth curved into a smile. Eyes blue as winter pansies sparkling, she moved away from the sparse shelter of the hedge to attract the driver's attention.

Andreas did not see the woman in the road until he rounded the corner and then there was no time to do anything but take instant avoiding action. The powerful sports model slewed across the road in a wild skid, spun round and ploughed back across the snowy verge to crash with a thunderous jolt into a tree. Ears reverberating from the horrible crunching complaint of ripping metal, Hope remained frozen to the same spot several feet away. Pale with disbelief and open-mouthed, she watched as the driver's door fell open and a tall black-haired male lurched out at speed. He moved as fast as his car, was her first embryonic thought.

'*Move!*' He launched at her, for the pungent smell of leaking fuel had alerted him to the danger. 'Get out of the way!'

As his fierce warning sliced through the layers of shock cocooning Hope, the car burst into flames and she began to stir, but not speedily enough to satisfy him. He grabbed her arm and dragged her down the road with him. Behind them the petrol tank ignited in a deafening explosion and the force of the blast flung her off her feet. A strong arm banded round her in an attempt to break her fall and as she went down he pinned her beneath him.

Winded, she just lay there, lungs squashed flat by his weight and struggling to breathe again while she reflected on the impressive fact that he had in all probability saved her life. She looked up into bronzed features and clashed with eyes the exotic flecked golden brown of polished tortoiseshell.

At some level she was conscious that her clothes had got very wet when she'd fallen, but the damage was done and it seemed much more important to recognise why those stunning eyes of his struck such a chord of familiarity with her. As a child she had visited a zoo where a splendid lion had been penned up behind bars, which he had fiercely hated and resented. Tawny eyes ablaze, defying all those who had dared to stare, he had prowled the limits of his humiliating cage with a heartbreaking dignity that had made her tender heart bleed.

'Are you hurt?' he asked in a dark, deep accented drawl that would have made her toes curl had she been able to feel them.

Slowly, carefully, she shook her head to express her continuing health. The fact that he was flattening her into a wet ditch was meaningless when she met those gorgeous eyes. She spread her visual net to appreciate the lush spiky black lashes that provided a fitting exotic frame for his deep-set gaze. He had a lean, hard-boned face that was angular and uncompromisingly male, yet possessed of such breathtaking intrinsic beauty that she could do nothing but stare.

Andreas looked down into the bluest eyes he had ever met. He was convinced they could not be naturally that bright turquoise colour and was equally suspicious of the spill of shiny pale blonde hair tumbling round her heart-shaped face like tangled silk. 'What the hell were you doing in the middle of the road?'

'Would you mind letting me up?' Hope mumbled apologetically.

With a stifled curse as he registered in rare embarrassment that he was still lying on top of the woman responsible for the death of his car, Andreas wrenched himself back from her. A faint tinge of colour demarcating his superb cheekbones as he questioned his own uncharacteristic loss of concentration, he sprang upright and reached down a lean, long-fingered hand to assist her. An unsought thought emerged out of nowhere: she had skin as smooth, soft and tempting as whipped cream.

'I wasn't in the middle of the road...I was scared you would drive on without seeing me,' Hope explained, wincing at the freezing chill of her clothing as she let him pull her upright. He was impossibly tall, so tall, she had to throw her head back on her shoulders to look up at him.

'You were standing in the centre of a very narrow road,' Andreas contradicted without hesitation. 'I had to swerve to avoid hitting you.'

Hope looked back down the road to where his car still smouldered. It was obvious even to her that when the last of the little flames died down, it would be a charred wreck fit only for the scrapyard. She could see that it had been a sports model of some kind and probably very expensive. That he appeared to be blaming her for the accident sent a current of guilty anxiety travelling through her.

'I'm really sorry about your car,' she said tautly, striving to sidestep the possibility of conflict. Having grown up in a family dominated by strong personalities, who had often been at loggerheads, she was accustomed to assuming the soothing role of a peacemaker.

Andreas surveyed the pathetic remains of his customised Ferrari, which he had only driven for the second time that day. He turned his arrogant dark head back to his companion and flicked his keen gaze over her at supersonic speed. He committed her every attribute to memory and dismissed her with every cold succeeding thought. Her clothes were drab and shabby. Of medium height, she was what his father would have called a healthy size and what any of his many female acquaintances who rejoiced in jutting bones would have called overweight. But no sooner had he reached that conclusion than he recalled how soft and feminine and sexy her full, ripe curves had felt under him and a startling spasm of pure, unvarnished lust arrowed through him at shattering speed.

'It's such a shame that you weren't able to avoid the tree,' Hope added, intending that as a sympathetic expression of regret.

'Avoiding *you* was my priority. Never mind the fact that, in the attempt, I could easily have killed myself,' Andreas countered with icy bite at what he interpreted as a veiled attack on his skill as a driver. Having dragged his attention from her, he had felt the heat of that startlingly inappropriate hunger subside as swiftly as it had arisen. He decided that the crash had temporarily deprived him of his wits and caused his libido to play a trick on his imagination: she had to be the least attractive woman he had ever met.

'But mercifully,' Hope bravely persisted in her efforts to offer comfort, 'we both have a lot to be grateful for—'

'Educate me on that score,' Andreas sliced back in an invitation that cracked like a whiplash.

'Sorry?' Hope prompted uncertainly, turquoise eyes locking to him in dismay.

'*Theos mou!* Explain exactly what you believe that I have to be grateful for at this moment in time,' Andreas demanded with derision, snowflakes beginning to encrust his cropped black hair as the fall grew heavier. 'I'm standing in a blizzard and I'm cold. It's getting dark. My favourite car has been obliterated from the face of the earth along with my mobile phone and I am stuck with a stranger.'

'But we're alive. Neither of us has been hurt,' Hope pointed out through chattering teeth, still keen as mustard to cheer him up.

He was stranded with Little Miss Sunshine, Andreas registered in disgust. 'May I make use of your mobile phone?'

'I'm sorry...I don't have one—'

'Then you must live nearby...how far is it to your home?' Andreas cut in, taking an impatient step forward.

'But I don't live round here,' she answered ruefully. 'I don't even know where I am.'

Ebony brows drawing together, Andreas frowned down at her as though she had confessed to something unbelievably stupid. 'How can that be?'

'I'm not a local,' Hope explained, trying to still a shiver and failing. 'I'm only in the area because I was attending an interview and I got a lift there. Then I started walking...I followed this signpost and I thought I couldn't be that far from the main road but I must have taken a wrong turn somewhere—'

'How long were you walking for?'

'A couple of hours and I haven't seen any houses for absolutely ages. That's why I didn't want you to drive past. I was getting a little concerned—'

Watching her shiver violently, Andreas noticed that her coat was dripping. 'When did you get wet?'

'There's a stream in that ditch,' she told him jerkily.

'How wet are you?'

Having established that she was soaked through to the skin, Andreas studied her with fulminating intensity, brilliant eyes flashing tawny. 'You should have said,' he censured. 'In sub-zero temperatures, you're liable to end up with hypothermia and I don't need the hassle.'

'I'm not going to be any hassle,' Hope swore hurriedly.

'I saw a barn a couple of fields back. You need shelter—'

'Really, I'll be fine. As soon as I start walking again, I'll warm up in no time,' Hope mumbled through fast-numbing lips, for of all things she hated to make the smallest nuisance of herself.

'You won't warm up until you get those clothes off,' Andreas asserted, planting a managing arm to her spine to urge her along at a pace faster than was comfortable for her much shorter legs.

Her lips were too numb for her to laugh at the very idea of getting her clothes off in the presence of a strange man. But she was tickled pink by his instant response to what he saw as an emergency. In a flash, he had abandoned all lament about his wrecked car and his own lack of comfort to put her needs first. At a similar speed he had found a solution to the problem and he was taking charge.

Wasn't that supposed to be a typically male response? Only it was not a response that was as common as popular report liked to suggest, Hope reflected thoughtfully. Neither her father nor her brother had been the least bit tempted to help her out by solving problems. In fact both the men in her life had beat a very fast retreat from the demands placed on them by her mother's long illness. She had been forced to accept that neither man was strong enough to cope with that challenge and that, as she *was* capable, there was no point blaming them for their weakness.

'What's your name?' she asked him. 'I'm Hope… Hope Evans.'

'Andreas,' Andreas delivered grimly, watching her attempt to climb a farm gate with incredulous eyes. With purposeful hands he lifted her down from her wobbly perch on the second bar so that he could unlatch the gate for their entry.

'Oh, thanks...' Wretched with cold as she was, Hope was breathless at having received that amount of attention and shaken that he had managed to lift her without apparent effort. But then she could not recall anyone trying to lift her after the age of ten. She would never forget, however, the cruel taunts she had earned at school for the generous bodily proportions that had been the exact opposite of the fashionable slenderness possessed by the most popular girls in her form.

As she lurched into a ditch by the hedge where the snow was lying in a dangerously deceptive drift Andreas hauled her back to his side. 'Watch where you walk...'

The numbness of her feet was making it well nigh impossible for her to judge where her steps fell. The natural stone building ahead seemed reassuringly close, however, and she tried to push herself on but stumbled again. Expelling his breath in an impatient hiss, Andreas bent down and lifted her up into his arms to trudge the last few yards.

Instantly, Hope exploded into embarrassed speech. 'Put me down, for goodness' sake...you'll strain yourself! I'm far too heavy—'

'You're not and if you fall, you could easily break a limb,' Andreas pointed out.

'And you don't want the hassle,' Hope completed in a small voice as he lowered her to the beaten earth floor towards the back of the dim barn, which was open to the elements on the side closest to the road.

Before she could even guess what he was doing, Andreas tugged off her coat. Her suit jacket peeled off with it. 'My goodness!' she gasped, lurching back a step from him in consternation.

'When you get the rest off, you can use my coat for cover,' Andreas declared, shrugging broad shoulders free of the heavy wool overcoat and extending it with decisive hands.

Hot pink embarrassment washed colour to the roots of Hope's hair. Grasping the coat with reluctance, she hovered. She was too practical to continue questioning his assertion that she had to take off her sodden clothing.

'I'll get on with lighting a fire so that you can warm up,' Andreas pronounced, planning that he would then leave her ensconced while he sought out a house and a phone. He would get there a hell of a lot faster on his own.

There was a massive woodpile stacked against the wall. She stepped to the far side of it, rested his coat over the protruding logs and began with chilled hands to clumsily undress. Removing her trousers was a dreadful struggle because her fingers were numb and the fabric clung to her wet skin. She pulled off her heavy sweater with equal difficulty and then, shivering violently and clad only in a damp bra, panties and ankle boots, she dug her arms into his overcoat. The coat drowned her, reaching down to her ankles, hanging off her shoulders and masking her hands as though she were a child dressing up in adult clothes. The silk lining made her shiver but the very weight of the wool garment bore the promise of greater warmth. Wrapped in the capacious depths of his carefully buttoned coat, she crept back into view.

Andreas was industriously engaged in piling up small pieces of kindling wood with some larger chunks of fuel already stacked in readiness. Again she was impressed by the quiet speed and efficiency with which he got things done. He was resourceful. He didn't make a fuss. He didn't agonise over decisions and he didn't moan and whinge about the necessity either: he just did the job. She had definitely picked a winner to get stranded with in the snow.

She studied him, admiring the trendy cut of his luxuriant black hair, the sleek, smooth and undoubtedly very expensive tailoring of the charcoal-grey suit he wore teamed with a dark shirt and a silk tie. He looked like a high-flying business executive, a real urban sophisticate, the sort of guy she would have been too afraid even to speak to in normal circumstances.

'One small problem...I don't smoke,' he murmured.

'Oh...I can help there,' Hope recalled, hurriedly digging into her handbag and producing a cheap plastic lighter. 'I don't smoke either but I thought my future employer might and I didn't want to seem disapproving.'

As he waited for her to complete that rather intriguing explanation Andreas glanced up and registered in surprise that she was very far from being the least attractive woman he had ever met. In the dim interior, her pale blonde hair, now loose and falling almost to her shoulders, glowed like silver against the black upraised collar of his coat. Her cheeks were flushed, her eyes bright. She was smiling at him and when she smiled, her whole face lit up. Lost in the depths of his coat, she looked startlingly appealing.

'Here...' Hope extended the lighter.

'*Efharisto*...' Andreas thanked her gravely, mentally querying her unexpected pull for him. She was blonde and rather short and he went for tall, leggy brunettes.

'*Parakalo*...you're welcome,' Hope responded with a weak grin, striving to move her feet to instil a little feeling back into her toes. 'So, you're Greek?'

'Yes.' Protecting the minuscule blaze of wood shavings from the wind whistling through the cracks in the wall, Andreas fed the fire. She was virtually naked below his coat. It was that knowledge that was making her appear appealing to him, he told himself in exasperation. He resisted a foolish urge to look at her again. Why would he even *want* to look at her again?

'I love Greece...well, I've only been there once but it was really beautiful.' When her companion failed to grab that conversational opener, Hope added, 'You're used to lighting fires, aren't you?'

'No, as it happens,' Andreas remarked, dry as dust. 'But I don't need to be the equivalent of a rocket scientist to create a blaze.'

Hope reddened. 'I'm talking too much.'

Andreas told himself that he was glad that she had taken the hint. Yet when he looked up and saw the stoic look of accepting hurt in her face, he felt as though someone had kicked him hard in the stomach. When had he become so rude and insensitive?

'No. I'm a man of few words and you're good company,' he assured her.

She gave him a huge surprised smile and, blushing like a schoolgirl, she threaded her hands inside the sleeves of his over-large coat and shuffled her feet. 'Honestly?'

'Honestly,' Andreas murmured, taken aback by her

response to the mildest of compliments and involuntarily touched.

He coaxed the fire into slow life. She was so cold she was shivering without even being aware of it. As the fire crackled he sprang up to his full height of six feet four and approached her. 'There's a hip flask in the left pocket of my coat.'

Hope reached in and lifted it out.

'Take a drink before you freeze.'

'I'm not used to it...I couldn't—'

Andreas groaned out loud. Taking the flask from her, he opened it. 'Be sensible.'

Hope sipped and then grew bolder. When the alcohol raced like a leaping flame down her throat she choked, coughing and spluttering.

Closing the flask for her, Andreas surveyed her and rueful amusement tilted his wide, sensual mouth. 'You weren't joking when you said you weren't used to it.'

Hope sucked in a jerky breath and wrapped her arms round herself. 'I didn't know I could feel this cold,' she confided in a rush.

Andreas uncrossed her arms, closed lean, strong hands over hers and slowly drew her close. 'Think of me as a hot blanket,' he urged.

Her lashes fluttered in confusion. 'I don't think I could...'

'Try. It will be a while before the fire puts out enough heat to defrost you.'

Hope lifted wide eyes as turquoise as the Aegean Sea on a summer day. 'I suppose...' she mumbled.

'Do you wear coloured contact lenses?' Andreas enquired, black brows pleating because even as he spoke he questioned the inanity of his enquiry.

'You must be joking… I can't even afford make-up!' Hope's state of nerves was betrayed by the tiny jerk she gave as he eased her into physical connection with his tall, well-built body. All of a sudden her heart felt as if it were jumping inside her chest and she could hardly catch her breath.

'You have perfect skin…you don't need it,' Andreas said thickly, his big, powerful body growing rigid. Even the separation of their clothing could not dull his high-voltage awareness of the tantalising softness of her lush, feminine curves. In spite of his every effort to freeze his own all-too-male reactions, his libido was rocketing into overdrive.

That close he turned her bones to jelly and Hope couldn't think straight. She looked up and connected with his mesmerising dark golden eyes. A dulled heaviness gripped her lower limbs while a tight, hard knot of agonising tension formed in her pelvis. He lowered his handsome dark head and she guessed what was going to happen before it happened but still couldn't believe that he would actually do it.

But Andreas confounded her expectations and captured her mouth with hungry urgency. That single kiss devastated her and as it began, it continued, his tongue delving between her readily parted lips to demand greater intimacy. She was defenceless against that wild, sweet tide of sensation, for her body flared into sudden desperate life. The tense knot low in her stomach spiralled into a drugging flare of heat that suffused her entire body with explosive effect. Only the need to breathe conquered that wicked heat and she had to pull her swollen lips free to drag in a great gulp of oxygen.

Andreas gazed down at her with heavily lidded

dark eyes and then, abruptly, he yanked his head up and colour delineated his hard cheekbones. '*Theos mou*...I had no intention of...' His handsome mouth clenched. 'I should never have touched you. I'm sorry.'

'Are you married?' Hope demanded, voicing her worst fear instantaneously and only contriving to drag her hands from him as she finished speaking.

'No.'

'Engaged?' Hope was no longer cold. Her entire body felt as though it were hot as a furnace with embarrassment.

His ebony brows pleated. 'No.'

'Then there's no need to apologise,' Hope declared half under her breath, scrupulously avoiding his scrutiny while she struggled to get a grip on herself. The way he had made her feel had been a revelation to her and she felt incredibly vulnerable and confused. Her fingers clenched into the cuffs of the coat sleeves to prevent her hands from reaching back to him. She turned away in an awkward semi-circle, so many thoughts and emotions and physical feelings bombarding her that she felt momentarily overwhelmed.

Her first real kiss and he had apologised. It would be terribly uncool to confess that he had thrilled the socks off her and that if he wanted to do it again he was more than welcome. Her face flamed with guilt and bewilderment. For goodness' sake, where had that shameless thought come from? With hands that trembled she made herself concentrate long enough to pick up and drape her wet clothing over the pile of logs.

'I've upset you,' Andreas breathed.

Hope whirled round, turquoise eyes bright as pre-

cious stones in her flushed heart-shaped face. 'No...
I'm not upset.'

She felt a hundred things but not upset: shocked,
bemused and exhilarated by the sheer strength of her
response to him. For too many years she had lived in
a world empty of any form of excitement. Andreas
was the most exciting thing that had ever happened
to her and so great was her fascination that it hurt to
deny herself the pleasure of looking at him.

'I planned to leave you here alone,' Andreas
drawled flatly, still struggling to get a handle on his
own inexplicable behaviour and somewhat stunned by
his loss of control.

Startled, Hope whirled round. 'Why? Where were
you planning to go?'

'I intended to try and find a house but it's too dark
now.'

'And I have your coat. Much better to wait until
daylight.' Hope snatched in a stark breath of the icy
air while she gazed out at the fast-swirling snow being
blown about by the wind. It was no longer possible
to see even the hedges bounding the road.

She drew nearer to the fire and then knelt down
beside it to take advantage of the heat the flames were
beginning to generate.

'Tell me about your interview,' Andreas invited,
having noted that she would no longer meet his gaze
and determined to eradicate her unease. 'What was
the job?'

'The position of live-in companion to an elderly
woman but the interview never happened,' Hope confided ruefully. 'When I got to the house I found out
that a relative had moved in with the lady instead and
there was no longer a job available.'

'So these people didn't bother to cancel your interview and left you stranded?' Andreas queried with disapproval.

'I asked why I hadn't been contacted but the woman who spoke to me said it was nothing to do with her because she hadn't placed the ad in the first place.' Hope just shrugged and smiled wryly. 'That's life.'

'You are far too forgiving,' Andreas told her. 'Why did you want work of that nature?'

'I'm not qualified for anything else...at least, not at present.' Hope wanted a stable roof over her head and a period of steady employment before she checked out what she considered to be the much more remote and ambitious possibility of winning a place on a design course. 'I also need somewhere to live and it would've suited me very well. Where were you travelling?'

'I was heading back to London.'

'Why did you kiss me?'

It was hard to know which of them was most surprised by that very abrupt question: Hope, who had not known that she was about to embarrass herself by asking for clarification on that score, or Andreas, who had never been faced with such a bald demand to know his motivation before.

Dark golden eyes surveyed her steadily. 'Why do you think?'

Face hot again, Hope studied her tightly linked hands. 'I haven't a clue...I was just curious.'

'You're very sexy.'

Her lashes swept up on her astonished gaze. 'Are you serious?'

'I should know...I'm a connoisseur,' Andreas asserted without hesitation.

Her lush, full mouth curved into a grin, for she liked his frankness. So, he liked women and no doubt in large numbers. And why should he not? He was gorgeous and women had to fall for him in droves. Naturally he took advantage and who could blame him? If deep down a little twinge of pain stabbed at her that that should be so, she ignored it.

After all, she was much more interested in what Andreas had said prior to that final statement. It seemed like a miracle to her but he had called her sexy. Hope was used to thinking of herself as plain, overweight and ordinary. She had spent years hating her own body and longing to be thinner. To that end she had dieted and exercised and her weight had fluctuated up and down while the slender figure she craved continued to elude her. Even the mother she loved had sighed over her daughter's lack of looks and lamented her keen appetite.

Yet Andreas, who was heartbreakingly handsome, considered her attractive. And not only that...he thought she was sexy. Even better he had proven his own conviction by succumbing to charms she had not known she had. She reckoned that she was probably going to love him until the day she died for allowing her to feel just once like a young and pretty woman. She had waited what felt like half a lifetime to hear such words and had truly believed that she would die without ever hearing them. He was the fulfilment of a dream and she studied him with massive and grateful concentration.

'So what do you do for a living?' Hope asked chattily.

'I deal with investments.'

'I suppose you're stuck at a desk all the time study-ing figures and it's a bit boring. Still, somebody has to do it.' Her turquoise eyes were warm with sym-pathy.

Andreas got a high out of his immensely successful career but he had met far too many women who faked an interest in finance in an effort to impress him. Hope, he recognised, was not tempted in that direc-tion. His rare smile illuminated his lean bronzed fea-tures, which in repose could seem grave and cold.

'Would you like some chocolate?' she asked, root-ing round in her capacious bag and emerging with a giant bar and only then seeing that smile and riveted by it. He had buckets of charisma and she was en-trapped.

'Yes…before you melt it,' Andreas laughed, hun-kering down to reach for the bar, which she was hold-ing perilously close to the fire. He broke off a piece and let his brilliant gaze sweep from her clear bright eyes and the fascination she couldn't hide to the ripe curve of her lips. He remembered the intoxicating taste of her and the laughter left him to be replaced by a disturbingly strong desire to haul her back into his arms. He put the square of chocolate he had in-tended for himself into her mouth instead.

'Oh…' Hope gasped in surprise and closed her eyes in slow, blissful appreciation as the cold choc-olate began melting against her tongue.

Andreas was transfixed by the expression she wore. He could not take his attention from her. He won-dered if she would react like that to him in bed. He tried to kill the thought. He tried to suppress the powerful tide of hunger she ignited in him, but his usually disciplined libido was behaving like a runaway train.

Her lashes lifted. 'I would do just about anything for chocolate...'

Her voice faded away and her mouth ran dry on the glittering blaze she met in his intent golden eyes. On a level of understanding she had not even known she possessed she recognised his hunger and she leant forward without even thinking about what she was doing and sought his hard, sensual mouth again for herself. With a hungry growl, Andreas came down on his knees and kissed her until the blood drummed at an insane rate through her veins and her head swam.

'I'll buy you chocolate every day,' Andreas promised huskily.

'You know...I wasn't meaning anything provocative,' Hope warned him anxiously.

'I know.' Long fingers framed her cheekbones while his eyes devoured her. 'I find that straightforward streak of yours very refreshing.'

'Other people call me blunt—'

'Whatever, I don't meet with much of it,' Andreas admitted thickly, his hands not quite steady on her. 'I also want you so much it hurts to deny myself. That's a first for me.'

Hope felt utterly unlike herself. It was as though at that first kiss she had become an alien inside her own once familiar skin. She felt wild and greedy and joyous and as tempting as Cleopatra. All the years of stoically repressed regret at the manner in which life was passing her by, all the wistful longings and fanciful dreams that crowded out the fertile imagination she hid behind a front of no-nonsense practicality finally got to break free. Andreas was the embodiment of her every fantasy.

'A first for me too,' she confided breathlessly.

He unbuttoned the coat and then froze, a rare glint of confusion in the wondering appraisal he gave her. He had no grasp of quite how the situation had developed but he couldn't make himself let go of her. 'We have to be out of our minds—'

Hope closed her fingers into the lapels of his suit jacket. 'Shush...don't spoil it,' she whispered pleadingly.

Andreas spread her back against his coat and let his mouth glide down the length of her throat. 'Tell me when to stop...'

With no intention of calling a halt at any point, Hope shivered with delicious tension and lay there. She booted the misgivings struggling to be heard out of her mind and slammed shut the door on them for good measure. For twenty-eight years she had been good and just once, and for the space of one stolen, secret night, she was going to be bad and what was more she was going to enjoy it.

He unsnapped the lace bra and groaned out loud at the creamy swell of her pouting breasts in the firelight. 'You have a body to die for.'

Hot with a mix of self-consciousness and helpless longing, she opened her eyes to see if he was teasing: his appreciation spoke for him. With reverent hands he toyed with the tender pink peaks already straining into thrusting points. Deep down inside she felt as if she were burning and her hips shifted in a pointless effort to contain the feeling. Within very little time the whole world centred on him and what he was doing to her.

He employed his knowing mouth on the stiff crests that crowned her breasts and the inner thrum of her body's response became so powerful she could not stay still. Her entire skin surface felt unbearably sensitive but more than anything she was aware of the damp ache at the swollen heart of her.

'Andreas...' She sounded his name in a throaty, pleading purr and at last he touched her where she most needed to be touched.

Sensation electrified her and took her to a place she had never been before, where all that mattered was the sensual glory of his touch and the wildness that was being born within her. She writhed, wrapped herself round him, lost in the hot, male scent of his skin and hair and the enervating roughness of his hard, muscular body against her.

'I can't wait...' Andreas confessed rawly, passion breaking through his formidable control at a level of excitement he had never known before.

The sheer overload of physical pleasure had driven her to a tortured peak and she was helpless in the hold of the powerful craving that controlled her. He pulled her under him and she was with him every step of the way. With an earthy groan he sank into the slick, hot heat of her and met with unexpected resistance.

'You're a virgin?' he breathed in stark shock.

'Don't stop...' she gasped, reaching up to lock imprisoning arms round him.

He yielded and swept her through the sharp little pain into a fast, frantic rhythm as primal as the overpowering sensations that had taken her over. Intolerable excitement pushed her into ecstasy and a cocoon of pleasure. In the aftermath, she felt amazingly silly and happy and buoyant.

Andreas gazed at Hope with wondering golden eyes and then he gathered her very carefully back into the warmth of his coat and tugged her into his arms. He kissed her brow. 'You're very sweet...but you should have told me I'd be the first.'

'It was my business,' Hope muttered, burying her face into his shoulder, fighting off the shock of what she had just done.

'But now's it mine,' Andreas asserted, determined fingers tipping her chin up so that he could look at her again in the flickering light cast by the burning logs. 'I think that in the very near future you will decide to move to London and I will be your lover.'

'Why would I do that?' Hope dared to ask although sparkles of joy were running through her like precious gold dust.

His hard, sensual mouth slashed into a sudden smile of breathtaking assurance. 'Because I will ask you to and you won't be able to resist.'

Her heart was bouncing like a rubber ball inside her chest and she smiled up at him with all the natural warmth that was the very core of her character.

CHAPTER ONE

ALMOST two years later, Hope sat in a fashionable London café waiting for her friend Vanessa's arrival.

Her thoughts were miles away and centred entirely on Andreas. She was dreamily wondering how she could best celebrate the second anniversary of that first eventful meeting. By seeking out a snow-bound barn? That would not be a good idea, she conceded with a grin. Andreas disliked inconvenience, cold and, indeed, had a very low tolerance threshold for any form of discomfort.

'Sorry I'm late.' A slim redhead with sharp but attractive features and bright brown eyes sank down into the seat opposite and settled a heavy camera case down. 'If that hair of yours grows any longer,' she remarked, surveying the pale blonde hair Hope wore secured at her nape but which reached halfway to her waist, 'people are going to start wondering if you've got Rapunzel fantasies.'

Hope blinked. 'I beg your pardon?'

'You know...the lady in the fairy tale who got locked up in the tower and let her long hair down to be used as a ladder to rescue her,' Vanessa clarified. 'Only unfortunately for her, it wasn't the handsome prince who climbed up, it was the witch. Be warned.'

Hope laughed and they ordered coffee. She was accustomed to her more sophisticated friend's cynical outlook on life. The daughter of a famous artist, Vanessa had survived a Bohemian and unstable childhood to become a gifted photographer. But the red-head still bore the scars inflicted by parents who had enjoyed tempestuous love lives.

'So, how is *your* handsome prince?' Vanessa en-quired a tinge dryly.

Hope was impervious to that tone and her eyes sparkled. 'Andreas is great. Very busy, of course, but he phones me a lot when he's out of the country—'

'A mobile phone being Andreas's equivalent of a ball and chain,' her friend mocked. 'I seem to recall that if you switch it off he wants an explanation in triplicate.'

'He just likes to know where I am. He worries about me,' Hope countered equably. 'Do you realise that in ten days' time, Andreas and I will have been together for two whole years?'

'Wow. The guy who doesn't commit is going for gold. You could be making gossip column headlines. Of course,' Vanessa murmured wryly, 'the world would first have to know you existed and you remain a very well-kept secret.'

'Andreas hates media attention and he knows I wouldn't like it either. I'm a very contented secret,' Hope admitted, telling herself with the ease of long habit that what little time she had with Andreas would be very much diluted if she had to share him with a social whirl and lots of people as well. 'Right now, I'm trying to think of some special way to celebrate our anniversary.'

'Andreas didn't make the effort to mark the occa-sion last year, did he?'

'I doubt if it even occurred to him that we had been together an entire year. I shouldn't have sat around waiting for *him* to say or do something, I should just have reminded him,' Hope said ruefully

'Did he ever mention it afterwards?'

Hope shook her head.

'Then, let me offer you a piece of advice,' the younger woman remarked. 'If you want to hang onto Andreas Nicolaidis, resist the urge to celebrate your second anniversary in his presence.'

'But why?'

'The reminder that you've been around for two years might set the cold wind of change blowing.'

'What are you trying to say to me?' Hope prompted anxiously.

Vanessa compressed her lips and sighed. 'I just feel you're wasting your time with Andreas. He didn't even bother to show up the night you collected the top award for your design course.'

'His flight was delayed.'

'Was it?' The younger woman looked unimpressed. 'He has no interest in anything in your life unless it directly affects him.'

'Andreas isn't artistic...or into fashion. I don't expect him to take an interest in the handbags I design—'

'He hasn't introduced you to a single member of his family or to any of his friends. If he takes you out it's to some place where he won't be bothered by the paparazzi and where he won't be seen with you. He's kept his life separate from yours and he keeps you in a little restricted box. Why don't you face facts? You're his mistress in everything but name—'

'That's not true! Andreas doesn't keep me. I take nothing from him...OK, I live in that flat, but I pay all my own expenses and I don't accept expensive gifts or anything from him,' Hope reasoned in a low-pitched tone of urgency.

'But it's not a question of what *you* think, it's all about what Andreas thinks and how he treats you—'

'He cares about me...he treats me really well,' Hope argued tightly.

Vanessa gave her a concerned look but Hope felt far too raw to take comfort from a sympathy that could only further dent her pride. 'Why shouldn't he? You're devoted to him and he knows it and he uses it. He set the boundaries of your relationship way back at the beginning—'

'No...there were no rules set. I am not his mistress...I wouldn't *be* his mistress!' Hope stated in an almost fierce undertone.

'So he was too smooth an operator to put a label on it. Has he ever mentioned a future with you? Love? Marriage? Children?'

Battered down by those bold words, Hope almost flinched.

'You have a right to ask where things are going at any stage of a relationship,' Vanessa informed her and then she changed the subject.

Afterwards, Hope had no real idea what she had discussed with Vanessa beyond that point. She remembered having smiled a lot. She had been keen to reassure her closest friend that she was not offended by that blunt appraisal of her relationship with Andreas. But, in truth, those same comments had blown her peace of mind sky-high and caused her considerable pain. Vanessa's every word replayed again and again in Hope's troubled thoughts. She was devastated when she was forced to acknowledge that most of what the other woman had said had been based on unarguable fact rather than personal opinion.

Only hours earlier, Hope had felt supremely happy and perfectly contented with her life and with Andreas's central position within it. It had been Vanessa who had sowed discontent inside her. Yet she did not blame her friend. After all, Vanessa had only shown her a more disturbing interpretation of limitations that Hope had simply accepted. Slowly and painfully, Hope felt all the concerns that she had suppressed and all the questions she had never dared to ask Andreas rise like taunts to the surface of her mind.

Andreas had never taken her to Greece, although he knew that she longed to visit the country of his birth with him. Even though his one and only sibling, his younger sister, Elyssa, was married to an Englishman and lived in London, Andreas had not succumbed to Hope's gentle hints that she would like to meet Elyssa. Hope had always avoided dwelling on that omission and had told herself that in time Andreas would make that suggestion on his own account. In the same way, she had also convinced herself that she was unconcerned by her lack of contact with Andreas's family and friends. But he had never given her the option, had he?

It was equally true that Andreas had never been known to make a reference to the future as something they might share…at least not a future that extended further than a calendar month ahead in his highly organised schedule. Not once had he mentioned marriage or a desire for children. As for love, well, he was prone to making cutting comments on that topic and she had learned to avoid the subject.

Her eyes stung with a surge of rare tears as she entered the big penthouse apartment that had become her home. Andreas might be in no hurry to offer commitment, but that still did not mean that she was his mistress. *Did it?* By nature, Andreas was reserved and cautious. Another doubt crept in to make itself heard: how could she even tell herself that they lived together? In the strictest sense they did not because Andreas continued to own and make occasional use of another, even more substantial city property. He had pointed out that the apartment was a necessary convenience for him because it was a lot closer to his office than his town house. His relatives also stayed at the town house when they visited London, as did he when it suited him. Furthermore, Hope had never set foot inside the town house…

Suddenly, Hope was seeing the foundations of her happiness wash away like sand on a beach. She adored Andreas. She had truly believed that their relationship was wonderful and well worth cherishing. But Vanessa's frankly offered opinion had lacerated Hope's pride and destroyed her confidence. Was it possible that she had been wilfully blind rather than face the harsh, hurtful truth? Was it possible that, like the penthouse apartment, she was really just a convenience to Andreas too? A sexual rather than residential convenience?

The phone in the echoing reception hall was ringing. After a moment of hesitation, she picked up.

'Why has your mobile been switched off for three hours?' Andreas demanded. 'Where have you been?'

'I was meeting Vanessa and…er…shopping and I forgot to put it on again.' Hope crossed two sets of fingers as she told that small lie and swallowed hard.

'I'll be with you by eight tomorrow night. So, talk to me,' Andreas invited, because he had taken a break for coffee and he could always depend on her to fill the space with the minutiae of her daily existence. No matter where he was in the world, he could pick up the phone and within minutes her tide of chirpy chatter would filter away all stress and entertain him. Hope had been very well named. She never said anything bad about anyone. She went out of her way to do favours for total strangers. She put a positive spin on every experience.

Her mind was blank. 'What about?'

'Anything and everything…how clothes are shrinking in size to fuel the diet industry…the addictive quality of chocolate…what a lovely day it is…how even wet days can be fun…what wonderfully pleasant people you have met in the apartment foyer, on the street, in the stores,' Andreas enumerated without hesitation. 'I'm used to a deluge of irrepressibly cheerful chatter.'

Hope's face flamed. Did he see her as a mindless babbler? What *did* he see in her? She had always wondered. It took huge effort but she managed to talk and it must have been mindless because, the whole time, one half of her was concentrated on the less-than-encouraging reflection she could see in the contemporary mirror on the wall opposite. How could any guy who looked like Andreas really care for a woman her shape and size? Stop it, stop it, *stop it*, the voice of common sense urged her. With resolute courage, she turned away from the mirror and assured herself that self-doubt was not about to make her bolt to the kitchen and use food as a source of comfort.

In Switzerland, Andreas set down his phone, a

frown dividing his ebony brows as his analytical brain
homed in on the question of what had upset Hope.
She was not prone to moods. Indeed her temperament
was remarkably even and upbeat. When something
bothered her, she shared it with him. In fact, she told
him immediately and appreciated his advice. What
kind of problem would she choose not to share with
him?

Although she remained blissfully unaware of the
fact, Hope was currently enjoying very discreet
twenty-four-hour protection. Andreas, in common
with many wealthy individuals, had suffered threats.
Concerned that Hope might also be targeted, Andreas
had hired security professionals to watch over her.
Initially he had planned to tell her. But he had feared
that the safeguards he had put in place might frighten
her. She was friendly and trusting and thought the
very best of everyone she met. He did not want that
to change and had decided that it was kinder to leave
her in ignorance. Only for an instant did he consider
contacting her security team to find out where she had
been and whom she had been with. That would be
taking advantage of the situation and he respected her
privacy. Even so, a sense of annoyance that Hope
should for once have given him cause for disquiet
made Andreas icy cold and tough with the executives
who at his signal returned to the conference table.

Hope always dressed up for Andreas. Staring into her
wardrobe, she was mentally dividing it into three separate collections of clothes. Of the three, usually only
one set fitted her at any one time. The first had enjoyed a brief but glittering life after a crash diet and
the second was filled with all the replacement clothes

in different sizes that she had had to buy while she'd steadily regained the weight she had lost. The third was full of stalwart outfits with forgivingly stretchy proportions. Almost everything was bright in colour. As she yanked out a dress her head spun a little and she felt momentarily dizzy enough to sink down on the edge of the bed. It had not been the first time that she had felt that way in recent weeks but she reckoned that the light-headed feeling was an irritating hangover from a virus she had found hard to shake off during the autumn. No doubt the bug was still working its slow way out of her system and she would be wasting her doctor's time if she approached her with such a vague symptom.

In an hour, Andreas would be with her again and excitement was leaping through Hope in intoxicating waves. She refused to torment herself with Vanessa's gloomy forecast of doom and disappointment. Her friend had only wanted to put her on her guard, had in short spoken up out of pure, disinterested kindness. But Hope was equally well aware that Vanessa, who had had several unfortunate experiences, cherished a pronounced distrust of men and their motives. Furthermore, Vanessa had never met Andreas, had not even had the opportunity to appreciate what a wonderful guy he was.

Andreas kept the media at arm's length and suffered accordingly for his determination to protect his privacy. It took a great deal to anger Hope but she had been very much annoyed by several magazine articles and newspaper columns that had utilised old photos and old stories to enable their continued unjust depiction of Andreas as a ruthless, callous womaniser who was merciless in business. Had Vanessa read those items and been influenced by them?

As Hope brushed her hair she was thinking about the male she knew. Strong, generous, wildly passionate, literally everything she wanted in a man wrapped up in one fantastic package. Even though Andreas hated roughing it, he took her on picnics because he knew she loved them. Sightseeing bored him to death but he had flown her out to Paris, Rome and a host of other fabulous cities so that she could explore her passion for history in his company. Whenever she had been scared, discouraged or in need of support, he had been there for her. She loved him with her whole heart and soul for a host of very understandable reasons. On the debit side...? No, no, she wasn't going there, she was determined not to allow foolish negativity to creep in and wreak havoc with her happiness.

Andreas called her from the airport.

'I'm counting the minutes,' she told him truthfully.

He called her from the limo when it got stuck in city traffic.

'I can't bear it...' she gasped strickenly.

'Have you any idea how much I've missed you?' Andreas finally broke through his cool to demand in his final call made as he stepped into the lift to come up to the apartment.

By that stage, Hope was in a heady fever of anticipation. The front door opened: she saw him and all intelligent thought ceased. Her knees felt weak. She leant back against the wall to steady herself. Everything about Andreas thrilled her to death. From the stubborn angle of his proud dark head to the lithe, leashed power and grace of his hard, muscular frame, he was spectacularly male. Lamplight burnished his cropped black hair and cast his lean, bronzed features into tantalising angles of light and shade. He was breathtakingly handsome and he still only had to walk through the door to make her heart threaten cardiac arrest.

Andreas kicked the door shut behind him and powered on across the hall to haul her into his arms. For an endless moment of bliss she was lost in the glorious touch and feel of him. Her nostrils flared on the familiar male scent of his skin overlaid with a faint tang of designer lotion and her responses went into overdrive. 'Andreas...' she breathed unsteadily.

'If you could travel with me, we would have more time together.' Brilliant dark golden eyes entrapped her misty gaze, his accented drawl husky and reasonable in tone, for he chose his moments with care. 'Think about that. You could let your artistic endeavours take a back seat for a while.'

And lose her independence, which was quite out of the question, Hope acknowledged while she agonised with guilty longing over the seductive idea of being able to see more of Andreas. 'I couldn't...'

His hands closing over her smaller ones, and content to have planted yet another seed, Andreas pinned her back against the wall with all the single-minded purpose of a male guided by lustful intent. She succumbed to the allure of his hard, sensual mouth with the same fervour she would have employed in a life-or-death situation. He tasted like heaven, like something addictive she could not do without, and she clung. The tight knot of excitement in her belly fired her every nerve ending into an eager blaze of expectation. He dropped her hands to curve possessive fingers to the full, feminine swell of her hips and lift her into stirring connection with his bold erection.

'Oh...' she moaned, melting like honey in sunlight while the wicked throb of helpless hunger shimmied down into her pelvis and made her ache.

Plastered to every line of his big, powerful frame, she dragged her mouth free to snatch in a necessary gulp of oxygen while dimly her mind prompted her to recall an important ritual that she could not afford to overlook. 'Your mobile...' she gasped.

Andreas tensed.

'It's me or the phone,' Hope reminded him reluctantly.

One-handed, Andreas wrenched the phone from his jacket, switched it off and tossed it down on the hall-stand. He returned to plundering her mouth with devouring hunger and then wrenched himself back from her, dark colour scoring his aristocratic cheekbones. 'For once, we are going to be cool and make it out of the hall.'

Dazed by passion, Hope slowly nodded.

With determination Andreas angled her away from the wall and backed her towards the bedroom. 'If I surrender my phone, you have to make it worth my while, *pedhi mou*.'

'Oh...' Hope gazed back at him, soft mouth pink and tingling from the heat of his, her legs unsteady supports. The blaze of sexual challenge in his eyes imprisoned her as surely as a chain. A blinding wave of excitement sizzled through her.

Andreas surveyed her with scorching satisfaction. He ran down the zip on her turquoise dress and shimmied it down over her hips to expose the pink lace bra and panties that moulded her ripe curves. He vented a husky masculine sound of appreciation. 'You're superb…'

Self-conscious colour flushed her cheeks and even burnished the slope of her full breasts. Scooping her up, he deposited her on the bed, his rare charismatic smile flashing across his lean dark features, and her heart leapt as though it had a life of its own.

'Don't move,' he told her with urgency.

'I'm not going anywhere,' she whispered, her attention locked to him like a magnet as he peeled off the tailored jacket of his business suit.

He looked sensational. Lithe, dark and arrestingly handsome, he emanated the prowling, lethal sexiness of a predator. Butterflies were fluttering in her tummy and she was on a helpless high of anticipation. But on another level, she suddenly discovered that she was fighting off a sense of shame that she should be lying on a bed in her underwear for his benefit. She had not been raised in a liberal home and when Andreas had come into her life she had not just thrown away the rulebook, she had virtually burned it. Did she mean anything to him? Or was what they had just a casual thing on his terms?

'Do you think about me when you're away?' Hope blurted out.

His shirt hanging loose on his bronzed muscular chest, Andreas came down on the bed and laughed out loud. 'After two weeks without sex?' he teased in his dark deep drawl. 'By this week, I was thinking about you at least once a minute!'

Hope flushed to the roots of her pale hair, hurt and disappointment scything through her that he should be so literal. 'That wasn't what I meant.'

Andreas hauled her up against him with strong

hands, and golden eyes ablaze with arrogant confidence assailed hers. 'Don't ask a Greek trick questions,' he warned her. 'You're my lover. Of course I think about you.'

Without hesitation, he plundered her mouth and her uneasy thoughts blurred. Fire sparked low in her belly and a wave of tormenting hunger consumed her. Two weeks without Andreas felt like half a lifetime. Even as she doubted his commitment, she could not resist her need to take refuge in his passion. Her body was taut with sensitivity, begging for sensation. The expert caress of his hands on her breasts made her moan. The rosy buds crowning her tender flesh tingled and when he utilised his teeth and his tongue on those inflamed peaks, she writhed, control slipping from her as steadily as any form of rational awareness.

Her heart was racing, the breath catching in her dry throat. He was pure bronzed elemental male and he knew exactly what inflamed her. He found the hot, swollen secret at the heart of her and clever fingers drove her to ever more desperate heights of longing. The passion took over, roaring through her twisting, turning length like an explosive fireball.

'This is how I like to picture you,' Andreas rasped with raw satisfaction. 'Out of your mind with the pleasure I give you.'

He sank into her with ravishing force and her body leapt and clenched. The frenzy of excitement mastered her with terrifying immediacy. Delirious with desire, she was way beyond any hope of mastering the tempestuous surge of her responses. Her need for Andreas was almost painfully intense. His passion pushed her to a wild peak of unbearable pleasure and then she fell down and down and down into a state of turbulence that bore no resemblance to her usual languorous sense of peace and happiness. Her body was satisfied but her emotions were raw. Tears lashed her eyes and overflowed before she even knew what was happening to her.

Andreas rolled over onto his back. In the act of rearranging her on top of him, he pushed her hair gently off her face and his fingers lingered on her damp cheekbone. 'What's wrong?' he demanded.

'Nothing's wrong.' Hope gulped. 'I don't know why I'm crying. It's silly.'

Foreboding nudged at Andreas, who excelled at second-guessing those who surrounded him. She buried her head in his shoulder. He smoothed her hair. Handsome mouth taut, he closed his arms round her. If he were patient she would tell him what was wrong. She was quite incapable of keeping anything important from him. Her confiding habits were engrained, he reminded himself.

'I'm sorry…I suppose I've just come over all emotional thinking about our anniversary,' Hope mumbled in a muffled voice.

Lush black lashes lifted on guarded dark golden eyes. 'Anniversary?'

'Don't you know that in another few days we'll have been together for two whole years?' Hope lifted her tousled head, a happy smile of achievement on lips still swollen from his kisses. 'I want to celebrate it.'

Two years? His gaze narrowed, his lean, darkly handsome face impassive, concealing his stunned reaction to that news. Had she really been in his life that long? He was appalled that he had neglected to notice her staggering longevity. Two years? Marriages didn't last that long. When had she become the equivalent of a fixture? She had inserted herself into his daily routine with astounding subtlety. She was just… *there*. She didn't cling but the tendrils of her existence were as meshed with his as ivy round a tree. That was not an inspiring analogy. But when had he last slept with another woman? He squashed the instant sliver of guilt that even the thought ignited. He had been incredibly faithful to her. Acknowledging that reality set his even white teeth on edge. Inexplicable as it seemed to him, she had infiltrated his freedom like an invisible invading army and conditioned him in ways that were foreign to him. Angry surprise turned him to ice as though he were in the presence of the enemy.

'I'm not into anniversaries with women,' Andreas delivered, brilliant eyes dark as coals and diamond-bright. 'I don't do the sentimental stuff.'

Hope could hardly breathe. She wanted to put her hand over his beautiful mouth and prevent him from saying anything more. She could not bear that he should fulfil any part of Vanessa's disparaging forecast, yet she was equally unable to let that laden silence lie. 'But it's special to me that you've been a part of my life for so long.'

Andreas shrugged a muscular bronzed shoulder and firmly lifted her off him. 'We have a good time together. I value you. But it would be inappropriate to celebrate an anniversary. That's not what we're about.'

Hope felt like someone tied to the railway tracks in front of an express train and the roar of the metal monster was his words crushing the dreams she had cherished and ripping apart her illusions. In one lithe, powerful movement, he sprang off the bed and headed into the bathroom. She lay there cold and shocked and shattered. In her presence he had changed from the guy she loved into an intimidating stranger with cold eyes and a harsh, unfeeling voice and he had pushed her away. She got up to pull on the ice-blue wrap lying on a nearby chair. But she was forced to sink back down onto the bed because her head was swimming. It was that stupid dizziness again, she thought wearily. Perhaps it was an ear infection that was interfering with her sense of balance.

I value you. What sort of a declaration was that? That Andreas knew the exact extent of her worth? In terms of convenience? No, he didn't do sentimental but, perhaps more tellingly, he had not cared whether or not he wounded her feelings. He had to be very sure of her to put a blanket ban on even a minor celebration. Biting her lip and with a knot of fear forming inside her, Hope tightened the sash on her wrap. But anger was also slowly stirring out of the ashes of the hurt caused by his humiliating response to her perfectly innocent remarks.

Taut with angry, frustrated tension, Andreas leant back against the limestone wall in the power shower and let the water stream down over his magnificent bronzed body. Usually he was still in bed with Hope at this stage of the evening. His chill-out time with her had been wrecked. Taken by surprise, he had been tactless. He wanted to punch something. Their relationship was as near perfect as he had ever hoped to achieve on a casual basis. Hope never made unreasonable demands and appeared to have no greater ambition in life than to make him happy. And she was bloody brilliant at making him happy, Andreas acknowledged grudgingly. He did not want to lose her. But what did he do with a mistress who did not know she was a mistress? A mistress who wanted to celebrate anniversaries as if she were a wife? *Theos mou...* He winced. What had come over her?

Most probably, Andreas reasoned with a surge of fierce resentment, Hope's shrewish friend, Vanessa, was responsible. Was it she who had destroyed Hope's sunny contentment? Who else could it have been? Once or twice Hope had repeated Vanessa's revealingly acidic remarks about men. Andreas had gained the distinct impression that Hope's best friend would fry him alive in hot oil if she ever got the chance.

That his association with Hope should be so misjudged and so undervalued outraged Andreas. He was proud of the way he treated Hope. He looked after her. She was a very happy woman. Why? He kept all the nasty realities of life at bay. He even made her dreams come true. Although she had no suspicion of the fact, eighteen months earlier it had been his influence that had won her a place on a design course at a leading art college. Thanks to him she had since graduated and begun fashioning handbags that he was secretly convinced no sane woman would ever wish to buy. He had a shuddering recollection of the one shaped like a ripe tomato. But the point was, Hope was cheerfully content...or, at least, she had been until the serpent had entered Eden.

Andreas was towelling himself dry when Hope entered the bathroom. She drew in a slow, deep breath to steady herself and fixed turquoise blue eyes bravely on him. 'So if we can't have anniversaries, what can we have?'

Six feet four inches tall, black hair still wet from the shower and crystalline drops of water still sparkling on the ebony curls defining his powerful pectoral muscles, Andreas froze. He had not expected a second assault in that line. The first had been startling enough. Winged ebony brows drew together. 'I don't believe I follow…'

Hope realised that there was a lump in her throat, a lump that was swelling with every second that passed with the threat of tears. 'I…I suppose I'm asking is this it for you and me?'

'Clarify that,' Andreas instructed in the cool tone he used in the office to make underlings jump. But his dark golden eyes shimmered with intensity. He could not credit the idea but for a split second he wondered if she was threatening to dump him.

'Once you told me that nothing stays the same and that everything must progress,' Hope reminded him unsteadily. 'You said that the things that remain static wither and die. Yet from what I can see, in the last two years we haven't changed at all.'

Right there and then, Andreas decided that in the future it would be wiser to keep all words of wisdom on the score of goal-orientated achievement targets and healthy change to himself.

Every word Hope spoke came from her heart and nothing was pre-planned or judged for its effect. She was very upset. Horribly conscious of his cool distance, she was desperate to make sense of what was happening between them. She needed the reassurance of finding out exactly where she stood with the man she loved.

'So what about us?' Hope continued half under her breath, doggedly pushing the question out, refusing to surrender to her inner fears. 'Are we going anywhere?'

Incredulous that Hope should be subjecting him to such an onslaught, Andreas snatched in a charged breath and reached for her with determined hands. Gathering her small, curvaceous body to him, he reclaimed her mouth in a fierce, sweet invasion that left her quivering with disconcertion. 'Back to bed?' he murmured with hungry intent as he finally lifted his arrogant dark head.

Her pale face flamed as though he had slapped her. Indeed she felt as though he might as well have done, for she was bitterly ashamed that he had found it so easy to distract her. 'Is that my answer? I want to feel like I'm part of your life, not just someone you sleep with,' she confided painfully.

Golden eyes ablaze with displeasure, Andreas spread lean brown hands wide in emphasis. 'You *are* part of my life!'

'If that's true, why do I never get to meet your friends?' Her voice was rising with stress in spite of her efforts to keep it level. 'Are you ashamed of me?' she gasped strickenly.

'When we're together, I prefer to keep you to myself, *pedhi mou*. I won't apologise for that,' Andreas fielded smoothly. 'Calm yourself. You're getting hysterical!'

'I'm not...I'm just fighting with you!'

Andreas dealt her a stony appraisal. 'I won't fight with you.'

'Is that something else you're not into?' Hope heard herself hurl in shock at her own daring. Backing away from him, she jarred her hip painfully on a corner of the vanity unit behind her.

'Are you hurt?' Lean, strong face taut, Andreas strode forward.

In the room next door the phone started ringing. The untimely interruption made Andreas swear in exasperated Greek, but Hope was grateful for the excuse to escape and answer the call.

'Get me Andreas...' Elyssa Southwick's imperious voice demanded.

'Hold on, please,' Hope said gruffly.

If Elyssa couldn't raise Andreas on his mobile phone when he was in London, she called the apartment instead. The Nicolaidis siblings were close, for their parents had died when Elyssa was barely a teenager. Still only in her mid twenties, Elyssa leant heavily on her big brother for support. The young Greek woman, however, seemed to have no inkling of Hope's identity, for she always spoke to Hope as though she were a servant on telephone duty.

Andreas accepted the phone Hope extended. But his attention was on Hope, who looked like glass about to shatter, her warm blue eyes cast down and her generous mouth taut with strain. He was furious with her. Why was she doing this to them? The phone dialogue continued in Greek. Hope understood the gist of it for she had been learning the language at night class for many months and had planned to surprise Andreas with her proficiency. Elyssa was reminding her brother that she was throwing a housewarming party the next week. Hope left the room.

Of course, she would not be invited to the party. Andreas was in no hurry to take her out and show her off. Was that because he was only using her for sex?

Easy, uncomplicated sex with a woman who had been weak and foolish enough to give herself freely on that basis from the very outset of their acquaintance? How could she complain on that score when Andreas had never promised anything else and she had never had the courage to ask for anything more?

Pure anguish threatened to take hold of Hope. She wanted to weep and wail like a soul in torment and the power of her own distraught emotions scared her. Her mouth wobbled and she pinned it flat. Terrified as she was of breaking down while Andreas was still in the apartment, she fought to keep a lid on all distressing thoughts.

But her mind marched on with relentless cruelty. Andreas thought nothing of making love over and over again. He was all Greek, an unashamedly passionate guy with an insatiably high libido. But he was more into work than leisure and a woman who required little in terms of romance or attention was a necessity. No doubt, she suited him on those scores. She had always tried to be independent. She didn't create a fuss when he was late or business kept him from her. She had accepted her backstage role in his life.

Why? Andreas was so much what she was not and never could be. It was not that she suffered from low self-esteem; simply that she could not ignore or forget the reality that Andreas outranked her in so many ways. He was the gorgeous, sophisticated product of a world of immense privilege and even more immense wealth. If it rained on a summer day, he thought he was suffering and he had once flown her halfway across the world to spend three hours on a hot beach. He was highly educated and shockingly clever. Far too clever for his own good, she had often thought, she recalled ruefully, for he was a perfectionist, obsessively driven to achieve, but rarely satisfied even by superlative results.

What had she to offer in comparison? Basic schooling, an ordinary background and at best what she deemed to be only average looks and intelligence. How could she ever have dared to dream that some day he might fall in love with her? Or that he might eventually choose to offer her a more secure place in his life? But she had been guilty of harbouring exactly those dreams. She loved Andreas, she loved him a great deal, and right from the beginning that had been a handicap to any form of restraint or common sense.

Hope tilted up her chin as if she was bracing herself. Andreas might be satisfied with the current status quo, but she needed to have a good hard think about whether or not she could cope with a relationship that had no future. And presumably none of the commitment she had taken for granted that she already had. Her tummy flipped. She felt sick at the very idea that she might have to walk away from Andreas. But if she meant nothing more to him than a casual bed partner, wasn't that her only option?

On the other hand, was it possible that she had chosen the worst possible moment to mention something that Andreas seemed to find so controversial? Maybe the very word 'anniversary' struck horror into his bones. Maybe she was overreacting to her own anxieties, concerns that she had contrived to ignore until a friend had voiced similar reservations.

Here she was fighting with Andreas for the very first time. Here she was putting their entire relationship in jeopardy. Her hands knotted into fists and her eyes swam with hot tears. She never cried. What was the matter with her? So much emotion was swilling about inside her, she felt frighteningly on edge. She had almost shouted at him. He had been astonished. She pressed trembling hands to her cool cheeks. She breathed in slow and deep in an effort to recapture the tranquillity that had until very recent times been so much a part of her nature.

'Hope...' His long, lean, muscular body garbed only in a pair of cotton boxers, Andreas found her by the window in the elegant sitting room. Looking incredibly male and sexy, he strolled across the handsome oak-planked floor and closed firm hands over her knotted fingers to pull her close. His brilliant golden eyes snared her deeply troubled gaze and held her entrapped. 'How would you like to go to my sister's party next week?'

Her surprise and pleasure linked and swelled into a sensation of overwhelming joy and relief. 'Are you serious? My goodness, I'd love to go!'

Andreas watched the glow of happiness reanimate in the instant generous smile that lit up her face. Situation defused: it had been the right gesture to make. A weekend in Paris would have compromised his principles in regard to anniversaries. That Elyssa would barely notice Hope's existence among so many other guests was irrelevant. There was no reason why Hope should not attend, but he had no intention of making a habit of such invitations.

Eventually, he would have to do his duty by the Nicolaidis name and marry to father an heir. In the light of that prospect, it was wise to make a distinction between his public and his private life and be discreet. Hope would be hurt but, the longer she had been part of his life, the harder she would find it to break away and the more easily she would adjust to the inevitable restrictions and accept them, Andreas reflected with hard determination.

Her heart beating very fast, Hope curved into the gloriously familiar heat of his big, powerful frame. She felt very guilty over her temporary loss of faith in him. Obviously, she should have spoken up sooner. Perhaps he had just needed a little nudge in the right direction.

'Now…' Long brown fingers curved to her cheekbones and her breath began coming in quick shallow bursts. His scorching golden eyes dazzled her. Excitement leapt even before he tasted her readily parted lips with devastating hunger and swept her up into his arms to carry her back to the bedroom.

CHAPTER TWO

ENTERING the imposing mansion that Elyssa and her wealthy husband, Finlay Southwick, had renovated at reputedly vast expense, Hope smoothed her V-necked black dress down over her hips with damp palms.

The party was already in full swing, for Andreas did not believe in early arrivals. She was very nervous and was resisting a powerful urge to stick to him like superglue. She had been so scared of wearing the wrong thing that she had opted to play it safe with black, but women all around her were wearing rainbow colours and she felt horribly drab and unadventurous. In addition, her plan to spend half the day grooming herself to her personal best in the presentation stakes had been interrupted, cast into confusion and pretty much destroyed by Andreas arriving three hours early.

Warm colour blossomed in Hope's cheeks. A business meeting had been cancelled, leaving Andreas free to finish early. The intimate ache between her thighs testified to the enthusiasm with which Andreas had taken advantage of that rare gift of extra time with her.

A youthful blonde caught up in the crush stared at Hope in surprise and stopped dead. 'It *is* you, isn't it? You're the handbag lady who does the stall in Camden market...aren't you?'

'I think you will find that you are mistaken,'

Andreas interposed in a cool, deflating tone that would have crushed granite.

Hope tensed. The teenager already reddening with embarrassment had vaguely familiar features. 'Yes... that's me,' she confirmed with a warm smile to ease the girl's discomfiture.

'My mother adores the bag I gave her for her birthday and loads of her friends are desperate to find out where she got it from! I'll be calling back soon,' the blonde promised.

Before Hope could confide that she had given up on selling at the market, Andreas had curved a firm hand to her spine to urge her past. The foyer was big and crowded with noisy knots of chattering guests. He pressed her into a doorway to say in an icy undertone, 'Is it true? Have you been flogging merchandise from a stall?'

Taken aback, Hope looked up at him in dismay. His gleaming dark eyes were hard and cold. 'Yes. Initially, I was doing market research to find out what sells to which age groups. It helped me keep in touch with current trends—'

'You've been keeping a market stall,' Andreas sliced in, cold, incredulous disapproval etched into the hard angles of his lean, strong face. 'Trading in the street as though you were penniless and without means of support! How *dare* you affront me in such a manner?'

Hope was paralysed to the spot. Astonishment had leached all the natural colour from below her skin. 'It never occurred to me that you might be so snobbish about it,' she muttered unevenly.

'I am not a snob.' Andreas rejected that accusation out of hand.

Anxious turquoise eyes clear as glass rested on him. 'I'm afraid you are, but with your privileged background that's perfectly normal and understandable—'

'*Theos*...what has my background to do with this?' Andreas grated, his annoyance fuelled to anger by the expression of gentle and compassionate forgiveness that she wore. 'Why did you not tell me that you were working as a street trader?'

'For goodness' sake, it was only an occasional casual thing. I had no idea you would feel like this about it. I didn't even think that you would be interested,' Hope murmured unhappily. 'As it happens, I'm not doing the market any more—'

'You should never have stooped to such a level. From now on you will respect the standards required to conserve your dignity.' Devastatingly handsome features set in grim lines of intimidating impassivity, Andreas reined back his temper with difficulty.

'I don't think I've got any to conserve,' Hope confided apologetically, deciding that it might not be the best time to tell him that she had only given up the market in favour of craft fairs.

Sometimes, the cocoon of his own stratospheric wealth made Andreas hopelessly impractical, she thought ruefully. After all, she *was* virtually penniless. She had lived like a church mouse on her student loan and had since stretched her meagre earnings to paying for all her outgoings but it was a real uphill battle. Only the fact that she had no rent to pay for the roof over her head had enabled her to manage. Was he even aware of the contribution she made to the household bills? Or did one of his staff deal with all his domestic expenditure at the apartment?

'But I *have*, so cultivate dignity for my benefit,' Andreas delivered with cutting clarity, refusing to be softened by the playful light in her gaze.

His pride was outraged by the very idea of her rubbing shoulders with market traders and serving customers. Such a milieu was beneath her touch and she ought to know that without being told. She was too naive and she lacked discrimination. How much over-familiarity and coarseness had she endured without complaint? What other foolish things did she get up to that he didn't know about? His unquestioning trust in her was shaken. For the first time he acknowledged the inherent flaw in his own all too regular absences abroad. If he had been around more, he would have found out about the market-trading project and he would have suppressed it. In the future he would need to take a much closer interest in her activities.

Hope knew Andreas too well not to recognise his distaste and it cut her to the quick at a moment when she was already feeling vulnerable. He was disappointed in her. It was plain that he believed she had embarrassed him and that really hurt. The cool distance stamped in his stunning dark golden eyes hit her hardest of all.

At that point she registered that the crush had magically cleared to allow them a clear passage. But she was discomfited by the discovery that they appeared to be the cynosure of all eyes. A perceptible ripple of excited awareness was travelling round the big reception room, turning every head in their direction. Eyes skimmed over her with curiosity but lingered with fascinated awe on the tall, authoritative male at her side. Andreas was the main attraction and the crowds parted before him as though he were royalty. Certainly, he was royally indifferent to the power of his own presence. He ignored all but a tiny number of the hopeful and gushing greetings angled at him.

A beautiful young woman with sultry dark eyes and long brown hair, her slender figure displayed to advantage in a strappy iridescent pink dress, was hurrying towards them. Hope, who had often seen photos of Elyssa in gossip magazines, recognised Andreas's sister instantly and smiled. Her tummy felt tight with nerves. She so much wanted her meeting with the other woman to go well. Elyssa focused her attention on her brother and kissed him on both cheeks in ebullient welcome even as she uttered a spirited barrage of complaint about his late arrival.

Untouched by that censure, indeed laughing, Andreas flicked a glance at Hope as though he was about to introduce her to his sibling. However, a heavily built older man approached him just then and addressed him in a flood of Greek. 'Excuse me a moment,' Andreas said to both women, his mouth tightening with impatience as he stepped to one side.

'I'm Hope,' Hope confided as she extended a friendly hand to Elyssa. 'I've been looking forward to meeting you.'

A glittering smile pinned to her burgundy-tinted mouth, Elyssa fixed sullen dark eyes on her, ignored her hand and murmured with stinging scorn, 'You're my brother's whore. Why would *I* want to meet *you*?'

As Elyssa walked away, her smile brighter than ever, Hope struggled to conceal her shock. Her face burning, she was gripped by a sick sense of humiliation. That Andreas's sister and closest relative, a woman who did not even know her, should attack her with such venom appalled her. She told herself that she would not think about the offensive label the brunette had applied to her. She had been mad keen to come to Elyssa's party, she reminded herself doggedly, and she had to make the best of the event for Andreas's sake. Andreas was very fond of his kid sister. There was no way she could tell him what Elyssa had said to her. She would just have to take it on the chin.

Across the room, a man in his twenties with fair, angelic features at odds with his bloodshot eyes and tousled spiky blond hair raised his hand to her in nonchalant greeting. Grateful to see a face she knew in that sea of daunting strangers, Hope beamed at him.

'Do you know who that guy is?' Andreas enquired flatly.

'Ben Campbell...he's Vanessa's cousin,' Hope told him, her face shadowing as she once again fought off the recollection of the name Elyssa had applied to her. *Whore*...no, she refused to even think about that.

Andreas spared the younger man a chilling glance and made no effort to acknowledge him. Campbell had a sleazy reputation for wild parties and indiscriminate womanising. He was very much disconcerted by the evident fact that Hope should be on friendly terms with him.

'I don't want you associating with Campbell,' Andreas imparted with succinct clarity.

Hope stiffened in surprise, chewed at her lower lip and then dropped her pale head. When had Andreas begun to talk as though his every word, unreasonable or otherwise, ought to be her command? She might only have met Ben a few times but she liked him.

'Which means,' Andreas extended very dryly, for

he was less than impressed by her lack of response and the way she appeared to be avoiding his gaze, 'as of now, you no longer know him.'

Hope said nothing. How could she cut Ben dead and offend her best friend? Apart from anything else, it would be ridiculous overkill for a casual acquaintance that only encompassed a handful of meetings at Vanessa's apartment.

A woman glittering with diamonds swam up to speak to Andreas. She paid Hope the barest minimum of attention and was the forerunner in a long and constant procession of people frantic to get a chance to talk to him. In comparison, Hope felt as interesting as a wooden chair and would not have been surprised to find coats being draped over her.

Her confidence already smashed to bits by her hostess, Hope retreated into an alcove nearby. From that safe harbour, she watched the female contingent gush and flatter and hang on every word that fell from Andreas's beautifully sculpted lips. The men were loud with nerves, unerringly deferential and eager to hear his opinion.

His whore. Without the slightest warning, that dreadful tag leapt back into her mind and had much the same effect on her as an axe wielded by a maniac. A whore was a promiscuous woman, she thought sickly. A woman who bartered sex for reward. A woman who made a special effort to please men sexually. Could she be described in those terms?

Andreas did not give her money, but she lived in an apartment worthy of a princess and it did rejoice in a designer décor, fancy furniture and fantastic art works. Even if she worked a thousand years she would never be able to afford such luxury on her own income. But she was not promiscuous. When she had met Andreas, she had been a virgin. She had only ever slept with Andreas. He had taught her everything she knew. But Andreas being Andreas and a demanding perfectionist in all fields had doubtless ensured that she had learnt exactly what pleased him in bed. Did that make her a whore?

Feeling claustrophobic in her dim corner and too tormented by her own fears to stay still, Hope wandered off into the next room. Only then did she appreciate that her eyes were awash with tears. Ashamed of her lack of self-control, she hurried on in her exploration of the big, crowded house, afraid that if she lingered anywhere someone would notice that her emotions had got on top of her. A sob was clogging up her throat. She wished she had never come to the party. She felt duly punished for daring to crave what she had naively believed would be an important stepping stone in her relationship with Andreas. Finding herself alone in a quiet branch corridor, she paused, listened outside a solid panelled door and, reassured by the silence within, pressed down the handle.

The door creaked wide on a low-lit room and a startling spectacle. Andreas's sister, Elyssa, was passionately kissing a dark-haired man, who bore no resemblance whatsoever to her husband, Finlay Southwick.

Consternation momentarily froze Hope on the threshold. Shocked eyes veiling, she pulled the door closed again in a nerveless harried movement and sucked in air to steady herself. But before she could even breathe out again and move on, the door flew open again to reveal Elyssa.

'Don't you *dare* tell Andreas!' the young Greek woman hissed in a tempestuous mix of revealing fear and fury. 'If this gets back to my brother, I'll know who to blame and I'll destroy you!'

Barely able to credit the extent of the other woman's aggression, Hope murmured tightly, 'There's no need to threaten me—'

'There's every need,' Elyssa condemned furiously. 'What were you doing snooping? Did you follow me in here?'

'Of course I didn't!' Hope protested in disbelief. 'I wasn't snooping either. I was just looking for somewhere quiet where I could sit down. I thought the room was empty—'

'Did you really?' Elyssa sneered.

'Yes, I did. Look, I have no intention of telling anybody anything. I always mind my own business—'

'Just you see that you do, you fat cow!' the enraged brunette spat at her spitefully.

Reeling from that second attack, Hope walked away with a rigid back. Tears were blinding her: it was a nightmare party with the hostess from hell. She cannoned into someone and looked up with a stifled apology to focus on Ben Campbell.

'What's up?' Ben asked, his voice a trifle slurred.

'Nothing!' Brushing past him, Hope took refuge in the cloakroom. Secure then from prying ears and eyes, she punched out Vanessa's number on her mobile phone and said wretchedly, 'Everything's going horribly wrong. Elyssa hated me on sight!'

'Good. Andreas must be even keener than I suspected,' her friend responded with disconcerting good cheer.

'How do you make that out?' Hope swallowed back another sob and decided that she did indeed look very large in the black dress. All that dark unbroken colour was less than flattering. In fact her reflection seemed to fill the whole dainty mirror above the vanity unit.

'Elyssa's a spoilt little brat of an heiress and she's possessive of her big brother. She must have some idea how long you've been with him and I bet she's worried that he's serious. Did she say anything nasty? Anything you could make decent mileage out of?'

Hope frowned, for where Andreas's sister was concerned she felt honour-bound to preserve a discreet silence. 'Why?'

'Because you could use it as ammunition and confide tearfully in Andreas. Only a week ago, I would have said that that was a major no-no, but with impressively little effort you miraculously persuaded Andreas to take you to the party of the year,' the redhead mused thoughtfully. 'I'm now convinced that you have more influence over Andreas Nicolaidis than either he or you appreciate.'

'Do you really think so?' Hope encouraged, desperate to have her spirits raised even with what she deemed to be a false hope. 'But I wouldn't dream of saying anything that would cause trouble between Andreas and his sister. That would be dreadfully mean of me and certain to fail—'

'If Elyssa is planning to be your enemy, you may not have much choice,' Vanessa warned.

'Don't be so pessimistic.' Hope sighed. 'She may well think that I'm not good enough for her brother—'

'Oh, please, don't start making excuses for her!' Vanessa groaned in despair.

Finishing the call, Hope returned the phone to her bag. She hadn't been able to bring herself to tell her best friend that she had been called a whore. She was too afraid that Vanessa might secretly think that Elyssa had had some justification for voicing that cruelly humiliating opinion. Emerging from the cloakroom, she saw that Ben was now lounging up against the wall a few feet away.

'Let's talk...' he urged, holding out a languid and rather wavering hand, which made her suspect that he was drunk. 'Who stole your big happy smile? I want you to tell me what's wrong. Van would kill me for walking by on the other side.'

Cheeks hot with self-consciousness as envious female eyes locked to her, Hope hurried over. 'Shush... there's nothing wrong...please keep your voice down—'

Ben locked both arms round her as much to keep himself upright, she suspected, as to prevent her walking away. 'Would you like me to take you home?'

'Thank you but no—'

'I got droves of women,' Ben confided lazily, bloodshot green eyes mocking her as she blushed and attempted to tug free of his hold. 'Do you think I could seduce you away from your Greek billionaire?'

'No chance. Nothing and nobody could,' Hope swore with fervour.

'Never say never...it's like challenging fate.' Scanning her pale, troubled expression, Ben sighed and dropped an almost paternal kiss down on top of her head. 'You're way too sweet and straight for Nicolaidis.'

Andreas was the restive centre of a crowd. He was bored: even at a distance she could tell. His stunning dark golden eyes picked her out when she was still moving towards him. Lean, extravagantly handsome face intent, he abandoned his audience without hesitation and strode forward to intercept her. 'Where the hell have you been?' he demanded.

'When the dialogue turns to gold prices and pork bellies, I feel a bit surplus to requirements.'

'Let's go, *pedhi mou.*' Closing a determined hand over hers, Andreas trailed her in the direction of the hall and remained wonderfully impervious to every fawning attempt to slow down his progress. 'We should never have got out of bed...'

As he hurried her down the steps into the cool night air the shameless sexual sizzle in his skimming appraisal made her tummy clench and her mouth run dry. Suddenly everything that had upset her seemed utterly unimportant. She loved him to death. What else mattered? In a spontaneous movement, she stretched up on her tiptoes to press a kiss to a bronzed cheekbone and she breathed in the heady male scent of his skin with the delight of an addict.

'Andreas? Please wait,' a soft voice interposed from behind them in Greek. 'I need to speak to you.'

Andreas tensed, ebony brows drawing together. He tucked Hope into the waiting limousine with scrupulous care and an apologetic smile. 'Give me five minutes...I'll say your goodbyes for you.'

Elyssa's approach had made Hope tense as well, but she was grateful to be released from the challenge of dealing with his volatile sister again. She had been surprised at how quiet and hesitant the brunette had sounded until it occurred to her that perhaps Elyssa

intended to confide in her brother and admit that all
was not well in her marriage. Hope liked that idea,
for she felt bad about withholding what she had seen
from Andreas. After all, he was very attached to his
sister and her two young children. Cynical he might
be, but Hope was convinced that he would make considerable effort to keep his sister's family together.

Perhaps Elyssa, who had married when she was
still very young, had allowed a flirtation to get out of
hand. Whatever, Hope reminded herself that the situation was none of her business. But even so the
whole wretched tangle was liable to put Andreas in a
very bad mood. Andreas was not tolerant of female
mistakes in the fidelity line, Hope reflected ruefully.
More than once she had heard him pass distinctly
judgemental comments on that score.

It was fifteen minutes before Andreas joined her.
In the artificial light his vibrant olive skin tone had
an unusually pale aspect. His brilliant eyes were dark
and screened to a brooding glitter. Convinced that his
sister had told him what had happened, Hope was
unsurprised by his silence during the drive back
through the city streets. He was fiercely loyal to his
own flesh and blood and he had never discussed
Elyssa with her.

When Hope recognised the tension in the atmosphere, she thought she had to be imagining it. Then
doubt crept in. Had Elyssa accused her of snooping?
Surely Andreas was too sensible to pay credence to
that far-fetched idea? Her brow tightened even more
with tension.

In the lift on the way up to the apartment, she met
bold dark eyes cold as the Atlantic in winter. 'What's
the matter?' she asked instantly.

'Why are you asking?' Andreas murmured sibilantly.

Hope had never heard that daunting inflection in his rich dark drawl before. Entering the hall, she kicked off her shoes as was her wont and hesitated.

'Hope…?'

Slowly she turned round and stared back at him. Andreas was still lodged at the far side of the spacious hall. Lethally tall and exotically dark and sexy, he looked so drop-dead gorgeous he took her breath away. Yet her sense of being under threat at that moment was so intense that she felt slightly queasy.

Andreas strolled fluidly towards her. Brilliant dark eyes flashed shimmering gold. 'Did anything happen tonight that you would like to tell me about?'

CHAPTER THREE

HOPE gulped. Why was Andreas acting as if she had done something wrong? She had no desire to whinge about Elyssa's unkindness or indeed to tell tales about the younger woman. Yet if Andreas knew that she had seen his sister with another man, why was he making a mystery of that embarrassing event?

'No, nothing comes to mind,' Hope answered uneasily, wishing she did not feel quite so guilty about keeping quiet on Elyssa's behalf.

'You were seen with Ben Campbell,' Andreas imparted icily, but there was a dauntingly rough and unfamiliar edge to his intonation.

Disconcerted by that reference to Ben, Hope turned pink and shifted uncomfortably, but she could see no reason to be the slightest bit apologetic on that score. 'Yes, I did speak to Ben for a couple of minutes.'

'Finlay, my brother-in-law, saw you with him. You were in Campbell's arms.'

That particular choice of wording sent a stab of sincere annoyance travelling through Hope. Could something so minor and innocent in every way be responsible for causing so much bad feeling? She had not even met Elyssa's husband. But she could not help thinking that there was surely something rather mean-spirited about a man capable of reading anything suspect into her brief chat with Ben. 'It wasn't quite as you make it sound—'

Andreas elevated a black brow. 'Wasn't it?'

Her usual calm chipping away at an ever-faster rate, Hope stared back at him in an effort to comprehend the mystery of his unusual behaviour. He had never shown signs of being unreasonably jealous or possessive. Now all of a sudden he was acting like a stranger. 'Of course it wasn't. For a start there were at least half a dozen other people nearby,' she pointed out. 'Ben wasn't even flirting with me, he was just fooling around.'

His lean bronzed features remained maddeningly uninformative. 'Was he?'

'For goodness' sake, Andreas,' Hope continued with gathering force, for a cascade of little mental alarm bells was beginning to go off inside her head. 'Ben probably put his arms round me because he had to hang onto me to stay upright. He *was* rather merry. There certainly wasn't anything else to it. In fact, I'm finding it very hard to believe that we're having this conversation.'

'We're having this conversation because five minutes after Finlay saw you getting cosy in public with Campbell, Elyssa surprised you getting cosier still in private,' Andreas delivered with grim clarity.

Hope stilled, the animated pink draining slowly from her shaken face. 'Say that again…'

'Surely I don't need to repeat it,' Andreas said, his disgust unconcealed. 'You went into a private room with Campbell.'

A tiny pulse had begun to go bang-bang-bang at Hope's temple and she was so stiff she might have been fashioned out of stone. 'I did not go into any room to be alone with Ben—'

Something flashed in his hard, dark gaze: a sizzle of golden fury. 'This is grubby…this is beneath me!'

Andreas incised with a raw, slashing derision that cut her to the bone. 'At least admit the truth. When such behaviour is witnessed, there is no scope to lie or make excuses.'

'But I'm not lying or making excuses,' Hope fielded breathlessly, for sheer shock was making her feel as if she had been punched squarely in the solar plexus. 'What am I supposed to have been doing with Ben?'

'You were kissing him—'

'I wasn't!' Hope gasped. 'Your sister is—'

Andreas spread his arms in a sudden violent movement that shook her into silence. 'Don't offend me even more by daring to question my sister's integrity. She saw what she saw. You abused her hospitality and embarrassed her.'

'I did not...I *swear* I did not,' Hope muttered in bewilderment, her head swimming with too many thoughts at once. As she finally grasped how cruelly manipulative and unashamedly deceitful Elyssa Southwick had been, she felt sick to the stomach. For an instant she was simply shattered that someone she barely knew could be prepared to tell a lie of such appalling magnitude about her.

'Elyssa was very upset and she didn't know what to do. But after discussing the matter with her husband, she decided that I had a right to know that you were behaving like a slut behind my back!' Andreas bit out rawly, his wintry cool and control starting to crack.

Hope trembled. 'But it's not true. Not a word of it is true—'

'I want to hear you admit the truth before I leave. You owe me that at the very least,' Andreas growled.

Even as she saw that her world was falling apart, Hope was sickly fascinated by the callous ruthlessness that Elyssa had employed to bring about the destruction she had threatened. 'I've been a real fool,' she mumbled in a daze. 'I always try to overlook other people's mistakes and not stand in judgement because I know I'm not perfect either. But I overlooked one very dangerous fact...your sister is as clever as you are and it seems she decided that I was a threat to her security.'

His handsome mouth curled. 'That's offensive nonsense. Have the decency to leave Elyssa out of this unpleasant business.'

'I don't think I can.' Yet Hope was also asking herself how she could possibly stage a creditable counter-accusation. Having got her story in first, Elyssa had backed it up most impressively with her husband's reference to having previously seen Hope in Ben Campbell's arms. It didn't matter that that latter incident had taken place in the most innocent of circumstances. The other man's additional testimony had made the case against Hope look irrefutable. On the other hand, she reasoned, perhaps the story might have looked unarguable to a stranger, but should Andreas not know her better?

'Don't you know me better than this?' she whispered out loud.

That question hit Andreas as hard as a blast of dynamite detonating inside a giant rock. Rage was like a clenched-tight fist inside him and it took all his concentration to keep it contained. He could not stand to look at her; yet somehow he could not make himself look away. He had trusted her. Until his sister had blown away his illusions he had had no idea just how deep his trust in Hope had run. The sleazy truth had come as a body blow. But then placing that amount of faith in a mistress was asking for trouble, he reflected bitterly. He had kept her around too long. He had let her rosy, cosy sentimentality infect him like a virus and blur the boundaries of what they shared: great sex, nothing more, and he could find equally great sex elsewhere.

'Andreas?' Hope breathed unevenly, a tumult of emotions thrust down as she fought a fierce battle not to lose control. 'Do you really think that I would do something like that?'

Insolent golden eyes zeroed in on her. 'Is it beyond impossible?' Andreas drawled smooth as silk. 'You did it with me in a barn the first night we met.'

All the natural colour bled from Hope's complexion to leave her pale as parchment. Pain exploded inside her. But on some level, she welcomed the hurt inflicted by his cruel derision. Perhaps it was a long overdue punishment for her recklessness that night. Evidently that bad beginning had come back to haunt her. He didn't respect her; he had obviously never respected her. Virgin or not, she had been too easy a conquest and he was now looking back at that as though it had been the first betraying symptom of her being a slut in the making. It was incredibly cruel of him to throw that first night back in her teeth. She had cherished the memory of the night she fell in love with him as the very essence of romance. But he had slung that same recollection back to her as a base and humiliating insult.

Her eyes felt horribly hot, dry and scratchy. Shock seemed to have driven all desire to cry out of her.

'Yes I did, didn't I?' she managed gruffly. 'But even if it wasn't special for you, it was for me.'

Emanating pure indifference on that issue, Andreas shrugged a broad shoulder in a gesture that was as careless as it was wounding.

Hope tried again. 'You have to listen to me—'

'No, I don't.'

'I didn't do anything tonight and I'm not lying to you. I have never kissed Ben Campbell,' Hope declared with vehemence.

'I expect you to find alternative accommodation by the end of the month. It's over,' Andreas countered with supreme derision.

Hope realised he was about to leave and horror galvanised her out of her paralysis into sudden action. She placed herself between Andreas and the front door. 'You can't leave!'

'Watch me—'

'No, I won't. I want you to stop and think about the person you know me to be. Ask yourself if I'd throw what we have away just for the chance to snog Ben Campbell!'

His strong jaw line clenched. 'Other women have. He's wrecked several marriages with his little-boy-lost act. He's also famous for going after women who belong to other men—'

'But I don't fancy him...I never have. I imagine half of London has got to snog Ben when he's drunk. He's not exactly exclusive,' Hope pointed out in growing desperation, praying that the very tenor of her comments would force Andreas to see that she had never even thought of Ben Campbell as a potentially fanciable male. All he had ever been on her terms was Vanessa's rather dissolute and amusing cousin. 'If you won't believe me, ask Ben if anything happened tonight.'

Outraged by that suggestion, Andreas vented a harsh laugh of incredulity. 'Why would I lower myself to that level? Had you been my wife, I would have confronted him. I would've torn him apart for daring to lay a single finger on you!' he proclaimed with a disconcertingly vicious edge to his dark, deep drawl. 'But you're *not* my wife, you're my mistress and, as such, expendable with the minimum of fuss.'

Ashen-pale beneath the lash of his naked contempt, Hope looked back at him, distraught turquoise eyes sparkling with sudden angry denial. 'I am not and I have never been your mistress.'

'Then what are you?' Andreas purred like a panther ready to flex his claws and draw blood.

'A woman who fell in love with you and who never stopped to count the cost,' Hope quantified jerkily, her generous mouth compressing. 'Some people would judge me harshly enough for that or call me a fool. But that doesn't make me your mistress—'

'A lot of women have told me they loved me,' Andreas murmured with sizzling scorn. 'Invariably they love what I can give them more.'

Her spine ached with tension. 'But I've never let you give me anything. With the exception of this apartment, I've kept your money out of our relationship and I never once looked for or accepted expensive gifts. Don't try to bundle me up with other women when I've always been true to you!' she told him, hearing the sharp, accusing undertone in her voice and unable to suppress it. 'And you can also stop insulting me for what I haven't done and talking at me in that bored, sneering way!'

'If I stop sneering, I might lose my temper,' Andreas asserted with a lethal quietness that made gooseflesh prickle at the nape of her neck. 'Now get out of my way…I'm leaving.'

Hope backed up against the door in a panic. 'Over my dead body. I won't let you leave until you listen to me. This is like a living nightmare and I won't let it happen to us—'

'There is no us now.' Without further ado, Andreas lifted her bodily out of his path and strode through the door.

Hope could not believe he was gone any more easily than she could accept what had just happened. Only a few hours earlier when they had left for the party, she had been so happy and secure. To accept that Andreas had dumped her, walked out on her, indeed finished with her absolutely and for ever was more than she could bear to deal with at that moment.

Like someone lost in a strange land, she wandered round the big, empty apartment. Elyssa had told horrible lies about her. Such behaviour was so inexplicable to Hope that for the space of an hour she strove frantically to plan out how she might approach Andreas's sister and what she might say to persuade the young Greek woman that she had to retract her false accusation. But even an optimist like Hope could not cling to such a remote prospect for long.

After all, even before she had had the misfortune to catch Elyssa in compromising circumstances, Elyssa had made it clear that she despised her. The brunette had too much to lose from telling the truth and had triumphed with her lies. She had managed to destroy Hope's relationship with her brother and ensure that Hope was banished from his life.

Hope's hands closed tight in on themselves. She recognised that she was still in a stupor of shock. But she was already thinking that she ought to have told Andreas that she had seen his sister with another man. Whether he believed her side of the story or not, she needed to speak up in her own defence. Yet what realistic chance of success did she have? Any attempt she made to clear her own name would entail accusing Elyssa of, not only being a liar, but also being an unfaithful wife. She shivered at the prospect. Andreas was very proud and protective of his younger sister. Honour and family were all-important to the Greek male. Any attack on Elyssa would outrage him.

She tripped over the black shirt lying discarded by the bed and swept it up, burying her face in its crumpled cotton folds to draw in the scent of Andreas. He was gone. How could someone who felt like the other half of her leave and how could she still function? Terror spread into the void inside her for she could not imagine living without Andreas. A passion of grief dug nasty talon claws into her shrinking flesh. Her aching eyes finally overflowed and she threw herself down on the bed and cried until her throat hurt and she could hardly see through her swollen eyes. In the silence that followed, she was overwhelmed by a terrible sense of loss and emptiness.

In the limo that ferried him back to the town house, Andreas worked his way through two brandies. What Elyssa had seen admitted no possibility of error. Hope's foolish pleas of innocence had only deepened his anger. He concentrated on that anger, letting it rise like a red mist and suppress all other thoughts. He would prove that she was lying, he decided grimly.

Lifting the phone, he called his security chief and, with a perfunctory apology for the late hour, he requested a detailed rundown of Hope's daily itinerary in recent months.

Somewhere around dawn, Hope had drifted into an uneasy slumber disturbed by dreams. Wakening, she sat up, and as the awful events of the previous night rolled back to her her tummy seemed to roll queasily in concert. In the aftermath of that rare bout of nausea, she stumbled into the shower and slumped. With or without Andreas, her life had to go on, she reminded herself dully. There was no point being wimpy about it. From somewhere she had to find the strength to concentrate on the practicalities of life. She had to find somewhere else to live. It was also time to redouble her so-far-unsuccessful efforts to get a loan that would enable her to set up her own business. When she was finally in a position to design and produce her own small select line of handbags, she would be working night and day. Yes, she would be so incredibly busy she wouldn't have the time to agonise over Andreas.

She noticed a small decorative gold box resting on a console table in the hall. When he'd arrived the day before, Andreas had tossed something down before he'd hauled her into his arms. As always it would be chocolate, superlative, incredible, melt-in-the-mouth chocolate purchased abroad at an extortionate price. And as well? Opening the box, she lifted out the tiny gold charm that he had included as a surprise. Only it wasn't really a surprise any more for one by one Andreas had given her an entire collection of unusual charms for her bracelet. This particular one was her name picked out with tiny glittering stones. Some lucky charm this one had proved to be...*hope*? Without warning her eyes flooded again and she squeezed them tight shut in an agony of loss. Blinking back tears, she realised that misery appeared to have deprived her of her usual love of chocolate. Instead the image of an olive and the prospect of that sharp rather than sweet taste came to mind and her taste buds watered. Bemused, for she had never liked olives, she frowned, but a moment later she headed into the kitchen.

On the way to the airport and a flight to New York, Andreas studied the security reports that detailed Hope's recent movements. His initial sensation of complete disbelief swiftly mounted to hot-blooded fury. He knew that if he put his private jet on hold he would never make his transatlantic meeting in time. But for once, emotion took strong precedence over efficiency and discipline and he told his chauffeur to turn round and head for the apartment instead.

Hope disposed of the now-empty jar of olives that Andreas had recently disdained to eat. Perhaps being sick had done something odd to her taste buds, she was reasoning in some confusion just as she heard the slam of the front door. Her heart leapt into her mouth and instant optimism seized her in a heady tide. Andreas had come back...Andreas had realised that she could never have been unfaithful to him!

'I'm down in the bedroom!' she called when she heard him say her name with all the impatience that was so much a part of his abrasive character.

Pale blonde hair tumbling round her shoulders in silken disarray, Hope focused turquoise eyes bright with expectation on the doorway and wished she had had time to get dressed and do something about the redness of her eyes. Her restive hands fiddled with the sash of her wrap.

Stunning golden eyes blazing, Andreas strode in. Garbed in a dark designer suit that accentuated his superb masculine physique, he looked heartbreakingly handsome. In a gesture of high voltage intensity that she would never have associated with his cool, controlled nature, he pitched a whole handful of documents down on the carpet at her feet. 'You lying slut!' he raked at her in raw condemnation. 'You've visited Campbell's apartment on countless occasions! You've even stayed the night there. You've been screwing him for months!'

Dumbfounded by the naked aggression of that full-frontal verbal attack, Hope was paralysed to the spot. 'What on earth are you talking about?' she framed in bewilderment. 'I've never been in Ben's apartment. I don't even know where he lives.'

'Like hell you don't! Take a good look at the quality of the evidence I have!' Andreas enunciated from between even white teeth.

'Evidence?' Hope bent down to lift several of the sheets of paper and frown down at the neat lines of computerised entries. 'What are these?'

'Surprise...surprise. You've had round-the-clock security for most of the past year. Those are the most recent reports of your activities,' Andreas informed her grittily.

'I've had round-the-clock security?' Hope parroted in total astonishment. 'Are you saying you've been having me watched?'

'I would argue that watched *over* would be a more fair and accurate description.'

'Who's been watching me?' Hope queried tightly, the physical recoil of genuine revulsion assailing her at the very thought of strangers taking note of her every move while she went about her daily business in sublime ignorance of their presence in her life.

'One of my own security teams. Top-notch professionals, who can do the job without attracting attention or interfering with your freedom. They don't make mistakes,' Andreas declared in a ferocious undertone, 'so don't waste your time trying that line on me.'

Hope surveyed him with huge perturbed eyes. 'I'm horrified that you could have distrusted me to that extent. You actually paid people to spy on me. That's absolutely horrible.'

The faintest tinge of dark colour demarcated the angular bronzed planes of the aristocratic cheekbones that enhanced his superb bone structure. 'That isn't how it was. Anonymous threats were made against me. Naturally I was concerned that through your association with me you could be at risk. I considered it my duty to protect you and I *did*. End of story.'

Hope wasn't listening. She was very much shocked by what he had revealed. 'The very idea that strangers have been spying on me gives me the creeps. I never realised until now just how much I took my right to privacy for granted.'

The confrontation was travelling along unanticipated lines that were utterly infuriating Andreas. How dared she focus on a trivial and obscure angle and ignore the giant sin of her own infidelity? What the hell was her right to privacy worth when set beside the gross betrayal of her affair with another man? Where did she get the nerve to look at him in that reproachful way as if he had done something shameful?

'Until last night I never once requested a copy of the reports on your movements. I *did* respect your privacy one hundred per cent,' Andreas countered with grim exactitude, his sculpted masculine mouth firming. 'But I wanted to satisfy myself with the proof of your infidelity. The number of visits you have made to Campbell's apartment corroborated the accusation made against you in full.'

Hope was still studying the papers in her hand. A slight sound was impelled from her parted lips when she recognised the familiar address that appeared several times over in the daily reports. She began to understand how the latest misunderstanding had come about. She breathed in deep, glancing up with rueful turquoise eyes to say quietly, 'Ben does own that apartment. But he throws a lot of parties and the residents' committee made life difficult for him. He moved out last year and Vanessa lives there now.'

Andreas was unmoved. Hard-as-granite golden eyes clashed with hers. 'I don't believe you. But I've no doubt that your best friend would back up a cover story for your benefit.'

On that score he could not have been more wrong. Having grown up with parents who had frequently cheated on each other, Vanessa heartily despised the deceit that went hand in hand with infidelity. She was the last woman alive likely to lie to conceal a friend's affair.

Taken aback as she was by Andreas's instant dismissal of her explanation about the apartment, Hope swallowed hard. She was very pale. '*Vanessa* lives at that address,' she stressed in her determination to make him listen. 'I hardly know Ben Campbell and I have not been unfaithful to you. I appreciate how dreadful all this must look to you but surely the two years we've been together at least buys me the right to a fair hearing—'

Andreas studied her with raw contempt. 'It buys you nothing.'

He swung on his heel and strode out of the bedroom.

'Wait!' Hope called down the corridor after him.

Slowly and with a reluctance she could feel, Andreas turned his arrogant dark head and looked back at her.

Hope snatched in a jagged breath. Her nerves were so fraught that she had to immediately pull in another deeper breath. The terrifying finality and obduracy she saw stamped in Andreas's lean, hard face frightened her to the edge of panic. She saw that she truly had no choices left. She saw that keeping quiet about Elyssa's behaviour was no longer a sustainable stance. It was wrong that she should be afraid to tell the truth, she reflected unhappily. Unfortunately, the truth would be most unwelcome to Andreas. He might well dismiss what she said out of hand and hate her even more for making damaging allegations against his sister. But Hope felt that she should not let that daunting awareness prevent her from speaking out in her own defence. After all, she might never have another opportunity. As that reality sank in on her, as she was finally forced to confront the possibility that she might never see Andreas again, Hope was impelled into sudden speech.

'Let me give you my version of events last night. It was me who walked into a room and saw your sister in a clinch!' she admitted with all the abruptness of severe stress.

Outrage firing his brilliant gaze, his lean features clenching taut with disgust, Andreas fell very still. '*Theos*...don't say another word; stop right there—'

Hope thrust up her chin. 'I can't. Elyssa came after me and swore that I would suffer if I told you what I'd seen—'

'How dare you speak of my sister in such a way?' Andreas was white with anger below his olive skin.

'I had no intention of telling anybody what I'd seen...to be honest, I just didn't want to be involved,' Hope continued doggedly.

'You've said enough to make me your enemy for life. The Nicolaidis family have honour—each and every one of us and I am proud of that,' Andreas proclaimed in fierce dismissal. 'It is deeply offensive that you should soil Elyssa's reputation in a pointless attempt to rescue your own. Were you a man I would not have stood here and let you talk about my sister like that. Don't take advantage of the fact that you're a woman.'

'You're the one who's been taking advantage!' Hope protested, a floodtide of anger and agony breaking loose inside her because he had immediately dismissed her account of what had happened at the party. 'You've called me a liar and a slut...you're refusing even to listen to my side of the story.'

'What's to listen to? What's to understand?' Andreas demanded, striding back down the corridor and cornering her against the wall outside the bedroom. 'You spread your legs for a pretty blond toy boy!'

'Of course I didn't!' Colour had run like a banner into her cheeks. 'Don't be crude—'

'That's nothing to what I would like to know.' Andreas slammed his hands to the hall on either side of her head, effectively holding her entrapped. Smouldering golden eyes as dangerous as dynamite challenged her. 'Did you do it in *our* bed?'

'It didn't happen!' she cried. 'I wouldn't even look at someone else, never mind—'

'You forget...I *saw* you looking at Campbell last night,' Andreas reminded her darkly.

Hope was trembling with the strength of her emotions. Her spine pushing into the wall, she was forced to tip her face up. 'But I wasn't looking in the way you mean—'

'What does he have that I don't?' Andreas demanded with savage force. 'Is he better in bed?'

'Andreas...' Hope gasped, fierce embarrassment and dismay at the tenor of that blunt question making her full lower lip part from the cupid's bow curve of her upper.

'Is he more inventive? More exciting? Kinky? What did he do that I didn't do? Didn't I satisfy you? Tell me...I have the right to know!' he launched at her, stunning eyes smouldering ferocious gold with dark sexual jealousy and dropping to the luscious pink swell of her mouth.

'There's nothing for you to know!' she cried in despair.

The tension in the atmosphere was electric. At first Hope did not understand its source. There was a warm, heavy feeling low in her tummy, a buzzing vibration of awareness holding her on a dizzy edge. Holding her indeed on the edge of an anticipation that left her mind frighteningly blank.

'And right now…it's *me* you want,' Andreas purred with silken satisfaction, lifting lean brown hands to skim a blunt masculine thumb over the distended buds of her nipples, which were clearly delineated by the thin wrap.

Hope gasped in helpless response and arched her back. Her entire body felt hot and super sensitive. Recognising her own sexual excitement shook her inside out. 'Yes, but—'

'In fact you're begging for it,' Andreas husked, dropping his hands to her hips and mating his passionate mouth to hers with a bold hunger that in its very intensity was overwhelmingly erotic.

Fire snaked sinuous seductive forays through her heated flesh. She melted like honey in sunshine, yielding to the plundering thrust of his tongue and the heady intoxication of her own response. In one powerful movement he lifted her off her feet and carried her into the bedroom. As he brought her down on the bed his mouth was still melded to hers with devouring passion.

Just as swiftly he relinquished his hold on her. Still lost in the fever of her own desire, Hope clung to his shoulders to draw him back to her.

With cool disdain, Andreas detached her arms from him and straightened to his full commanding height. Proud, dark head high, he stared down at her with icy derision. 'It's over. The instant you let Campbell touch you, it was over. I expect my mistress to preserve her affections exclusively for me.'

Her face drained of colour, Hope thrust herself up

into sitting position. 'I'm not and I never was your mistress!'

From the doorway, Andreas vented a sardonic laugh that scored her tender skin like a whiplash. 'Of course you were. What else could you have been to me?'

Hurt far beyond his imagining, Hope blanked him out and stared into space. She could no longer bear to see him. She listened to his steps recede down the corridor, the distant slam of the front door echoing through the apartment. It was over and he was gone and without apparent regret. He could never have cared a button for her, she thought in an agony of mortified pain.

CHAPTER FOUR

FRANTIC to conceal the fact that she had been crying, Hope utilised some eye shadow to draw attention away from her reddened lids. 'Smile…' she instructed her flushed and unhappy reflection and she practised curving her mouth up instead of down at the corners.

It was seven weeks since she had moved into Vanessa's spare room. Her friend had been marvellous in every way but Hope knew that misery made other people uncomfortable. Vanessa had told her that the end of a relationship was the perfect excuse for a week of tears and laments, but that after that point it was time to move on. Ever since that week had ended Hope had been pretending that she was well over Andreas and miles down the road to recovery.

Unhappily, however, she was finding that maintaining that pretence was the most enormous strain. She assumed that stress had caused the further bouts of nausea she had suffered. Mercifully that sickness had petered out the previous month and, apart from a rather embarrassing craving for olives at certain times, she was fine. If she had a problem, it was with her state of mind. For so long Andreas had been the centre of her universe. Now every day stretched in front of her like a wasteland. Determined to keep up her spirits, she had concentrated on developing a new and much improved business plan. She had visited various financial institutions and was doing her utmost to win a business loan. So far, admittedly, she

had not been lucky, but she kept on telling herself
that success lay just round the next corner. In the
meantime, to meet her bills, she was working in a
shop and selling bags at occasional craft fairs.

'Are you sure you don't want any lunch?' Vanessa
called from the kitchen.

Hope emerged from her room. 'No, I grabbed
something earlier,' she fibbed because her friend had
begun to nag her about how little she was eating.

Vanessa, who ate like a horse and never put on an
ounce, strolled into the ultra-modern lounge. In one
hand she held a sandwich the size of a doorstep. 'So,
how did you get on with that bank this morning?'

Hope almost winced. 'The guy said he'd be in
touch but I don't think I'll be holding my breath.'

'Let Ben back your business,' Vanessa urged impatiently. 'Your funky handbags are a much better
risk than the racehorses he keeps on buying!'

Hope smiled to show that she was appropriately
grateful for Ben's offer of financial assistance.
However, her smile was a little tense round the edges,
for if being dumped by Andreas had taught her anything it was that caution and common sense should
be heeded. 'I don't think that would be a good idea.'

'Why not? Five different banks have turned down
your loan application,' the redhead reminded her
baldly. 'Ben's got money to burn and he's eager to
help. In your position I wouldn't think twice about
it.'

'Ben's your cousin. You see him from a slightly
different perspective,' Hope murmured gently.

Hope felt that she had learnt the hard way that there
was no such thing as a free lunch. She had lived rent-
free in Andreas's enormous apartment and that had

come back to haunt her. Instead of maintaining total independence, she had allowed herself to be seduced by the concept of pleasing Andreas and had become, in his eyes at least, a 'kept' woman. As a result, Andreas had found it impossible to see her as an equal. Instead he had regarded her as his mistress: an object and a possession rather than a lover whom he respected. Hope now felt that she understood how rich men looked on less financially successful women. At the same time, she was beginning to value Ben's friendship and did not want to muddy the waters by borrowing money from him.

Vanessa grinned. 'Of course. Ben treats me like a mate but he definitely has the hots for you. I think it's great that he's finally getting tired of the party girls and wakening up to the idea of a *real* woman.'

'I don't think Ben feels that way about me.' Hope was emanating embarrassment in visible waves. 'He likes me and, although he shouldn't, he feels a little guilty that Andreas made wrong assumptions about how well we knew each other.'

'Nah…' Vanessa elevated a mocking brow in disagreement. 'Ben's not that nice. He gets a kick out of having rattled Andreas's cage. We both think Andreas has acted like a callous bastard. But Ben also genuinely wants a chance with you—'

'Even if that's true, and I don't think it is…Ben loves to tease people. Well, I'm not in the notion of anything else right now anyway,' Hope fielded awkwardly.

Vanessa fixed exasperated brown eyes on her. 'Ben won't be interested for ever. Andreas isn't coming back, Hope. He's history.'

Hope's creamy skin was pale as milk. 'I know that—'

'I don't think you do. Have you any idea how worried I've been about you? Instead of living in your little world, you should be facing some hard facts—'

'I think I've faced quite a few of those in recent times,' Hope slotted in ruefully, wishing the other woman would just stand back and give her the time to heal.

'But let's recap,' the other woman said with determination. 'Andreas accused you of sleeping with Ben and he wasn't interested in letting you defend yourself—'

'He believed his sister,' Hope countered tightly. 'I can be very hurt about that but I can't hate him for trusting his own flesh and blood.'

'I reckon Andreas was ready for a change and his sister's lies gave him a fast and easy exit.'

Hope thought back to the fierce emotion that Andreas had betrayed at their last encounter and pain squeezed her heart so hard that she could hardly breathe. Had only his ego been stung by the belief that she had betrayed him?

'Take a look at this…' Vanessa settled a newspaper in front of her. It was folded open at the gossip page and a photo of Andreas with a beautiful skinny blonde. Hope felt as if someone had pushed her below the surface of a pool without giving her the chance to first take in a breath.

'I don't want to look at that,' she whispered shakily.

The redhead grimaced. 'I didn't want to do this to you but you've given me no choice. You won't even open the papers I keep on leaving around for you. But you need to know…Andreas is out partying like mad here in London *and* in New York. He's been seen out with a string of gorgeous models and celebrities. He's not grieving, he's not sitting in nights missing you—'

'I get the message…OK?' Hope breathed chokily. 'I didn't expect him to grieve. I doubt if many men grieve over a woman they think slept with some other man and Andreas is too proud.'

'I just want you to know and accept that you've seen the last of him.' Her friend squeezed her arm in a show of affection. 'It'll help you get over him more quickly.'

The doorbell buzzed. Momentarily, Hope shut her eyes: she had been plunged into the most terrifying tide of despair by Vanessa's lack of patience and tact. In what way was the excruciating spectacle of Andreas in the company of a breathtakingly lovely blonde supposed to help her heal?

'I'm Vanessa…isn't it amazing that we've never actually met until now? Hope's not expecting you, is she?' Vanessa was saying in a curiously loud and incredibly cheerful tone from the hall. 'She's only just got out of bed. In fact, she's wrecked and you'll be lucky if she can string two words together in a single sentence. She's been out to dawn every night this week!'

Transfixed by the sound of her friend giving vent to that rolling tide of outrageous lies, Hope lifted her lashes. What she saw paralysed her to the spot: Andreas stood in the doorway. *Andreas isn't coming back…you've seen the last of him.* Shock seemed to bounce her heart inside her, making it a challenge to catch her breath. Feeling the race of her heartbeat, she trembled. The breeze had tousled his cropped black hair. His lean, strong features were bronzed, his gleaming golden eyes veiled but intent. He looked every inch the heartbreaker he was.

'Thank you,' Andreas drawled smoothly as he snapped the door shut in Vanessa's madly inquisitive face.

'I wasn't expecting you,' Hope framed unevenly and she could have winced at the inanity of unnecessarily stating the obvious.

Andreas watched the light catch the faint track left by a tear on her cheek. Although her eyes still had the luminous intensity of turquoises, her familiar happy glow was gone. In response, the razor edge of his cold, aggressive mood mellowed. If she was miserable, it was only what she deserved. If she was missing him, regretting what she had stupidly thrown away, even better. If she were ready to beg for forgiveness, he would enjoy it even more.

Vanessa poked her head round the door that communicated with the kitchen. 'Would you like me to stay, Hope?'

For all the world as though she were a little kid in need of support around the grown-ups, Hope reflected in an agony of mortification. Recognising Andreas's derisive disbelief at that interruption, Hope almost cringed and took immediate action to avoid any further embarrassment. 'No, thanks. Actually, we're going into my room.'

'Don't be silly, there's no need for that! Naturally you can stay in here,' her friend exclaimed in an offended tone while treating Andreas to a sharp and unfriendly appraisal. 'I just thought you might need support.'

'I'm fine.' Mortified as Hope was by Vanessa's behaviour, she was determined to speak to Andreas in private and without fear of being overheard. She pulled open the door that led into the hall. 'This way,' she urged him in a rather harried undertone.

'We could always go and sit in the limo,' Andreas drawled sibilantly, flicking a chilling glance at Hope's friend. An interfering brazen bully, who he could see walked all over Hope in hobnail boots.

'No, really, that's not necessary, ' Hope declared breathlessly.

It was becoming obvious to Andreas that on one score at least Hope had not lied to him: Ben might own the apartment but his cousin, Vanessa Fitzsimmons, did indeed appear to be the current tenant. Of course the flat could still have been regularly used to facilitate Hope's affair with Campbell. Only as time passed and his powerful intellect continued to dwell on and question the few facts at his disposal, Andreas was finding it increasingly hard to credit that a lengthy affair had even taken place.

For a start, Hope had appeared to be her usual sunny self right up until the week before his sister's party. Hope had an honest and open nature and it would be wildly out of character for her to have engaged in long-term serious deception. He found it much easier to believe that she had simply succumbed to temptation that evening. He was also highly suspicious of the fact that the male involved was closely related to her best friend. After all, before he had even met Vanessa, Andreas had guessed that the woman was hostile to his relationship with Hope. Had Ben Campbell been encouraged to target Hope with his attentions? Had Campbell pretended to be a friend to

win Hope's trust and wear down her defences? In
short, had Hope been set up to fall?

'In here...' Hope pushed open the door of her bedroom and hoped it wasn't in too much of a mess. Why
had Andreas come to see her? Even the most vague
and far-fetched possibility that Andreas might want
her back reduced her mental agility to zero. Her
tummy filled with fluttering butterflies of nervous tension.

Andreas studied his surroundings with eyes so
keenly intent and precise that after ten seconds he
could have accurately enumerated every visible item
right down to the tiny corner of the chocolate wrapper
protruding from a drawer. His tension dropped several
degrees and his vigilance relaxed as he appreciated
that there was nothing in the room that suggested
even occasional male occupation. In fact the bed was
clearly only occupied by one person. One person with
a fondness for cuddly toys. He could not credit that
any male would willingly share space with the shabby
pink rabbit that had survived Hope's childhood.

As Hope stepped away from the door the disturbingly familiar scent of her herbal shampoo flared his
nostrils. Her pale silky blonde hair shimmered across
her shoulders like a fall of satin. His every physical
sense suddenly on full alert, he studied her. Her fabulous hourglass curves looked more pronounced than
ever but he assumed his memory was playing tricks
on him. Of recent he had been surrounded by some
very thin women, he reminded himself absently,
while he fought the treacherous buzz of his powerful
sexual arousal. Such comparisons could only make
Hope seem more luscious in contour. Regardless, the
bountiful swell of her generous breasts below her pink

T-shirt was nothing short of spectacular. His even white teeth gritted.

'Would you like to sit down?' she asked nervously, bending down to scoop a pile of magazines off a chair. Her top rode up a few inches at the back to reveal a slender strip of pale creamy skin.

'No...' His drawl was thickened by his Greek accent and his hands clenched into defensive fists. He wanted to touch that smooth, tantalising stretch of naked flesh in view. In fact he wanted to do a whole hell of a lot more than just touch Hope. After weeks of enduring a worryingly uninterested libido, he was rampant. He wanted to drag her down on the bed, rip off her clothes and have sex with her. Hot and deep and fast, out of control...mind-blowing as it was only with her.

Rigid with the force of the appetite he was containing and the temptation he was resisting with every aggressive fibre of his body, Andreas backed away until she was out of his natural reach. In an effort to control the biting heat of his unsated hunger, he focused on the magazines she had pushed onto the carpet. Evidently she was still obsessively reading interiors magazines. Publications stuffed with photos of period country dwellings groaning with oak beams and crammed with anachronistic kitchens and bathrooms. She was mad about houses. Her nest-building instincts would have terrified a weaker man. Andreas had contrived quite happily to ignore them. But now a taunting, infuriating voice was coming out of nowhere inside his head and asking him why he hadn't given her that fantasy and bought her a country house. Had he given her the opportunity to wallow in chintz and walled gardens, he was willing to bet that she would still have been with him.

'Coffee…?' Hope mumbled, her mouth running dry at the high-wire tension in the atmosphere. She could not take her eyes from his extravagantly handsome features.

A tinge of dark colour highlighting his striking high cheekbones, Andreas lowered thick black lashes over his brilliant eyes. 'I won't be here that long.'

'Are you sure? I'd like you to stay,' she heard herself say without any forethought or pride whatsoever. 'A while…' she added jerkily, hoping it made her sound a bit less desperate.

His lashes lifted, revealing his sizzling golden gaze. A combination of sexual desire and fierce resentment held him fast. If he dragged her down on the bed, would she say no? She had never, ever said no to him. Like an executioner letting the guillotine blade fall, he clamped down on that dangerous train of thought.

'I just want to know how you're doing…' Hope flinched, thinking of the blonde in that newspaper photo with all her bones on display. She breathed in hurriedly, afraid that he might already have noticed that her stomach was not as flat as it had been. Once comfort eating had kindly bestowed its largesse in less noticeable amounts on her hips and her breasts, but now visible surplus flesh was creeping onto her middle section as well.

'I've only one reason for being here. I couldn't get in touch any other way,' Andreas asserted with chilling cool, his beautiful mouth compressed with impatience, his defiant libido willed into subjection. 'What happened to your mobile phone?'

'It broke,' she confided.

'The number here is ex-directory,' he pointed out.

'Why did you want to get in touch with me?' Her nerves could no longer stand the suspense of waiting.

'Your brother has left several messages for you on the phone at the apartment. I believe he's visiting London next week. When he couldn't raise you on your mobile phone, he got worried.'

'Jonathan? Oh...' The colour in Hope's cheeks evaporated as severe disappointment claimed her. She felt very foolish and rather humiliated. Andreas had had the most pedestrian of reasons for coming to see her and his visit had no personal dimension whatsoever. But she could not have foreseen the likelihood of her brother suddenly trying to get in touch with her. As a rule she only heard from Jonathan with a card at Christmas and a catch-up phone call after New Year. If Jonathan were visiting London, he would be on a business trip, she thought dully.

'Make sure that you call him. That line has now been disconnected.'

Her brow indented. 'But why?'

'The apartment is for sale.'

That news hit her like a slap in the face. It made everything so dreadfully final. The apartment had been her home for two years. For her, it was still a place full of happy memories. Only now was she forced to acknowledge that she had still cherished secret hopes of returning to live there. She tried and failed to find consolation in the evident fact that at least he wasn't moving some other woman in.

'Don't you still need it?' she prompted tightly.

In silence, Andreas lifted and dropped a broad shoulder in continental dismissal of the topic.

Her turquoise eyes lifted and she noticed the way his gaze was welded to her mouth. Her lips tingled, felt dry. As the tip of her tongue snaked out to provide moisture his golden eyes smouldered and he reached for her in a sudden movement that stripped the breath from her lungs with a startled gasp.

'A-Andreas...?' she stammered, feverishly conscious of the lean, strong hands clamped to her wrists and the scant few inches separating their bodies.

'Don't make yourself cheap trying to turn me on,' Andreas delivered with derisive bite, setting her back from him in a mortifying gesture of rejection and releasing her from his hold.

Hope reeled back in shock from that icy rebuff. Somehow, heaven knew how, the distance between them had narrowed. Had she unconsciously drifted closer to him or was he the one responsible? Whatever, she had never been made to feel more humiliated than she did at that moment. 'You actually *think*...but I wasn't trying to—'

'It's such a waste of your time,' he murmured silkily. 'I'm over you.'

'I *wasn't* trying to turn you on!' Hope persisted, writhing with horror at the charge. Her temper surged up in response to her discomfiture. 'It's ridiculous to accuse me of that. You're the last guy in the world I'd want to make a play for. You're lucky that I'm even willing to still speak to you!'

Dark deep-set eyes gleaming gold, Andreas angled his arrogant head high and loosed a derisive laugh that gave her a shocking desire to kick him. 'And how do you make that out?'

'Well, for a start, you've insulted me beyond any hope of forgiveness. You misjudged me and you

dumped me for something I didn't do. The night of
that party, I hardly knew Ben Campbell but you refused to listen to me,' she condemned with helpless
bitterness. 'When Ben found out what happened between us, he said he was willing to go and speak to
you for me—'

Unimpressed, Andreas grimaced. 'How cheap…is
he now wishing he had kept his hands off my property?'

'I'm not and I never was your property!' Hope
shouted back at him so shrilly and in so much distress
that her voice broke. 'Now get out of here!'

Ben had made a grudging offer to speak to Andreas
on her behalf but she had decided that dragging the
younger man into her personal problems would have
been unfair, embarrassing and probably pointless.
Andreas's derisive crack about Ben had confirmed
Hope's conviction that Ben's intervention would have
been unsuccessful. Andreas believed his sister's version of events and would discount any other. He had
swallowed his sister's lies hook, line and sinker.
Nothing she could do or say would alter that.

'With pleasure,' Andreas spelt out.

As Andreas strode to the door it opened, framing
Ben Campbell. 'Are you OK?' he asked Hope, ignoring Andreas.

Tears were dammed up inside her like a threatening
floodtide. She thought if she let them out, she might
wash both Ben and Andreas away. For the space of
a heartbeat, the two men were side by side. With his
slighter build, fair hair and fine features, not to mention his trendy jeans, Ben looked boyish next to
Andreas, but the concern in his eyes warmed her.

Andreas subjected her to a chilling glance of contempt as if Ben's mere presence was an offence.

'I hate you...' Hope mumbled tautly. 'I've never said that to anyone before...I've never felt this way before either. But what you've done to me and the way you've treated me has changed me.'

'You shouldn't be here upsetting Hope. Leave her alone,' Ben said abruptly.

And the glitter in Andreas's stunning eyes blazed as hot as the heart of a fire. A satisfied smile driving the inflexible hardness from his shapely mouth, he stepped back and hit Ben so hard that the younger man went crashing out into the hall where he fell back against the wall.

'*Theos*...I owed you that,' Andreas growled with seething emphasis, aggression etched into every taut and ready line of his big, powerful body.

'How *could* you do that?' Hope gasped in horror, appalled at his violence and guilty that she should have been the cause of it.

'If I wasn't averse to spilling blood in front of women, I'd kill him,' Andreas intoned without a shred of shame.

Grimacing, Ben hauled himself up out of his slump with a groan. Flushed with anger, he launched himself away from the wall, but before he could attempt to strike a blow in retaliation Hope had stepped between him and Andreas.

'I'm so sorry about this. But please don't sink to *his* level,' Hope begged Ben frantically, terrified that masculine pride would press him into a fight that she was certain he would lose.

'Spoilsport,' Andreas growled between clenched teeth, outraged by the sight of her rushing to protect the other man, the freezing cool of his innate strong will icing over the outrage and denying it.

'And to the winner goes the spoils,' Ben countered, closing his hand over Hope's to anchor her to his side in a deliberately provocative statement. 'I don't need to hammer anyone into a pulp to impress her.'

'That is fortunate. You're usually too drunk even to try,' Andreas riposted with lethal distaste.

Shell-shocked by the amount of bad feeling between the two men, Hope watched Andreas stride out of the apartment and out of her life all over again. He did it without a backward glance or a word. She shivered, feeling cold and crushed and bereft.

With a rueful sigh, Ben released Hope's limp fingers. 'I guess I shouldn't have said that. But Nicolaidis is an arrogant bastard. I couldn't resist the urge to give him the wrong impression. He deserves to think we're together.'

Hope tried to twitch her numb lips into a smile of agreement. Ben had got punched because of her. Ben had got punched for being kind and supportive. If he had chosen to save face by implying that they were in a relationship, he had only been confirming what Andreas already believed. Anyway, Hope reflected wretchedly, what did what Andreas thought matter any more?

Vanessa had been right. She had been hiding her head in the sand, living in the past, shrinking from the challenge of the present. Now she had to face the future and accept that Andreas was gone for good. Andreas had moved on. He was seeing other women, taking advantage of his freedom. A brief, shattering image of that lean, bronzed body she knew so well wrapped round that gorgeous blonde in the newspaper threatened to destroy her self-control. If that image hurt—well, it did hurt; in fact it was a huge hurt that hit her so hard she felt traumatised. But the point was, she had to get used to dealing with that hurt.

'Andreas doesn't care about what I'm doing any more,' Hope muttered, wondering if it was possible to teach herself to fancy Ben. Loads of females found Ben madly attractive and witty. He was around a great deal more than Andreas had ever been. Of course, he did party a little too much and too often and in comparison she was really quite a staid personality. But with some give and take, who knew what might be possible? Perhaps she needed to keep in mind just how many compromises she had made on Andreas's behalf...

When had she ever dreamt of living in the city without a garden and beside busy, noisy roads? When had she dreamt of loving a guy who did not return her love and who made her no promises? A guy who was often abroad and who was so busy even when he was not that she hardly saw him. She might be breaking her heart for Andreas but that did not mean he had been perfect.

He had acted like a Neanderthal if she'd interrupted the business news. He had woken her up for sex at dawn and referred to the candles she had placed round the bath as a fire hazard. He had ignored St Valentine's Day. He had given her a pen that first Christmas. It had been an all-singing all-dancing pen that was solid gold and jewelled and could be used for writing at the bottom of the sea, but it had still been a pen. She had also been left alone while he'd enjoyed the festive season in Greece. Why had it taken her so long to appreciate that Andreas had treated her rather as a married man would treat a mistress?

He had agreed that they could live at the apartment without servants, but had continued to live as though the servants were still invisibly present. He had never been known to pick up a discarded shirt or bath towel. Like a domestic goddess to whom nothing was too much trouble when it came to the man in her life, she had cooked, tidied and laundered. And not once had he noticed, commented or praised. In fact Andreas was so domestically challenged that when she had asked him to make her a cup of tea he had ordered it in. Her eyes were filmed with tears but she told herself it was regret for the two years she had thrown away on such an arrogant specimen of masculinity. He had not deserved her love and it was time she got over him. If she went out with someone else, wouldn't that be the best way to speed up her recovery?

Ben regarded her with lazy aplomb. 'Come down to the cottage with Vanessa this weekend,' he suggested. 'There'll be a crowd. We could have a blast.'

'Just friends?' Hope breathed tautly, tempted by the welcome prospect of being able to escape the city for a couple of days.

'Kissing friends only,' Ben traded teasingly, but there was an edge of seriousness in his tone.

Hope turned a hot pink and embarrassment claimed her. 'Thanks, but no, thanks— I don't know you well enough—'

Before she could turn away, Ben closed a hand over hers. 'I'm not expecting you to sleep with me yet—'

She was really embarrassed. 'No? But—'

'I know my reputation but I'm willing to go slow for you,' Ben promised.

Evading his eyes, Hope nodded. She did not know what to say. She did not think that there was the remotest chance of her *ever* wishing to become that intimate with Ben Campbell or indeed anyone else. Yet, without hesitation, Andreas had slammed shut the door on the past they had shared, she reminded herself doggedly. Presumably Andreas suffered from none of her sensitivities. But then Andreas had never loved her. That was the bottom line that she needed to remember, she told herself painfully. Sitting around alone and feeling sorry for herself would not improve her lot or her spirits. Perhaps if she went through the motions of enjoying herself, enjoyment would begin to come naturally.

The following week, Hope met her brother for dinner at his hotel. More than two years had passed since their last meeting. She was grateful that she had not had the opportunity to mention Andreas during the annual phone calls when Jonathan had brought her up to speed on what was happening in his life. At least she did not now have to announce that she had been dumped, she told herself in consolation. Seeing her brother's fair head across the quiet restaurant, she smiled warmly, wanting to make the most of so rare an occasion.

'You haven't got something to tell me, have you?' Jonathan enquired, arranging his thin features into an exaggerated grimace as he stood up and raising a mocking brow.

'Sorry?' Hope stepped back from him with an uncertain look. 'What's the joke?'

'Well, I suppose it's not that funny.' Her older

brother sighed heavily. 'But when I first saw you walking towards me, I honestly thought you were pregnant. Don't you think it's time you went on a diet?'

Hope reddened with hurt and embarrassment. She had forgotten just how critical Jonathan could be of a body image that was not as lean as his own. His wife, Shona, was a physical education instructor and the couple and their children led a formidably healthy lifestyle. Although it had been some time since Hope had had the courage to approach the bathroom scales, she was already painfully aware that she had put on weight and she could have done without her brother's blunt comments. At present only the larger sizes in her wardrobe were a comfortable fit. *I thought you were pregnant.* How could he say that to her? Did she really look that large? Tears burned the backs of her eyes.

'You're letting yourself go. It's time for a wake-up call,' her sibling continued without a shade of discomfiture. 'A good diet and exercise regime would transform you. Did I tell you that Shona has opened a fitness salon?'

'No...'

'Business is good, *very* good,' Jonathan asserted with satisfaction. 'I'll get Shona to send you a copy of her favourite diet.'

Pregnant. Hope was lost in her own feverish thoughts. She was thinking of the new bras she had been forced to buy and considering her tummy's more rounded profile. She was gaining weight in a pattern that was different from her own personal norm. Then there were those secret binges on olives. Hadn't she once read that some women were afflicted by strange cravings during pregnancy? But aside of all those vague factors, what had happened to her menstrual cycle in recent months?

'My firm is operating to full capacity. We can hardly keep up with the order book,' her brother informed her cheerfully. 'Life has been very good to Shona and I.'

'I'm happy for you,' Hope mumbled, transfixed by the alarming awareness that she could not recollect when she had last had a period. It was not something she took a note of or indeed looked for or had ever made welcome. But her cycle had always been a regular one. Yet if her memory served her well, her cycle had not been functioning correctly for several months at the very least. Did that mean that there *was* a possibility that she could be pregnant?

'I'll always be grateful that you had the generosity to allow me to inherit mother's estate,' Jonathan added squarely. 'At the time I needed that inheritance and I was able to make excellent use of it.'

It was only with the greatest difficulty that Hope could keep up with the conversation, for anxiety had turned her skin clammy. She was being forced to acknowledge that there was a distinct chance that she could have conceived while she was still with Andreas.

'Hope…' Jonathan prompted.

'Sorry, I'm a bit preoccupied today,' Hope apologised weakly. 'But I was listening. I know you'll have made good use of that money.'

'But it's been on my conscience ever since and it's only fair that you should get the same opportunity. After all, you cared for our mother for a long time and you sacrificed your education and prospects.'

With a look of distinct pride Jonathan laid a cheque down on the table in front of her. 'I can now afford to return the original inheritance to you. If you're still planning to open your own business, a cash injection should help.'

Hope stared down at the cheque open-mouthed and blinked in astonishment. Her sibling had managed to thoroughly disconcert her. Below the level of the table she had splayed her fingers across the soft swell of her stomach while she'd focused on the shattering idea that she could be carrying a baby. But now she had to concentrate on the very large cheque that her brother had just presented her with.

'My goodness...' she said shakily.

'If you're about to embark on a new business, you'll need to be super fit,' Jonathan warned her. 'I still think a diet should be at the very top of your agenda.'

CHAPTER FIVE

ANDREAS saw the artistic photo of the three handbags first. The shot was part of a feature in a Sunday magazine devoted to Vanessa Fitzsimmons's deeply trendy photographic exhibition. There was a miniature silver-on-black Hope label in the seam of the tiny lime-green bag and it was a dead giveaway to Andreas. Courtesy of Vanessa, the handbags had been arranged against a rough stone wall as though they were works of art. His handsome mouth curled. He wondered why he was even looking at such superficial rubbish.

Flipping the page, however, Andreas was wholly entrapped by a shot of Hope sitting on a rock by a river. Several other faces that were far more well known on the social scene featured in the same study, which was called simply 'My friends' but Andreas initially saw only Hope. A multicoloured gypsy-style top open at her creamy throat, her face bathed in golden sunlight and her turquoise eyes luminous, she looked knock-down stunning. A tiny muscle jumped at the corner of his clenched jaw line. His brilliant dark gaze slashed from Hope to the male standing to one side of her: that smug-looking bastard, Campbell, who had a proprietary hand resting on her shoulder.

A boiling tide of rage filled Andreas. He wanted to smash something. Instead he poured himself a drink. It was only ten in the morning. Self-evidently, he was on edge because he had been working too hard for too long, he reasoned grimly. Rage had no place in his disciplined world. All emotion, irrational and otherwise could be controlled, suppressed and ultimately nullified by intelligence. He drained the glass and smashed the crystal tumbler in the Georgian fireplace. The deed was done before he was even aware of his intention.

Hope emerged from the doctor's surgery on rather wobbly legs.

Vanessa leapt up and groaned. 'You *are*, aren't you? I can tell by your face!'

Hope nodded and did not speak until they reached the street. She had been told that she was more than five months pregnant and she was in complete shock. 'The oddest thing is,' she mused helplessly in the fresh air, 'I'm a healthy weight for a pregnant woman. I'm not too heavy. Can you believe that?'

'Andreas Nicolaidis has ruined your life,' her friend lamented in a tone of unconcealed resentment. 'You've just started seeing Ben, you're just about to look for business premises and then it all goes pear-shaped on you. How could you be so careless?'

Hope went pink and cast down her eyes. She had not been careless; Andreas had been, though. Several different types of contraceptive pill had failed to agree with her and Andreas had been concerned that she would be damaging her health if she persisted. For that reason, about nine months earlier, he had said that he would take full responsibility in that field. Unfortunately he had been rather forgetful on at least a couple of occasions that came to mind. Certain methods of birth control could put a breaker on spontaneity and Andreas was a very spontaneous guy, she reflected with a pained stab of recollection.

'So how far along are you?' Vanessa enquired gloomily.

Hope sucked in her tummy guiltily, for she could see that the sight of her changing shape depressed her friend. 'I'll be a mother in just over three months.'

Vanessa stopped dead in the middle of the street and surveyed her in wonderment. 'But you can't be *that* pregnant!'

'I am...'

'But how could you not have noticed?' The redhead gasped, standing back to subject Hope's stomach to a distinctly embarrassing appraisal. 'I mean, give your brother a medal. You *do* look pregnant and yet none of us noticed!'

'I've been wearing loose clothing,' Hope pointed out. 'And people only see what they expect to see.'

When she had first fallen pregnant, her life had been incredibly busy and she had been so wrapped up in Andreas that she had failed to notice that her menstrual cycle had come to a mysterious halt. The other signs of pregnancy had also passed her by. Her health had never given her cause for concern and she had shrugged off the slight nausea and the dizziness she had experienced, believing neither symptom worthy of a visit to the doctor. In more recent months her personal woes had acted like a cocoon that had blinded her to everything outside her own thoughts and feelings, she acknowledged ruefully.

'What are your plans?'

'I have to tell Andreas.'

Vanessa pulled a sour face. 'Let Ben know first.'

But Hope did not fall for that suggestion. For the

first time in two and a half months, she rang Andreas on his mobile phone and left a message on his voicemail asking if she could see him to discuss something important.

It was three hours before he returned her call. 'What is it?' he breathed coldly without any preliminary greeting.

'I need to see you and I can't talk about it on the phone. Where are you?'

Somewhere close by, a woman giggled and muttered something in a low, intimate voice. 'In the UK and busy,' Andreas said dryly.

She squeezed her aching eyes tight shut. She did not want to speak to Andreas and hear his dark, deep drawl and she especially did not want to listen to another woman speaking to him in the teasing tone of a lover. In fact she really could not bear that torment at all.

'I'm also leaving for Athens tomorrow morning,' Andreas informed her coolly. 'This is your one chance to speak to me. Use it or lose it.'

'No, I have to see you in person and in private,' Hope countered tautly. 'I don't think that's such a huge thing to ask.'

'Perhaps not but the prospect is not entertaining,' Andreas fielded, smooth and sharp as a shard of glass cutting into tender skin. 'In short, I don't want to see you.'

'Do you expect me to beg you for five minutes of your time?' Hope demanded painfully, angry, humiliated tears clogging up her throat, for she had not been prepared for that level of bluntness.

'OK. If you're that keen, you'll find me at the gym

tomorrow morning at seven.' He finished the call without another word and left her staring into space.

How was she supposed to tell a guy that cold and unfriendly that she was carrying his child? He was not going to be happy about that. Even when they had still been together, Andreas would not have been happy about that. How much worse would it be to break such shattering news now that they were apart? It had been a long time since they had broken up as well. What male was likely to be even remotely prepared for such an announcement weeks and weeks after the relationship had ended? How could he be so cruel as to demand that she come to the gym where he trained at practically the crack of dawn? He knew the one thing she had always hated was getting out of bed early.

Andreas enjoyed extensive private facilities at an exclusive sports club and visited it several times a week. He had a fitness room at his town house but rarely managed to use it. He had once explained that the club offered him the advantage of sparring with an instructor and training without distractions.

As Hope walked past the limousine in the car park his chauffeur acknowledged her with a polite inclination of his head. What did it matter *where* she was when she made her announcement? she was asking herself ruefully. His office would not have been any more suitable and she would not have felt comfortable at the town house, which he had never invited her to visit even when they had been together. Furthermore, it was foolish to suspect that some slight was inherent in his suggestion that she meet him at his club. After all, Andreas had very little free time and she had to accept the reality that she no longer enjoyed special status in his life.

The weathered older man presiding over Reception asked to see proof of her identity and then told her where to find Andreas. Smoothing damp palms down over the long black wool coat she wore, Hope pushed back the swing door on the gym.

Clad in black boxing shorts and a black vest, Andreas was pounding a speedball with so much energy that he remained unaware of her entrance. She had always been madly curious about exactly what he did at the sports club. Now she remembered him telling her that he had boxed at university. Her attention clung to him. He looked drop-dead gorgeous, she thought helplessly. Every lean, muscular and bronzed line of his long, powerful physique emanated virile masculine strength. She missed looking at him, being with him, touching him, talking to him. She even missed the pleasure of being able to think about him without feeling guilty.

'Andreas…' she croaked.

Although she would have sworn he could not have heard her above the racket of the speedball, his hands dropped down to his sides immediately and he swung round as though his every sense had been primed for her arrival. Veiled dark deep-set eyes with the brilliance of black granite inspected her from below inky, spiky lashes.

It was a bad moment for Andreas. He had picked the club with care. He had thought it an inspired choice of venue where Hope was unlikely to linger or stage an emotional scene. But there she was, garbed in a big black coat and reminding him very much of how she had looked in his overcoat in the barn when they had first met: all silky soft blonde hair and huge bright eyes above that ripe pink unbelievably kissable mouth. That was Ben Campbell's territory now, came the thought, and he went rigid. He hung onto that alienating awareness and welcomed the return of the cold, bitter aggression that slaughtered at source any suggestion of sexual desire.

'So...' Andreas murmured, secure again in his emotion-free zone and cold as a polar winter. 'How can I help you?'

'Well, it's not something you can help me with exactly,' Hope declared in an odd little breathless voice that made her want to wince for herself. Without warning the entire opening speech she had planned to make had vanished from her memory. Her brain now seemed to have all the speed and creative enterprise of a tortoise trapped upside down.

Andreas discovered that like a schoolboy he was picturing her naked below the coat. Angry colour outlined his proud cheekbones and his beautiful mouth curled. He was well rid of her, he decided furiously. He loathed the effect she had on him. 'I haven't got much time here,' he reminded her flatly. 'But maybe you just came here to look at me.'

'No, I came here to tell you something that I find very difficult to say,' Hope advanced jerkily.

'At this hour of the day I'm not in the mood for a guessing game!' Andreas derided and he stripped off the fingerless mitts and flexed long, lean brown fingers.

Hope tried a limp smile. 'Actually I do wish you would guess but it's not the sort of thing you're likely to think of on your own. Although you always look on the dark side of things, so I suppose that ought to provide some guidance.'

Exasperated golden eyes lodged to her anxious face, Andreas murmured dryly, 'What's the matter with you? You never used to have a problem getting to the point.'

'That was back when you looked at me as if I was still a human being instead of a waste of space!' Hope dared, appalled to find that without even the tiniest warning her eyes were suddenly ready to overflow with tears.

Andreas was in the act of pulling on boxing gloves but he stilled and shot a stern look of gleaming golden enquiry at her. His stomach had performed a back flip and he had broken out in a sweat. 'Are you ill? Is that what you're trying to tell me?'

'No...not, not at all,' she asserted, taken aback by that dramatic flight of fancy on his part.

Relief washing over him, Andreas dragged in a long, deep breath to refresh his lungs. He strode towards the leather punchbag. 'Then talk before I run out of patience,' he urged.

'I'm pregnant.'

Andreas froze two feet away from the punchbag. Stunned by her declaration, he did not turn his arrogant dark head. 'If that's a joke, it's in bad taste and I'm not laughing.'

'I wouldn't joke about something like that.'

Andreas discovered that he could not make himself look at her again. He believed he already saw the whole scenario and what he assumed could only leave a very nasty taste in his mouth. Bitter anger slashed through his wall of determined indifference and reserve. Hope had fallen for Campbell. He had come to terms with that. But that Campbell should have stolen her and used her and ditched her again when she proved to be inconveniently fertile enraged Andreas. He did not trust himself to speak. If he spoke he knew he would make comments that she would consider cruel and wounding and that those words would ultimately prove to be of no profit or consolation to either of them.

How the hell could she have been so stupid? Hadn't she learned anything while she was with him? Of course, she had been able to trust him to look after her, Andreas reflected grimly. She had not had to look out for herself. That was just as well because, in his considered opinion, when shorn of his protective care she had all the survival power of a goldfish swimming with piranhas. She gave her trust indiscriminately. But Campbell had been a very poor bet. He was a spoilt and immature playboy with too much money and no sense of responsibility.

Was it so surprising that Hope should have come back to him for support? What did she want from him? Or expect? Advice? It would be very biased. Money? Suddenly, Andreas was grateful that she was fully covered by her coat. He did not wish to see the physical evidence of her pregnancy. *Theos*…she had another man's baby inside her womb! The very concept of that filled him with antipathy and another even more powerful reaction that he flatly refused to acknowledge. Out of disgust and denial rose rage and frustration. An image of Campbell and his pretty-boy looks before him, Andreas pounded the leather punchbag with fists that had the impact of blows from a sledgehammer.

Paralysed to the spot ten feet away, Hope surveyed

Andreas with a sinking heart. He was furious and fighting it to stay in control. He was saying nothing because he was too clever to risk saying the wrong thing. She watched him fall back from the punchbag and pull off and discard the boxing gloves. Raking blunt fingers through his short damp black hair, he swore half under his breath and peeled off his sports vest to let the air cool his overheated skin.

'I need a shower,' he breathed grittily. 'Come on.'

He wanted her to accompany him to the shower? Hope would have gone anywhere he asked her to go. Even in such tense circumstances it felt amazing to be with Andreas again. There was an electric buzz in the air. As she preceded him into a luxurious changing area flanked by a walk-in wet room for showering, she was as nervous as a kitten.

'Aren't you going to say anything at all?' she prompted tautly, disconcerted that he should be dealing with her news so much more calmly than she had expected.

Scorching golden eyes lit on her squarely for the first time in several minutes. The burn of his ferocious anger needed no words. Her mouth running dry, she tried and failed to swallow. Hurriedly she tore her gaze from the condemnation in his.

'I know you have to be very surprised. I was too,' she muttered, unable to stifle her need to fill every silent, tension-filled moment with chatter. 'But I'm trying to view this development in a positive light—'

'What else?' Andreas ground out in a disturbingly abrupt interruption.

Hope fixed strained turquoise eyes on his lean, darkly handsome features. 'This baby was obviously meant to be.'

'That's a hellish sentiment to throw in my teeth!' Andreas raked at her, his Greek accent so thick she could hardly distinguish the individual words.

Aghast, Hope fell silent. He bent down and extracted a bottle of water from the mini fridge, wrenched off the lid and tipped it up. He drank thirstily, the strong muscles in his brown throat working. As he wiped his mouth dry again she could not help noticing that his hand was not steady. He was, she registered with a piercing sense of love and empathy, as on edge as she was.

'Maybe I should go,' she mumbled. 'I've said what I came to say and I'm sure you must want to think it over in private.'

'I didn't intend to raise my voice. Sit down,' Andreas instructed, grimly acknowledging that the last thing he wanted was to be left alone with the bombshell she had dropped on him.

'I should leave you to have your shower,' she said uncomfortably.

'Sit down,' Andreas repeated, striding past her to snap shut the lock on the door. His reaction to her suggestion that she depart was instinctive. '*Please…*'

Soothed by the rare sound of that word, Hope became a little less tense. 'It's warm in here,' she remarked and began to unbutton her coat.

'Keep your coat on!' Andreas growled as if she had threatened to strip naked, parade around and make a dreadful exhibition of herself.

Andreas decided that an ice-cold shower would settle his tension. He felt as if he were hanging onto his usual cool by a single finger. She was carrying a child and an honourable man did not lose his temper with a woman in that condition. 'Give me five minutes and then you can have my full attention.'

Hope sat down in her coat. She was overheating but in infinitely better spirits: he had locked the door to keep her with him. She had understood that gesture just as she understood that he needed some time to consider what she had told him. She was well aware that he did not like the unexpected. He liked everything cut and dried and organised. He had never, ever mentioned children to her. It was perfectly possible that he disliked children. Some people did. And even if he did not dislike children, he might still want nothing to do with her baby. He might ask her to consider adoption. He had the right to make his own views known and she had to accept that she might not like what she was about to hear, she told herself firmly.

Andreas stripped off his boxing shorts and strolled into the shower. Hope stared and reddened and glanced away and then glanced back again in a covert but mesmerised appraisal. He was incredibly male and from his wide shoulders, magnificent hair-roughened chest to his lean hips and long, powerful thighs he was quite divinely well built. She had always loved to look at him. But she knew she no longer had the right to do so and that his complete lack of inhibition in the current climate merely emphasised how shattered he was by the news of her pregnancy. Her eyes ached and burned and she averted her gaze from him while he towelled himself dry with unselfconscious grace. She was remembering how happy she had once been and appreciating how desperately fragile and fleeting happiness could be.

Andreas dressed with speed and dexterity in a dark blue suit. Exquisitely tailored to a superb fit on his lean, powerful frame, it was very fashionable in style. He looked sleek and rich and gorgeous and distinctly intimidating.

'Tell me…what do you want from me?' he asked softly, opening the door and standing back with innate good manners to allow her to leave first.

Her brow indented, her tension climbing again. 'I don't want anything. I have no expectations. I just knew I had to tell you.'

His beautiful stubborn mouth quirked. 'Thank you for that consideration at least. I would not have liked to find out from someone else. How did Campbell react?'

'Ben?' Hope repeated in surprise, struggling to keep up with his long stride as they crossed the foyer. 'He doesn't know yet. I don't know what I'll say—'

Ebony brows pleating, Andreas stared down at her with incisive dark golden eyes. 'You chose to tell me…*first*?'

'Who else? I mean…strictly speaking, what's Ben got to do with this?' Hope asked uncomfortably.

'He is the father of your baby,' Andreas drawled flatly.

On the steps outside, Hope came to a sudden halt and stared up at him. As that most revealing statement sank in on her she stiffened in appalled disbelief. 'My goodness, is that what you think? That Ben is the father? Oh, that's too much altogether!' she exclaimed angrily. 'How dare you assume that? How blasted dare you? I'm very sorry to disappoint you but you are the man who is responsible!'

Andreas vented a rough, incredulous laugh, for he could not believe what she was now telling him. 'You've got to be kidding…is that why you had to see me? You think you can pin this baby on me? What would prove to be the longest pregnancy on record? I dumped you months ago!'

By the time he had finished making that derogatory and insulting speech, Hope was pale as snow. But shocked though she was, she was also furious. 'I've no intention of lowering myself to the level of arguing with you and particularly not in a public place!' she hissed in a fierce undertone he had never heard her employ before. 'I've done my duty: I've told you. I will not tolerate your offensive personal comments—'

'But what you just said is ridiculous!' Andreas ground out at a lower pitch, closing a domineering hand to her elbow to herd her in the direction of his limousine. 'I assume Campbell has shown his worth in the crisis by bolting. But accusing me in his stead is not a win-win tactic.'

In a passionate temper new to her experience, Hope slapped his hand away from her arm and backed off several steps. 'I'm ashamed I ever loved you and you can stop being so superior about Ben—'

His stunning golden eyes were blazing. 'Get a grip on yourself.'

'At least Ben didn't try to seduce me before we even got out on a first date! At least he's looking for a girlfriend, not a mistress…you know something?' Hope demanded shrilly. 'I wish this was Ben's baby because I bet he'd be a lot nicer about it than you're capable of being!'

'Hope…' Andreas grated from behind her as she stalked away.

'Leave me alone…just stay away from me!' she launched back over her shoulder, not even caring about the fact that her raised voice and distress had attracted attention.

CHAPTER SIX

FOR the second time in as many months, Andreas made a last-minute change to his plans and turned back from the airport.

He did not feel that he had a choice: Hope was seriously distressed. In fact she seemed to be coming apart at the seams. She had slapped out at him, lost her temper and shouted at him, and she had done all of that in front of an audience of interested by standers. It was as though she had had a personality transplant. Yet he knew her as a kind, gentle and unassuming woman, who was slow to anger and blessed with a cheerful outlook on life. Clearly, Ben Campbell was responsible for the appalling change in Hope. He had destroyed her tranquillity and plunged her into so much misery and confusion that she was making wild accusations.

Of course Campbell was the father of her baby! But evidently, Hope did not want Campbell in that role. It seemed obvious to Andreas that Hope's toy boy had cut and run from the threat of paternity and left her in the lurch. So how was that *his* business? And why was he getting involved? Hope was in trouble and she had approached him for help. Who else did she have to turn to? Why shouldn't he demonstrate that he was more of a man when the chips were down than Campbell would ever be?

Back at Vanessa's apartment, Hope was tumbling a jumble of clothes into a squashy bag and asking feverishly, 'Are you absolutely sure it's OK for me to use your family's cottage?'

'Stop fussing. My mother's in Jersey and my aunt, Ben's mother, is far too grand for the cottage now. At least you'll keep it aired,' Vanessa remarked. 'But is it such a good idea for you to leave London right now?'

'I need peace...I have to think.'

Vanessa gave her a wry look. 'Well, not about what you'll be doing with the baby. You're crazy about babies, so I feel it's fairly likely that you'll be keeping the sprog. This sudden departure from city life, however, feels more like you're running away—'

Hope lifted her head, turquoise eyes defiant at that charge. 'I'll only be at the cottage for a few days. I'm not running away. I just don't want to see Andreas—'

'I don't see him around to bother you. I gather by your attitude that he's not going to be pitching for the Father of the Year award?' Vanessa could not hide her curiosity.

'Not while he thinks Ben fathered my baby—'

'He thinks Ben knocked you up?' the redhead queried in lively astonishment.

'I hate that expression. Please don't use it—'

'Didn't you tell Andreas *how* pregnant you are?'

'No, I didn't stay around to exchange conversation after he had made it clear that he was convinced Ben was the guilty party,' Hope admitted heatedly. 'Oh yes, Andreas also accused me of trying to pin my baby on him because Ben didn't want to know!'

Her friend gave an exaggerated wince. 'When Andreas gets it wrong, he gets it *horribly* wrong.'

Hope threaded a restive hand through the pale blonde strands of hair falling across her brow. 'I tried to understand that he trusted his sister and believed in her. I tried to be fair to him but I don't feel like being understanding any more,' she confessed in a driven rush. 'I've put up with enough. I thought that Andreas had a right to know about the baby but now I wish I had stayed away from him.'

'I have a confession to make.' Vanessa stretched her mouth into a wry look of appeal. 'I told Ben about the baby...I know, I know, it wasn't my business. Unfortunately I let something slip accidentally over lunch and when he picked up on it, I couldn't lie, could I?'

'No...you couldn't lie.' But Hope guessed that Vanessa had quite deliberately chosen to break the news of her friend's pregnancy to Ben. Had her friend been afraid that, on the spur of the moment, Ben might say something hurtful? Or had Vanessa decided that it was unfair that Ben should be left in ignorance while Andreas was put in the picture? Whatever, Vanessa had interfered and perhaps she shouldn't have done. At that moment, however, Hope was guiltily grateful not to be faced with the embarrassing prospect of having to tell Ben that she was expecting Andreas's child. Informing Andreas had been upsetting enough. Yet Ben, whom she had been seeing for just three short weeks, was entitled to hear the same announcement.

'Ben was gobsmacked.' Vanessa heaved a sigh and jerked a slim shoulder. 'He's keen on you but I don't think he has a clue how to deal with this situation.'

'I'm not stupid. I'm not expecting Ben to deal with it and stay around.' Hope forced a laugh at the very idea. 'What guy would?'

Vanessa reflected on that question. 'A very special

one,' she said finally. 'But I'm not sure Ben is up for the challenge.'

'Why on earth should he be? Within another month at most I'll be a dead ringer for a barrel in shape!' Hope quipped.

The doorbell went.

Both women stilled.

'It's probably for you,' her friend forecast.

Hope finished zipping her bag and then, tilting her chin, she went to answer the bell.

Andreas levelled steady dark golden eyes on her. 'Invite me in.'

'No.'

Andreas angled his handsome dark head to one side. 'Why not? Is your watchdog home?'

'That's no way to refer to my best friend.'

'Are you saying she has never maligned me?' Andreas fielded with lethal effect.

Hope flushed to the roots of her hair and deemed it wisest to say nothing. But she did very nearly confide that she had always warmly defended him from every hint of criticism. Only now she felt ashamed rather than proud of her once-unswerving loyalty. After all, that very day she had been forced to appreciate that Andreas had never had a similar level of faith in her. He found it easy to accept that she had done all sorts of unforgivable things, didn't he?

He believed she had slept with Ben and carried on an affair with the other man behind his back. He believed she had lied about her infidelity and engaged in all the deceits that would have been required to conceal that betrayal. He believed she had made up a nasty, sordid story about his sister, Elyssa, in an effort to save her own skin. He also believed that, having found herself in the family way, she had been desperate enough and foolish enough to try and lie about who had put her in that condition in the first place.

Injured pride and deep pain warred inside Hope and produced anger. 'Andreas...I don't see any point in you being here. I've nothing more to say to you.'

'You approached me first.'

'Yes and I said what I had to say.' Her heart-shaped face pale with strain, Hope folded her arms in a jerky movement.

'But I've barely got warmed up,' Andreas fenced, leaning into the apartment to call, 'Vanessa?'

Startled, Hope exclaimed, 'Why are you—?'

Her friend strolled out to the hall.

'I was convinced you would not be far. Hope and I are going out—'

'No, we're not. I have a train to catch,' Hope protested.

'I should be in Athens right now and you screwed it up for me,' Andreas delivered, lean, strong face taut with fortitude.

Hope was laced with equal determination. 'I'm not going anywhere with you. I'm not even speaking to you—'

'That's not a problem,' Andreas drawled, smooth as silk. 'I'm perfectly happy to do all the talking. I enjoy it when people just listen to me.'

'I'd know that without even hearing you,' Vanessa chipped in.

If her friend had been hoping to put Andreas out of countenance, she had misjudged her man. Ablaze with confidence and purpose, Andreas vented an appreciative laugh. 'Good.'

His amusement cut through Hope's sensitive skin

like a knife. That was how much her current crisis meant to Andreas Nicolaidis. He had refused to credit that the baby was his and he didn't really need to care about her predicament. She studied him with helpless intensity. Getting by without him was agony and seeing him only increased her craving to be with him again. She had to get over that.

'I don't want to see you...or have anything to do with you,' Hope breathed unevenly, and she reached forward and slowly, carefully closed the front door in his darkly handsome face.

'I can't believe you just did that!' Vanessa gasped, wide-eyed. 'He's the love of your life and your idol!'

'I need to cultivate better taste. That was the first step and overdue.' Hope retreated back to her bedroom to retrieve her bag. She felt as if she were bleeding to death. She wanted to run out the door and chase after him like a faithful pet. For the very first time she was learning to say no to Andreas and it did not feel good to go against her own nature. In fact it hurt like hell.

Four hours later, she was climbing out of a taxi clutching the key for the picturesque country cottage that belonged to the Fitzsimmons and Campbell families. It lay down a leafy lane and was sheltered by tall, glossy hedges of laurel. Cottage was a bit of a misnomer for a property containing more than half a dozen bedrooms. It was a substantial house.

In the charming bedroom she chose for herself below the overhanging eaves she looked out over the back garden towards the gentle winding river and the open countryside beyond. The silence and the sense of peace were wonderful. Her train had been packed and noisy and she had not initially been able to get a seat. Exhaustion was making her droop.

'Carrying a baby is a tiring business,' the doctor had warned her. 'You have to be sensible and take extra rest if you need it.'

It didn't help that it had been weeks since she had benefited from an unbroken night of sleep. Bad dreams and worries had haunted her. Shedding her clothes where she stood, she pulled on a thin white cotton nightdress and sank between the sheets on the comfortable bed as heavily as a rock settling in silt.

Wakening refreshed the following morning, Hope felt her mood lift in tune with the sunshine filtering through the curtains. It was a beautiful day. She put on a light summer dress, attempted unsuccessfully to suck her tummy in and still breathe, and finally went downstairs to satisfy her ravenous appetite for food. She blessed Vanessa when she found that the fridge already contained a few basic foodstuffs. A local woman acted as caretaker and Vanessa had evidently contacted her.

Hope ate her toast on the sun-drenched terrace beside the river and then allowed herself five olives. She had so many decisions to make. But her friend had been right on one score: whether or not to keep her child was not one of them. She had the lucky advantage of being cushioned by the cash her brother had given her. Only now she was no longer sure of what to do with that money. Perhaps putting it into property might be the wisest move.

Her business plans would have to go on the back burner for a while. Too many new businesses failed. Having a child to care for would change her priorities. She was less keen to take on financial risk. Setting up a viable enterprise to craft handmade bags and employing even a couple of workers would always have been a risky venture. But to set herself such a task with a new baby on the way and single parenthood looming would be downright foolhardy.

Ben arrived when she was working on new ideas for bags, an exercise that never failed to relax her. Lost in creative introspection, she did not hear his car arriving. When she glanced up, she just saw Ben standing at the corner of the house watching her. Thrusting aside her sketch pad, she scrambled up, taut with apprehension. With his fair hair fashionably tousled into spikes and his green eyes usually serious, he had a rakish, boyish attraction, she acknowledged. He wasn't a bad kisser either. Only her heart didn't go bang-bang-bang when she saw him and the almost-sick-with-excitement sensation, which she associated with Andreas, did not happen for her around Ben.

'You didn't need to come down to see me,' she said awkwardly.

'I did.' Ben dug restive hands deep into his pockets. 'You should have been the one to tell me about the baby.'

'Vanessa didn't give me the chance.' Hope sighed.

'This was one of the times when she should've minded her own business. She made me feel like I had no place in your life.' Ben subjected her anxious face to a rueful appraisal. 'I'm not going to pretend that this development hasn't knocked me for six...it *has*. But however this pans out, we'll still be friends.'

Her soft mouth wobbled and she compressed it. But it was no good—her eyes overflowed and, with a sound that veered between a laugh and a sob, she groaned. 'The slightest thing brings tears to my eyes at the minute. It's so embarrassing...please ignore me!'

Ben draped a comforting arm round her shoulders but he did not draw her close as he would have done only days earlier. 'You've had a rough week. Don't be so hard on yourself. Vanessa says that you and Andreas are engaged in major hostilities. That's my fault—'

'How can it possibly be your fault?'

'I could've put him right about us a couple of months back but I didn't see why I should. I wanted a chance with you and if you stayed with your Greek tycoon, I wasn't going to get it. I took advantage. I'm admitting it,' Ben said bluntly. 'But even I draw the line at continuing to muddy the water when you're expecting his kid! That has to be sorted out.'

Ben insisted on taking her down to the medieval pub in the village and treating her to lunch. His unexpected plain common sense had left her conscience uneasy. Her own behaviour seemed less sensible. Feeling horribly hurt and humiliated, she had shut the door in Andreas's face and refused to talk to him. It might have been what Andreas deserved and it might have made her feel less like a doormat, but important issues still had to be resolved. Andreas could not be allowed to retain the impression that Ben might have fathered her child. She was not to blame for the misunderstanding. But for Ben's sake and for the baby's, she needed to keep on trying to ensure that Andreas accepted the truth.

Early evening that same day, Andreas brought the powerful Lamborghini to a throaty halt in front of the thatched cottage.

He had leant on Vanessa until she had buckled and told him where Hope was. Hope might well be in need of a break in which to recoup her energies, but he was not willing to accept that she had to be protected from him. Even though he had missed a family christening in Athens, he was feeling good about what he was doing. In fact he was aware of a general improvement in his mood. That was no surprise to him. When had he ever done anything quite so unselfish? Naturally he was proud of himself. Although Hope had no claim on him and even less right to his consideration, he had set aside his perfectly justifiable anger and understandable distaste to check that she was all right.

Hope clambered out of the bath because she was terrified of falling asleep in the water. Wrapping her streaming body in a velour towel imprinted with zoo animals, she padded back into the bedroom. From the low window there she saw Andreas springing out of an elegant long, low silver car. He hit the knocker on the front door.

'Oh, heck…' Her first glance was into the mirror to note that, yes, her hair was damp and messy and piled on top of her head where it was anchored by a canary-yellow band. And her face was hot pink. And nobody was ever likely to suggest that her figure was enhanced by a bulky towel in primary colours. Was her tummy really *that*…? She flipped sideways and wished she hadn't bothered. Sometimes ignorance could be bliss.

Yet even in profile, Andreas looked stunning, his bold, bronzed features vibrant with dark, intrinsically male beauty. Tall and well built, he emanated powerful energy. Her hand flew up to tug off the band restraining her hair. In a panic, she finger-combed the resulting tangle. The door knocker went a second time. Breathless and reckless as a teenager, terrified he would decide she was out and leave if she did not hurry, she raced down the stairs as though her feet had wings and dragged open the door.

His dark, deep-set gaze narrowed below thick black lashes and roamed from the lush pink cupid's bow of her mouth to the voluptuous creamy swell of her breasts. Not even the sight of a pink elephant marching across the towel could dim Andreas's appreciation of her fabulous shape. His eyes flared to smouldering gold.

Her mouth ran dry. 'How did you find out where I was?'

'Vanessa told me.'

Hope was amazed. 'She...*did*?'

'I said I was concerned about you. That unnerved her. Suddenly she didn't want the responsibility of withholding information from me,' Andreas explained lazily.

'I'm glad...we do need to talk,' Hope conceded quietly, backing towards the stairs. 'If you wait in the sitting room, I'll get dressed.'

'Why bother?' Andreas was tracking her every tiny move with keen male attention.

'Because I'm not wearing enough clothes,' she mumbled uncertainly, finding it incredibly hard to concentrate beneath Andreas's steady appraisal.

'You're not wearing *any*,' Andreas contradicted huskily. 'Do you hear me complaining?'

'Don't talk like that,' she begged, her tension rising because she knew she wanted him to talk like that to her. In fact her protest was a truly appalling lie when she knew that more than anything else in the world at that moment she wanted him to kiss her.

Her retreat from the door had exposed the jacket slung down carelessly across the window seat. Andreas treated the garment to a fulminating scrutiny. His hard jaw line clenched taut. 'Whose jacket is that? Daddy Bear's?'

Disconcerted, Hope followed the path of his eyes. Her fine brows pleated when she saw that Ben, who had departed a couple of hours earlier, had forgotten to take his jacket with him.

'*Hope?*' Andreas prompted icily. 'That's a man's jacket.'

Never in her life until then had Hope been so tempted to tell a lie for the sake of peace. While she was wondering whether an elderly gardener with expensive tastes could be the likely owner of a designer leather jacket, time ran out.

'Is Campbell here?' Andreas slung at her wrathfully. 'Upstairs in the bedroom?'

Hope exploded into emotive speech, 'No, of course not. He's not here but he would have every right to be if he wanted to be! Vanessa may have given me permission to be here but the cottage belongs to her family *and* Ben's.'

Andreas paced forward a step. His lean, strong face was set like stone, his brilliant eyes hard as steel. 'When was Campbell here?'

'That's none of your business,' Hope dared shakily.

His intent gaze flared to a volatile gold. 'You made it my business again. Either you're with him or you're alone. If you're still with him, I want to know about it!'

'I'm not discussing Ben with you. You have no right to ask me these questions—'

'If you're still involved with Campbell, why did you approach me?' Andreas launched at her in raw condemnation.

Hope lifted her head high, turquoise eyes dark with stress. 'This is your baby. It's got nothing to do with Ben, so just leave him out of things—'

'That's a fantasy...I finished with you months ago. How the *hell* could it be my baby?' Andreas thundered at her in fierce frustration.

Hope flinched from the violence flaring like a silent lightning strike in the atmosphere. 'In another week, I'll be six months pregnant. Six months ago I hadn't even met Ben Campbell.'

Andreas had fallen very still. He fixed sceptical eyes on her and stared. 'You can't be six months pregnant.'

'The doctor says that some women...of my build,' she selected with care, 'don't look like they're expecting until the last couple of months.'

His normal healthy colour noticeably absent below his bronzed skin, Andreas coiled his restive hands into powerful fists and half lifted his arms in emphasis. 'There's no way you can be six months pregnant,' he repeated, less stridently it was true, but the repetition of that assurance broke the thin hold she had on her control.

'Isn't there?' Hope gasped, angry pink blooming in her cheeks. 'You could not be more wrong. Furthermore, if it's anyone's fault I'm going to be a mother, it's yours!'

'*Mine?*' Andreas echoed. 'You start telling me this crazy story—'

'What crazy story would that be? You got me pregnant. Who was it who said that *he* would take care of the precautions?' Hope shouted at him in a tempestuous fury of frustration and pain. 'Who assured me that I could safely leave everything to you? And then who didn't bother when it didn't suit him? In the shower, in the middle of the night, on the bathroom floor…that time in the limo…'

A slow, dulled rise of blood below his olive skin demarcated the superb slant of his high cheekbones

'How is it that you took that kind of risk with me? Over and over again? How is it that you then have the cheek to repeatedly insist that some other man must be the father of my child? You've got a very short memory, Andreas—'

'No…I remember that time in the limo,' Andreas breathed thickly, fabulous golden eyes not quite focused, a frown line between his ebony brows as though he were literally looking back through time. 'I had flown in from Oslo…I called you to meet me…that…that was pretty much unforgettable.'

Her small fingers curved like talons into her palms. 'I'm so glad it was memorable enough for you to recall.'

Andreas studied her stomach as covertly as he could. But he could not look away. *His* baby. It could be; it might be. He was in shock. 'Now that you've said how far along this pregnancy is, I can see there's a stronger possibility that the baby is mine.'

'You're so generous,' Hope said in a small, tightly restrained voice.

'I'll still want DNA testing after the child's born,' Andreas assured her, not wishing to seem a pushover while he skimmed his gaze over Ben Campbell's jacket. His stubborn jaw line hardened. He still had to deal with Campbell. He wasn't prepared to accept Campbell's inclusion in any corner of the picture. A miniature Nicolaidis, a son or daughter, his first child, his baby would soon be born. It was amazing how different a slant that put on things.

Pale and stiff, Hope inwardly cringed at the threat of DNA tests. He would take nothing on trust. All over again, she felt hurt and humiliated. 'That's up to you but it won't be necessary.'

'What's the state of play between you and Campbell?'

Hope coloured in embarrassment and compressed her lips. 'Take a guess.'

The inference that her pregnancy had wrecked her affair with Campbell put Andreas on a high. Satisfaction zinged through him in an adrenalin rush. He had to resist the urge to smile in triumph. 'I imagine you don't qualify as ideal playmate material with my baby inside you.'

'Ben doesn't see me in that light. He's a friend—'

'Whereas I never wanted to be your friend,' Andreas incised with a look of unashamed challenge in his clear gaze. 'I wanted you in my arms, by my side and in my bed. I didn't feed you any rubbish lines about friendship.'

'Nor did you mention the fact that you thought of me as your mistress.'

'Labels aren't important.' Andreas angled back his arrogant dark head, refusing to award her the point. 'Many women would be proud to be called my mistress.'

'But you *knew* I wouldn't be proud because you

never once mentioned that word to me until after we broke up,' Hope reminded him doggedly.

Andreas strolled with fluid grace across the hall. 'Don't argue with me. There is no longer any need. For the moment I will accept your word that the child you carry is mine.'

Hope shifted a casual shoulder as if the matter were immaterial to her. However, grudging though his concession was, it was a source of great relief to her.

'Why did it take you so long to realise you were pregnant?' he questioned.

'I didn't pick up on the signs. I had too much else on my mind over the last few months.'

'That's all in the past,' Andreas asserted, gazing down at her. She met dark golden eyes and her tummy turned a somersault in response. The beginnings of a smile chased the ruthless quality from his beautifully sculpted mouth. Her heart began to beat to a very fast tempo.

'You've been very unhappy, *pedhi mou*.'

She nodded in uncertain agreement. She was struggling to drag her attention from him but she was mesmerised by the sexual spell he could cast without even trying. A helpless rush of yearning shimmered through her. It had been so long. Her breasts stirred below the towel, her rosy nipples becoming prominent. An embarrassing ache pulsed between her thighs and her face burned with shamed awareness.

'I like what I do to you,' Andreas confessed huskily. 'But you have very much the same effect on me.'

'Do I?' She gave way then to her weakness and let herself touch him again. Her fingers fluttered up to smooth across a hard, taut masculine cheekbone and then flirted with his luxuriant black hair. The wonderfully familiar scent of him that close intoxicated her. Her legs felt wobbly.

'How could you doubt it?' He bent down and let his warm tongue delve into the moist centre of her mouth and caress the soft underside of her lips. Way down low in her throat a moan escaped. She stretched up on her tiptoes and kissed him back with fervent, eager need. He reached down and lifted her up into his arms and then he took the stairs two at a time.

She let her hands sink into the springy depths of his hair. Joy was dancing through her in a heady tide of celebration. He laid her down on the bed. Her hunger for his touch felt almost unbearable. He stood over her, discarding his jacket and tie, ripping open his shirt while he kicked off his shoes. His impatience thrilled her. She lay there, anticipation a wicked spiral twisting down deep inside her.

'I'm so hot for you,' Andreas growled like a hungry tiger as he came down to her.

She opened her arms wide. He tugged away the towel and she gasped and tried to cover herself again, suddenly remembering that she had rounded up in places she had had no need to fill out and stricken by the fear that he would be repulsed.

'I've died and gone to heaven...' Andreas groaned, settling that concern instantly with his bold masculine appreciation of the lush swell of her breasts.

He uncrossed her arms to bare her for his scrutiny.

'Close your eyes...' she pleaded. 'I've expanded.'

'Gloriously,' Andreas declared raggedly, scorching golden eyes glittering with admiration. 'You look like a pagan goddess...very, very sexy.'

Her spine arched a little. He used his thumbs on

the tender crests of her breasts and followed with the sweet, erotic torment of his expert mouth. She whimpered, her hips shifting on the mattress.

'I didn't think to ask…' Andreas stared down at her, taut with sudden anxiety. 'Can I? Is it safe to make love?'

'It's OK…it's no problem…oh, I want you so much,' she gasped.

He traced the swollen, sensitive heart of her femininity and she jerked and writhed, losing control as the exquisite sensations came quicker and faster. The most devastating need had taken her over. She was liquid as honey heated to boiling point. He was a fantastic lover and he had primed every sensitised inch of her to the peak of sensual torment. Suddenly he was kissing her again in a deep, wild, drugging melding of their mouths that excited her beyond bearing.

'Please…please…' she cried.

He told her in Greek how much he needed her, his hands spread to cup her face. Lean, strong face stamped with desire and an intensity that was new to her, he tipped her back. 'I'll be very gentle.'

Slow and sure, he thrust into her hot, damp core, taking her by aching degrees. He stretched her and possessed her with long, hard strokes that drove her out of her mind with incredible pleasure. The tight sensation welling at the heart of her sent her excitement racing higher and higher. The surge of ecstasy she experienced plunged her into sobbing abandonment. It took a long time for the pulsing waves of delight to drain from her languorous body. Full of joy at the wonder of being with him again, she felt her eyes flood with tears and she kept her head buried in his shoulder. But she succumbed to the temptation of pressing tiny little kisses against his damp, bronzed skin, tickling him and making him laugh.

Grinning, Andreas closed both arms round her and breathed in the fresh herbal scent of her hair, revelling in the return of the harmony and satisfaction that had eluded him for months. He smoothed possessive hands over the smooth, soft curves of her highly feminine derrière. He wondered if it would seem uncool and if she would be offended if he examined the tantalising swell of her formerly flat stomach. He decided not to chance it and dropped a kiss down on the crown of her head. The unwelcome recollection of Ben Campbell's jacket slunk into his mind like a depth charge from the deep.

Had she slept with Campbell in the same bed? What do you think, Andreas? A snide, cynical inner voice mocked. Don't the guy's relatives part-own the property? His sleek muscles drew taut. Suddenly a tidal wave of doubts and unease was assailing him. How could he ever trust her again? All men were vulnerable to false paternity claims. Even if DNA testing were to prove the child was not his, wouldn't she still be able to plead that she had made a genuine error? After all, how could she know for sure that it was his baby? At best she was probably hoping like mad that it was his. The last thing she was likely to do was admit anything that might reawaken his worst suspicions.

In the course of seconds his mood had dive-bombed from the heights to subterranean-cellar level. He had dragged her off to bed as if the past few months could be wiped out. But the bitter memory of betrayal remained. Could he really be contemplating the concept of forgiving her? How could he ever forgive her for what she had done? He knew there were sad guys who did do stuff like that. Sad, weak men who let their even sadder dependency on a lying, deceitful woman overpower their brains and their pride. But he wasn't one of those guys. His only weakness around her was lust, Andreas reasoned. That was sex, though; that was allowable. He would sleep with her as and when he liked. That was harmless. But forgiveness was impossible.

'If you pack now, I'll take you back to London with me,' Andreas murmured flatly, hauling his long, powerful frame up against the pillows while at the same time shifting her off him onto the mattress. 'The apartment already has a buyer. I'll have to find you somewhere else to live.'

His cool detachment was as shocking to Hope as a bucket of icy water drenching her overheated skin. He had cut short the affectionate aftermath of their intimacy, Hope registered with a stark sense of panic and loss. Had she really believed that a nightmare could be eradicated and their former relationship reinstated? Why on earth had she fallen back into bed with him again? After all, she was now painfully aware of the deficiencies of what she had once mistakenly seen as a wonderfully happy relationship. Would she really sink so low as to accept being his mistress?

'I'm not that fussed about diamonds,' Hope pronounced grittily.

Halfway out of bed, for he was determined to remove Hope from her present accommodation as fast as he possibly could, Andreas stilled with a frown. 'Say that again?'

Hope shot him a pained glance. 'A mistress is sup-posed to have diamonds but I don't want any. I *never* wanted any.'

Andreas deemed silence the best response to those incomprehensible statements. Nor did he see it as the best moment in which to confess that some of the charms on her bracelet were ornamented with dia-monds of the very highest quality.

'You never ate a grain of food in that apartment that I did not pay for...does that make you a kept man?' Hope enquired curtly.

Stark naked, Andreas swung back at that facetious question. 'What's that supposed to mean?'

'I bought all the food. My small contribution to our shared life,' Hope informed him, her turquoise eyes overbright. 'But you thought you had bought me.'

'No, I never thought that.' Andreas frowned. '*Did* you buy the food? I had no idea—'

'I wish I'd poisoned you when I got the chance!' Hope hissed and, grabbing up her nightdress, she pulled it over her head, leapt off the bed and vanished into the *en suite*.

Andreas listened to the bolt shooting home on the other side of the door and swore under his breath while looking heavenward in vague hope of divine intervention. She had seemed perfectly happy, but he was learning that he could no longer depend on that superficial calm. She could fly from apparent tran-quillity to screeching fury with him now in the space of seconds. Was that his fault? Campbell's fault? Was she only back with him because Campbell had re-jected her? He could not afford to take anything for granted this time around, he reminded himself harshly.

Hope could not bear to meet her own anguished eyes in the vanity mirror. She had acted like a slut and his coolness afterwards had ensured that she felt like one too. She really hated herself. As long as she behaved like that she would never win his respect. Once again she had been too easy. How could Andreas have sunk so low as to take advantage of her again? And how could she have allowed that to happen?

She had to forget that she loved Andreas. Her baby should be her only priority now. She should never, ever have got back into bed with him again. All that was likely to do was complicate things. Andreas still believed she had slept with Ben. No affair with Andreas had the faintest hope of a promising future. He would not make any commitment to her. Such a relationship would be doomed to failure and their child would also suffer in that breakdown. Sleeping with Andreas had been a serious mistake, but it was not a mistake she had to go on repeating, was it?

Hope emerged from the *en suite*.

Fully dressed, only his tousled black hair revealing that he had not spent the last hour in the average business meeting, Andreas surveyed her. 'All I want to do is take you out of here and back to London where you belong.'

'But I don't belong there. I always preferred the country and that's where I'd like to live if I get the chance. Look…' Hope shifted an awkward hand, inhibited by the need to conceal her true emotions from him with a show of indifference. 'We slept together and we shouldn't have. I regret it very much.'

'You didn't regret it while you were doing it, *pedhi*

mou,' Andreas spelt out with dangerous bite. 'So, what's changed?'

'I'm trying to be sensible for the baby's benefit. I don't want to be your mistress and I don't think you're facing how complicated things could get with a child in the midst of it all.'

Andreas pinned smouldering golden eyes of censure on her and proved that he was not listening. 'This is about Campbell, isn't it?'

Hope winced, for with that one question he fulfilled her every fear. 'It's not even me you want—'

'What on earth is that supposed to mean?'

'I think you just want to take me away from Ben to prove that you can do it. And, yes, you *can* do it. I'm no good at saying no to you...but that doesn't mean I don't know how dangerous you are to my peace of mind,' she confessed gruffly.

Andreas dealt her a look of stark and savage impatience. 'This is all nonsense. You fell into my arms...you came back to me—'

'No...I had sex with you,' Hope rephrased in a mortified undertone, her face reddening as she pushed out that contradiction.

Andreas studied her in angry disbelief. 'Don't be coarse—'

'You had sex with me. Are you saying that meant anything special to you?' Hope was striving not to look hopeful.

Put on the spot, Andreas refused to yield. His stubborn mouth firmed. 'I'm not saying anything right now. It's too soon.'

Unbearable sadness welled up inside Hope. 'We don't have any kind of a future.'

'If that baby is mine, you'll have a role to play in

my life for years to come,' Andreas pointed out impressively.

'A backstage role that you define: a convenient mistress. I don't want my baby to grow up and despise me. If there's a chance that I could be the main event in some guy's life…I want to be free to take that chance,' Hope answered shakily. 'And if I end up alone, so be it. I'll take that risk.'

That was the definitive moment that Andreas appreciated that she had raised the stakes, changed the game, if game it was, and altered the rules without telling him. Either he offered her more or he walked away. He had never surrendered to blackmail in his life. Outrage slivered through him as he angled a brooding glance at the tumbled bed. Just two years ago Hope had been a clueless virgin. But this evening she had had rampant sex with him and then announced that she intended to keep her options open in case some other man presented her with a better deal. For some other man, read Ben Campbell, Andreas reflected in volcanic fury.

'Please say you understand,' Hope muttered tautly. 'I want to try to be the best mother I can be—'

'Naturally. If your child is mine, I'm willing to acknowledge the blood tie and accept a parental role.' Andreas refused to think about how the advent of an illegitimate Nicolaidis heir or heiress would strike the more elderly of his conservative Greek family. 'I will also cover all your expenses and settle money on both of you so that your future is secure. Those arrangements would be separate from any more intimate bonds we shared.'

Hope was very pale and her strained eyes lowered

from his to hide her pain. 'I'm not talking about money, Andreas.'

'I didn't suppose you were,' he drawled flatly, his brilliant gaze cold and level, his handsome mouth set in a hard line. 'But financial security is the most I intend to put on the table. I have no plans to marry you. Not now, not ever.'

She hadn't been talking about marriage either. She had been hoping for some verbal acknowledgement of reconciliation between them and the hint that a degree of caring and commitment could exist in the future. But he was not even prepared to concede the possibility that over time something deeper might develop.

'I wasn't referring to marriage. There are options which go beyond mistress and don't stretch as far as matrimony,' Hope framed with weary dignity. 'Please don't be offended but I'm going to have to ask you to leave. I'm feeling incredibly tired and I'd like to lie down for a while.'

Belatedly noticing her pallor, Andreas descended from his icy tower of reserve at supersonic speed. Concern in his troubled gaze, he strode across the room. With careful hands he scooped her up and rested her down again gently on the bed. 'Let me take you back to London with me. You don't even need to get dressed. I could wrap a blanket round you,' he heard himself suggesting.

'Don't fuss. I'm too tired to go anywhere,' she muttered sleepily.

'*Theos*…I think I should get a doctor to check you over,' Andreas continued.

'Don't be daft. I'm only pregnant,' she mumbled soothingly, heavy eyelids already drooping.

Andreas had always admired Hope's robust good health. She was never sick. Any condition capable of flattening her to a bed before nine in the evening was the equivalent of a serious illness in Andreas's book. She looked exhausted and the translucence of her skin lent her a disturbingly fragile air. Guilt threatened to swallow him alive. He tugged the bedding up over her and tucked her in as she slid over onto her side. He had subjected her to a great deal of stress. That had to stop right now.

He shouldn't be throwing Ben Campbell up and upsetting her either. But had he been a substitute for Campbell in the bedroom this evening? he wondered rawly. Understandably, Campbell had backed off once he'd realised Hope was carrying Andreas's child. That would have been a distinct turn-off for the other man. Was the fact that Andreas had been a substitute the reason why Hope had referred to their recent physical encounter as being just sex?

His mobile phone vibrated. He walked out to the landing and pulled across the door before answering it.

'Where are you?' Elyssa demanded stridently. 'You've got to come and sort Finlay out!'

Andreas raised a wry ebony brow and said nothing. He had never made the mistake of interfering between his sister and her husband. Elyssa was volatile and could be quite a handful. Finlay might worship the ground his beautiful wife walked on but he was no pushover.

'This is serious!' his sister gasped and an uncharacteristic sob broke up her voice. 'Finlay says he's leaving me!'

Switching off his phone a couple of minutes later,

a grim expression stamped on his darkly handsome features, Andreas strode back into the bedroom.

Hope's feathery lashes fluttered up on drowsy turquoise eyes. 'Sorry...did I drift off?'

'Come back to London with me,' Andreas urged forcefully. 'I don't like leaving you here alone.'

With a shake of her blonde head, she burrowed deeper into the pillow. Andreas adjusted the sheet again and resisted an almost overpowering need to just grab her up and stow her in the front of his car. His life had been so smooth when she had just done as he'd asked. Now everything was a battle and he hated it.

He needed an edge. He needed a country house, something Hope would take one look at and fall hopelessly in love with. Cue: listed building of historical interest, oak beams, walled garden, loads of bathrooms. At least it would be a good investment. He contacted a top city estate agent and passed on his requirements.

CHAPTER SEVEN

THE strident call of the phone wakened Hope the following day. In her dream she was wearing a billowing evening frock and drifting gracefully across a vast green lawn towards Andreas, who had never looked more like a movie star. Then all of a sudden the dream turned into a nightmare for Andreas got fed up waiting and walked off. Even though she tried frantically hard to catch up with him, he kept on getting further and further away from her. She sat up with a start and his name on her lips, her heart pounding with panic.

When she snatched up the phone, she somehow assumed that it would be Andreas and was guiltily but deeply disappointed when she realised that the caller was Vanessa. Her friend was so thrilled by the news she had to relate that it was several minutes before Hope grasped what the other woman was talking about. A London fashion designer had seen Vanessa's photographic study of Hope's handbags and, having been hugely impressed by Hope's sense of style, was eager to meet Hope in person and see more of her work.

Hope called the number that Vanessa gave her and agreed to an appointment late that same day. She had to leap out of bed, pack her bag and ring a taxi to take her to the train. Her relaxing country break had lasted less than forty-eight hours. But she was very excited that her designs had attracted the attention of a real trendsetter in the fashion world.

Just before she locked up the cottage, a courier delivered a brand new mobile phone to her courtesy of Andreas. It was her favourite colour of lilac and it was incredibly cute as well as being possessed of every technological development known to man, most of which she would never use, but which Andreas would take the first opportunity to explain and demonstrate in detail. Of course, she knew she shouldn't accept the phone, but she absolutely craved the sense of connection she experienced at the frequent sound of his dark, deep drawl.

Establishing less fraught relations with Andreas made good sense, she reasoned inwardly. After all, they would soon be parents even if they were no longer together. Her throat filled with an immoveable lump. Had she been a little hasty rejecting him the night before? Hurriedly she squashed that weak rebellious thought.

But there was no denying that the tranquillity she had achieved had been slaughtered by Andreas's arrival and consequent departure. She felt bereft and empty and unhappy and that made her so angry with herself. She had to learn to live without Andreas. A positive development on the career front that would also keep her busy had never been more necessary.

Her new phone rang. 'Yes,' she answered all breathless, and on edge.

'It's me...' Andreas imparted unnecessarily, the dark timbre of his sexy voice shimmying down her sensitive spine.

All of a sudden she was reliving the crash-and-burn effect of his gorgeous mouth on hers, his wildness in bed and the complete impossibility of ever replacing him with anyone even human.

'I have some family stuff to deal with this evening.' He sighed with audible regret. 'But I would like to see you tomorrow.'

She breathed in deep and held her breath to prevent herself from saying yes too quickly. 'OK...' she said finally, trailing out the word as if she were still considering the idea.

'I'd appreciate your advice on a house I'm thinking of buying.'

Hope was vaguely surprised that she didn't swoon. Andreas wanted *her* advice? That was a huge compliment. And the advice related to a house? She adored houses. Was he moving? Whatever, it felt marvellous and cosy and confidence-boosting to be approached for an opinion. It was respect...in a small way, she told herself. Suddenly the glitz and the sparkle had returned to her day.

'What right did Finlay have to take Robbie and Tristram to his mother's house?' Elyssa demanded shrilly of Andreas for at least the tenth time.

'You're very upset.' Andreas released his breath in a soundless hiss. 'Perhaps your husband thought he was doing you a favour.'

Finlay often took his sons to their grandmother's with Elyssa's blessing. On this occasion, however, Elyssa was making a drama out of the event. Although Andreas had been at the Southwick home for almost an hour he still had no idea why his sister's husband had left the marital home. Elyssa had been in hysterics when he'd arrived and it had taken Andreas a phenomenal length of time to calm her down.

'Isn't it time you told me why Finlay has walked out?'

'I don't *know* why!' Elyssa slung petulantly.

'There has to be a reason,' Andreas murmured steadily. 'Why are you so afraid that Finlay might have deliberately removed the children from your care?'

'Maybe he's bored with me...maybe he's got someone else. He could be planning to make up insane lies about me in an attempt to gain custody of my boys!' Elyssa cast a sidelong glance at her brother to see how he reacted to that very specific concern on her part.

From the outset, Andreas had been aware that his sister was determined to win every possible atom of his sympathy. Now he grasped that he needed to hear the precise nature of what she termed lies. 'Tell me about the lies,' he encouraged softly.

Her sullen brown eyes flicked warily back to him. 'Finlay had the nerve to imply that I was a neglectful mother just because I left the boys with the nanny overnight.'

'For how long was the nanny left in charge?'

'Only over a few weekends...and once for a week when I went to Paris.'

Reluctant to risk provoking her hysteria again, Andreas struggled to be tactful. 'I understand Finlay's concern. Couldn't you have taken the children with you?'

'I'm only twenty-five years old,' Elyssa responded heatedly. 'Surely I'm entitled to a life of my own?'

'You have a good life,' Andreas told her levelly.

'Now why won't you tell me why your husband has left?'

Elyssa tossed her head. 'I don't want you preaching at me,' she warned him thinly. 'All right... I had an affair.'

Sincerely shocked by that truculent admission, Andreas stiffened. He attempted to keep an open mind. 'Are you in love with this man?'

Her earlier distress apparently forgotten now that she had confessed, Elyssa rolled pained eyes. 'It was only a fling. I can't believe the fuss Finlay is making. As if anyone needs to break up a marriage over a casual affair!'

'I would if you were my wife,' Andreas responded without hesitation.

'You're Greek...your vote doesn't count. You're angry with me but I need you to *make* Finlay see sense. He has huge respect for you. He'll listen to you.'

Distaste gripped Andreas. He could see no evidence that Elyssa even regretted her infidelity. 'How long did the affair last?'

Elyssa gave him a sulky look. 'I suppose I have to tell you because if I don't Finlay will...there's been more than one affair.'

Andreas surveyed the young woman in front of him with incredulous disdain.

Elyssa pouted. 'I can't help it if men find me irresistible.'

Her vanity even in the face of the damage she had done was deeply offensive to Andreas. Somehow he had overlooked the reality that his once-vulnerable little sister had grown to adulthood and full independence. It was not a good moment to discover that he did not like the woman she had become.

'The night that you threw your housewarming party,' Andreas murmured abruptly as it occurred to him that his sibling was not at all the reliable and truthful witness he had believed her to be, 'you said that you found Hope with Ben Campbell. Was that true?'

Her surprise patent at that unexpected change of subject, Elyssa coloured. 'Why are you asking?'

'That story about Hope was a wind-up, wasn't it?' Determined to get the truth out of his sister, Andreas let a deceptively amused smile curve his handsome mouth.

His sister regarded him uncertainly and then she relaxed when she saw the smile. 'How did you guess?'

At Elyssa's confirmation that she had concocted the tale about Hope, Andreas fell very still. 'Why did you do it?'

'I had to protect myself. She caught me kissing another man. I decided to discredit her before she got the chance to tell anybody what she'd seen.' Elyssa lifted a shoulder in a careless shrug of dismissal.

Cold condemnation was stamped on her brother's lean, hard-boned face. 'I'll never forgive you for hurting her.'

'You tricked me into telling you...' Pale with consternation as that truth sank in, Elyssa started to scramble upright. 'That's not fair!'

'How fair were you to Hope?'

'Surely you didn't expect me to *like* her?' his sister snapped with furious resentment. 'From the minute you met Hope Evans, you had no time for me any more. You were always with her playing house. Yet who was she? A vulgar little upstart from nowhere! I couldn't believe that you would bring a woman like that to my home and show her off!'

'Your spite turns my stomach,' Andreas breathed in disgust.

When he emerged from his sister's home, he did not climb back into the limo. He wanted to walk for a while in the fresh air. Elyssa's vicious attack on Hope and the jealousy that had powered her abuse appalled him. Nothing could excuse his sister's cruel lies or her complete lack of guilt. How could he have been so blind to the younger woman's true nature?

Elyssa had always needed to be the centre of attention. From babyhood she had thrown tantrums to ensure she got what she wanted. Of recent Andreas had become less patient with her constant demands and had encouraged her to rely on her husband for support. Naturally he had wanted to spend more time with Hope. Once or twice he had wondered why his sibling had so little apparent interest in his private life. Now he suspected that Elyssa's resentment had grown in direct proportion to the longevity of his relationship with Hope. Yet he had failed to notice that anything was wrong. He had also made the fatal mistake of introducing Hope to his sister. It was *his* fault that Hope had become the innocent victim of her malice. How was he supposed to make that up to Hope?

He phoned her five minutes later. 'I have to see you.'

'Why?' Hope said a little prayer that he would answer that he was missing her.

'Something's happened. I don't feel right about waiting until tomorrow to discuss it with you,'

Andreas admitted. 'It's late...you could stay the night.'

'At the town house?'

'Yes.'

Hope entered a large tick on the mental scorecard she was running on him. 'That would be OK,' she said as lightly as she could. 'But I couldn't actually stay *with* you...if you know what I mean.'

'I'll send the car to pick you up.'

A manservant ushered her into the elegant hall of the big Georgian terraced house and into an imposing drawing room where Andreas awaited her. He looked very serious and her apprehension shifted up another notch on the scale.

'What's wrong?' she asked immediately.

Andreas read the strain in her clear turquoise eyes and reached for both her hands. 'Stop worrying right now,' he told her firmly. 'I think that what I have to say qualifies as good rather than bad.'

'That's great.' Some of her tension evaporated. Her hands trembled in the grip of his and she tugged them free again. Either she was his mistress or she tried to be a friend, even though he had once told her that he didn't do friendship with women. She could not be a mixture of both and there had to be boundary lines. So this was not the moment when she should be noticing that the dark stubble beginning to shadow his sculpted mouth and hard jaw line made him look outrageously sexy. In fact just thinking that forbidden thought made ready colour warm her complexion.

With a distinct air of concern, Andreas urged her down onto a sofa. 'You look tired.'

Hope decided being pregnant was deeply unsexy. Only three months ago, he would have urged her down onto a sofa solely to take rampant, masculine advantage of her horizontal state. But now he was more keen for her to rest.

'Tonight I found out something that shocked me.' Lean, strong face taut, Andreas launched straight into the confession he knew he had to make. 'As you've probably already worked out, Elyssa has been having affairs with other men. This evening, I also learned that my sister lied when she claimed to have seen you in Ben Campbell's arms at her party.'

Hope closed her eyes and breathed in slow and deep. Relief made her feel dizzy. That part of the nightmare was over: Andreas was finally accepting that she had told him the truth all along. 'I'm glad. I really thought that I was going to have to live with that nonsensical story for ever.'

'I wish I could tell you that Elyssa is very sorry for what she's done. But I'm afraid my sibling appears rather lacking in the conscience department,' Andreas derided harshly. 'Before tonight, I had no idea that Elyssa resented your place in my life.'

'She called me your whore at the party,' Hope mused with a little shiver of reluctant recall.

Andreas groaned, his vexation unconcealed. 'Why didn't you tell me?'

'I knew how fond you were of her and telling tales would only have made her dislike me even more. I suppose that even then I wasn't sure that you would take my word over hers...' Hope worried at her lower lip and let her pent-up breath escape softly. 'Of course, by the end of the evening I found that out for a fact.'

Andreas tensed at that reminder. 'I thought I knew Elyssa inside out but I had idealised her. I wasn't seeing her as she really was...spoilt, selfish, shallow in her affections,' Andreas enumerated with a heavy regret that she could feel. 'OK. I admit it. I didn't want to see those traits in my closest relative—'.

'You were proud of her...it was natural that you would want to think only good things about her,' Hope told him gently. 'I don't hold that against you. You had no reason to doubt her word if she hadn't lied to you before.'

Andreas rested his brilliant dark eyes on her heart-shaped face. 'You're being very generous about this.'

'I don't think so. I just want to be fair.'

'I'm sorry I didn't believe you, *pedhi mou*. I don't know where to begin apologising for some of the things I've said or for the way I've treated you,' Andreas admitted with roughened honesty. 'But I was so angry that that whole week is virtually a blank. It was a very unfortunate coincidence that you had indicated your dissatisfaction with our relationship shortly before that party.'

That angle had not occurred to Hope before and she was dismayed that she had not guessed that he would inevitably forge a link between those two apparent events.

Andreas spread lean brown hands, his darkly handsome features clenched taut. 'I thought you weren't happy with me any longer. It made the idea that you had sought consolation with someone else seem much more likely.'

'Yes, I imagine it would have done.' But Hope also felt that, having known her so well, he should at least have cherished some doubt of her guilt. But then she had long since reached her own conclusions as to why he had been so quick to misjudge her and saw no good reason to share those thoughts. 'Well,' she added with a typically warm and soothing smile, 'I'm grateful that you know nothing happened between Ben and I...'

'That night anyway.' Andreas could not silence that qualifier. He was fishing, he knew he was, regardless of his awareness that he had no right to ask her what had happened since then between her and the other man. But he was unable to resist his own powerful need to know.

Tensing below that laser-sharp dark golden appraisal, Hope lowered her uneasy gaze to her linked hands where they rested on her lap. Hot pink was blooming over her cheekbones. It was dreadful but she felt as though every kiss she had exchanged with Ben were written above her head in letters of fire and shame. They had really been very innocent kisses but anything she had shared with Ben ought to remain private. In any case Andreas was not entitled to that sort of information, she reminded herself sternly. After all, could she believe that *he* had behaved in an equally innocent manner with the beautiful, sophisticated women he had been seen out with in recent times? No, she could not credit that. She had lain awake a lot of nights while she'd struggled not to torment herself with agonising images of Andreas making the most of his newfound sexual freedom.

As Andreas watched her fair skin turn pink a cold, heavy sensation settled like concrete in his stomach. He knew how unreasonable he was being but he had very much hoped to hear her say that, challenging though the circumstances had been, she had stayed loyal to him in spite of everything. Intelligence told him that was unlikely. Intelligence told him that blush was as good as a signed confession in triplicate. She had slept with Campbell. Of course she had.

Andreas endeavoured to put the entire controversial subject out of his mind. He was a pragmatic man. What had been done could not be undone. He offered Hope a soft drink, which she declined. He poured a whisky that he drank down in two minimal gulps. Pragmatic though he believed himself to be, he was assailed by another unfortunate reflection: there was no point hoping that at some future stage she would tell him that Campbell had been absolute rubbish in bed. She was not that kind of woman. He would never, ever know whether she compared them.

'I feel that I should make an effort to clear the air,' Hope remarked hesitantly, fixing anxious turquoise eyes on Andreas.

'As regards what…exactly?'

'As regards Ben,' Hope proffered gently.

Andreas froze. His imagination went into a loop. In the name of honesty, she was about to talk like a canary, telling everything right down to the tiniest and most insignificant detail. He wanted to know but feared that knowing would torture him. He breathed in deep. 'Hope…'

'No, please let me say what I want to say first,' Hope interrupted apologetically. 'Ben's been so very kind to me. I want you to understand that he's a much nicer person than people seem to appreciate. I think you'd really like Ben if you got to know him…'

That was the moment when Andreas knew that he should have drunk all the whisky in the decanter in the hope of anaesthetising his sensibilities into a stupor. Hope was engaging in a more refined form of torture than he had even envisaged. She was keen for him to get to know Ben. In the eternally sunny world she inhabited they were probably all destined to become the very closest of mutually supportive friends. There was just one small problem. He could not think of Ben Campbell without wishing to wipe him with maximum violence from the face of the earth.

'I'm fond of Ben and he's been a terrific friend.'

'That's cool,' Andreas breathed between clenched teeth.

'I would like him to stay a friend,' Hope advanced.

Valiantly, Andreas shrugged while conceding that the eating of humble pie was his equivalent of eating rat poison. But he had screwed up badly. She was expecting his baby and he had put her through hell and this was his penance. Presumably, if he agreed with even the most fanciful and unreasonable requests and expectations, all her fears would be soothed and everything would finally go back to normal. Normal. That was his only ambition. 'Why not…?'

Hope wondered why he was so tense. Was he annoyed because she had said earlier that she believed that she ought to sleep alone? The belief was not set in stone. She was open to clever argument and even downright seduction. Had she hurt his feelings with her embargo? His ego? Was that why he was chucking whisky down his throat as if there were no tomorrow? What was wrong? As a rule, he was a very occasional drinker.

'You should go to bed,' Andreas suggested rather abruptly. 'We have an early start in the morning.'

'Oh, my goodness, I never even asked you about the house—'

Andreas opened the door into the hall. 'It'll keep until tomorrow.'

Hope swallowed back a yawn. In truth she was very tired. 'I haven't even told you my own news yet.' She laughed on the way up the imposing stairs. 'Guess what? I've been discovered by the fashion world. I met Leonie Vargas this afternoon and I'm being offered the chance to design bags for her next collection!'

'That's great.' Andreas thought about what he knew about Leonie Vargas. In his conservative opinion, she was a very eccentric lady who wore even stranger outfits. Even so she had become spectacularly rich designing clothes for the young and hip. Hope had really found her niche, Andreas thought with satisfaction and considerable relief. The Vargas woman would probably be delighted with a bag that resembled a tomato. His biggest fear had always been that Hope would meet with the kind of rejection that crushed a vulnerable creative personality.

'See you in the morning...' Hope whispered, hovering within reach.

Andreas resisted temptation. She had taken the trouble to warn him off before she had even agreed to stay. In the light of that prohibition, testing the boundaries would be a bad move. Tomorrow, however, after he had proposed and she had the engagement ring on her finger, he would probably bulldoze down the boundaries. Gently bulldoze, he adjusted, thinking about the baby. In any case he still had one or two arrangements to put in place for the next day.

Hope surveyed the beautifully decorated guest room. She had finally made it into the town house. A barrier had been crossed. But she remained far more aware that she had been carefully kept from the same door for two years.

Since Andreas had dumped her she had learned some hard lessons. Andreas had always viewed her as his mistress, probably still did and was very unlikely to ever see her in any other light. For the moment, her pregnancy had brought down several barriers but she suspected that in time the same barriers would be reinstated. So, although she was horrendously weak where he was concerned and changed like the wind according to the level of his proximity, she needed to be sensible and keep her distance.

When Andreas had told Hope that he wanted her opinion on a house, she had had no real idea what to expect. But she had nonetheless assumed that he would only be interested in a city property within easy reach of his office. Instead she was tucked into a helicopter and informed that their destination lay outside London. Mesmerised by his pronounced air of mystery, she was a really good sport about the fact that the seat belt had to be loosened to fit her.

When the helicopter came in to land at Knightmere Court, Andreas was experiencing the high of a male convinced that he had picked a sure-fire winner. He had picked Knightmere from a selection of six large country properties. It ticked every box on the list of desirable qualities he had drawn up and Hope was already staring out the window with an appropriately transfixed expression pinned to her face.

'My goodness...' Hope exclaimed weakly as he lifted her out of the craft.

Andreas took her on a very brief outside tour just to ensure that she got a tantalising flavour of the extensive grounds, which included a knot and topiary garden, the all-important walled garden and a park as much ornamented by a pedigree flock of sheep as by the trees. He drew her attention variously to the dove-cote, the clock tower and the lake in the distance. He had picked a building that fairly bristled with historic features.

'The estate comes with a considerable amount of land, sufficient to ensure that the superb views will remain unaltered,' Andreas informed her, having read and inwardly digested every packed and detailed page of the glossy sales brochure.

Hope blinked and wondered what was the matter with him. She was not aware that he had ever shown any interest in country life. But his disinterest in his surroundings embraced city living too, she reflected with a slight frown. As long as the luxury comforts, services and privacy he took entirely for granted were available, Andreas was maddeningly indifferent to his home environment. Yet now all of a sudden he sounded rather like an enthusiastic estate agent.

Round the next corner she was treated to her first full view of the south front of the ancient Tudor manor house. 'My goodness…' she said again, utterly charmed by the soft mellow colour of the bricks and the latticed windows sparkling in the sunshine. 'It's beautiful.'

'Indoors you'll have to exercise your imagination,' Andreas remarked, nodding acknowledgement of the discreet older man who appeared at the entrance and spread the door wide for them. 'Knightmere has been empty for more than three years, although it has been extensively renovated.'

'Was it originally owned by one particular family?'

'Yes. The family line died out with an elderly spinster. A foreign businessman bought it but the repairs took longer than expected and he never lived here. He's now moved abroad again and the house is back on the market.'

'Wouldn't this place be too far from the city for you?'

'I'd use the helicopter.'

Her turquoise eyes were perplexed. 'It's just not the sort of property that I would've expected you to be interested in. I thought possibly you were thinking of converting it into a hotel or apartments or something—'

'No.'

'Then if you bought it, this would actually be your home?'

'My country home and where I would spend most of my time…yes,' Andreas confirmed. 'I like space around me.'

'There's certainly plenty of that,' Hope conceded. 'It's a huge house. How many bedrooms are there?'

'A dozen or so.' Andreas shifted a casual shoulder. 'But I have a large family circle. On special occasions those rooms would be easy to fill.'

Hope scanned the panelled walls, massive overhead oak beams and the huge elaborate fireplace, which bore the carved date of a year in the sixteenth century. She was fascinated. 'This must have been the Great Hall. It's so old and yet so wonderfully well preserved,' she whispered in frank awe of her surroundings.

Andreas surveyed her rapt profile and decided it was a done deal; she was reacting exactly as he had hoped. He allowed her to roam where her fancy took her and watched her enchantment grow. No nook and no cranny remained unexplored. An ancient range had been left intact at one end of the vast kitchen and she went into raptures over it and the beautifully carved free-standing units. Inspecting a procession of stream-lined opulent bathrooms almost emptied her of superlative comments.

Andreas walked her back outside through the courtyard. 'Do you think I should buy it?' he asked, confidence riding high.

'Oh, yes…it's fantastic,' Hope murmured dreamily.

Andreas pushed open the cast-iron gate into the walled garden, which was a riot of early summer roses and lush greenery. 'Close your eyes,' he urged softly. 'I have a surprise for you.'

Obediently she let her lashes dip and then lifted them again at his bidding. A traditional canvas canopy screened the sun from the tumbled cushions that were piled invitingly on the elegant striped rug spread across the manicured grass. A wicker hamper sat invitingly open with linen napkins, a chrome wine cooler and crystal glasses already lined up in readiness. It was a picnic Nicolaidis style, she registered in wonderment, so perfect in presentation and backdrop that she felt as if she had wandered into a picture in a magazine. It would no doubt knock her home-made picnics of the past into a cocked hat.

Her generous smile lit up her lovely face. 'Oh, this is a glorious surprise.'

'I wanted to do something special that you'd really appreciate, *pedhi mou*.'

Her mobile phone rang. Wishing that she had thought to switch it off, she dug it out. It was Ben.

Ready embarrassment coloured her cheeks and she half turned away to speak. 'Ben…hi.'

Ben was ringing to congratulate her on the offer she had received from Leonie Vargas.

'Don't mind me,' Andreas breathed very dryly.

'Could I call you back later?' Hope asked Ben in a whisper that sounded to her own ears like a shout. 'I'm so sorry but I can't really chat right now.'

As she put the phone away again the silence fairly bulged with hostile undertones. Andreas was furious. At the optimum wrong moment, Campbell phoned. Was he expected to accept that? Being haunted by the ex-boyfriend? With difficulty he suppressed his annoyance by reminding himself that Hope was friendly with everybody she met.

'Let's eat,' Andreas suggested.

The hamper was packed to the brim with delicious items. Hope sipped fruit juice and ate until she could eat no more. She told him what Leonie Vargas was like in the flesh and made him laugh. Resting back against the tumbled cushions, she relaxed and feasted her eyes on his lean, powerful face.

Andreas stretched out a lean, long-fingered hand to her. 'Come here…' he urged huskily.

A quiver of forbidden excitement tugged at her. After a split second of hesitation, her hand reached out to close into his. He tugged her close, leaning over her to scan her with brilliant golden eyes. 'Let's get married and make Knightmere our home,' he murmured smoothly.

CHAPTER EIGHT

HOPE's mouth ran dry and shock tore through her tensed body. Andreas had taken her by surprise. She closed her eyes tight against the intrusion of his and let herself savour just for a moment the sheer joy of actually being asked to be his wife. There was nothing she wanted more but she knew that it would not be right for her to say yes unless he said the right words. Unfortunately those same words were words she had long since accepted that she would never hear from him.

'Why?' she questioned tightly. 'Why are you asking me to marry you?'

His ebony brows pleated. 'Isn't that obvious?'

The first twist of disappointment tore at her and she opened strained turquoise eyes. 'You're thinking about the baby.'

'Of course. No Nicolaidis that I know of has ever been born outside the bonds of matrimony,' Andreas informed her with considerable pride.

His reasons for asking her to become his wife were fairly piling up, Hope conceded unhappily. One, she was pregnant. Two, he was keen to respect the conventions.

'It's only two days since you told me that you would *never* marry me,' Hope reminded him very quietly.

'That was when I was still under the impression that you had been unfaithful,' Andreas asserted without discomfiture. 'I think we should go for a quick, quiet ceremony and throw a big party afterwards. What do you think?'

Slowly, Hope withdrew her fingers from his and sat up. 'I think you're not going to like my answer.'

Andreas misunderstood. 'If you prefer a more traditional wedding, I don't mind. Have as many frills as you like. *How* we do it isn't important as long as we do it before the baby's born.'

Hope pushed herself upright. 'I'm afraid the answer has to be…no.'

'No?' She saw that it had not once occurred to Andreas that he might meet with rejection.

'I love the house, love the picnic—' Love you too, Hope reflected painfully but kept that admission to herself '—but unfortunately you don't want to marry me for the right reasons.'

Utterly taken aback by that criticism, Andreas sprang upright, dark golden eyes incredulous. 'What are the right reasons?'

'If you don't know, there's no point in me spelling them out for you,' she said heavily.

'Are you still determined to keep your options open? Is that what this is all about?' Andreas ground out.

Her brow indented. 'I don't know what you're getting at.'

'Or are you punishing me for listening to my sister three months ago and letting you down?' Andreas demanded in a raw undertone.

Hope studied him with pained intensity. 'I wouldn't behave like that. But I am afraid that you were so willing to believe Elyssa's lies because you wanted your freedom back—'

'I always had my freedom. I made a free choice to be with you!' Andreas contradicted.

'And when I made the mistake of reminding you that we'd been together almost two years, you were in no mood to celebrate.' Hope sighed. 'There was no question of your making a commitment to me then—'

His even white teeth gritted. 'Everything's changed since then—'

'Yes. But you don't need to put a ring on my wedding finger because I fell pregnant,' Hope told him gently.

'How are you planning to manage without me?'

Hope lost colour at that crack. 'Are you saying that if I don't marry you, you'll break up with me again?'

An electrifying silence fell.

His beautiful dark deep-set eyes struck sparks from hers. 'No, I'm not saying that. I'd have to be a real bastard to abandon the mother of my child in any circumstances.'

'For goodness' sake, I know you're not that.' Hope felt as though she were standing on the edge of a chasm in the middle of an earthquake. If she wasn't careful she might tumble into the chasm and lose everything. Was she being foolish? Should she be willing to settle for a marriage of convenience with a guy who didn't love her? Or was it that she was more scared of Andreas marrying her and then regretting it?

While she was frantically questioning whether or not she was making the biggest mistake of her life, Andreas closed his arms round her. 'I made you happy before...I can do it again,' he intoned fiercely.

'I know, but—'

'*Theos*...Just you try and find this same fire with someone else!' He bent his arrogant dark head and crushed her ripe mouth under his, unleashing a passion that took her by storm. His lips were firm and warm and wonderful on hers and she could not get enough of his kisses.

Breathless and trembling, she knotted her fingers into the shoulders of his jacket to hold him close. She did not want to set him free to find someone else. She did not want to be alone.

'Andreas...?' she framed through reddened lips, turquoise eyes clinging in urgent appeal to his. 'Don't get the wrong idea about what I'm about to say. I'm not suggesting that I be your mistress. But could we live together instead of getting married?'

Andreas was a long way from happy with that proposition. His smoothly laid plans had been derailed when he'd least expected it. He felt hollow, bewildered by his failure, quite unlike himself.

Had he rushed her too much? He always moved fast and made decisions at the speed of the light but she did not. Once, though, she had had touching faith in him and his judgement. Now, however, she was wary, unsure of herself and of him. For the first time he recognised how much he must have hurt her when he'd dumped her. He could hardly blame her for being afraid to trust him again.

He saw that there had been a fatal flaw in his approach. He had put more effort into marketing the house than himself. Having recognised the problem, he saw the solution and came up with a fresh strategy. That disturbing sense of disorientation that had afflicted him mercifully vanished. All he had to do was demonstrate that he would make a perfect husband and a fantastic father.

'Andreas…' Hope prompted worriedly, afraid she had offended him.

The brooding light in his dark reflective gaze ebbed and his slow, charismatic smile curved his handsome mouth. 'I'll buy the house this afternoon. How soon will you move in?'

She blinked, thrown by his immediacy. 'Whenever you like.'

'I like it best when you're not out of my sight for longer than five minutes, *pedhi mou*,' Andreas told her, tugging her up against his lean, powerful frame and anchoring her below one strong arm while he called the agent to negotiate.

'No, you're not to look at that,' Andreas scolded, flipping an offending newspaper out of her reach six weeks later.

'Why not?' Hope watched him lounge back against the crisp white pillows. The sheet had dropped to below his waist, exposing the hard, hair-roughened expanse of his bronzed torso and the sleek, muscular strength of his superbly fit body. He looked breathtakingly handsome.

'There's an entry about us in the gossip column…I don't want you lowering yourself to look at trash like that,' Andreas delivered in a tone of finality.

Unimpressed, Hope put out her hand. 'Give it to me,' she told him.

A raw masculine grin slashed his beautiful mouth. 'No…'

'Stop being bossy!' Levering herself up, Hope flung herself across him in an effort to wrest the paper from him. Laughing with rich appreciation, he caught her in his arms and pressed her gently back against the pillows. Teasing golden eyes met hers. 'Behave yourself!'

'You can't censor what I read—'

'If there is the tiniest risk that something might upset you it's my duty to protect you from it. I'm Greek. You're my woman and I look after you. Learn to live with what you can't fight,' Andreas warned with unblemished good humour.

'I'll just walk down to the village and buy another copy.'

'You're supposed to be taking it easy.' Frowning, Andreas handed the disputed item over. 'That was blackmail.'

'I know.' Far from ashamed of herself, Hope wriggled up again, snuggled back into him for support and opened the paper. Sometimes it was rather sweet to be treated like impossibly fragile spun glass, but other times it made her feel horribly like a burden. It was bad enough that he should be full of energy and vitality while she was falling asleep in the middle of the day. In addition, anything more intimate than a hug was off the menu as well. When her cautious gynaecologist had said that her exhaustion could become a source of concern, Andreas had decided that sex was absolutely out of the question.

Having leafed through the newspaper, Hope found a most unflattering photo of herself that seemed to concentrate rather cruelly on her pregnant stomach. She looked like a large woman overfilling a little black dress, an archetypal ship in full sail trundling across the pavement. The photo had been taken two days earlier as they'd left the well-known restaurant where Andreas's grandfather, Kostas, had entertained them to dinner and initially trying questions. She had soon warmed to the blunt-spoken older man, however. Kostas Nicolaidis had made it clear that, although he would much prefer them to marry, he was overjoyed that she was carrying his grandson's baby and that Andreas was finally settling down.

'Oh, no…' Hope exclaimed, aghast, as she started reading the article beside the photo.

'So what's wrong with my grandson that you won't make an honest man of him?' Kostas had asked baldly, and there were those exact same words in print, clearly overheard and passed on to the columnist. Below the execrable title, BAG LADY REFUSES NICOLAIDIS HEIR, virtually every female that Andreas had ever dated was listed, the suggestion being that he had been turned down because no sane female would seek to tie down a rampant womaniser.

'Kostas will be thrilled. He loves to see his name in newsprint,' Andreas commented cheerfully.

'But I look simply *huge*!' she wailed in embarrassment.

Andreas stretched appreciative hands across the rounded swell of her stomach, stretched them just a little more and contrived to link his fingers. 'You look fantastic, really, really pregnant now. Ripe like a peach, *pedhi mou*.'

'Very round and squashy?' Hope refused to be comforted. 'Aren't you angry that everybody knows that you proposed and I said no?'

'You must be kidding.' Andreas laughed off that idea with disconcerting verve.

Her brows pleated, for she had assumed that he

would be furious that something so private had been accidentally brought by his grandfather into the public domain. 'You don't mind?'

'Not in the slightest,' Andreas asserted silkily. 'And when you get to meet the rest of my relatives this weekend you'll understand why. I'm the golden boy because I tried to get a wedding ring on your finger and you'll be—'

'The horrible witch who doesn't appreciate you!' she slotted in, cringing at that new awareness.

'Nonsense. My great-aunts will be very keen to talk me up. You are destined to spend the entire weekend listening to stories that represent me as Mr Wonderful—clean-living, kind to old ladies and animals and stupendous with children. I'll bet you right now that nobody mentions my late father and his three divorces. He's the family skeleton and would give the wrong impression.'

An involuntary gurgle of laughter escaped Hope and she relaxed. The past six weeks had been just about the happiest and busiest of her life. They had managed to move into Knightmere the previous month. Andreas had pulled strings, called in favours and brought in an interior design firm as well as a project manager to ensure that the wonderful old house had been made habitable in the least possible amount of time. A full quota of domestic staff had been hired and Hope had been left with little more to do than design bags.

That had proved to be just as well because pregnancy was slowing her down. Just occasionally her worries got on top of her. Had saying no to the proposal been the right thing to do? He had not mentioned the subject since, which suggested that he was quite content with things as they were. How could a guy so gorgeous cheerfully settle for a woman who was the shape of a very ripe peach? Was it guilt that was making Andreas so perfect? Guilt that he had misjudged her and left her alone for several months?

Perfect was not an exaggeration of his attitude towards her or his behaviour. He had begun working much shorter hours and cutting down on his trips abroad. He had attended all her pre-natal appointments with her. He had read a book on pregnancy with the result that he descended into pure panic if she experienced the slightest twinge of pain in any part of her body. When she'd got a cramp in her leg one evening he had wanted to take her to Casualty and when she'd refused he had sat up all night watching over her. He had also been pleasant to her friend, Vanessa, and had tolerated her receiving regular phone calls from Ben, who had been travelling round Europe for several weeks.

In addition, Andreas had been kind, affectionate, supportive and, as always, wonderfully entertaining. Being sexy came naturally to him so she didn't count that. But although he could well have aspired to sainthood, not one word had Andreas said about love. So there it was, Hope thought heavily. She had to accept that she just did not have what it took to inspire Andreas with love. As long as there was no other woman out there who had the power that she lacked, she supposed she was all right. After all, she loved him and she was living with him and she would soon give birth to his child. Wasn't it rather greedy to want more?

'I have a couple of things I need to deal with at the office before we leave for Greece. I'll meet you

at the airport at six,' Andreas murmured above her
head, wishing he could take her to the office with him
and then frowning in bemusement at the seriously uncool and embarrassing oddity of that last absent-
minded thought.

He assumed that he was always stressing about her
because she was pregnant. She was always on his
mind. When he was away from her, he found it particularly difficult to concentrate on work. Reading that
gruesome book had been a serious error. He had not
slept for a couple of nights after it and the worst thing
of all had been the necessity of keeping quiet about
the concerns that had been awakened by what he had
read. He had dumped the book. He didn't want *her*
reading scary stuff of that nature.

'Hope...?' Andreas probed.

He tugged her to one side and bent over her. She
was fast asleep. He listened to hear her breathing just
in case it didn't sound normal. With great care he
settled her down on the pillows. He would warn the
housekeeper to check on her.

Hope was really annoyed when she realised that
she had drifted off and missed Andreas's departure.
Having completed her packing the day before, she
donned the lilac tunic and cropped trousers she had
decided to travel in. Andreas phoned an hour later.

'Make sure you eat some lunch,' he instructed.

'Stop fussing...' She walked over to the window
of the room that she used as a design studio. It overlooked the courtyard where a car was pulling up. It
was a Porsche and she grinned when she saw a familiar tousled blond head emerging from the driver's
seat. 'Oh, my goodness, Ben's here...sorry, I have to
go!' she told Andreas in a rush.

In his London office, Andreas stared fixedly down at the phone in his hand. She had been so overjoyed to see Campbell she had ended the call. He endeavoured to return his attention to the report on his desk. Campbell had been out of the country for weeks. Hope seemed to think he simply enjoyed travel but Andreas suspected that Ben had gone abroad in an effort to come to terms with losing Hope. Now Campbell was back and what was his first action? He went to see Hope in the middle of the day when he knew he was most likely to find her at home and on her own.

Andreas breathed in deep but the sick sense of rage threatening him did not abate. He leapt upright. Exactly what was he going to do? Go home. He rang his helicopter pilot and told him he needed to get there as soon as possible. Would it look odd if he just arrived back at Knightmere? He raked an uneasy hand through his cropped black hair. Hope might think he didn't trust her. He did trust her, he trusted her absolutely. But how could he possibly trust Ben Campbell?

Campbell might try to make a move on Hope. A guy didn't get over losing a woman like Hope that easily. Andreas knew that from painful personal experience. He had dumped Hope and lived in hell for endless weeks that were a blur of alcohol and misery. He did not want to go through that again *ever*. If Campbell attempted to lure Hope back to him, he was going to get a fight he would never forget.

On the top of the Nicolaidis building, Andreas boarded the helicopter. He felt out of control. That unnerved him. But he was quick to assure himself that there was no way he would lose his temper and get physical with Campbell. Hope would not like that and he was determined not to do or indeed say anything that might distress her. Possibly he should tell her how her seeing Campbell made him feel. He felt angry. He felt jealous. He felt threatened. Of course, he felt threatened! He was on like…continual probation. She wouldn't marry him. The one thing that would give him a sense of security, she denied him and she would not tell him why.

Maybe he should make a special effort to explain just how important she was to him. That was something he had always been careful to keep to himself, but now he was afraid that he had kept quiet for too long and missed his chance. She was very, very important to his peace of mind. He could not bear the idea that anything might ever harm her. He thought he was incredibly lucky to have got a second chance with her. Was that love? How was he supposed to know what love was? Before he had met her, he had never been in love. He was morosely convinced that Campbell wouldn't hang back from saying he loved her.

Hope tensed when she saw the helicopter coming in to land. Why had Andreas changed his plans and returned to the house? Was it because he was unhappy about Ben coming to visit? She really hoped it wasn't that.

'Andreas…' she murmured as he strode into the drawing room, his lean, strong face shuttered and taut. 'Did you forget something?'

'Ne…yes,' he breathed in Greek, his eyes smouldering gold as his expressive mouth curved into a smile that was purely for her.

'Let me introduce you to our visitors,' Hope said warmly.

Visitors in the plural? Disconcerted, Andreas turned his head and saw to his surprise that Ben had his arm wrapped round a tiny exquisite brunette. A perceptible air of intimacy clung to the other couple.

'Of course, you know Ben...this is Chantal,' Hope informed him.

Andreas extended a hand to Ben and kissed the brunette on both cheeks French style.

'I'm afraid we have to make tracks,' Ben told them. 'My mother's expecting us this afternoon.'

Having watched them drive away, Andreas closed a hand tightly over Hope's. 'I was really scared that Campbell was back to make a play for you,' he admitted half under his breath.

Hope dealt him a startled glance. 'Andreas...at this moment, I'm the size of a medium-sized house,' she pointed out gently. 'I don't think there's much risk of any guy making a play for me right now.'

'I've had a problem handling your friendship with him.' Dulled colour scored his high cheekbones. 'If you hadn't been pregnant, you'd probably still be with him—'

'No, slow up there!' Hope inserted in dismay. 'As far as I'm concerned I'm with you by choice and our baby has very little to do with it.'

'But you had something good going with Campbell—'

'I liked him very much but he's not you and he was never going to be.'

Encouraged by that statement, Andreas bit the proverbial bullet. 'I've been jealous as hell—'

Hope looked up at him in amazement. 'But why?

There's no need. I had only started seeing Ben when I found out I was expecting. It's not as if I slept with him or anything like that!'

The silence sizzled.

'You...*didn't* sleep with him?' Andreas prompted fiercely. 'Have you any idea how much knowing that means to me?'

'If you had asked, I would never have lied. You didn't ask.'

Andreas flexed lean brown fingers, shrugged broad shoulders, compressed his beautiful mouth and nodded into the bargain. It took all those separate gestures to express the intensity of his response. 'It always meant a lot to me that I had been your only lover—'

'You never said.'

'I took you for granted. You were there. Life was good and then...pow! It's gone,' he breathed in a roughened undertone, pulling her close as though to combat that unhappy memory.

'Elyssa,' she sighed.

'Her lies tore me apart. I have never been so wretched in all my life. I didn't understand what you meant to me until you were gone,' Andreas confessed raggedly above her head, his strong arms tightening expressively round her. 'Then I couldn't admit to myself that I hated my life without you in it.'

'Honestly?' Her head came up, turquoise eyes focusing on him.

'Honestly.'

'But what about all the women you were seen about with?'

Andreas grimaced. 'Window dressing.'

Hope snatched in a stark breath. 'Did you undress any of the windows?'

Andreas winced. 'Couldn't...'

Her eyes rounded. *'Couldn't?'*

'I couldn't because...' Andreas dragged in a sustaining breath before he pushed himself on to the crux of the matter. 'I couldn't because I only turn on for you. Didn't you notice how hot I was for you at the cottage?'

'You've been faithful.' A huge sunny smile lit up her heart-shaped face.

'I'll always be faithful...' Andreas hesitated. 'I love you, *pedhi mou.*'

Her lashes fluttered up on wide, disbelieving eyes.

'It's true...I do!' Andreas stressed as if she had argued the score with him. 'When I feel this weird, it's got to be love!'

'You love me...' Hope felt buoyant with happiness. 'I love you too—'

'So why won't you marry me?' Andreas demanded fiercely. 'Being single is driving me mad!'

'Oh, I think I could do something about that and save your sanity for you,' Hope whispered teasingly. 'If you love me—'

'I love you like crazy!' Andreas launched, cupping her cheekbones with his spread fingers.

'I'll marry you just as soon as you can get it organised,' she told him happily. 'That was what I was waiting and hoping for. I didn't want you to marry me unless you loved me.'

Andreas did not let the grass grow under his feet. The relatives assembled to meet Hope that weekend extended their stay and got treated to a big splashy wedding in Athens. Hope's grasp of the Greek language was finally revealed and much admired. Hope took centre stage in a pink off-the-shoulder dress and a bag in the shape of a lucky horseshoe. Vanessa acted as her bridesmaid. Ben attended with Chantal. The paparazzi turned out in large numbers but were prohibited any wedding pictures by tight security arrangements.

The happy couple returned to Knightmere for their honeymoon because the bride did not feel up to anything more strenuous. When she lamented that truth, Andreas just laughed and reminded her that they had their whole lives in front of them.

Karisa Nicolaidis was born five weeks later. Andreas had to get Hope to the hospital in the middle of the night, an event he had planned for with split-second timing. It was an uneventful and quick delivery. Karisa came into the world at dawn with her mother's lack of fuss. With her crisp head of dark curls, she was a very pretty infant and she was christened when she was four weeks old.

Elyssa sent a gift. Andreas returned it without discussing the matter with Hope. When Hope found out, she told Andreas that she thought it was time that hostilities ceased. By all accounts, Elyssa was having a rough enough time. Her husband, Finlay, was divorcing her and contesting custody of their two little boys. Hope encouraged Andreas to at least consider the idea of speaking to his sister again as, while he was unwilling, Elyssa was receiving the cold-shoulder treatment from most of his family.

The collection of bags that Hope designed for Leonie Vargas sold like hot cakes and catapulted her name to fame. Instead of being called the 'bag lady' by the press, she was referred to as the 'reclusive accessory designer, Hope Nicolaidis.' Her bags sold for a small fortune. Andreas was impressed to death by her profit margins but he never did comprehend the attraction of most of her designs.

Several months after the birth of their daughter, Andreas flew Hope to Paris for a very special meal. When they got back to their exclusive hotel suite he presented her with a fabulous pair of diamond earrings. 'This is our third anniversary since we met, *agape mou*.'

After a night of wild passion they lay talking way into the small hours. Curved beneath his arm, Hope loosed a blissful sigh. 'I'm so happy…'

'And I intend to devote the rest of my life to ensuring that you stay that way,' Andreas promised, his dark golden eyes full of love resting on her smiling face.

The Purchased Wife

MICHELLE REID

Michelle Reid grew up on the southern edges of Manchester, the youngest in a family of five lively children. But now she lives in the beautiful county of Cheshire with her busy executive husband and two grown-up daughters. She loves reading, the ballet, and playing tennis when she gets the chance. She hates cooking, cleaning, and despises ironing! Sleep she can do without and produces some of her best written work during the early hours of the morning.

Don't miss Michelle Reid's new novel,
The De Santis Marriage, out in September 2008
from Mills & Boon® Modern™!

CHAPTER ONE

GETTING from flight arrivals to the airport's main exit was like taking a long walk through hell. The whole route was lined with baying reporters, flashing light bulbs and a cacophony of questions aimed to provoke an impulsive response.

Xander kept his mouth clamped tightly shut and ignored provocations like, 'Did you have anything to do with your wife's accident, Mr Pascalis?'—'Did she know about your mistress?'—'Did she run her car off the road to kill herself?'—'Is there a good reason why you withdrew her bodyguard last week?'

With his eyes fixed directly ahead Xander just kept on going, six feet two inches of mean muscle power driving long legs towards the airport exit with no less than three personal-security men grouped around him like protective wolves guarding the king of the pack.

Through it all the questions kept on coming and the camera bulbs flashed, catching his severely handsome dark features locked in an expression of blistering contempt. Inside, his fury was simmering on the point of eruption. He was used to being the centre of media interest, speculation—scandal if they thought they could make it stick. But nothing—nothing they'd said about him before had been as bad or as potentially damaging as this.

He hit the outside and crossed the pavement to the waiting limousine where Rico, his chauffeur, stood with the rear door open at the ready. Dipping into the car, the door shut even before he'd folded his long frame into the seat, while outside his security people dispersed in a prowling circle that kept the reporters back until Rico had safely stashed himself back behind the wheel.

5

Ten seconds later the car moved away from the kerb and another car was pulling into its place to receive his men.

'How is she?' he lanced, rough toned, at the man sitting beside him.

'Still in surgery,' Luke Morrell replied.

The granite set of Xander's jaw clenched violently on a sudden vision of the beautiful Helen stretched out on an operating table, the object of a surgeon's knife. It was almost as bad as the vision he'd had of her slumped behind the wheel of her twisted wreck of a car with her Titian-bright hair and heart-shaped face smeared with blood.

His jaw unclenched. 'Who is with her at the hospital?'

There was a short hesitation before, 'No one,' Luke Morell answered. 'She refused to allow anyone to stay.'

Turning his dark head, Xander fixed his narrowed gaze on the very wary face of his UK-based personal assistant. 'What the hell happened to Hugo Vance?'

'Nell dismissed him a week ago.'

The simmering silence which followed that tasty piece of information began to burn up the oxygen inside the luxury car. 'And you knew about this?'

Luke Morrell swallowed and nodded. 'Hugo Vance rang to let me know what she'd done.'

'Then why the hell was I not told—?'

'You were busy.'

Busy. Xander's lips snapped together. He was always busy. Busy was a damned bloody way of life! 'Keep something like that from me again and you're out,' he seared at the other man with teeth-gritting intent.

Luke Morrell shifted tensely, wishing to hell that the beautiful Helen had remained locked away behind the gates of their private country estate instead of deciding it was time to venture out and take a look at life.

'It was an accident, Xander. She was driving too fast—'

A pair of wide shoulders shifted inside impeccable dark suiting. 'The point is—*why* was she driving so fast?'

Luke didn't answer. In truth he didn't need to. Xander could put two and two together and come up with four for himself. Yesterday his name had been splashed all over the tabloids alongside a photograph of him standing outside a supposedly discreet New York restaurant with the beautiful Vanessa DeFriess plastered to his front.

His skin contracted against tightly honed face muscles when he thought of the incident. Protecting Nell from embarrassing scenes like that was a duty from which he never shirked. But his bodyguard of the evening had been distracted by a drunk trying to muscle in on them, and by the time the drunk had been hustled away and the frightened Vanessa had been peeled off Xander's front, a convenient reporter had already got his sleaze-grabbing photograph and slunk away.

Nell would have been upset, angry—who the hell knew what went on inside her beautiful head? He'd stopped trying to find out a year ago when she'd married him to a fanfare of 'Romance of the New Century' then promptly refused to share his bed. By the time she'd finished calling him filthy names ranging from *power-driven fiend* to *sex-obsessed moron*, he no longer wanted her anywhere near him.

Liar, jeered a voice inside his head. You just had no defence ready when you were hit with too many ugly truths, so you backed off to hide behind your pride and arrogance.

Photographs of his relationship with Vanessa had been the catalyst then, he remembered. Tasty snippets of truth printed in with the lies that had made it impossible for him to defend himself. He *had* been with Vanessa the week before his marriage. He *had* wined and dined her at a very fashionable restaurant then taken her back to her apartment and gone in with her. The fact that he'd been doing it on the other side of the Atlantic made him stupidly—*naively* believe he was safe.

But back here in the UK, his young, sweetly besotted future bride had been avidly following his every move as it was recorded in the New York gossip columns via the internet.

The sneaky little witch had told nobody. His mouth gave a grim, uncontrolled twitch. She'd come to him down the aisle of the church dressed like an angel in frothy silk tulle and gossamer lace. She'd smiled at him, let him take her cool little hand, let him place his ring on her slender white finger, let him vow to love, honour and protect. She'd even allowed him that one traditional kiss as they became man and wife. She'd smiled for their wedding photographs, smiled throughout the long wedding breakfast that followed and even smiled when he'd taken her in his arms for their traditional bridal dance. If there had ever been a man more ready to be a willing slave to his lovely young bride then, by the time they reached the hotel suite where they were to spend their wedding night, he, Alexander Pascalis, was it.

She'd waited until then to turn on him like a viper. A cold, glassy-eyed English version of a viper, who'd spat words at him like ice picks that awoke this handsome prince up from his arrogant dream-world instead of the prince awakening his sleeping beauty with the kind of loving that should have made her his slave for life.

And sleeping beauty she was then—too innocent to be real. That same innocence had been her only saviour on their miserable wedding night. Still was, did she but know it.

Because his marriage might have turned into a disaster even before he'd got around to consummating it but his desire to possess the beautiful Helen had remained a strong, nagging entity amongst the rubble of the rest.

'I suppose you know why she dismissed Vance?' he queried now, dragging his mind back to the present crisis.

There was a tense shift beside him. Xander turned his dark head again and a warning tingle shot across the back of his neck when he saw the new guarded expression on his employee's face. Luke was wary—very wary. There was even a hint of red beginning to stain his pale English cheeks.

'Spit it out,' he raked at him.

Luke Morrell tugged in a breath. 'Hugo tried to stop her,' he claimed defensively, 'but Nell took offence—'

'Tried to stop her from doing what?'

Luke lifted up a hand in a helpless gesture. 'Listen, Xander,' he said in an advisory voice that sounded too damn soothing for Xander's liking, 'it was nothing serious enough to need to involve you but Hugo was concerned that it might…get out of hand, so he…advised Nell against it and she—'

'Advised her against doing what?' Xander sliced right through all of Luke's uncharacteristic babbling, and by now every bone in his body was tensing up as his instincts shot on full alert. He was not going to like this. He was so damn certain of it that his clenched teeth began to sing.

'A man,' Luke admitted reluctantly. 'A—a friend Nell's been seeing recently…'

Nell felt as if she were floating. It was a really strange feeling, all fluffy and soft yet scary at the same time. And she couldn't open her eyes. She had tried a couple of times but her eyelids felt as if they'd been glued down. Her throat hurt when she swallowed and her mouth was so dry the swallowing action was impossible anyway.

She knew where she was. Had a vague recollection of the car accident and being rushed by ambulance to hospital, but that pretty much was the sum total of her recollection. The last clear thing she remembered was gunning the engine of her little open-top sports car and driving at a pace down the long drive-way at Rosemere towards the giant iron gates. She could remember the wild sense of elation she'd felt when the gates had swung open with precision timing to let her shoot right through them without her having to drop her speed. And she could still feel the same sense of bitter triumph with which she'd mocked the gates' efficiency as she'd driven past them. Didn't the stupid gates know they'd just let the trapped bird escape?

Escape. Nell frowned, puzzled as to why the word had jumped into her head. Then she was suddenly groaning when the frown caused a pain to shoot right across the front of her head.

Someone moved not far away. 'Nell…?' a deep, darkly rasping voice said.

Managing to open her eyes the small crack that was all they would allow her, she peered out at the shadowy outline of a man's big, lean, dark-suited bulk standing stiffly at the end of her bed.

Xander, she recognised. Bitterness welled as her heart gave a tight, very painful pinch. What was he doing here? Had corporate earth stopped turning or something? Nothing less would give him the time to visit her sickbed.

Go away, she wanted to say but did not have enough energy, so she closed the slits in her eyes and blocked him out that way instead.

'Nell, can you hear me?'

He sounded unusually gruff. Maybe he had a bad cold or a sore throat or something, she thought hazily. How would she know? She'd barely set eyes on him for months—not since he'd turned up like a bad penny on her birthday and dragged her out to have dinner with him.

The candlelit-table-for-two kind of dinner with good wine and the requisite bottle of champagne standing at the ready on ice. Her fuzzy head threw up a picture of his handsome dark image, the way the candlelight had played with his ebony hair and the golden sheen of his skin as he'd sat there across the table from her with his slumberous dark eyes fixed on her face. Sartorial elegance had oozed from every sleek skin pore. The smooth self-confidence, the indolent grace with which he'd occupied his seat that belied his height and lean muscle power. The lazy indifference with which he'd dismissed the kind of breathless looks he received from every other woman in the room because he was special and he knew he was special, and there was not a person in that restaurant that didn't recognise it. Including Nell, though she was the only one there that refused to let it show.

'Happy birthday,' he said and used long, tanned fingers to push a velvet box across the table towards her. Inside the box was a diamond-encrusted bracelet that must have cost him the absolute earth.

If she was supposed to be impressed, she wasn't. If he'd presented her with the crown jewels she still would not be impressed. Did he think she didn't know that a bracelet like that was the kind of thing a man like him presented to his mistress for services rendered?

Where was his sensitivity? Where it had always been, locked up inside his impossible arrogance, as he proved when he dared to announce then that he wanted to renegotiate their marriage contract as if some stupid trinket was all it would take to make her agree.

She pushed the box back across the table and said no—to both the bracelet and the request. Did it faze him? Not in the slightest. He took a few minutes to think about her cool little refusal then nodded his disgustingly handsome dark head in acceptance, and that was basically that. He'd driven her back to Rosemere then drove away again to go back to his exciting life as a high-profile, globe-trotting Greek tycoon and probably given the bracelet to some other woman—the more appreciative Vanessa, for instance.

'I hate him,' she thought, having no idea that the words had scraped across her dry lips.

The sound of furniture moving set her frowning again, a pale, limp hand lifting weakly to the pain that stabbed at her forehead. Another hand gently caught hold of her fingers to halt their progress.

'Don't touch, Nell. You won't like it,' his husky voice said.

She opened her eyes that small crack again to find Xander had moved from his stiff stance at the bottom of the bed and was now sitting on a chair beside it with his face level with hers. A pair of dark eyes looked steadily back at her from between unfairly long black silk fringes, a hint of strain tugging on the corners of his wide, sensual mouth.

'How do you feel?' he asked.

Pain attacked her from the oddest of places—her heart mainly, broken once and still not recovered.

She closed her eyes, blocking him out again. He shouldn't even be here; he should be in New York, enjoying the lovely Vanessa with the long dark hair and voluptuous figure that could show off heavy diamond trinkets while she clung to someone else's husband like a sex-charged limpet.

'Do you know where you are?' Xander persisted.

Nell quivered as his warm breath fanned her face.

'You are in hospital,' he seemed compelled to inform her. 'You were involved in a car accident. Can you hear me, Helen?'

The *Helen* arrived with the rough edge of impatience. Xander did not like to be ignored. He wasn't used to it. People shot to attention when he asked questions. He was Mr Important, the mighty empire-builder aptly named after Alexander the Great. When he said jump the whole world jumped. He was dynamic, magnetic, sensational to look at—

Her head began to ache. 'Go away,' she slurred out. 'I don't want you here.'

She could almost feel his tension slam into her. The gentle fingers still holding hers gave an involuntary twitch. Then he moved and she heard the sound of silk sliding against silk as he reached up with his other arm and another set of cool fingers gently stroked a stray lock of hair from her cheek.

'You don't mean that, *agape mou*,' he murmured.

I do, Nell thought, and felt tears sting the backs of her eyelids because his light touch evoked old dreams of a gentle giant stroking her all over like that.

But that was all they were—empty old dreams that came back to haunt her occasionally. The real Xander was hard and cold and usually wishing himself elsewhere when he was with her.

How had he got here so quickly anyway? What time was it? What day? She moved restlessly then cried out in an agonised, pathetically weak whimper as real physical pain shot everywhere.

'Don't move, you fool!' The sudden harshness in his voice rasped across her flesh like the serrated edge of a knife—right here—and she pushed a hand up to cover the left side of her ribs as her screaming body tried to curl up in instinctive recoil. The bed tilted beside her, long fingers moving to her narrow shoulders to keep her still.

'Listen to me…' his voice rasped again and she arched in

agony as pain ricocheted around her body. He tossed out a soft curse then a buzzer sounded. 'You must try to remain still,' he lashed down at her. 'You are very badly bruised, and the pain in your side is due to several cracked ribs. You are also suffering from a slight concussion, and internal bleeding meant they had to operate. Nell, you—'

'W-what kind of operation?'

'Your appendix was damaged when you crashed your car; they had to remove it.'

Appendix? Was that all? She groaned in disbelief.

'If you are worrying about a scar then don't,' Xander clipped. 'They used keyhole surgery—barely a knick; you will be as perfect as ever in a few weeks.'

Did he really believe that she cared about some silly scarring? Down in A&E they'd been tossing about all kinds of scenarios from burst spleen to ovaries!

'I hate you so much,' she gasped out then burst into tears, the kind of loud, hot, choking tears that came with pure, agonising delayed shock and brought people running and had Xander letting go of her to shoot to his feet.

After that she lost sight of him when a whole army of care staff crowded in. But she could still hear his voice, cold with incision: 'Can someone explain to me, please, why my wife shares a room with three other sick individuals? Does personal dignity have no meaning here…?'

The next time Nell woke up she was shrouded in darkness other than for a low night lamp burning somewhere up above her head. She could open her eyes without having to force them and she was feeling more comfortable, though she suspected the comfort had been drug-induced.

Moving her head on the pillow in a careful testing motion, she felt no pain attack her brow and allowed herself a sigh of relief. Then she began to take an interest in her surroundings. Something was different, though for the life of her she couldn't say what.

'You were moved this afternoon to a private hospital,' a deep voice informed her.

Turning her head in the other direction, she saw Xander standing in the shadows by the window. Her heart gave a help-less little flutter then clenched.

Private hospital. Private room. 'Why?' she whispered in con-fusion.

He didn't answer. But then why would he? A man like him did not leave his wife to the efficient care of the National Health Service when he could pay for the same service with added touches of luxury.

As she looked at him standing there in profile, staring out of the window, it didn't take much work for her dulled senses to know his mood was grim. The jacket to his dark suit had gone and he'd loosened the tie around his throat. She could just pick out the warm sheen of his golden skin as it caught the edges of a soft lamplight.

For a moment she thought she saw a glimpse of the man she had fallen in love with a year ago.

The same man she'd seen on the evening she'd walked into her father's study and found Xander there alone. He'd been standing like this by her father's window, grimly contemplating what lay beyond the Georgian glass with its hand-beaten dis-tortions that had a knack of distorting everything that was hap-pening in the world beyond.

That was the night he had asked her to marry him; no fan-fare, no romantic preliminaries. Oh, they'd been out to dinner a couple of times, and Xander tended to turn up at the same functions she would be attending and seem to make a beeline for her. People had watched curiously as he monopolised her attention and she blushed a lot because she wasn't used to having such a man show a desire for her company.

Twenty-one years old and fresh back from spending three years high up in the Canadian Rockies with a mother who preferred getting up close and personal with pieces of drift-wood she found on the shores of the Kananaskis River than she did with living people. Nell had gone to Canada for her annual two-week visit with the reclusive Kathleen Garrett and stayed to the end when her mother had coolly informed her that she didn't have long to live.

Nell liked to think that her quiet company had given her mother a few extra years of normal living before it all got too much. Certainly they became a bit more like mother and daughter than they'd been throughout Nell's life when previous visits to her mother had made her feel more like an unwanted distant relative.

Coming back to England and to her father's busy social life-style had come as a bit of a culture shock. She'd gone to Canada a child who'd spent most of her life being shunted from one boarding-school to another with very little contact with the social side of her industrialist father's busy life. Three years' living quietly with her mother had been no preparation for a girl who'd become a woman without really knowing it until she met Alexander Pascalis.

An accident waiting to happen... Nell frowned as she tried to recall who it was that had said those words to her. Then she remembered and sighed because of course it had been this tall, dark, silent man looking out of the window who'd spoken those words to her. 'A danger to yourself and to anyone near you,' he'd rumbled out as he'd pulled her into his arms and kissed her before sombrely asking her to marry him.

She looked away from his long, still frame, not wanting to go back to those days when she'd loved him so badly she would have crawled barefooted over broken glass if that was what it took to be with him. Those days were long gone, along with her pride, her self-respect and her starry-eyed infatuation.

Her mouth was still dry, the muzzy effects of whatever they'd given her to stem the pain making her limbs feel weighted down with lead. When she tried to lift her hand towards the glass of water she could see on the cupboard beside her, she could barely raise her fingers off the bed.

'I need a drink,' she whispered hoarsely.

He was there in a second, sitting down on the bed and sliding an arm beneath her shoulders to lift her enough to place the glass to her lips. She felt his warmth and his strength as she sipped the water, both alien sensations when she hadn't been held even this close to him since the day of their marriage.

'Thank you,' she breathed as the glass was withdrawn again.

He controlled her gentle slide back onto the pillows then sat back a little but didn't move away. Something was flickering in his dark eyes that she couldn't decipher—but then he was not the kind of man who wanted other people to read his thoughts—too precious, too—

'Your car was a write-off,' he remarked unexpectedly.

Her slender shoulders tensed in sudden wariness. 'W-was it?'

He nodded. His firmly held mouth gave a tense little twitch. 'You had to have been driving very fast to impale it so thoroughly on that tree.'

Nell lowered her eyes on a wince. 'I don't remember.'

'Nothing?' he questioned.

'Only driving through the gates at Rosemere then turning into the lane. After that—nothing,' she lied huskily.

He was silent for a few seconds and she could feel him studying her. Her cheeks began to heat. Lying had never been her forte. But what the devil did not know could not hurt him, she thought with a stab at dry sarcasm that was supposed to make her feel brave but didn't.

'W-what time is it?' She changed the subject.

Xander sprang back to his feet before glancing at the gold watch circling his wrist. 'Two-thirty in the morning.'

Nell lifted her eyes to watch the prowling grace of his long body as he took up his position by the window again.

'I thought you were in New York.'

'I came back—obviously.'

With or without Vanessa? she wondered. 'Well, don't feel like you have to hang around here for my benefit,' she said tightly.

He didn't usually hang around. He strode in and out of her life like a visiting patron, asked all the right polite questions about what she'd been doing since he'd seen her last and sometimes even lingered long enough to drag her out with him to some formal function—just to keep up appearances. He occupied the suite adjoining her bedroom suite but had never slept in it. Appearances, it seemed, only went as far as delivering her to her bedroom door before he turned and strode out of the house again.

'It is expected.'

And that's telling me, Nell thought with another wince. 'Well, I hereby relieve you of your duty,' she threw back, moved restlessly, which hurt, so she made herself go still again. And her eyelids were growing too heavy to hold up any longer. 'Go away, Xander.' Even her voice was beginning to sound slurry. 'You make me nervous, hanging around like this...'

Not so you would notice, Xander thought darkly as he watched the little liar drop into a deep sleep almost before her dismissal of him was complete.

The night-light above her bed was highlighting her sickly pallor along with the swollen cuts and bruises that distorted her beautiful face. She would be shocked if she knew what she looked like.

Hell, the miserable state of her wounded body shocked him.

And her hair was a mess, lying in lank, long copper tangles across the pillow. Oddly, he liked it better when it was left to do its own thing like this. The first time he'd seen her she'd been stepping into her father's house, having just arrived back from taking the dogs for a walk. It had been windy and cold outside and her face was shining, her incredible waist-length hair wild and rippling with life. Green eyes circled by a fascinating ring of turquoise had been alight with laughter because the smallest of the dogs, a golden Labrador puppy determined to get into the house first, had bounded past her, only to land on its rear and start to slither right across the slippery polished floor to come to a halt at his feet.

She'd noticed him then, lifting her eyes up from his black leather shoes on one of those slow, curious journeys he'd learned to recognise as a habit she had that set his libido on heat. By the time she'd reached his face her laughter had died to sweet, blushing shyness.

What a hook, he mocked now, recalling what happened to him every time she'd blushed like that for him—or even just looked at him.

Xander looked away and went back to his grim contemplation of the unremarkable view of the darkness outside the window, not wanting to remember what came after the blushing look.

He should have backed off while he still had a chance then— right off. If he had done they would not be in the mess they were now in. It was not his thing to mix business with pleasure, and the kind of business he'd had going with Julian Garrett had needed a cool, clear head.

Sexual desire was neither cool nor clear-headed. It liked to catch you out when you were not paying attention. He'd had a mistress, a beautiful, warm and passionately sensual woman who knew what he liked and did not expect too much back, so what did he need with a wild-haired, beautiful-eyed *ingénue* with a freakish kind of innocence written into her blushing face?

A sigh ripped from him. Nell was right and he should leave. He should get the hell away from here and begin the unpalatable task of some very urgent damage control, only he had a feeling it was already too late.

The tabloid Press would already be running, churning out their damning accusations cloaked in rumour and suggestion. The only part of it all that he had going for him was the Press did not know what Nell had been in the process of doing when she crashed her car on that quiet country lane.

His pager gave a beep. Turning away from the window, he went to collect his jacket from where he'd tossed it on a chair and dug the pager out of one of the pockets.

Hugo Vance was trying to reach him. His teeth came together with a snap.

And so to discover the truth about his wife's new *friend*, he thought grimly, shrugged on his jacket, sent Nell one final, searing dark glance then quietly let himself out of the room.

CHAPTER TWO

FOR the next few days Nell felt as if she had been placed in purdah. The only people that came to visit her belonged to the medical staff, who seemed to take great pleasure in making her uncomfortable before they made her comfortable again.

The first time they allowed her to take a shower she was shocked by the extent of her bruising. If anyone had told her that with enough applied pressure you could achieve a perfect imprint of a car safety belt across your body she would not have believed them—until she saw it striking across her own slender frame in two ugly, deep bands of dark purple bruising. She had puncture holes and stitches from the keyhole surgery and her cracked ribs hurt like crazy every time she moved. She had bruises on her legs, bruises and scratches on her arms and her face due to ploughing through bushes in an open-top car— before it had slammed into the tree.

And the miserable knowledge that Xander had seen her looking like this did not make her feel any better. It was no wonder he hadn't bothered to come and visit her again.

Her night things had been delivered, toiletries, that kind of thing. And she'd even received a dozen red roses—Xander's way of keeping up appearances, she supposed cynically. He was probably already back in New York by now, playing the big Greek tycoon by day and the great Greek lover by night for the lovely Vanessa.

If she could she'd chuck his stupid roses through the window, but she didn't have the strength. She'd found that she ached progressively more with each new day.

'What do you expect? You've been in a car accident,' a nurse said with a dulcet simplicity when she mentioned it to her. 'Your body took a heck of a battering and you're lucky that your injuries were not more serious. As it is it's going to be weeks before you begin to feel more like your old self again.'

The shower made her feel marginally better though. And the nurse had shampooed her hair for her and taken gentle care as she blow-dried its long, silken length. By the time she'd hobbled out of the bathroom she was ready to take an interest in the outside world again.

A world in which she had some urgent things to deal with, she recalled worriedly. 'I need a phone,' she told the nurse as she inched her aching way across the room via any piece of furniture she could grab hold of to help support her feeble weight. 'Isn't it usual to have one plugged in by the bed?'

The nurse didn't answer, her white-capped head averted as she waited for Nell to slip carefully back into the bed.

It was only then that she began to realise that not only was there no telephone in here, but the room didn't even have a television set. What kind of private hospital was it Xander had dumped her in that it couldn't provide even the most basic luxuries?

She demanded both. When she received neither, she changed tack and begged for a newspaper to read or a couple of magazines. It took another twenty-four hours for it to dawn on her that all forms of contact with the outside world were being deliberately withheld.

She began to fret, worrying as to what could have happened out there that they didn't want her to know about.

Her father? Could something have happened to him? Stunned that she hadn't thought about him before now, she sat up with a thoughtless jerk that locked her into an agonising spasm across her chest.

That was how Xander found her, sitting on the edge of the bed clutching her side and struggling to breathe in short, sharp, painful little gasps.

'What the hell...?' He strode forward.

'Daddy,' she gasped out. 'S-something's happened to him.'

'When?' He frowned. 'I've heard nothing. Here, lie down again...'

His hands took control of her quivering shoulders and carefully eased her back against the high mound of pillows, the frown on his face turning to a scowl when he saw the bruising on her slender legs as he helped ease them carefully back onto the bed.

'You look like a war zone,' he muttered. 'What did you think you were doing, trying to get up without help?'

'Where's my father?' she cut across him anxiously. 'Why haven't I heard from him?'

'But you did.' Xander straightened up, flicking the covers over her in an act she read as contempt. 'He's stuck in Sydney. Did you not receive his flowers and note?'

The only flowers she'd received were the...

Turning her head, Nell looked at the vase of budding red roses and suddenly wished she were dead. 'I thought they were from you,' she whispered unsteadily.

He looked so thoroughly disconcerted by the idea that he would send her flowers that being dead no longer seemed bad enough. Curling away from him as much as she dared without hurting herself, Nell clutched her fingers round the covers and tugged them up to her pale cheek.

'You thought they were from me.' He had to repeat it, she thought as she cringed beneath the sheet. 'And because you thought the flowers were from me you did not even bother to read the note that came with them.'

Striding round the bed, he plucked a tiny card from the middle of the roses then came back to the bed.

'Shame on you, Nell.' The card dropped against the pillow by her face. It was still sealed inside its envelope.

And shame on you too, she thought as she picked it up and broke the seal. Even a man that cannot stand the sight of his wife sends her flowers when she's sick.

Her father's message—brief and to the point as always with him—read: 'Sorry to hear about your accident. Couldn't get back to see you. Take care of yourself. Get well soon. Love Pops.'

Saying not a word, she slid the little card back into its envelope then pushed it beneath her pillow, but telling tears were welling in her eyes.

'He wanted to come back,' Xander dropped into the ensuing thick silence. 'But he is locked in some important negotiations with the Australian government and I…assured him that you would understand if he remained where he was.'

So he'd stayed. That was her father. Loving in many ways but single-minded in most. Money was what really mattered, the great, grinding juggernaut of corporate business. It was no wonder her mother had left him to go back to her native Canada. When she was little, Nell had used to wonder if he even noticed that she'd gone. She was a teenager before she'd found out that her mother had begun an affair with a childhood sweetheart and had returned to Canada to be with him.

Like mother like daughter, she mused hollowly. They had a penchant for picking out the wrong men. The duration of her mother's affair had been shorter than her marriage had been, which said so much about leaving her five-year-old daughter behind for what was supposed to have been the real love of her life.

'You've washed your hair…'

'I want a telephone,' she demanded.

'And the bruises on your face are beginning to fade…' He spoke right over her as if she hadn't spoken at all. 'You look much better, Nell.'

What did he care? 'I want a telephone,' she repeated. 'And you left me with no money. I can't find my purse or my clothes or my mobile telephone.'

'You don't need them while you're lying there.'

She turned her head to flash him a bitter look. He was standing by the bed, big and lean, taking up more space than he deserved. All six feet two inches of him honed to perfection like a piece of art. His suit was grey today, she noticed. A smooth-as-silk gunmetal grey that did not dare to show a single crease, like his white shirt and his silk-black hair and his—

'They won't let me have a newspaper or a magazine.' She cut that line of thinking off before it went any further. 'I have no TV and no telephone.' She gave a full list of her grievances. 'If it isn't my father, then what is it that you are trying to hide from me, Xander?' she demanded, knowing now that her isolation had to be down to him. Xander was the only person with enough weight to throw about. In fact she was amazed that it hadn't occurred to her to blame him before now.

He made no answer, just stood there looking down at her through unfathomable dark eyes set in his hard, handsome face—then he turned and strode out of the room without even saying goodbye!

Nell stared after him with her eyes shot through with pained dismay. Had their disastrous marriage come down to the point where he couldn't even be bothered to apply those strictly polite manners he usually used to such devastating effect?

It hurt—which was stupid, but it did and in places that had nothing whatsoever to do with her injuries. Five days without so much as a word from him then he strode in there looking every inch the handsome, dynamic power force he was, looked at her as if he couldn't stand the sight of her then walked out again.

She wouldn't cry, she told the sting at the backs of her eyes. Too fed up and too weak to do more than bite hard on her bottom lip to stop it from quivering, she stared at the roses sent by that other man in her life who strode in and out of it at his own arrogant behest.

She hated Alexander Pascalis. He'd broken her heart and she should have left him when she'd had the chance, driven off into the sunset without stopping to look back and think about what she was leaving behind, then she would not be lying here feeling so bruised and broken—and that was on the inside! If he'd cared anything for her at all he should not have married her. He should have stuck to his—

The door swung open and Xander strode back in again,

catching her lying on her side staring at the roses through a glaze of tears.

'If you miss him that much I will bring him home,' he announced curtly.

'Don't put yourself out,' she responded with acid bite. 'What brought you back here so quickly?'

He didn't seem to understand the question, a frown darkening his smooth brow as he moved across the room to collect a chair, which he placed by the bed at an angle so that when he sat himself down on it he was looking her directly in the face.

Nell stirred restlessly, not liking the way he'd done it, or the new look of hard intensity he was treating her to. She stared back warily, waiting to hear whatever it was he was going to hit her with. He was leaning back with his long legs stretched out in front of him and his jacket flipped open in one of those casually elegant attitudes this man pulled off with such panache. His shirt was startlingly white—he liked to wear white shirts, cool, crisp things that accentuated the width of his powerful chest and long, tightly muscled torso. Black handmade shoes, grey silk trousers, bright white shirt and a dark blue silk tie. His cleanly shaved chin had a cleft that warned all of his tough inner strength—like the well-shaped mouth that could do cynicism and sensuality at the same time and to such devastating effect. Then there was the nose that had a tendency to flare at the nostrils when he was angry. It wasn't flaring now, but the black eyes were glinting with something not very nice, she saw.

And his eyes weren't really all black, but a dark, dark brown colour, deeply set beneath thick black eyebrows and between long, dense, curling lashes that helped to shade the brown iris black.

Xander was Greek in everything he thought and did but he got his elegant carriage from his beautiful Italian mother. And Gabriela Pascalis could slay anyone with a look, just as her son could. She'd done it to Nell the first time they'd met and Gabriela had not tried to hide her shock. 'What is Alexander playing at, wanting to marry a child? They will crucify you the moment he attempts to slot you into his sophisticated lifestyle.'

'He loves me.' She'd tried to stand up for herself.

'Alexander does not do love, *cara*,' his mother had drily mocked that. 'In case you have not realised it as yet, he was hewn from rock chipped off Mount Olympus.' She had actually meant it too. 'No, this is more likely to be a business transaction,' her future mother-in-law had decided without a single second's thought to how a statement like that would make Nell feel. 'I will have to find out what kind of business deal. Leave it to me, child. There is still time to save you from this…'

'Finished checking me out?' The mocking lilt to his voice brought her eyes back into focus on his face. She wished she knew what he was thinking behind that cool, smooth, sardonic mask. 'I am still the same person you married, believe me.'

Oh, she believed. Nothing had changed. His mother had been right but Nell hadn't listened. Not until Vanessa DeFriess had entered the frame.

'Want do you want?' She didn't even attempt to sound pleasant.

He moved—not much but enough for Nell to be aware by the way her senses tightened on alert to remind her that Xander was a dangerously unpredictable beast. He might appear relaxed, but she had an itchy suspicion that he was no such thing.

'We need to talk about your accident,' he told her levelly. 'The police have some questions.'

Nell dropped her eyes, concentrating her attention on her fingers where they scratched absently at the white sheet. 'I told you, I don't remember anything.'

'Tell me what you do remember.'

'We've been through this once.' Her eyebrows snapped together. 'I don't see the use in going through it a—'

'You would rather I allow the police to come here so that you can repeat it all to them?'

No, she wouldn't. 'What's to repeat?' Flicking him a guarded look, she looked quickly away again. 'I remember driving down the driveway and through the gates then turning into the lane—'

'Left or right?'

'I don't remember—'

'Well, it might help if you said where it was you were going.'

'I don't remember that either.'

'Try,' he said.

'What for?' she flipped back. 'What does it matter now where I was going? I obviously didn't get there.'

'True.' He grimaced. 'Instead of arriving—wherever it was—you left the road at speed on a notorious bend we all treat with respect. You then proceeded to plough through a row of bushes and concluded the journey by piling head-on into a tree.'

'Thanks for filling in the gaps,' she derided.

'The car boot sprang open on impact,' he continued, unmoved by her tone. 'Your possessions were strewn everywhere. Sweaters, skirts, dresses, underwear…'

'Charity!' she declared with a sudden burst of memory. 'I remember now, I was taking some of my old things to the charity shop in the village.'

'Charity,' Xander repeated in a voice as thin as silk. 'Well, that explains the need to drive like a maniac. Now explain to me why you dismissed Hugo Vance…'

Nell froze where she lay curled on her side, her moment of triumph at her own quick thinking fizzling out at the introduction of her ex-bodyguard's name. She moved, ignoring the creases of pain in her ribs to drag herself into a sitting position so she could grab her knees in a loose but very defensive hug, her hair slithering across her slender shoulders to float all around her in a river of rippling Titian silk.

'I don't need a bodyguard,' she muttered.

'I have three,' Xander replied. 'What does that tell you about what you need?'

'I'm not you.' She sent him an acrid look. 'I don't stride

around the world, playing God and throwing my weight around—'

His eyes gave a sudden glint. 'So that is how you see me—as a god that throws his weight around?' The silken tone gave her no clue as to what was about to come next. 'Well, my beautiful Helen,' he drawled in a thoroughly lazy attitude, 'just watch this space—'

In a single snaking move he was off the chair and leaning over her. The next second and he was gathering her hair up and away from her face. A controlled tug sent her head back. A stifled gasp brought her startled eyes flicking up to clash with his.

What she saw glowing there set her trembling. 'You're hurting—'

'No, I'm not,' he denied through gritted teeth. 'But I am teetering, *cara mia*, so watch out how many more lies you wish to spout at me!'

'I'm not lying!'

'No?' With some more of that controlled strength he wound her hair around his fingers, urging her head back an extra vulnerable inch so as to expose the long, creamy length of her slender throat.

'You were leaving me,' he bit at her in hard accusation. 'You were speeding like a crazy woman down that lane because you were leaving me for another man and you got rid of Vance to give yourself a nice clean getaway, only that damn tree got in the way!'

Caught out lying so thoroughly, she felt hot colour rush into her cheeks. His eyes flared as he watched it happen. Defiance rose in response.

'So what if I was?' she tossed back at him. 'What possible difference was it going to make to the way you run your life? We don't have a marriage, we have a business arrangement that I didn't even get to have a say about!' Tears were burning now—hot, angry tears. 'And I dismissed Hugo a week ago, much that you noticed or cared! I have a right to live my own life any way I want—'

'And let another man make love to you any time that you want?'

The raking insert closed Nell's throat, strangling her breath and the denial she could have given in answer to that. Her angry lips followed suit, snapping shut because she didn't want to say it. She did not want to give him anything that could feed his mammoth ego.

The silence between them began to spark like static, his lean face strapped by a fury that stretched his golden skin across the bones in his cheeks as their eyes made war across a gap of barely an inch. Then his other hand came up to cover her throat, light-fingered and gentle but oh, so menacing.

'Say it, *yenika*,' he encouraged thinly. 'Live dangerously…'

He thought she was holding back from admitting she had taken a lover, Nell realised, and felt the triumph in that tingle all the way down to her feet. She moistened her lips—tempted, so desperately tempted that she did not know how she managed to keep the lie back. Their eyes continued to war across several taut, suffocating seconds. It was exciting, knowing that she had the power to shatter his precious ego with a single soft word like *yes*.

The tips of his long fingers moved on her throat, locating a wildly beating pulse. Nell needed to take a breath, her ribs were hurting under the pressure she was placing on them, and in the end she managed a short, tense tug of air into her lungs before improvising shakily, 'If you want to strangle m-me then go ahead; I'm in no fit state to stop you.'

Surprise lit his face. He glanced down to where his fingers curved her throat, dark lashes curling over his eyes before lifting again to view the way his other fingers were knotted into her hair. There was yet another second of taut, breathtaking stillness in which the entire world seemed to grind to a halt. Then the fingers began to slide again, moving almost sensuously against stretched, smooth, creamy flesh as they began to make a slow retreat.

Relief quivered through her, parting her lips on a small, soft gasp. The fingers paused, she held her breath again, felt a dif-

ferent kind of excitement erupt as she flicked a look into the
deep, dark, swirling depths of his eyes and saw what she'd
always seen there.

Xander had always desired her and Nell had always known
it. Whatever else had motivated him into marrying her, the
desire had always been the added incentive that made the deal
worthwhile.

'You remind me of a sleeping siren,' he murmured. 'It is the
only thing that has kept you safe for the last year. Give me
one small hint, *cara*, that you have given to someone else that
which I have resisted and you will spend the rest of your days
regretting it.'

It was just too tempting to resist this time. Defiance back in
her eyes, she opened her mouth 'I—'

His mouth arrived to stop whatever she had been about to
utter. Shock hit her broadside, sheer surprise at the unexpect-
edness of it holding her utterly transfixed. He hadn't kissed her
once since their wedding night and then he'd been so angry—
hard and punishing with frustrated desire. This was different,
the anger was still there but the rest was warm, deep and sensually tantalising, the way he used his lips to prise hers apart
then stroked the inner recesses of her mouth.

It was her very first tongue-to-tongue experience and the
pleasurable sensations it fed into her tapped into one of her
many restless, hopeless dreams about moments like this. The
warm, clean, expensive scent of him, the smooth, knowing expertise with which he moulded her mouth to his, the slight
rasping brush of his skin against her soft skin, the trailing,
sensual drag she could feel on her senses that made her relax
into him.

He drew back the moment he felt her first tentative response
to him. Eyes too dark to read watched the soft quiver of her
mouth before he looked deeply into the swirling green confusion mirrored in her eyes. Then he smiled.

'There,' he murmured with silken huskiness. 'I have just
saved you from yourself. Aren't you fortunate to have a caring
husband like me?'

As she frowned at the comment, he brushed a contemptuous kiss across her still parted mouth then drew right away, fingers trailing from her throat and untangling from her silken hair while she continued to puzzle—until she remembered what she had been about to say before the kiss.

She shivered, horrified at how easily she had let herself be diverted. Resentment poured into her bloodstream. 'I still intend to leave you the moment I get out of here,' she said.

'You will not.' He was already on his feet and replacing the chair back from where he'd got it. 'And I will tell you why.' He sent her a cold look down the length of his arrogant nose. 'We still have a contract to fulfil.'

Nell lifted her chin to him, green eyes wishing him dead now. 'I signed under duress.'

'You mean you signed without reading it.'

Because she'd loved him so much she was blind! 'How many women would expect to be duped by both their own father and their future husband?' she defended her own piece of stupid folly.

Xander nodded in agreement. 'I offered to renegotiate,' he then reminded her. 'You turned the offer down, so the contract stands as written and signed.'

'And all for the love of money,' she said bitterly.

'A loan of fifty million pounds to haul your father out of trouble is a lot of money, Nell. Have you got the resources to pay me back?'

He knew she hadn't. The only money Nell had even a loose connection to was tied up in trusts left by her grandmother for any children Nell might have. And what her mother had left would not even pay back a tenth of what was owed to Xander.

'But I was not referring to the money,' he slid in smoothly. 'I was referring to the other clause—the one which involves me protecting my investment by you providing me with my son and heir to inherit from your father.'

Effectively putting Nell right out of the inheritance loop! 'Not with my permission.'

'With your permission,' he insisted. 'And at my time of choosing…'

He came back to the bed to lean over her again, ignoring her defensive jerk as he began plumping up the pillows behind her back. 'I have been very patient with you until now, *yenika mou*—'

'Because you had more—interesting things to do.'

As a direct shot about Vanessa, it went wide of its mark.

'Because,' he corrected, 'when we married you were nothing but a wounded babe in arms only a monster would have forced himself upon. The arrival of another man on the scene tells me I may well have been too patient with you.' Taking her by the shoulders, he gently urged her to lie back. Then his eyes were pinning her there, relentless and hard. 'Your growing time is up, Nell. I want a proper wife. Renege on the contract we made and I will take you, your father and your boyfriend to the cleaners and hang you all out to dry.'

'And cause yourself a nasty scandal involving yourself, your mistress and your lousy unfaithfulness?'

'Is that why you thought you could leave and get away with it?' Black silk eyebrows made a mocking arch. 'You think that because Vanessa has suddenly arrived back on the scene it gives you a tasty weapon to wield? I will let you into a little secret,' he murmured, a taunting fingertip making a swipe of her full bottom lip before he replaced it with the casual brush of his mouth. 'Vanessa has never been off the scene,' he informed her smoothly. 'I am just very discreet—usually.'

It was like being kicked while she was already down on the ground. It didn't help that her lips had filled with soft, pulsing heat. 'I hope you both rot in hell,' she breathed thickly.

'But you still want me, as that beautiful, quivering, hungry mouth is telling me.' He smiled a very grim smile. 'And if you were not so battered and bruised I would show you how much you want me.'

'I—'

He saw the lie coming, the tight repudiation of his arrogant confidence, and he swooped, claiming her parted mouth and pressing her back into the pillows. The long length of his torso followed, exerting a controlled power that stopped just short of crushing her beneath his weight. Nell felt taken over, overwhelmed, besieged. The scent of him, the heat, the way he used this kiss to demonstrate the difference between taunting and a full sexual onslaught. Hot tingles of sensation flared up from nowhere with the stabbing invasion of his tongue. Fierce heat rushed through her bloodstream, desire like she'd never known before set her groaning in protest and lifting up her hands to push at his chest.

But Xander was going nowhere, the unyielding contours of his body remaining firm as he deepened the kiss with an unhidden hunger that had Nell stretching beneath him in a wild sensual act that arched her slender shape from breasts to toes. He moved with her, a very male thigh finding a place for itself between her thighs. The bedcovers should have lessened the coiling spring of intimacy she was experiencing but did nothing of the kind.

She tried to drag in some air but found that she couldn't. She tried to separate their mouths but he had control. His tongue slid across her tongue and set it quivering as it hungrily began to follow his lead. Nothing had prepared her for a kiss like this. A kiss that sparked senses alive in every intimate place she had. When his hand covered the arching thrust of one of her breasts she almost shattered into little pieces, writhing and gasping as the rosebud nipple stung as it tightened to push into his palm.

He muttered something, went to move away, her hands stopped pushing at his chest and slid up to bury themselves in his hair so she could hold this amazing, sensational mouth clamped to her own. She didn't know she had the ability to behave like a wanton, but wanton she felt and wanton she acted, writhing beneath him, ignoring the many twinges of physical agony because everything else that was happening to her was oh, so much more important. When his thigh pressed into greater contact with the apex of her thighs she went up like tinder, a thick cry of pleasure coiling in her throat.

A knock sounded at the door. Xander drew back like a man bitten. Eyes like burning black coals scorched her a blistering look. Two hot streaks raked his high cheekbones; his mouth pulsed visibly even though it was suddenly stretched taut. She was panting and still clinging to his hair, the green of her eyes glazed by the stunning shock of her own loss of control.

'This had better be your awakening, *cara*, or you're dead,' he blasted down at her, voice rusted by jealous desire.

Before she could construct any kind of answer he had moved away, landing on his feet beside the bed. He did not look at her again until he'd stridden to the door and grasped the handle. The pause he made then sang between them, stretched taut and raw by that final rasping threat.

He was angry—*still* angry. The kiss had been delivered in anger, the deliberate assault of angry passion that left her lying here hot and trembling, shaken to her core by her own response, her mouth, her body, her deserted breast with its stinging nipple feeling utterly, shamefully bereft.

'Hypocrite,' she heard herself whisper across a throat thickened by the bubble of tears to come.

The charge swung him round to lance her with a hard, glinting look. 'And primitive with it,' he extended grimly. 'Forget the lover,' he warned thinly. 'You will not be laying eyes on him again.'

The note in his tone brought Nell upright. 'Why—w-what have you done to him?' she demanded in alarm.

'As yet—nothing.' His eyes blackened dangerously. 'His fate rests in the future when I have more time to discover if he taught you more than just how to kiss.'

Nell blinked then blushed at his thinking behind that revealing comment. He thought it was Marcel who'd taught her to kiss as she'd just done! Her kiss-numb lips parted to speak a denial then closed again. Let his primitive side twist his gut, she thought angrily, lowering her gaze from the piercing hardness of his. Let him learn what it felt like to imagine her locked in naked passion with another man as she had spent the last year imagining him with Vanessa the tramp!

'I will be away for the next few days but will be back in time to collect you from here on Saturday.'

This final piece of news brought her eyes flickering up again as he opened the door and left without another word, allowing whoever had knocked on the door earlier to come into the room.

It was one of his personal bodyguards, his polite greeting spoiled by the tough look on his face. He placed something down on the bedside cupboard. 'Mr Pascalis gave his permission for you to have these,' he said, then went to leave the room.

'H-how long have you been standing out there?' she asked, horrified that he might have heard or—worse—seen what had been going on in here through the little window in the door!

'Since you arrived in this hospital,' Jake Mather replied.

Nell stared at the door closing behind Jake Mather's bulky frame. She'd been under guard without even knowing it. She was in prison. She had been completely surrounded and isolated from the outside world. A shiver shot through her. It was like being back at Rosemere only worse.

Mr Pascalis gave his permission... She turned her head to look at what Xander had kindly given his permission to.

It was a neat stack of papers—tabloids—broadsheets—magazines. Reaching out to pick the top one of the stack, she let it unfold so she could see the front page in all its damning glory. 'Greek tycoon's wife tries to kill herself after he flaunts his mistress.'

No wonder he saw no threat in a scandal—it was already here!

She plucked up another paper and another, swapped them for the magazines. Scandal galore was splashed across the pages. There were even photographs of her wrecked car! She turned the page on those pictures quickly as nausea swam up inside.

But there was no mention of Marcel anywhere, which told her exactly what Xander was doing. Her imprisonment here had nothing to do with contracts or primitive demonstrations of ownership—but with damage control, pure and simple damage control!

He didn't want it reported that his wife had been leaving him for another man when she crashed her car!

He would rather they report that she was attempting to kill herself. What did that say about the size of his ego?

Kill herself? Where had they dragged up that big lie from?

Had Xander himself put it out there?

She hated him. Oh, God, she hated him. No wonder she was being so thoroughly isolated. He didn't want her retaliating with the truth!

Leaving him for another man… Oh, how she wished she'd managed to go through with it. She would have written her own headline. 'Wife of philandering Greek tycoon leaves him for Frenchman!'

CHAPTER THREE

STANDING unnoticed in the doorway, Xander watched Nell's trembling fingers grapple with the intricacies of fastening the tiny pearl buttons on the silky white blouse he'd had delivered to her along with a blue linen suit that did amazing things for her slender shape.

Someone had fixed her hair for her and it lay in a thick, shining, sandstorm braid to halfway down her back. She looked very pale, though the bruising on her face had almost disappeared. But it was clear to him that even the simplest of tasks still came as an effort.

She was not recovered, though the doctors had assured him that she was fit to travel and for now that was all he cared about: getting her away from here and to a place void of tabloid gossip—and the temptation to contact her lover the first opportunity she was handed.

His blood began to boil when he thought about the elusive Marcel Dubois. The Frenchman had disappeared into the ether like the scarlet pimpernel, and maybe showed some sense in doing so—sense being something he had not shown when he'd decided to make his play for the wife of Alexander Pascalis.

Wife... He could almost laugh at the title but laughing was not what was lurking inside him. His hooded eyes took on a murderous glitter as he watched Nell struggle with those tiny pearl buttons. Had his wife in name only lain with her Frenchman and allowed him to touch what Xander had not touched? Had Dubois seen power in her soft, willing body and those little confidences a woman like the love-vulnerable Nell would reveal to a lover about the emptiness of her marriage?

She turned then and noticed him standing there. His libido instantly kicked in to join the murderous feelings as her eyes began to make their rise up from his shoes to the casual black brushed-cotton chinos covering his legs and the plain white T-shirt moulding his chest. No other woman had ever looked at him the way Nell looked at him, with a slow, verdant absorption that drenched him in hellishly erotic self-awareness. She could not help herself, he knew that, which made the idea of her giving those looks to another man all the more potent. When she reached his shoulders, covered by the casual black linen jacket he was wearing, he could not halt the small recognising shift of muscle that sent a shower of pleasurable static rushing through his blood.

One day soon he was going to give this awareness true substance, he promised. He was going to wipe out all memory of her other man and introduce her to his power with all its naked, hot passion.

He was no neanderthal; he did not need a woman to be a virgin to enjoy her. But this one, this beautiful freak of modern living with her innocence steeped in womanly desire for him that she still did not have the tools to hide whatever the Frenchman had taught her, was going to open up like a chrysalis under his guidance and fly with him into ecstasy. She owed him that much.

She'd reached his face at last and Xander lost the murderous look to give her the benefit of a slow, easy smile, which she dealt with by flicking her eyes away. Nell was no fool. The last time he was here he had thrown down the sexual gauntlet and the smile was to remind her of it.

'Ready to come with me?' he enquired with the kind of soft challenge that had her breath feathering a quiver across the thrust of her breasts.

'I have no make-up,' she complained. 'You forgot to send it.'

'You don't need make-up. Your beautiful skin does not need it.'

'That's a matter of opinion.' Her chin lifted, eyes pinning him with an arctic green look. 'I've seen the waiting Press out there,' she said with a flick of a hand towards the window.

'Witnessing me leaving here looking black and blue won't help your cause, Xander.'

'And what cause is that?' The sexy smile was beginning to fade, Nell noticed.

'Damage control,' she replied. 'I presumed you would want me to look utterly love-blind and radiant for the cameras.'

'Your tongue is developing an aspish tone that does not suit it,' he drawled, moving further into the room with his graceful stride. 'Can you manage that last button on your blouse or do you need assistance?'

'I can manage.' Her chin dipped, her fingers moving to quickly close the button. 'The fact that I'm unhinged and suicidal does not make me totally useless.'

Xander hooked up her jacket from where it lay on the bed. 'You must admit, Nell, it made hilarious reading.'

'You think it's a big joke?'

'You clearly don't.'

Neither did he by the look on his grim face. The jacket arrived around her slender shoulders, held out absolutely perfectly for her to slide her arms into the sleeves without needing to strain herself.

'They presented me as a spiritless fool.'

'And me as the ruthless womaniser.'

'Better that than a man that cannot keep his wife happy—hmm?'

Nell turned to face him with that aspish challenge, but it was the first time she'd actually stood in front of him in goodness knew how long and it came as a shock to be reminded of his overpowering six feet two inches of pure masculinity compared to her own five feet five inches' more diminutive build.

Black eyes glinted narrowly down at her. 'Are you deliberately goading me into proving you wrong?'

Remembering the kiss of a few days ago, she felt her stomach muscles give a hectic quiver. 'No,' she denied and lowered her eyes in an attempt to block him out as his long fingers smoothed the jacket fabric into place.

'Then take my advice and hold back on the barbs until we can achieve guaranteed privacy.'

As if on cue, the door swung open and the doctor who'd been overseeing her recovery strode into the room. He and Xander shook hands like old friends then proceeded to discuss her as if she wasn't standing right beside them.

So what was new there? Nell asked herself as she stood with her eyes lowered and said not a word. From the moment he'd stepped into it, Xander had been arranging her life for her as if she wasn't a part of it. Their very odd courtship, the contract he had discussed with her father but not with her that she didn't bother to read. The marriage that had taken place in her local church but was put together by his efficient team with very little input from her. So why bother to make a fuss that he was discussing her health with the doctor he'd probably hand-picked to go with the private hospital he'd moved her to without her approval?

The only time he'd ever really listened to her was on their wedding night, when she'd refused to make their marriage real. She might have been upset, angry—hysterical enough to be a turn-off for any man, but she also knew that when he agreed to leave her alone, the final decision had been his. He could have changed her mind. He could have seduced her into weakening to him.

But no, what Xander had done was walk away—easily. Nell cringed inside as she thought it. He'd gone back to his life as if she was not in it, other than for those few token visits aimed to keep up appearances.

As the discussion about her needs went on around her Nell began to feel just a little light-headed because she'd been standing up for longer than she'd done since the accident. Her legs felt shaky and the solid prospect of the nearby chair was almost too tempting to resist. But if she showed signs of weakness now they might decide to keep her here and the risk of being incarcerated for another single hour was enough to keep her stubbornly on her feet.

By the time the doctor turned to say his farewell to her, her fixed smile was wavering though. Xander reached out to take her arm, had to feel the fine tremors shaking her and abruptly cut the goodbyes short.

Two minutes later she was walking down the corridor with his grip like a vice and his grim silence ominous. They entered a lift, the doors closed behind them. Xander propped her up against the wall then remained standing over her as they shot downwards, his grim face strapped by tension. The moment the doors slid open again, he was taking her arm and guiding her out of the lift.

Nell showed a brief start of surprise when she realised they had not arrived in the hospital foyer but in a basement car park and she had never felt so relieved about anything. Not only had Xander pre-empted the Press pack but his black Bentley stood parked right there in front of them with Jake Mather standing to attention by the open rear door.

Nell sank with trembling relief into soft leather. The door closed as another opened. Xander arrived at her side and within seconds they were on the move.

So what came next? she wondered wearily when, a short minute later, Xander was on his mobile phone, lean dark profile wearing its power mask as he talked in smooth, liquid Italian then switched to rich, sensual Greek for the second call he made.

Uttering a small sigh, she closed her eyes and just let the sound of his voice wash over her—only to open them again with a start when her door came open and she found herself blinking owlishly at Xander, who was leaning into the car and unlocking her seat belt.

She must have fallen asleep. As she was too disoriented to do more than let him help her out of the car, it took a few more seconds for her brain to register that she was not standing outside Rosemere.

'What's going on?' she questioned.

'Nothing.' With a coolness that belied the alarm that was beginning to erupt inside her, he turned her round so she could

see the sleek white private jet standing on tarmac a few yards
away. 'We are going home, that's all.'

'By air?' She blinked again as he drew her across those few
yards towards the waiting flight steps. 'But it's only an hour
by car back to Rose—'

'Greece,' he corrected. 'I need to be in Athens on Monday
morning, and if you think I am leaving you alone at Rosemere
to plot assignations with your Frenchman then think again.'

Greece, Nell repeated and stopped dead at the entrance to
the plane. Her heart gave a punch against her sore ribs. 'No,'
she refused. 'I don't want to go—'

'Don't make a fuss, *agapita*.' The flat of his hand at the base
of her spine gave her a gentle push forward. Before she knew
it, she'd been hustled inside the plane and the door was being
closed.

Staring bemusedly at her luxury surroundings, she turned
suddenly to make a protest and cannoned right into Xander's
chest. The breath left her body on a tense little whoosh and
she tried to take a defensive step back, but his arms came
around her, strong and supportive. It was like being surrounded
by the enemy, frightening and suffocating.

She breathed in anxious protest. 'Please…'

'Please what?'

His voice had deepened and roughened. Glancing up, Nell
saw the dark, simmering spark in his eyes and tried one final
breathless, 'No…'

But his mouth found hers anyway, moulding her lips and
prising them apart to allow his tongue to make that slow, sensual slide against moist inner tissue that made her breath quiver
as her senses tingled with pleasure. She wanted to pull away
but instead her mouth crushed in closer. She wanted to deny
this was happening at all but once again her mind was not in
control. He murmured something, she didn't know what. But
his tongue when it delved deeper sent her hands up to clutch
at his chest and, as strong male muscle rippled beneath her
fingers, he eased her even closer to him.

His thighs pressed against her thighs, the solid evidence of his desire pushing against the tense flatness of her lower stomach. Damp heat sprang out all over her and on a very masculine growl he deepened the kiss some more. Dizzily she clung to him, her breathing coming faster as the intensity of the kiss increased. Her head tilted backwards, arching her breasts into the solid wall of his chest. Her nipples sharpened like stinging arrows against him and she could feel the uneven thump of his heart and the fine tremor attacking him as he used long fingers to draw her more tightly against the sensual movements he was making with his hips. It was all so sexual, so overwhelmingly physical and exciting. A shimmering, quivering shower of desire dragged at inner muscles that seemed to scoop out the strength from her legs.

Then the plane's engines gave a sudden roar, breaking them apart with an abruptness that left Nell staring dizzily up at his face. She saw the tension there, heat streaking across his cheekbones, the flaring nostrils, the predatory burn in his eyes, and quivered out a constricted gasp.

He dipped his dark head and caught the sound, burnt this kiss onto her pulsing lips—then without warning took hold of her shoulders, turned and dumped her unceremoniously into the nearest seat then spun away in an odd jerky movement that kept her eyes fixed on him in giddy fascination.

He really wanted her. Badly. Now. The knowledge ploughed a deep furrow of heat down her front and held her utterly, breathlessly entrapped. When he suddenly twisted back round to look at her his eyes were so black she didn't even try to look for the brown. That one glance at her expression and he was growling out some kind of harsh self-aimed curse and coming down on his haunches to grimly belt her in. Her eyes clung to his taut features as he did so. She didn't even breathe when he moved away to take a seat on the other side of the aisle and strapped himself into it.

Nothing going on inside was making any sense to her any more; everything was just too new. The plane engines gave another roar then they were shooting forward with rocket propulsion that only helped to heighten the awareness pulsing back and forth.

'If you ever let another man touch you again I will kill you,' he rasped into the charged atmosphere.

Kill her—kill Marcel. The primitive man in him was beginning to take on a life of his own. Is this what untrammelled lust did to men—turned them all into angry, murderous, primeval beasts?

'Speak!' Xander lashed out, stopping her thought processes stone dead as he seared a blistering look across the aisle.

He wanted her to retaliate. To spit something back at him about Vanessa so he could shoot her down with some cruel remark. It was all to do with a need to finding an alternative release for all of this tension, but she turned her face away and refused to respond.

Couldn't respond; she was too locked up inside with what she was feeling herself.

They were already in the air and still shooting higher; the pressure in the cabin hummed in her head. Lifting a set of trembling fingers, she touched the place above her nose where the last and worst bruise on her face still lingered. She thought it would be throbbing, it felt as if it was but it was all over that was throbbing.

A click followed by an angry hissing sound came at her from across the aisle and she dropped the fingers back to her lap— only to find that Xander had moved with the speed of light, unfastening his belt to come to squat down in front of her again, his own long, cool fingers coming up to cover where her own had just covered.

'You are hot and in pain,' he muttered angrily. 'I apologise for my—thoughtlessness.'

Sounding stiff and very foreign to her now, 'I'm all right,' she managed on a shaken breath.

'You are not.' His fingers moved to one of her burning cheeks. 'Don't give me that stiff upper-lip stuff, Nell. I treated you roughly. You now think I am crass and uncivilised,' he brusquely pronounced. 'Did I hurt you anywhere—your injured ribs?'

Nell reached up to curl her fingers around his wrist to pull it away from her cheek so she could give a negating shake of her head and was instantly assailed by the sensation of strong bone and warm skin peppered with crisp dark hair. This was mad, she tried to swallow, found her eyes lifting to clash with his. Darkened emerald-green showing a complete helplessness as to what was happening to her. She'd spent so many months blocking out what she used to feel for him; now it was all pounding about inside her and she didn't like it.

She tugged her hand down again. 'Let me go home to Rosemere,' she whispered unsteadily.

'No.' It came out hard and gruff. 'Where I go you go from now on. I want you with me.' Eyes no longer black with passion but dark—dark brown and swirling with feelings that shattered the breath she tried to take.

'So you can protect your investment?' she hit out. 'Your bodyguards can do that just as well in England.'

'So I believed. You proved me wrong.' He sprang to his feet. 'We will not discuss this again.'

She only had herself to blame for what was happening to her now, in other words. She looked away from him, and had never felt so trapped in her life.

They landed in Athens to a blistering heatwave that almost sucked her of her remaining strength as they transferred to a waiting helicopter and immediately took off again. Three and a half hours on a plane, too much tension and stress, and she was beginning to feel so wiped out she could barely sit up straight.

'Where to now?' she asked as they swung out over a glistening blue ocean with this now daunting man at the controls.

'To my private island.'

Spoken like a true Greek billionaire, with an indifference that suggested that all Greeks owned their own island. Nell was too tired to do more than grimace at his arrogance.

But she couldn't stop the tip of her tongue from running an

exploratory track across her still warm and swollen full bottom lip, unaware that Xander witnessed the revealing little gesture and the way he had to clench hard on a certain part of his anatomy to stop the hot response from gaining in strength.

The island turned out to be a tiny baked brown circle of land floating alone in a crystal blue ocean. Nell caught sight of two white crescents of sand, a fir-covered hill in the middle, and a beautiful two-storeyed whitewashed villa with a swimming pool nestling in between the two sandy beaches.

They landed in an area close to the pool. Jumping out, Xander had to stoop as he strode round to the other side of the machine to open her door, then held out his hand to help her alight. She stumbled as he hurried her from beneath the rotors. A sharp frowning glance at the exhaustion wrenching at her pale face and he was scooping her off the ground.

'I can walk—'

'If you had to,' he agreed tersely. 'Which you don't.'

With a sigh, Nell gave in because she didn't have the energy to argue with him never mind the strength to put up a physical fight. Her head lolled onto his shoulder, his warm breath brushed her face as he carried her past the glinting blue pool and up a set of wide, shallow steps towards the house. A wall of plate-glass stood open ready for them and a tiny woman dressed in black waited to welcome them with a warm, crinkly smile.

She said something in Greek. Xander answered in the same language, his tone short and clipped. The old woman lost her smile and turned to hurry inside ahead of them, tossing long sentences over her shoulder that sounded to Nell as if Xander was being thoroughly scolded, like a child. He seemed to take it without objection, allowing the woman to lead the way across a cool hallway and up a flight of stairs.

They entered a beautiful room with pale blue walls and white drapes billowing at the floor-length windows covered by blue slatted shutters that helped to keep out the worst of the afternoon heat. Setting Nell down on the edge of a pale blue covered soft, springy bed, Xander clipped out an order and the woman hurried away, leaving him squatting down in front of Nell, whose head was just too heavy to lift off his shoulder.

'The journey was too much,' he hissed. 'I apologise.'

Again? Nell thought. 'I just want to go to bed.'

At any other time Xander would have jumped on such an appealing statement. But not right now, when it was clear she was totally wasted and he was worried and feeling as guilty as hell for putting her through such a journey before she had recovered her strength.

Reaching between them, he unbuttoned the lightweight blue summer jacket and slid it carefully from her shoulders then tossed it aside. The white blouse was silky, the tiny pearl buttons more difficult to negotiate from this position and he frowned as his fingers worked, the frown due more to her silent acquiescence. It was a good ten seconds before he realised that she'd actually fallen asleep.

The blouse came free and landed on top of the jacket, working by stealth, he gently laid her down against the pillows then shifted his attention to removing her shoes then the slippery silk-lined skirt and lace-edged stockings that covered her slender legs. Leaving her dignity intact with her lacy bra and panties, he was just grimacing to himself because this was as naked as he had ever seen his wife of a year—when he saw what he had missed while he'd been busy undressing her and it straightened his spine with a stark, rigid jerk.

She was so badly bruised he could not believe the doctor had dared to say that she was fit to travel! One whole side of her ribcage was a mass of fading purple and yellow, and he just stared in blistering horror at the two thick seat-belt lines, one that ran from her left shoulder diagonally across her body to her waist, where the other took over, strapping straight across her hips.

What the hell kind of speed had she been doing when she hit that tree to cause such bruising?

Had it been deliberate?

His blood ran cold at an idea he dismissed instantly. But the cold shock of the thought lingered much longer than that. And the guilt he had been feeling at the rough way he'd handled her on the plane grew like a balloon in his chest.

Someone tutted beside him. 'Oh, poor wounded child,' Thea Sophia murmured. 'What kind of man have you become, Alexander, that you bring her this far in this state?'

It was not a question he cared to answer. He was struggling enough with it for himself. Setting his mouth, he bent down to gather Nell into his arms again with as much care as he could manage.

'Pull back the covers, Thea,' he instructed gruffly. Ten seconds later he was resettling his wounded bride against the cool sheets of their marriage bed.

Did she but know it, he thought as he straightened a second time and stepped back to allow Thea to gently fold the covers back over Nell's limp frame. Her hair lay in a thick braid beside one of her cheeks and she had never looked so pale—or so vulnerable.

God give me strength, he thought grimly, glad that only he knew what plans he'd made for the beautiful Helen involving this island, some serious seduction, this room and this bed.

Shelved plans. He turned away, grim face mask-like as he watched Thea fuss around picking up Nell's discarded clothes and folding them neatly on a chair.

He made a decision. One of those quick-thinking, business-minded decisions he was more familiar with. It was called a tactical retreat.

Nell slept on through the sound of rotor blades stirring up again, slept through the whooshing din the helicopter made as it took off. She had no idea at all that while she slept Thea Sophia sat in the chair beside the bed, quietly working her lace with gnarled, nimble fingers while a maid just as quietly unpacked and put away Nell's clothes. The afternoon sun slowly turned the room golden. She only stirred when the sound of rattling crockery made her dry throat and her empty stomach demand she take note.

Opening her eyes, she took several long seconds to remember where she was, and a few more seconds' sleepily watching the old lady in black as she fussed around a table by the window across the room. Then the old lady turned.

'Ah, you are awake at last!' she exclaimed and came across the room with her crinkly face full of olive-toned smiles. 'My name is Sophia Theodora Pascalis,' she introduced herself. 'I am Alexander's great-aunt. You may call me Thea Sophia and I will call you Helen—such a proud Greek name.'

Was it? Nell had never given much thought to her name's origin.

'Of course, if Alexander were here he would have made the formal introductions,' Thea Sophia continued. 'But welcome—welcome to our beautiful island and our beautiful home, Helen.' Nell found her face being clasped between two hands in a warm, affectionate gesture, and released again.

'Th-thank you. I'm very happy to meet you, Thea Sophia,' Nell returned politely and it was impossible not to smile back in response.

'Ah, it is I who is happy to see you here at last.' The old lady stood back to beam a very satisfied smile then turned to walk back to the table by the window. 'We will become very good friends, you and I, *ne*? You will like it here,' she promised. 'When that stupid boy Alexander decides to get his priorities right and come back here you will makes lots of babies between you in that bed as is Pascalis tradition and we shall be a very happy family, *ne*?'

The baby part floated right by Nell, pushed out by the much more disturbing part of Thea Sophia's chatty speech. 'Xan—Alexander has…gone?' she prompted unsteadily.

'He took one look at your poor bruised body and took to his heels,' his aunt informed her in disgust. 'You would not believe that such a big strong man could be so squeamish, but there you go.' She added a very Mediterranean shrug. 'It will be his guilty conscience taunting him, of course. He was brought up to protect his loved ones. In this, with you, he failed. He will come back when he has come to terms with his…'

Nell had stopped listening. She was pushing the covers away from her body and staring down at her near-naked flesh. Hot colour poured into her cheeks then paled away again when she saw what Xander had seen.

'W-who undressed me?'

'Alexander, of course.'

'Then he left...'

'*Ne.*' China chinked against china.

Nell sat up with a jerk and drew her knees up to her chin so that she could hug herself. Tears were burning, hurt tears, angry tears.

Xander had brought her to this island to seduce her—he'd left Nell in no doubt whatsoever about that. One glance at her miserable body and he'd seen his plans thwarted so he'd done what he always did.

He'd walked away. Left her. Marooned her on this tiny island with this sweet but *old*, old lady, while he returned to his busy, important life, the seduction of his wife shelved—again.

'You ready for a nice cup of English tea now...?'

CHAPTER FOUR

NELL stepped barefooted onto the sand, dropped her book and her sunglasses down at her feet then removed the wide-brimmed straw hat Thea Sophia had insisted that she wear to shade her face from the fierce rays of the sun.

Using the hat as a fan, she wafted it to and fro as she stood looking around the small cove she'd found during her first week here and since then made it her very own. It meant a stiff climb up and down the tree-covered hill to get here but it was worth it. The sand beneath her feet was sugary soft and hot, the sea a crystal-clear, smooth as glass, glistening blue, and in between the two lay a strip of cooler damp-silk sand kept that way by the flow and ebb of a lazy tide.

It was the stillest day since she had arrived here two weeks ago. Hot, breathlessly calm, exotically pine-scented and so exquisitely hush-quiet you could hear an ant move a leaf fifty feet away.

A wry smile played with her mouth as she stooped over again to place the hat over the book and sunglasses, paused long enough to scoop up a handful of warm sand then straightened again, green eyes fixed thoughtfully on her fingers as she let the sand filter through them while she tried to decide what she was going to do.

She was being watched. Not only was she very aware of that pair of eyes fixed on her, but she also knew to whom they belonged. She'd heard the helicopter fly overhead as she'd been strolling up the path that led over the pine-shaded hill on her way here. She also knew how he had found her so quickly. Yannis, the bluff, gruff odd-job man on the island and her latest guard would have told him where to look.

It made her curious as to whether it had ever occurred to

Xander that having her watched for every waking hour of the day meant that Yannis often saw what he was seeing right now as he stood beneath the shade of one of the trees that edged the little cove.

If her instincts were sending her the right messages, that was, and she knew that they were. Only one man had ever filled her with this tingling mix of anger, resentment and excitement just by looking at her.

There were two things she could do next, she pondered thoughtfully. She could turn round and confront him or she could ignore him and continue with what she'd come here to do.

The smile on her lips stretched wider. It was not a pleasant smile. The first option had never been a real contender, Nell had known it from the moment she'd heard his first footfall on the woodland path behind. There was no way that she was going to turn and let him know that she knew he was standing there.

It did not suit her purposes because she was about to show him just what it was he had been consistently rejecting for the last year. Show him how she looked without the bruises he'd turned his back on in favour of Athens and probably Vanessa's perfect, unblemished, *willing* charms.

Her fingers shook a little, though, as she began to untie the knot holding her sarong in place across the warm rise of her breasts. Her heart pumping a bit too thickly as she let the fine white Indian cotton slide away from her body to land softly on the top of the hat.

Underneath the sarong the new honey-gold tan she had been carefully cultivating shone softly beneath a protective layer of high-factor oil. Exercising three times a day by swimming in the pool or here in the sea had toned her up quite impressively—not that she'd been a slouch before the accident, but physical injury had taken a toll on her weight and her muscles.

Now, as she stood looking down at herself, a lazy finger absently rubbing in a previously missed smear of oil across the flat slope of her stomach, she was quietly impressed with how she looked even if it was vain to think it about herself. Whoever it was who'd packed her clothes for her in England must have been in romantic mood because they'd more or less picked out everything she'd bought for her non-starter honeymoon, like this bikini for instance, bought along with several others to seduce a husband who should have been her lover by the time she'd worn one of them.

The bikini consisted of a tiny white G-string that made only a scornful play at covering what it should, and a skimpy top made of two tiny triangles of silky fabric held together by two bootlace straps, one knotted around her neck and the other around her back. If she swam too energetically she came out of the top but—who cared? she thought with a large dose of defiance. She felt slinky and sexy and the G-string wasn't going to go anywhere because of the way it was held in place in the tight cleft of her buttocks.

So eat your heart out, Alexander Pascalis, she told him as she tilted her face up to the sun. Because here stands the unbattered version of the woman you turned your back on two weeks ago. And on that rebellious thought she moved into a long, slow, sensual stretch that accentuated every slender line of her figure from arms to spine to smoothly glossed buttocks and long, slender legs, held the pose for a few seconds then released it and began running lightly down to the sea.

In the shade of the tree, Xander watched the start of her little exhibition from a lazy, relaxed stance with one shoulder resting against the tree trunk.

She knew he was here, he was almost certain of it. She had to have heard his footfall on the path on such a still day. So, what was she thinking about as she stood there sifting sand through her fingers? Was she contemplating how he would react to a handful of the sand thrown in his face?

He knew she was angry with him. He knew she felt dumped and deserted when he'd left her here the way that he did. But what other choice had he had at the time? He had a wife who was not yet a wife and a marriage bed that was not yet a marriage bed that his aunt fully expected them to share.

Playing the loving husband who'd had a whole year to lose the edge to his sexual desires for this woman had not been an option he had been able to take. Put him in a bed next to Nell and despite the bruises he would not have been able to keep his hands to himself.

She was beautiful—look at her, he told that nagging part of his conscience that kept on telling him he could have sorted something out which had not involved shifting himself across the Aegean in a bid to put temptation out of reach.

The long, slender legs, the slender body hidden beneath the white sarong she had tied round the firm thrust of her breasts. The pale copper hair left free to ripple across slender shoulders tanned to a smooth honey colour since he'd seen them last.

Turn to look at me, *yenika*, he urged silently. Give me that slow, sensual glide with your eyes that turns up my sexual heat. I don't mind paying the price of the sand in my face.

But she didn't turn. Leaning there against the tree while willing the little witch to turn, Xander watched through eyes narrowed against the sunlight as she untied the knot holding the sarong in place then allowed the scrap of fine white Indian cotton to slide away from her body and fall on top of the hat.

His heart stopped beating. His shoulder left the tree trunk with a violent jerk. He could not believe what he was seeing. In fact he refused to believe it. It was the sun playing tricks with his eyes, he decided as he watched her move into a long, lithe stretch, which lifted her arms up as if in homage to the sun.

'*Theos*,' he breathed as his senses locked into overdrive. He'd seen many women in many different stages of undress. He'd seen them deliberately playing the temptress in an effort to capture his interest but he never expected to see this woman do it—never expected to see her wearing anything so damned outrageous!

Maybe she did not know of his presence. Maybe she was playing the siren like this because she truly believed there was no one to see!

Then he remembered Yannis—warned to follow her every

move because he did not trust her not to find some way to flee again. The idea of any other man enjoying the sight of his wife parading herself in what could only be called a couple of pieces of string had a red-hot tide of primitive possessiveness raking through him and sent his head shooting round, glinting black eyes flashing out a scan around the area, hunting out places a silent guard could watch unseen.

Then she dropped out of the stretch and his attention became riveted on Nell again as she began to run down to the sea, light steps kicking up soft, dry sand then leaving small footprints in the wet as she went. She hit the water at a run, her beautiful hair flying out behind her. In a smooth, graceful, curving dive, she disappeared beneath the smooth crystal water, leaving him standing there hot, damp in places, feeling as if he had just imagined the whole thing!

Nell swam beneath the surface until her lungs began to burst then she bobbed up like a seal, took in a deep breath then struck out with a smooth, graceful crawl towards the edge of the little cove where the rocky landscape on this side of the island rose up in a sheer slab for several feet she'd always thought would be great to dive from but had not yet found a way to reach the edge up there.

The tiny cove was perfect for swimming in because its two flanking outcrops gave her something to aim for when she swam across the cove. Making a neat racing turn, she started back in the other direction. She loved swimming, always had from being small. She'd swum for her school and won a few gold medals too. In Canada she'd scared her mother by swimming in the Kananaskis River, and before getting married had been a regular visitor to the local public swimming pool. When she'd married Xander, he had changed all of that by closeting her at Rosemere, which had its own pool, so she did not have to leave home to swim. On the rare occasions he'd turned up at the house unexpectedly to find her using the pool, she'd glimpsed him standing by the bevelled glass doors watching her cut a smooth line through the water—not that she'd ever let him know that she'd known he was standing there. When you hated and resented someone you ignored them as much as possible then they could never know what was really fizzing around your insides.

She made sure she did not look his way now, though the fact that she knew he was there watching her filled her with a mad, crazy, excited exhilaration as she cut through the water with smooth, darting strokes that barely caused a ripple on the ocean surface.

She was halfway across the cove when he struck, swimming beneath her and closing his hands around her waist. Nell let out a shrill, high-pitched scream and almost drowned as she gulped salt water into her lungs just before Xander lifted her high out of the water, rising like a big, black-eyed Poseidon out of the sea with his catch gripped between his hands.

'You shameless, ruthless provocateur!' he bellowed at her, then brought her sliding down the length of his body until her face was level with his.

Still coughing and choking, and almost hyperventilating with shock, Nell felt her skin slither against hard, tough, hair-roughened skin, legs, breast—*hips*! 'Oh, my God,' she gasped out. 'You've got no clothes on!'

'*I* have no clothes on?' he bit out angrily. 'What the hell do you think it is that *you* are wearing?'

Clutching at his satin-tight shoulders because she had to clutch at something, Nell lowered her eyes from the fury burning in his, then wished she hadn't when she saw to her horror that the two wet triangles of silk that should be covering her breasts had shifted and now two tight pink nipples were pouting at her like reckless taunts. Colour pouring into her wet cheeks, she flicked her wide eyes back to his blazing eyes and opened her mouth to retaliate with something—but he got there first, slamming his mouth onto hers with all the angry passion that had driven him through the water, submerged and unseen until he could grab her from underneath.

It was a kiss like nothing she had ever experienced. Open-mouthed, hot, frenzied and deep. It didn't help that they were both still panting from their energetic swim, both hearts pounding like thunder, both straining wildly against each other, her fingernails digging into his shoulders, his like clamps around her slippery waist.

The rough sound of masculine desire ground from his throat and he broke the kiss to lift her high again, eyes like burning black coals as he dipped his head and latched his mouth onto one of her breasts. The greedy suck dragged a shocked cry of pleasure from her, and sent him in search of the other breast.

When he lowered her to recapture her mouth he moved his hands to her wriggling hips, used long, sensually sliding fingers to urge uselessly flailing legs apart then wrapped them firmly around his hips. She took the new intimacy with a breath-gulping quiver, felt the bold thrust of his penis, rock-solid and probing against her flesh. The G-string was no barrier. She was going to lose her virginity right here in the ocean to a man balanced on the edge between violence and passion, and what was worse, she didn't care.

His hands were moulding the tight curve of her bottom now, her fingers buried in the wet silk of his hair, fingernails clawing at his scalp. The kiss was so wild and hot and urgent she felt dizzy from it, then it was gone.

With an angry growl he thrust her from him, sending her floundering into the sea. She dropped beneath the surface. By the time she'd gathered enough sense to make the push back to the surface he was already pounding his way back to the beach.

It was the worst, most devastating rejection he had ever dealt her. For a horrible few seconds Nell thought she was going to faint. If she could she would be turning and swimming out to sea just to get away from the fresh burn of rejection she was feeling but he'd sapped her strength, taking it with him like some lethal, heartless virus, leaving her with this hot, sensual, dragging feeling that was so new to her she didn't know what to do to ease herself out of its grip.

She watched him rise out of the water, a beautiful, wide-shouldered, long-bodied, bronze-skinned male without a hint of shame in his own nakedness. Toned muscles that moved and flexed in lithe coordination were caught to perfection by the water clinging to his flesh and the loving glint of the sun. He did not look back, and Nell could feel his anger emanating towards her back across the calm ocean and she hated herself for responding to him. Her breasts felt heavy, their tips tingling and tight. Even as she trod water in an effort to keep herself afloat her thighs had clamped together as if to hold in their first experience of a fully aroused man thrusting against the hidden flesh.

It took every bit of will-power she could drum up to make herself follow him, dipping beneath the water in an effort to cool the heat from her face and her body then angrily resettling her bikini top before she allowed herself to surface again then make deeply reluctant strikes for the shore.

By the time she reached it he'd pulled on a pair of smooth-fitting trousers, muscles clenching tightly across his glistening back when he heard the splash of her feet as she waded through the shallows to the beach.

Bending down, he scooped up her sarong, half turned and tossed it to her. It landed in a floaty drift of white on the damp sand at her feet, and he was already snatching up his shirt and dragging it on over his glinting wet skin.

Xander thought about apologising but he'd played that hand before and too often to give the words any impact. Anyway, he was not sorry. He was angry and aroused and he could still feel her legs wrapped around him, could still taste her in his mouth. He had an ache between his legs that was threatening to envelop him.

'You will not flaunt your body in get-ups like that excuse for a bikini,' he clipped out, heard the words, realised he sounded like a disapproving father, hated that, uttered a driven sigh that spun him about.

She was trying to knot the sarong with fumbling fingers. Her beautiful hair was slicked to her head. She had never looked more subdued or more tragic.

'And when we get around to making love it will not be out in the open for anyone to watch us,' he heard himself add.

'Behind a locked bedroom door on a bed, maybe,' she suggested. 'How boringly conventional of you.'

Subdued but not dead, Xander noted from that little piece of slicing derision. He could not help the smile that twitched at his mouth. It eased some of the passion-soaked aggression out of his voice.

'More comfortable too,' he agreed drily. 'I was treading water out there. I don't know how I kept us both floating. Add some of the really physical stuff and I would likely have drowned us in the process.'

'I can swim.'

'Not with me deep inside you, *agape mou*,' he drawled lazily. 'Trust me, you would have lost the will to live rather than let me go.'

She managed the knot. He had a feeling it cut off the circulation, it appeared so tight. And her cheeks went a deep shade of pink. He liked that. However, the look she sent him should have shrivelled his ego like a prune. It didn't though. The physical part of his ego remained very much erect and full.

'Such confidence in your prowess,' she mocked, stalking past him to scoop up the rest of her things. 'Don't they always say that those who boast about it always disappoint?'

'I will not disappoint,' he assured with husky confidence.

'Well, if you wait until it's dark to prove that, I can always pretend you are someone else, then maybe you won't.'

And with the pithy comment to cut him down to size where he stood she put the hat on her head and walked off towards the path.

A lesser man would react to such an insult. A lesser man, Xander told himself as he watched her walk away, would go after her and drag her down in the sand and make her take such foolish words back.

The better man picked up his socks and shoes and followed her at a leisurely pace, while he plotted his revenge by more—subtle methods.

Then a frown creased his smooth brow when he remembered something and increased his pace, only becoming leisurely again once he'd caught up with her and tempered his longer stride to hers.

Hearing him coming, Nell pushed her sunglasses over her burning eyes and increased her pace. She received a glimpse of sun-dappled white shirting, black trousers and a pair of long brown bare feet as he came up beside her, but her mind saw the naked man and her tummy muscles fluttered. So did other parts.

'I grew up on this island,' he remarked casually. 'As a small boy I used to walk this path each morning to swim in the cove before being shipped across to the mainland to attend school. Diving from the rocks is an exhilarating experience. The snorkelling is good out there, the fishing too—though I do not suppose the fishing part is of any interest to you.'

'You, used to fish?' Nell spoke the words without thinking then was angry because she'd been determined to say nothing at all.

'You think I arrived on this earth all-powerful and arrogant?' He mocked her lazily. 'In the afternoons I used to fish,' he explained. 'Having been transported back here after my school day was finished, with my ever-present bodyguard as my only playmate.'

Now he was playing on her sympathies by drawing heartstring-plucking pictures of a small, lonely boy protected and isolated from the world because of his father's great power and wealth.

'My parents were always off somewhere doing important things so I rarely saw them,' he went on. 'Thea Sophia brought me up, taught me good manners and the major values of life. The fishing taught me how to survive on my own if I had to. I used to worry constantly that something dreadful was going to happen to those who lived here on the island with me and I would be left alone here to fend for myself. I knew that my father had powerful enemies that might decide to use me in their quest for revenge. Before the age of six I had all my hiding places picked out for when they came for me...'

'Is there a point to you telling me this?' She would not feel sorry for that small, anxious boy, she wouldn't.

'*Ne.*' He slipped into Greek, which didn't happen often.

Xander was a man of many languages. Greek and Italian both being natural to him, the rest because he was good at them, and in the cut-throat, high-risk world he moved in it paid to know what the people around you were saying and to be able to communicate that fact.

'You think that you are the only one to have lived a strange, dysfunctional, sheltered life but you are not,' he stated coolly. 'I have lived it too so I can recognise the person you are inside because I am familiar with that person.'

Nell clutched her book in tight fingers and tried hard not to ask the question he was prompting her to ask, but it came out anyway. 'And what kind of person is that?'

'One who hides her true self within a series of carefully constructed shells as a form of self-defence against the hurts, the fears, the rejections life has dealt her from being small and vulnerable—like myself.'

Well, he certainly knows how to top up my feelings of rejection! Nell thought angrily. 'What rubbish,' she snapped out loud. 'And spare me more of this psycho-babble, Xander. I have no idea where you're going with it and I don't want to know.'

'Towards a deeper understanding of each other?' he suggested.

'For what purpose? So you can eventually get around to bedding me before you fly off to pastures new—or old,' she tagged on with bite. 'In case you didn't notice, I was easy prey out there in the water.' God, it stung to have to admit that. 'That means you don't need to achieve a greater understanding of me to get what you want.'

'You have always been easy prey, *cara*,' he hit back. 'The point at issue here is that I have always managed to avoid taking what has always been there to take.'

Nell pulled to a simmering stop. The hat and the sunglasses

hid her expression from him but there were other ways to transmit body language. 'I think you're into humiliation.'

'No,' he denied that. 'I was trying to...'

She walked on again, faster, her breath singing tensely from between her clenched teeth as she pumped her legs up the final stretch of the hill.

'Will you listen to me?' He arrived at her side again.

'Listen to you spelling it out for me that you married me because you saw your perfect soul mate? One you can pick up and drop at will and she won't complain because she's used to rejection, and all of this rotten isolation you prefer to surround her with?'

'I married you,' he gritted, 'because it was either that or take you to bed without the damned ring!'

Her huff of scorn echoed high in the trees above them. 'I was a business deal!' She turned on him furiously, brought her foot down on a sharp piece of gravel and let out a painful, 'Ouch!'

'What have you done?' he rasped.

'Nothing.' She rubbed at the base of her foot with a hand. 'And we've never shared a bed!' she flashed at him furiously. 'We've never even shared a bedroom!'

'Well, that's about to change,' he drawled.

I'm not listening to any more, Nell decided and dropped her foot to the ground to turn and start walking again, her legs and her body trembling with fury and goodness knew what else while her eyes still saw a tall, dark, *arrogant* man with tousled wet hair and a sexy damp shirt, dangling his shoes from his long brown fingers.

Topping the peak of the hill, she started down the other side of it. Below through the trees she could see the red-tiled roof of the house and the helicopter standing in its allotted spot by a glinting blue swimming pool.

All looked idyllic, a perfect haven of peace—sanctuary.

Sanctuary to hell! she thought. Her sanctuary had been in the isolation, not the place itself. Now Xander was back and the comfortable new world she'd created here was shattered.

She hated him so much it was no wonder her blood was fizzing like crazy as it coursed through her veins.

He did it again and took her by surprise, hands snaking around her waist to spin her round to face him. The shoes had landed with a clunk somewhere, her book went the same way. Next thing her hat came off, followed by her sunglasses, and were tossed aside. She caught a fleeting glimpse of a lean, dark, handsome face wearing the grim intent of what was to come, her breath caught on a gasp then that hard, hot mouth was claiming hers again and she was being kissed breathless while his hands roamed at will.

Her thighs, her hips, the smooth, rounded curve of her naked bottom beneath the covering sarong. He staked his claim without conscience, her slender back, her flat stomach, the still thrusting, pouting shape of her nipple-tight breasts. She was dizzy, narcotic, clinging to him, fingers clawing inside the shirt to bury into the tightly curling matt of hair on his chest.

It had all erupted without a warning gap now, as if one erotic encounter led straight into the next. He drew back from the kiss, face hardened by a burning desire that was no longer held in check.

'You want that we do it right here and now, Nell—up against the nearest tree maybe?' he gritted down at her. 'Or shall we go back to the ocean and complete what we started there? Or would you have preferred it if we had done it two weeks ago in the bed down there where you lay injured and weak? Or we could have whiled away the hours doing it on the flight over here. Or let us take this back to our wedding night, when you were so shattered only a monster would have tried. No,' he ground out. 'You will not turn away from me.'

His hands snaked her closer, cupping her behind to lift her into even closer contact. 'Do you understand now what I am trying to say to you? Look at us, *cara*,' he insisted. 'We are not what you would call passive about this. You hide your true self. I hide my true self. But here they are out in the open, two people with more passion for each other than they can safely deal with.'

'Only when you have the time to feel like it.'

'Well, I feel like it now!' he rasped. 'And if you refuse to listen to reason then maybe I will take you up against a tree, with your knees trapped beneath my arms and your heels digging into my back!'

Such a lurid, vivid picture made her push back from him, all big, shocked green eyes. 'You've done it before like that!'

Xander laughed—thickly, so thoroughly disconcerted by the attack that he discovered he had no defence.

The whooshing sound of a helicopter's rotor blades suddenly sounded overhead, saving him from having to defend himself. They both looked up then Xander uttered a thick curse.

'We have a visitor,' he muttered.

'Who?' Nell shot out as they watched the helicopter swoop down the side of the hill then come to a hovering stop beside the other one.

There was a moment of nothing, a moment of hovering stillness in Xander that brought her eyes back to his face. He didn't look happy. He even sent her a grimace.

'My mother,' he said.

CHAPTER FIVE

HIS mother…

Nell's heart sank to the soles of her bare feet. The beautiful, gorgeous, always exquisitely turned out Gabriela Pascalis was paying them a visit and Nell looked like this—wet, bedraggled, and more than half-ravished.

Her voice developed a shake. 'Did you know she was coming here?'

There was a sighed-out, 'No,' before he changed it to a heavy, 'Yes… She said she was coming. I told her not to bother. I knew she would ignore me—all right?'

Nell flashed him a killing look. 'You didn't think to warn me about that?'

'We were busy talking about other things—I forgot.'

He forgot…

'And I suppose I was hoping she would listen to me for once…'

Nell didn't even grace that with the spitting answer sitting on her tongue. Turning, she began striding down the hillside, leaving Xander cursing colourfully as he gathered up their scattered things.

She knew that mother and son did not enjoy a warm relationship, in fact the best she could describe it as was cool. They met, they embraced, they threw veiled but heavily barbed comments at each other; they embraced then parted again until the next time. It was like standing in the middle of a minefield when they were together. One step out of line and Nell had a feeling that they would both ignite and explode all over her, so she'd tended to keep very quiet and still in their company.

Not that it happened often. It wasn't as if with a relationship like that mother and son lived in each other's pockets. Xander had his life and Gabriela had hers—par for the course with Xander's relationships, she tagged on acidly. The very few times that Nell had come into contact with both of them together was usually at one of those formal functions Xander would drag her to occasionally—to keep up appearances while Vanessa hovered around somewhere in the murky background, awaiting her lover's return.

Her skin turned cold as she thought that.

A shriek of delight suddenly filled the hillside, dragging her attention down the hill towards the house. She saw that the helicopter had settled next to the other one and Gabriela was now standing by the pool with her arms thrown wide open while Thea Sophia hurried towards her clapping her hands with delight.

To witness the dauntingly sophisticated Gabriela dressed in immaculate lavender silk fold the little black-clad bundle that was Thea Sophia to her in a noisily loving hug came as almost as big a surprise as the way Nell had just behaved with Xander up on the hill.

Where had all the warmth and affection come from? She would never have believed Gabriela capable of it if she was not seeing it with her own eyes.

The two faces of the Pascalis family, she thought grimly as she maintained a brisk pace downwards. Behind her was a man who had been as cold as ice for ninety-nine per cent of their marriage, suddenly showing her he had passion hot enough to singe layers from her skin! Now here was the drop-dead sophisticated mother putting on a demonstration of childlike adoration that would shock her peers—though anyone would love Thea Sophia, she then had to add with a brief softening inside. The sweet old lady would make the devil want to give her a loving hug.

As the two embracing women dropped out of sight behind the red-tiled roof of the house, Nell felt the silly burn of tears sting her eyes. It was stupid to feel hurt by such an open display of affection from Xander's mother for his aunt, but that was exactly what she did feel. Gabriela had never greeted her like that, never welcomed her with open arms and shrieks of delight. On those few tension-charged occasions they had met just the brief air-kissing of Gabriela's perfumed cheeks had always made Nell feel as if she were desecrating holy ground.

Or was it the other way around and she was the one who repelled deeper displays of affection? Had those defensive shells Xander talked about kept her mother-in-law at arm's length? She didn't know. She didn't even know if Gabriela knew the full truth about the true disaster that her son's marriage was.

The two women had gone from the pool area by the time Nell reached it. Making directly for the rinse shower that occupied a corner of the patio area, she switched it on and began washing the dust from her feet. The bottom of her foot still stung from its contact with the sharp stone, but as she was about to lift up the foot to inspect it she saw Xander arrive a few paces behind her and her full attention became fixed on him.

He had gathered up their things and was now placing them on one of the tables, tall, dark, uncomfortably alluring with his shiny wet hair, loose clothes and bare feet. Nothing like the man she was used to seeing—nothing. The other Xander was all skin-tingling, sophisticated charisma; this one was all—sex.

She looked away as he turned towards her, stiffened like mad when his hands snaked around her waist to gently crush fine muslin against her skin. A long brown foot with long brown toes appeared next to her foot so he could share the water sprinkling down on them.

Next the smoothness of his cheek arrived against her cheek. 'We are being watched, *agapita*,' he warned huskily as she tried to pull away from him.

It was all he needed to say to halt her attempt to escape. So she clamped her teeth together, kept her chin lowered and swapped one cleaned foot for the other and felt the intimacy deep in her trembling bones in watching Xander do the same thing.

'You're trembling all over. I like it,' he remarked in a sexy, husky groan by her ear, felt the heat mount her cheek and laughed softly as he brushed his lips against that tell-tale heat.

'I'm trembling because I'm angry with you,' she said. 'Look at me, Xander,' she then said heavily. 'I'm all wet and salty and now I have to go in there and meet your mother looking like this. You should have given me more warning then at least I could have found time to shower and change before she arrived…and she will know, won't she,' she then added unhappily, 'what the papers have been saying about us?'

'And that bothers you.'

'It bothers you too or you would not have brought me here and hidden me away like you have.'

His foot disappeared and she sensed a new grimness in him as he reached over her shoulder to turn off the shower. 'I did not bring you here to hide you,' he denied.

'Yes, you did. The same as you've been hiding me away all year.'

'So you thought you would make me wake up and take notice by involving yourself with another man?'

'Isn't that just typically arrogant of you to think I was trying to grab your attention?' She tried to move away again but he still would not allow it, the flat of his hand resting lightly but firmly against her stomach to keep her trapped in front of him. She sucked in a short, tense breath. 'I was leaving you, Xander,' she stated bluntly. 'And I was going, hoping never to set eyes on you again.'

'You did more than set eyes on me a few minutes ago, Nell, and I don't recall you turning away. In fact…' He turned her to face him. His eyes wore a hard glitter. 'I would say that you could not get enough of what you saw.'

'That was just sex.'

'And you know so much about it to sound so dismissive?'

Nell didn't answer. She was glaring at the ribbon of hard brown skin dressed with crisp dark hair showing between his gaping shirt and wishing with all her heart that her tongue didn't tingle with a desire to taste.

'We were talking about your mother.' She slewed her eyes sideways to stare at the glinting pool.

'She's here to discuss some family business.'

'Well, maybe she will be kind enough to give me a lift off this island when she leaves.'

'You think I would allow it?'

Green eyes flashed into contact with his. 'Would you like to repeat that bit about not hiding me?'

He went several steps further and lowered his dark head and kissed her, not hot and driven like before but slow and gentle with just enough passion to elicit a response. 'That is why you're here, *agape mou*,' he murmured as he lifted his head again. 'We are going to kick-start this marriage. *Then* let us see if you still wish to leave.'

Xander could say this in *that* tone of voice because she'd responded. He could say it because her fingers were already in contact with his brown skin. This beautiful, defiant, contrary creature might not want to want him but hell, she did want him, Xander thought grimly.

Letting go of her, he strode off, leaving her standing there knowing that he had won that little battle without her putting up much of a defence.

Waiting in the coolness of the foyer, he viewed Nell's arrival in the open doorway through carefully hooded eyes and had to lock his jaw to keep other parts of him under control. Lit from behind by the sunlight, she looked like a sea nymph standing in the jaws of a hungry shark.

He was the hungry shark. If they had been alone here he would be closing those jaws and carrying her off to finish what he'd started out there. He'd laid down the gauntlet as to where this marriage of theirs was going to go from here and by the way she was hovering in the doorway he would say that she knew she did not stand a chance of changing that course.

She began walking forward. As he watched her come closer his head played a tempting little scene that involved him car-rying her up the stairs and laying her on the bed then stripping away the few scraps she wore.

Though maybe he would leave the G-string in place, he thought darkly, seeing his mouth tracing its skimpy white lines with a chain of tongue-tipped kisses that would have her begging him to take it off.

That was how he wanted her—begging. He wanted her spreading those slender golden thighs and inviting him in. He wanted her arms around his neck and her eyes pleading and—

A frown clipped his brows together. 'Go and make yourself presentable while I entertain our—guest,' he instructed.

'But your mother will think it rude if I don't—'

His eyes made a glinting sweep over the now damp strip of Indian cotton that was doing so little to hide the brevity of what was beneath. 'Trust me, you will feel better if you take time to change.'

A self-conscious flush mounted her cheeks. 'You don't look so presentable yourself,' she still had the spirit to hit back as she walked by him.

Xander just grinned. 'The difference being that I don't care what other people think when they look at me.'

Only because he still managed to look fabulous even with bare feet and his damp shirt lying open down his hair-tangled, muscle-contoured, bronzed front, Nell thought as she took to the stairs without further argument.

If she'd looked back she would have caught him quickly fastening buttons and combing long fingers through his hair. And the expression on his face had changed from lazily indifferent to grim.

He could have done without this intrusion from his mother today of all days. When she had rung his apartment in Athens this morning with an urgent request to see him, only to be told he was coming to the island, the last thing he had expected was for her to promptly invite herself and he'd told her not to come.

Though in truth, now she was here, he had some things of his own he needed to thrash out with his mother, things he preferred to get out of the way before his single-minded seduction of his beautiful wife continued along its present course.

Thinking about that exciting creature he'd met in the cove an hour ago set his nerves on edge. Nell had turned the tables on him with her provocative performance, and what was bothering him was why she had done it.

As the aggravating witch had just pointed out, three weeks ago she had been leaving him for another man.

A man, no less, that she'd been trying to contact via the telephone in his study here ever since she'd arrived on the island, but, like himself and the small army of people he had out there looking for him, Nell had discovered that Marcel Dubois had effectively disappeared from the face of the earth.

Scared of the repercussions when he heard of Nell's accident and knew that her husband was about to find out about them? If so, the Frenchman should have thought about those repercussions sooner—before he lured Nell into taking flight.

But that was not the point that was troubling Xander right now as he stood outside the salon door, grimly tidying himself. Nell was still trying to contact the cowardly swine yet she'd responded to him like a woman who'd been suppressing her desires for too long.

Hedging her bets? Using him as a substitute for her new love? Had that bastard woken her up to her own sexual desires and after three weeks without him she was hungry enough to let any man have her—even the one she believed was having an affair with another woman?

Anger bit its sharp teeth into him at the mere idea of another man taking what belonged to him. He threw open the salon door and stepped inside to the smell of his mother's perfume and to see an aunt who was all beaming smiles because her favourite person had come for a visit.

Shame that the son did not feel the same way. 'OK, Madre, let us make this brief. I have more important things to do than listen to your business troubles today.'

'I think you have already been dealing with your—business, *caro*,' his mother drawled with a swift up-and-down glance of his dishevelled state despite the attempt to tidy up. 'And there was I, thinking as I flew here that at last Alexander will know what it feels like when a marriage flounders on the rocks...'

'Your marriage did not flounder; you scuppered it,' he incised.

'If you two are going to fight I will leave you,' Thea Sophia put in and headed for the door, her beaming smile lost. 'You might also like to embrace each other *before* you tear each other to pieces,' she added sternly before she walked out.

Fifteen minutes later and Nell was coming down the stairs again after the quickest shower on record and with her freshly washed hair rough-dried by an urgent towel then left to do its own thing while she scrambled around for something suitable to wear. The fact that whoever had packed for her in England had chosen almost all of the clothes she'd bought for her non-existent honeymoon did not make the choice a simple one. One, the clothes had been bought with Xander and romance in mind. Two, they were now a full season out of date. So to have to put on one of the slinky off-the-shoulder short dresses in last season's rich jade colour did not give her confidence a major boost as she hovered outside the salon door, running nervous fingers down a mid-thigh-length dress that might do good things for her eyes and her figure but was going to look out-of-date to her super-elegant, fashion-guru mother-in-law.

That she'd stepped into a war zone took Nell about two seconds to register. Xander was lounging in one of the chairs, looking for the world like the king of all he surveyed even with bare feet—while he shot angry sparks at his mother.

Gabriela was sitting opposite him, giving the cool appearance that she did not notice the sparks. Heaven had left nothing out when they made this beautiful woman, Nell thought enviously. The sleek black hair, the sensational dark eyes, the long, slender figure which could pull off any fashion statement with panache.

As he turned his head to look at her, Nell felt a blush coming on as Xander let his eyes narrow then linger on her shining hair with its still damp, spiralling ends touching the hollow of her back. She'd tugged the dress up onto her shoulders as far as it would let her but it still looked low-cut at the front and slinky—as those too expressive eyes had already assessed.

'Ah, Helen, there you are.' Her mother-in-law's smooth voice brought her eyes swinging in her direction as Gabriela rose gracefully to her feet. 'You look delightful, *cara*,' she smiled as she came towards her, her expression revealing nothing as she swung her eyes down over Nell's dress, but the criticism was there, Nell was sure that it was. 'Enchantingly clean and fresh as you always look,' Gabriela added, then they air-kissed while Nell tried not to cringe at the 'clean and fresh' bit. 'And such hair! I am sure it grows two inches longer each time I see you. You know,' she eyed Nell shrewdly, 'with the touch of a gifted stylist I know in Milan it could be the most—'

'You will leave Nell's hair alone,' Gabriela's son interrupted as he rose to his feet. 'I like it exactly the way it is.'

'Don't be snappy, *caro*,' his mother scolded. 'I was only going to suggest that if you gave me a week with Helen in Milan I could truly turn her into—'

'I will extend on that,' Xander put in. 'You will leave Nell alone altogether. I like *all* of her exactly the way that she is.'

'Well, of course you do,' his mother agreed. 'But—'

'Exquisito, mi amore.' Placing his mouth to Nell's cheek, Xander spoke right over whatever Gabriela's but was going to be. 'Don't listen to her,' he advised. 'I do not need another fashion slave in this family.'

'I am not a slave to fashion!' his mother protested.

'The couture houses of Europe wipe their feet on you, Madre, and you know what makes it so crazy?' He looked down on her from his superior height. 'You would look amazing in whatever you chose to wear, be it sackcloth. They should be paying you to wear their clothes.'

'They do,' Gabriela informed him stiffly. Then because, like Nell, Gabriela clearly did not know if he was teasing or being cruel, 'Oh, go away and put some dry clothes on,' she snapped, wafting a slender white hand at him. 'You make a compliment sound like an insult and confuse me.'

Xander made no attempt to enlighten her as to which had

been his intention. He was angry, Nell noticed, so she had to assume the insult was what he'd meant.

He went obediently enough though, pausing long enough to assure Nell that he would be back before Thea Sophia arrived with refreshment for them all. The door closing behind him left Nell and Gabriela alone with a small silence to fill.

Gabriela did it. 'We were arguing when you came in, as I am sure you noticed. Alexander likes to have things all his own way but cannot always have it.'

The way her eyes slid away from Nell made her wonder if the argument had been about her.

Or the ugly rumours about their marriage seemed likely.

'Strong men are like that,' Nell found herself saying—as if she knew much about them.

'You think him strong?' Gabriela quizzed thoughtfully. 'I think him arrogant to believe that I should sacrifice my... Ah, but let us not talk about it.' She cut herself off from saying what she had been about to say right at the intriguing point, as far as Nell was concerned. 'Tell me about your accident and how you are recovering,' she invited. 'A much more interesting subject...'

By the time they'd done to death the scant details Nell was prepared to give about her accident and her ensuing recovery, which she suspected by the far-away expression Gabriela barely heard, Thea Sophia arrived and the odd mood lightened as Gabriela found a true smile as she went to take the heavy tray from the older woman.

There was a small tussle, which Thea won, as Nell knew from experience that she would.

'Leave me be, Gabriela,' she said. 'I must feel useful or I may as well take to my bed and wait for God to come and get me.'

'Wait for God indeed,' Gabriela mocked as she went to sit down and the older woman crossed the room to set down the tray. 'What you need, Thea, is to be taken out of yourself. When was the last time you left this brown dot of an island?'

'This brown dot is Pascalis land,' the old lady responded. 'And you might not have liked it here, but I love it.'

'Which did not answer my question.'

'I do not recall when I last left it.'

'Then it is high time that you did. Since Alexander refuses to let me make-over his wife, I think I will take you to Milan, Thea, and we will give you a complete make-over then find you a passionate man who will stop you talking about waiting for God.'

To Nell's surprise the old lady let out an amused chuckle. 'He will be too old to fulfil my hidden passions.'

'Not these days, *carisima*,' Xander's mother came back. 'Today the old men have the Viagra to maintain their flagging passions and will be very useful indeed to you. No, don't sit down right over there, Helen. Come and sit here beside me.'

'Wicked creature.' Sophia spoke over Gabriela's command while Nell meekly did as she had been told. 'If my nephew were still alive he would lock you in your room for speaking so disrespectfully to me.'

'Ah, four years and I still miss Demitri,' Gabriela sighed wistfully.

'I was twenty-three when the war took my Gregoris and made me a widow but I still miss him every single day.'

It was news to Nell that Thea Sophia had been married!

'You miss his *passions*, Sophia?' Gabriela prodded teasingly.

'Of course!' the old lady declared. 'He was a big, strong, handsome man—as with all the Pascalis men. My bed felt cold for years.'

'I understand the feeling,' Gabriela sighed. 'Maybe we should go to Milan to find ourselves a new man each. A cold bed is no pleasure, Thea. You would have liked my husband, *cara*.' She turned to include Nell in the conversation. 'Alexander is just like him—hewn from rock on the outside and deliciously protective by nature, but so jealously possessive of me that he rarely let me out of his sight. Yet what did he do but go and die in two short seconds while I was out of the room!'

'What is this—a wake?' Xander strode in on the conversation, wearing pale chinos and a fresh white shirt.

'Your father was my one abiding love,' his mother said sadly.

'Maybe he was, but you…'

The rest of the 'but' was completed in some cutting Italian that literally froze the discussion and turned Gabriela pale.

Thea Sophia recovered first, bursting into a flurry of chatter as she handed out the small cups of strong black Greek coffee and Nell puzzled over what Xander could he have said this time to destroy his mother as effectively as that.

She cast him a hateful look, which he returned with a grimace that seemed to say he was already regretting whatever he'd said. But no apology was offered and after giving him as long as it took him to lower himself into the chair he had been occupying earlier, Nell flicked him another hard look then turned to Gabriela.

'A trip to Milan sounds very exciting,' she said. 'I've never been there and I've had a yen to have my hair cut—short and spiky,' she added for good measure while Gabriela's eyes began to glow. She knew what Nell was doing and it was working. Xander shifted in his chair. 'Perhaps I could come with you,' she suggested. 'It would be fun to spend lots of money on new clothes and things, try out a new image—'

'Try for a full recovery before you make any plans,' Xander grimly put in.

'I am recovered,' Nell insisted. He was eyeing her narrowly, warning sparks glinting at her now instead of his mother. 'I've had two whole weeks under Thea Sophia's tender care to aid my recovery.'

'You were the good patient,' Sophia put in, bending to pat Nell's cheek fondly as she handed her a cup of coffee. 'You should have seen the extent of her bruising, Gabriela,' she declared in dismay. 'No wonder Alexander could not bear to look at them. Where were his protective instincts when this poor girl drove her flimsy car into a tree? She was bruised from here to here.' A gnarled hand drew a slashing left-to-right diagonal line in the air across Nell's chest then added the other line across her stomach.

Nell saw Xander's brows shift into a sharp frown as he watched the vivid demonstration take place.

'Car seat-belt burns, Helen called them,' his aunt continued in disgust. 'I call them criminal. Who would want to ever wear a seat belt again if they had suffered such damage?'

'Think of the damage without the belt, Thea,' her great-nephew pointed out. 'Nell lost her appendix, cracked her ribs and got off lightly into the bargain, if you want the truth.'

'While you were on the other side of the world getting your name in the newspapers and—'

'That is enough, Sophia…'

It was Gabriela's quiet command that brought a halt to it, her dark eyes flickering from Nell's suddenly pale face to her son's cold, closed one. The old lady resorted to mumbled Greek as she bustled back to her coffee tray, leaving a tense silence in her wake.

It screeched in Nell's head like chalk across a blackboard— a white chalk that had scraped itself across her cheeks. She wanted to jump up and run out of the room but she didn't think her trembling limbs would make it. So she stared down at the brimming cup of strong black coffee she balanced on its saucer and tried to swallow the lump of humiliation that was blocking her throat.

She'd known that her useless marriage was public property so why should she feel so upset that Thea Sophia was so willing to remark on it?

Xander shifted in his chair and she flinched a look at him from beneath her eyelashes. His eyes were fixed on her, narrowed and intense.

The lump in her throat changed into a burn as tears decided to take its place. In desperation she turned to Gabriela.

'How—how long do you plan on staying?' she asked in a polite voice that came out too husky.

Her mother-in-law was looking at her in dark sympathy, which hurt almost as much as Thea's thoughtless words had done. As Gabriela opened her mouth to answer, Xander got there before her.

'She will not be staying.' It was blunt to the point of rude.

Nell ignored him. 'It w-would be nice if you could stay a few days,' she invited. 'W-we could get to know each other better—'

'My mother does not do getting-to-know-you, *agape mou*,' Xander's hateful voice intruded yet again. 'She lives a much too rarefied life, hmm, Madre?'

Gabriela's lips snapped together then opened again. Like Nell, she was grimly ignoring her sarcastic son. 'I am afraid I cannot stay,' she murmured apologetically. 'I came because I need to discuss some business with my son.'

'Just business?' he mocked.

Nell couldn't take any more, ridding herself of the coffee-cup, she jumped to her feet. 'What is it with you?' she flashed at the sarcastic devil. 'Trying to have a polite conversation with you around is like living inside a tabloid newspaper—full of sarcasm and innuendo!'

'That just about covers it,' Xander agreed.

'Oh, why don't you just shut up?' she cried, making Thea Sophia jerk to attention, and Gabriela's eyes opened wide. 'You know what your problem is, Xander? You are still that resentful little boy who swam alone in the sea. You forgot to grow up!'

'*I* forgot to grow up?' Xander climbed to his feet. 'Where the hell have you been for the last year?'

'Right where you put me until I decided I'd had enough of it,' Nell answered fiercely. Cheeks hot now, green eyes alight with rage.

'So you decided it would be fun to drive you car into a tree?'

Fun? He thought she had done it for *fun*? 'Well, we all know what you were doing because you featured in the newspapers so prominently,' she tossed back. 'Would you like me to tell them what I was doing while I was having *fun* crashing my car?'

'Watch it, Nell.'

Now he was deadly serious. You could cut the tension with a knife. Nell's chin shot up. Xander towered over her by several intimidating inches but she faced up to his threatening stance.

Shall I tell them? her angry eyes challenged him while their audience sat riveted and the desire to unlock her aching throat and shatter his impossible pride to smithereens set the blood pounding in her head.

His face did not move, not even by an eyelash, hard, handsome and utterly unyielding like a perfectly sculptured mask. The cold eyes, the flat lips, the flaring nostrils—he was warning her not to do it—*daring* her to do it.

The pounding changed to a violent tingling. Taking Xander on was becoming a drug that sang like a craving she just had to feed. Her lips parted, quivering, and that stone-like expression still did not alter even though he knew it was coming—he *knew*!

Then another voice dropped cool, calm, curiously into the thrumming tension, 'Helen, darling, did you know you are bleeding from the base of your foot…?'

CHAPTER SIX

NELL broke vital eye contact with Xander to glance dazedly down at her foot, where, sure enough, blood was oozing onto the base of her strappy mule. The sharp stone on the hillside, she remembered, and was about to explain when Xander struck, seizing the opportunity to scoop her up off the ground!

'Get off me, you great brute!' she shot out in surprised anger.

'Shut up!' he hissed as he carried her from the room.

'I have never seen such fire,' Thea Sophia gasped into the stunned space they left in the tension behind them. 'The child has been as quiet and as sweet as a mountain stream all the time she has been here.'

'She's certainly found her voice now,' Gabriela drily responded.

'She's found more than her voice,' Xander bit down at her as the salon door swung shut behind them and he strode across the foyer, heading straight for the stairs. 'She's found a compelling desire for a death wish!'

'Not feeling so sarcastic now?' Nell hit right back, still fizzing and popping inside with fury.

He stopped on the stairs, blazing black eyes capturing sparking green. His wide, sensual mouth was tight with fury, nostrils flaring like warning flags. The cold mask had broken, she saw, and felt the hectic sting of a dangerous excitement vibrate just about every skin pore.

'You are goading me for some reason,' he ripped down at her. 'I want to know why!'

'Death wish?' Nell answered in defiance, only to bury her top teeth in her bottom lip when his glittering eyes narrowed for a moment, widened—then flared.

He caught that bottom lip with his own teeth and robbed it

79

from her. As she drew in a startled gasp he held on and sucked, turning the whole crazy thing into a very erotic kiss.

Downstairs in the salon Thea Sophia made a jerky move to follow them. 'They will need—'

'Stay where you are, Thea,' Gabriela murmured quietly. 'I don't think they will appreciate the intrusion right now.'

'Oh.' Thea stopped.

'Mmm,' Gabriela agreed with the older woman's dawning expression. 'Your calm mountain spring is about to turn into a raging torrent, *cara*,' she said thoughtfully. 'And our angry, high-principled boy is about to learn what it is like to be caught up in such an uncontrolled flood.'

'You sound pleased about that.'

'Pleased?' Gabriela considered. 'I suppose I am. He never forgave me my raging torrent. Let him learn and understand how I felt.'

'Those two are man and wife. Your torrent took place out of wedlock and devastated more people than you care to recall,' Thea said curtly.

The sighed-out 'Yes,' took place as Gabriela came to her feet then walked restlessly over to the window, where she stood staring out at the glinting swimming pool, beyond which lay a crescent beach and an ocean of glistening blue.

'I've had enough of this place,' she decided suddenly and, turning back to the room, went to collect her purse. 'Tell Alexander we will deal with our business some other time—'

'Oh, I did not mean to chase you away, Gabriela,' Sophia said anxiously.

'I know.' Gabriela kissed the old woman's worried cheek. 'But I should not have come. Alexander did warn me he had no time for my problems and now I know why.'

'They've been apart for two weeks, Gabriela.'

'They've been apart for much longer than that, Thea.' Gabriela smiled ruefully at the older woman's rose-tinted view of life. 'Those two might be married, my sweet darling,' she broke the news gently, 'but they are not yet man and wife...'

The kiss lasted all the way up the stairs and into the bedroom. Nell only thought to pull back from it when she heard the door slam behind them with the help of a foot. Xander watched the liquid bewilderment darken her beautiful eyes as she stared up at him. He could feel her heart racing beneath the flat of his palm.

'I'm going to ravish you senseless until you tell me what it is you are up to,' he bit out thinly.

The heart rate speeded up. 'I'm not up to anything!' she denied.

But her cheeks began to heat—a sure sign that she was lying, the little witch. 'You have been playing me hot and cold since I arrived here! Do you think I cannot tell when someone has a hidden agenda? And don't blink those innocent eyes at me,' he rasped. 'I know when my strings are being pulled!'

'*Your* strings are being pulled?' Nell tried to wriggle free of his arms but he was having none of it, strong muscles flexed in a show of pure male strength. 'You've been threatening to ravish me since you turned up at my sick-bed!'

'What a good idea,' he gritted out with a teeth-clenching smile and headed for the bed.

Oh, my God, Nell thought and started to tremble. 'My foot!' she jerked out in the wild hope it would pull him up short.

It did. He stopped in the middle of the bedroom, cleft chin flexing, tiny explosions of angry frustration taking place in his eyes. Without a word he changed direction, carrying her into the bathroom, where he slotted her down on the marble top between the his-and-hers washbasins.

Her hair stroked Xander's face as she straightened away from him, her fingers trailing a reluctant withdrawal from around his neck. Her heart was still racing, the fine tremors attacking her slender frame, making his teeth grit together because he couldn't decide if they were tremors of anger or desire.

It was novel; he didn't think he'd ever been in this kind of situation before in which he was having to out-guess the confusing signals he was being sent. Women usually fell on him— wholesale. Having this beautiful, contrary creature try her best to tie him in knots was stinging to life senses he'd had no idea he possessed.

A taste for the fight. A deeply grudging willingness to play the game for a while just to see where she thought she was going with it. He knew where it was going. Hell, he was already there. She might have earned herself some respite with the injured foot but that was all it was—a brief time-out while the rest of it throbbed and pulsed in the quickened heat of his blood.

Reaching above her head, he opened a cupboard and fished around for a clean cloth and some other bits and pieces he kept up there. He was standing between her legs, her thighs touching his thighs and she wasn't moving a muscle. Yet another surge dragged on his senses as he dropped his arms and saw the way she was staring at the flexing muscles beneath his shirt. Narrowing his eyes, he watched as the tip of her tongue sneaked out to moisten her upper lip as he ran his fingers lightly down her thighs to go in search of the offending foot.

Mine, he thought as he watched that nervy pink tongue-tip, and let his hands pause so his fingers could draw some light, experimental circles across the soft skin behind her knees. She jolted as if he'd shot her. Her chin came up, their eyes clashed, his carefully unfathomable, hers as dark and disturbed as hell.

'Foot,' he said.

Her teeth replaced the tongue-tip, burying into the full bottom lip as she lifted her knee so he could grasp her ankle and remove her shoe. One glance down and he realised she'd offered him the wrong foot.

'The left not the right,' he said then began to frown. Something was niggling him about the left and the right side of this aggravating woman. What could aggravate him when they both looked more or less the same?

Beautiful, perfect, ripe for seduction.

She offered him the other foot. Removing the shoe, he dipped his head and used the cloth to wipe away the blood so he could check out the cut.

'You did this on the hill,' he recalled and she nodded.

'It didn't bleed then. The hot shower I took must have aggravated it—ouch,' she added when he pressed the pad of her foot around the small cut in search of foreign bodies.

Her toes wriggled, small, pink, slender toes with a shading of gold across their tops from the sun.

Xander's tongue moistened. 'Feel anything in there?'

'No. It's just stinging a bit.'

'Clean cuts do.'

'Speaks the voice of experience,' she mocked huskily.

Swapping the cloth for a packet of antiseptic pads, he ripped a sachet open with his teeth.

'I wet-shave,' he answered, bringing those incredible eyes flickering curiously up to stare at his lean, smooth chin. That pink tip of a tongue returned to replace the teeth as she studied him with a fascination that set the skin all over his body tingling. If this wasn't the most intimate she'd ever been with a man—not counting the interlude in the cove—then he did not know women as he thought he did.

'I cut myself sometimes. Usually when I'm—distracted.'

The colour bloomed in her cheeks as she caught his meaning. 'Hence the antiseptic pads.' She sounded breathless.

'And wound strips.' He ripped the protective cover off a small plaster next and bent to press it over the cleaned cut.

But he didn't let go, his gaze recapturing hers as his thumb began lightly stoking the smooth, padded flesh at the base of her foot in the same circling action he had used on the backs of her knees. Silence followed. He didn't think she was even breathing. No two people had ever been more aware as to where this was leading and any second now she was going to disappear in a shower of her own prickling static.

'Xander…' His name feathered helplessly from her.

He responded by releasing the foot so he could run his hands back up the length of her legs—only this time he slid them beneath the clingy little dress.

'You are gorgeous, you know that?' he murmured softly.

'You don't have to say—'

'Gorgeous eyes, gorgeous hair, smooth, satin skin…' His

hands moved higher in a slow, sensual glide. 'You have the heart-shaped face of an angel and the mouth of a siren, the blush of a virgin and the teasing skills of a whore.'

'That isn't—'

With a controlled tug he slid her towards him across cold marble until she fitted neatly to his front. Her eyes widened when she felt the hardening thickness at his crotch. He felt her revealing little quiver, watched her breasts shift on a stifled little gasp. Then her thighs tightened against him, narrowing his eyes on her very—very expressive face.

'You like this, don't you?' he taunted lazily.

Nell dragged her eyes away. 'I don't know what you're talking about.'

'Sex, *agape mou*,' he named it. 'You are quivering with delight because you love to know you can affect me like this.'

'For all I know you're like this with any woman you come into contact with,' she tossed at him, making a jerky shift in an effort to move back.

His hands held her clamped to him. His hips gave a slow, smooth, sensual thrust. She quivered like a trapped little bird as damp heat spread across the exposed and vulnerable centre of her sex.

'Do I apply the same reasoning to your response?'

He knew what was happening to her, Nell realised. How could he not when she was so burning hot? A stifled gasp shot from her when he bent his head, his lips moulding hers and taking control of them, his tongue darting into her mouth. Each time they did this it got worse, she thought dizzily as she fell into it with a hopeless groan and let her slender arms snake up and around his neck.

She felt strong muscles flex in his shoulders as he lifted her up from the marble, felt the hard and pulsing sexual promise in his body as he flattened her to his chest. Her legs had wrapped themselves tightly around him and they might as well have been back in the ocean with no clothes on because she could feel everything that was happening to him.

It was only when he tipped her down onto the bed that she

realised where they were now. With a gasping drag on her unwilling lips she broke the kiss to look around her. With a swimming sense of disorientation noticed for the first time that since she'd taken her shower earlier someone had been in here and closed the shutters over the windows to keep out the fierce heat of the afternoon sun. The room had a warm, soft, sultry feel to it as if it had been deliberately set for making love.

Even the bedcovers had been drawn back, she realised. Her gaze flicked back to the man lying in a languid stretch beside her on the bed, lazily reading each expression as it passed across her face. He offered her a mocking smile. The air went perfectly still in her lungs. He'd done it. When he'd come up to take his own shower he'd come in here and made this room ready for seduction as if it had always been a forgone conclusion that it was going to happen this afternoon.

'No,' she pushed out across taut throat muscles.

He merely held on to the smile and brushed a stray lock of Titian silk from her suddenly pale cheek. 'I've spent a whole year imagining you lying here with your beautiful hair splayed out around you and your beautiful mouth warmed and pulsing as it awaits the pleasure of mine.'

Sensation trickled right down the front of her. 'We are not going to do this,' she insisted shakily.

For an answer he began to unbutton his shirt. Nell stared as warm, bronzed skin roughened by dark hair began to make its appearance. Everything about him said man on a course he would not be moved from. Real alarm struck her with a frightening clarity.

She drew in a taut breath. 'Y-your m-mother,' she reminded him. 'W-we—'

'I don't need her permission to do this, *agape mou*,' he drawled.

'But she—'

He moved, long fingers leaving the shirt to come and frame her heart-shaped face from pale cheek to trembling chin. Pinpricks leapt across the surface of her skin as he bent to brush his mouth across hers. 'No more reprieves,' he murmured very softy. 'This is it, my beautiful Helen. It is time to face your fate because it is here…'

Her fate. Nell stared at him. He was deadly serious. To her horror he began to stroke the hand down her throat and across her shoulder, fingertips pushing stretchy jade fabric out of his way.

'Stop it!' she choked out and at last found the sense to put up a fight.

Dark eyes lit with a kind of cold amusement that chilled her as he captured her flailing fists and flattened them to the bed above her head. 'The little game you've been playing with me is over,' he said grimly. 'Accept it, for you are about to get your just desserts.'

'You're angry,' she gasped in shocked realisation.

His tight grimace confirmed it.

'But—why?'

The innocent question locked his lean, handsome face. 'I've done nothing but treat you with respect since we married and you paid me back by leaving me for another man.'

With his free hand he went back to undoing shirt buttons in a grim display of intent.

'Just thank your lucky stars that you did not make it, my beautiful Helen,' he glinted down at her. 'Or you would not be about to enjoy Alexander Pascalis the lover, but the other Alexander Pascalis—the one that makes big men quake in fear!'

'How do you know I didn't make it?' she prodded recklessly, staring as more and more of that muscled, bronzed, hair-roughened chest appeared. 'How do you know I didn't *make it* a dozen times during the week Hugo Vance wasn't around to stop it from happening?' she choked up at him. '*Before* I decided to leave you for good!'

The fingers stopped working the buttons. Nell heaved in a wary breath of air as a *frisson* of alarm shot across her heaving breasts.

'But you didn't, did you?'

It was a very seriously driven warning to be careful what

she said next, making her wish her mouth would just shut up—
but it wouldn't. He might already be wearing the face that made
big men quake, but she had a whole year's-worth of unfairness
pounding away inside her, and it needed to be heard.

'Y-you left me alone on our wedding night,' she reminded
him, beginning to struggle again to get free. He subdued her
by clamping a leg across her thighs. 'You refused to make
excuses or defend yourself—you couldn't even be bothered to
lie! I've had to live with that, Xander, not you. Y-you just went
back to your life and didn't care what you left behind!' Tears
were threatening, making her soft mouth quiver and turning
her eyes into deep green pools of hurt. 'W-well, you left me
behind w-with a twenty-four-hour guard to do the caring for
you! If I went to the local village shop Hugo Vance came along
with me. He had to do—he was in charge of the remote control
for the wretched gates!'

'He was there for your safety,' he bit back impatiently.

'He was there to control your limp rag of a wife!' she cried.
'You said that you and I are alike; w-well, tell me, Xander,
would you have lived my life for the last year without doing
something about it?'

'But I repeat—you didn't, did you, Nell?'

Nell lay there beneath him heaving and panting, his leg
heavy across her legs and her shining hair caught beneath the
hands he still pinned above her head. She glared hotly into a
face that was coldly mask-like, reminding her of that rock his
mother had talked about. And the stinging pinpricks attacking
her flesh were the sparks of her mutiny bouncing right off him.

Hewn, hard, handsome and so threatening she shivered. Yet
backing down now just wasn't an option she was prepared to
take. 'Do you think you are the only one that can be discreet
about their lovers?' she heard herself dare to challenge. 'Do
you think that because you didn't want me I should think myself unfit for anyone else?'

Maybe she did have a death wish, she thought tensely as a
new level of stillness locked his hard eyes on her face with an
expression that was too frighteningly inexplicable to dare to

read. He was eleven years older than Nell and at that precise moment she felt every one of those years boring holes into her head.

'Are you telling me—without the guts to make the full statement,' he pushed out finally, 'that you have taken lovers since you married me?'

Nell's quivering upper lip had to fight to break free from her bottom lip. 'Would it make me a lesser person in your eyes if I said yes?' she quavered huskily. 'Perhaps totally unfit for you to touch?'

It was living on the edge, Nell knew that as she said it, feeling more afraid of what she was prodding here than she dared let herself think. But she needed to know. She'd lived the last year loving a man who'd locked her up in a glass bubble marked, 'Virgin. Sole possession of Alexander Pascalis', as if it was the only thing about her that made her worthy of the place she held in his life, while he blithely continued to bed his mistress as if that was perfectly OK.

But the real point she was making was, would he still want to be here with her without the provenance?

A stifled gasp escaped when his hand came to rest beneath her breast, where her heart was racing madly. It began a gentle stroking as he lay stretched out, half beside her, half on top of her, a look of grim contemplation taking charge of his face. She'd stop fighting to get free and had never felt more vulnerable because she just didn't know what he was going to say or do next. His eyes weren't telling her, his expression wasn't telling her, even the light stroke of this hand wasn't telling her anything because she wasn't sure that he was aware it was doing it.

It was a test, Xander knew that. He was not so blinded by those beautiful flashing eyes and this sensational body he had pinned to the bed that he could not recognise a challenge when it was being tossed at him.

What he could not decipher was if the reckless little witch was talking like this because she wanted to hit him hard with the truth or because she was taunting him with the possibility of it being the truth.

Was it the truth?

He still did not know. She had still not made that *yes* a full-blown, bloody statement of fact.

Did it make a difference to how he felt?

To wanting to make love to her? Not the slightest difference to the desire pounding away in his blood.

To this creature he had respected more than anyone else in his entire life? Hell, yes, it made a difference there. Nell belonged to him. She wore his ring on her slender white finger. She had loved him so much once that he refused to believe that she was capable of making love with any other man but him.

But he discovered he was scared that in a fit of rebellion she might have done.

He pulled in a deep breath. The atmosphere was so thick with his long silence that he could taste it on his tongue as he slid his hand up to cover her breast. Its receptive tip stung to life to push into his palm and another strangled gasp escaped her soft, quivering mouth.

He looked at her hair spread out across the cover like a burnished copper halo. Then at her face, heart-shaped, exquisite but wary as hell. His eyelashes glossed over his gaze, dipped lower, across the smooth-as-silk shoulder he had exposed that looked so sexy and inviting, then further to where his long fingers cupped her breast over sensually moulding jade-coloured fabric. The tips of his fingers were in tantalising contact with smooth flesh just above the dress, where a little pulse was beating wildly. He stroked, she quivered, his body tightened in response.

Then came the rest of her, slender, flat-planed yet deliciously curvy inside the hugging dress. She was stretched out beneath him like an offering. But what exactly was on offer? Experienced lover or the beguiling innocent he'd walked away from on their wedding night and since suffered so many hot dreams about?

He slid his eyes back to her eyes, capturing a deep look of anxiety that pricked the hairs around his groin. The sultry heat of the afternoon shifted around them as he released a hissing sigh.

Time to find out. 'The answer is—no,' he stated very huskily then before the next stifled gasp could escape her he trapped it with his hungry mouth.

Nell felt herself go up in a plume of sharp static. The wait, the breathtaking silence, the scouring inspection of her body followed by his answer had shattered her tension and sent her spiralling out of control. Sensation latched on to every nerve-end, making each muscle she possessed stretch in long, sensual response then collapse into the driving power of his kiss.

He responded without hesitation, taking that kiss even deeper. It was as it had been in the water only far more demanding, a wild, escalation of pleasure that would not let her be still and had her fighting to free her trapped hands so she could touch him as he was touching her.

He let the hands go, sliding his own hand over her hair to the side of her neck then the smooth skin of the shoulder he had exposed for himself. His mouth followed, pressing small kisses to her skin that had her fingers clutching at his head. Smooth, dark silk hair filtered through her fingers. The kisses reached the soft, pulsing mound of her breast. She released a tight groan then pulled at his hair, caught his mouth and began kissing him back so desperately it was almost frightening.

'Want me?' It was so harshly spoken that Nell thought he was still angry; opening her eyes, she expected to see the cruelty of rejection about to hit her once again, only to find herself drowning in the smouldering, dark depths of desire.

'Yes,' she breathed.

His masculine growl scored her cheek as he plundered that soft, breathy answer. His hand returned to her shoulder, took a grip on the dress and pulled it down to her waist.

No bra—had he known that? The next masculine growl said yes, of course he had known it and long before he'd cupped her breast. He'd known from the moment she'd walked into the salon that she'd dared to come there wearing less than she should. Even her nervousness towards his mother had not been able to quieten the little devil at work inside her that wanted to torment him as she had been doing since he arrived in the cove.

His mouth took possession of one pouting nipple while his fingers took possession of the other. The wet and dry rasping of tongue and fingers sent her into a paroxysm of gasping jerks and quivers. He knew what he was doing. He knew this was torture.

'Xander.' She groaned out his name in an anxious plea for mercy and received it when his warm, damp mouth came back to hers.

After that she lost touch with everything but her senses and him. He was an expert at this and so incredibly ruthless about it she barely had time to absorb one new exciting experience before he was overriding it with something else. Her flesh sang where he caressed it, her restless fingers digging into satin-tight flesh that rippled in response to the sharp edges of her nails.

His shirt had gone. Nell had no idea that she had removed it. Her dress lay in a discarded heap on the floor. He was kissing her breasts again, her stomach, her navel, tongue-tip sliding sensual moisture across her acutely alive and sensitised flesh. When he suddenly rose to his feet, she let out a cry of pained protest because she saw rejection coming yet again. When she realised what he was doing, she moved on her side to watch him unashamedly as his fingers worked to free himself of the rest of his clothes.

Eyes black with promise, he watched her watch him. Every movement he made was hard and tense—packed with sexual motivation that curled her up with excitement. The trousers were stripped from his body and deep green eyes made a slow, shy sweep of him that couldn't help but linger on the bold thrust of his erection. Arrogant, she thought, and, on the tight little sensation of alarm mixed with excitement, she gave it the right to be.

'The way you look at a man is going to get you into trouble one day,' he ground roughly into the tension.

'I only do it with you.'

It was an admission that brought him back to her side, his superior framework rolling her onto her back so he could cover her. Then the real seduction of his bride began. It was hot and it was deadly serious, an intoxicating journey into a dark new world that explored all her senses and tuned them to a thick, throbbing, aching pitch. No tormenting of her breasts now but long, deep suckling, hands stroking her everywhere, the knowing movements of his body keeping her floating on a desperate high. When he finally eased the briefs down her legs then stroked his fingers along her thighs she began whimpering uncontrollably because she knew what was coming, her body clenching and unclenching in a mad mix of uncertainty and need.

He took her mouth in a deep, drugging kiss as if he knew what she was feeling and was trying to soothe her fears as he reached that warm, damp, untouched place. Her head suddenly filled with dark noises, a swirling, whipping, throbbing pulsation that had her fingers clutching at him. He was hot, damp, tense and trembling, his breathing all over the place.

'Nell.' He said her name, hoarse and husky, then made that first gentle intrusion inside.

She went wild in a second, it was that devastating. Had her gasping and crying out as shocking, hot pulses of pleasure rushed into her blood. He was touching her in ways that sent her mindless, smooth, slick, knowing fingers dragging feelings from her she would not have believed could be as powerful as this. And she could feel the heat of his own desire feeding from hers with the plundering depth of his kisses and the shuddering pleasure he was getting from this.

'Theos,' she heard him utter in a deep, rasping growl, then he stretched, the length of his sleek, muscled frame sliding damply against her. 'Nell…' He breathed her name like a caress, trying to reach wherever it was she had gone off to. 'I need to know if this is the first time for you.'

The first time, Nell repeated hazily, and lifted heavy eyelids to see the intensity burning in passion-glazed eyes and the savage control locked into his beautiful face.

'Of course it is,' she answered softly as if he should know that—and smiled.

His response was dynamic, the heated power of his kiss and the return of his caresses that drew her like liquid into thick, melting heat. She was lost and she knew it, blown away by sensation and the power he possessed to make her feel like this.

'Xander,' she whispered, feeling oddly as if he was slowly shattering her into tiny pieces.

He moved again, overwhelming in his maleness as he slotted himself between her thighs then made that first careful thrust with his hips. She felt his heat, his probing fullness. The shuddering strength with which he controlled the slow force of his entry was an experience in itself. Nell opened her eyes, found herself trapped once again by the spellbinding intensity carved onto his lean, dark features. He was big and bronzed and glossed with perspiration. The scent of his desire permeated the air. Sweat beaded his tautly held upper lip, his black eyelashes heavy over the bottomless black glaze of his eyes.

'You tell me if I hurt.' His voice was hoarse and husky.

She nodded, soft mouth parted, breathing reduced to small, thick gasps of quivering anticipation.

She felt the increased burn of his slow intrusion, the hunger, the reined-in control. Silken muscles flexed and he was trembling. She lifted her head to crush a kiss against his parted lips.

'Take it,' she whispered and the potent flare of masculine conquest lit his eyes when he made that final long, smooth stab that sent her arching against the bed in a moment of hot, stinging agony.

He caught the sound in his mouth as if it belonged to him, lips fusing like their bodies as she tensed and clawed at his hot, damp flesh that rippled with each helpless dig of her nails. His breathing was ragged, the tension holding him showing in the tremor of his fingers as they did their best to soothe the moment of discomfort away with gentle strokes of her face.

Yet, 'Mine,' he still breathed in rasping triumph, then the pain was dispersing and she was shifting restlessly beneath him. With a groan that lost him the final grip on control, he began to move again, plunging ever deeper while she made the wild leap into a mindless pleasure, clinging not clawing, riding the ever-increasing pace of his passion as it grew and grew until it exploded in a sense-shattering whirl of electrifying release. He followed her into that amazing place with convulsive rasps, which tore from his chest.

Too stunned by it all to do more than listen to the pounding of his heart as he lay heavily on her, Nell lay quietly beneath him while he laid languid kisses across her face.

'You surprised me,' he murmured.

'In what way?' She couldn't even find the energy to open her eyes as she asked the question.

His tongue teased her kiss-swollen bottom lip. 'You put me out of my misery when you could have damned me forever by letting me take you without knowing the truth.'

'Whether you are my first lover or not should make no difference.' She could not resist sliding her tongue across the tip of his.

'I am not built for innocence, *agape mou*.' He made a move with his hips so she could understand what he meant. He was still inside her, a thick, pulsing entity that filled her. 'I hurt you anyway, but not as much as I would have done without your generosity to keep me in check.'

'And your arrogance is showing again.'

'*Ne,*' he acknowledged lazily. 'But admit it—I did not disappoint.'

The remark was to remind her of her cutting little quip at the cove. Nell gazed up at him, watched him return the gaze with a dark-eyed, warm-lipped, wryly knowing smile. Beautiful, she thought helplessly, so indolently masculine and sure of himself. Her heart gave a hopeless little squeeze to let her know how much she still loved him despite every attempt she'd made to shut the feeling out.

Did he have any idea that the sex wasn't enough for her?

No, she was sure of it. He saw power in his undoubted physical prowess but wouldn't think to look beyond it for something deeper than that.

So what had she gained here?

Nothing, the hollow answer came back. If, that was, she didn't count intimacy wrapped around the kind of physical pleasure she never knew it was possible to experience.

For that alone she reached up to kiss him on the mouth. 'You didn't disappoint.' She was willing to grant him that much. 'Now all we have to do is wait to see if *I* disappoint…'

A frown grabbed his eyebrows, muscles flexing as he levered himself up on his forearms so he could narrow a questioning look into her face.

'You did not disappoint.' It was rough-toned declaration that vibrated across the walls of his cavernous chest and set her breasts tingling.

He was about to recapture her mouth when she added, 'I was talking about your other goal…'

'Goal?'

'To make me pregnant.' She spelt it out gently.

The comment acted like a cold douche on his lingering passions. He withdrew then rolled away from her. 'That was not my intention,' he denied.

'No?' Sitting up, Nell came gracefully to her feet then walked towards the bathroom on legs that felt too trembly and weak to carry her there, leaving that questioning little *no* hanging in the sultry air she left behind.

CHAPTER SEVEN

WATCHING her go, with her hair tumbling down her slender back helping to hide her nakedness from him, Xander wondered grimly how the hell she had walked him into that silken trap.

His body responded to tell him how. He hadn't used anything. He had not so much as glimpsed the distant idea of using anything to protect her from the risk of pregnancy—and not because of some fixed agenda he had been working towards, though he allowed Nell the right to believe that had been his ultimate motive. No, for the first time in his long sexual history he'd found himself too locked in the thrall of how she'd made him feel.

And if anyone from now on ever dared tell him that a condom did not stunt the pleasure of sexual intercourse then he would know they had never experienced what he had just experienced.

'Theos,' he breathed, turning it into a sigh as he threw himself flat against the bed then glanced down at his body, where the length of his shaft lay tight and proud against the flat of his abdomen, impatiently demanding more of the same.

It knew the difference. *He* knew the difference. He turned his head to glance at the closed bathroom door and wondered what Nell would say in response if he went in there and informed her that she had not been the only one enjoying a virgin experience in this bed.

Not one of his better ideas, he thought ruefully as that highly active part of his body gave another impatient tug. A confession like that would still not alter the fact that his intoxicating wife might be a virgin no more but her cynical view of him was still very much in tact.

And—hell, what could he say to make her believe that he'd harboured no deliberate intentions but had simply lost his head? The way his body was acting, it was not going to back him up. *It* wanted more—and more of what they'd just had. Prolific, rampantly free and potently unprotected sex shared with the beautiful, excitingly responsive woman who'd just left this bed.

Not just any woman—his woman.

His wife...

Sensation flipped a running ripple down his body. Turning his head on the pillow, he stared up at the ceiling where the lines of sunlight reflected on it filtered in through the slatted shutters then released a deep sigh of satisfaction at how good those two words sounded and felt.

His wife in fact and at last now in body. Why not enjoy sowing the seeds of that union? Why not tie the beautiful if cynical Helen to him so tightly she would never be free to attempt to leave him again?

See her walk away from their child-to-be with her Frenchman, he challenged grimly and felt hot, grinding jealousy stir in his chest. Who the hell was the guy that he believed he could poach his wife from him in the first place? *What* the hell did he have that made Nell want to go away with him so badly that she planned her escape a whole week before she crashed her car?

Then worse came, shifting him restlessly on the bed. Had the lily-livered swine chickened out at the last minute and Nell had been driving so fast because she'd been nursing a broken heart?

Did she love the guy?

Had she only let him make love to her here because she was thinking, what did it matter now?

It did not matter, he told himself. The Frenchman did not get her. He, Alexander Pascalis, did. Their marriage was consummated at last and whatever else came after this day, the one thing that would never change was that Nell now belonged to him right down to the last silken strand of hair on her beautiful head.

He settled back against the pillows, a look of grim calcula-tion glinting behind his slowly drooping eyelids. The agenda was real. His cynical wife would have to get used to it because he was going to keep her barefooted and pregnant and too damn busy making love with him to pine for some fickle Frenchman who'd dared to break her heart.

That decision made, he relaxed his body, the sunlight glint-ing through the slats soothing in the soft, drowsy heat. In a second or two he would get up and join her in the shower he could hear running—consolidate his place with some very pas-sionate seed-sowing and at the same time he would make Nell fall in love with him again. He could do it. She had loved him once. All it would take was some of his famous, single-minded ruthlessness to make her love him again...

Wrapped in a bathrobe, Nell stepped back into the bedroom to find the man of her dreams lying spread out on the bed and fast asleep. Her tummy muscles quivered at the picture he pre-sented of bronze-muscled abandonment with his quietened sex still very much a daunting sight.

She'd half expected him to barge into the bathroom and de-mand she believe him that he had not deliberately set out to make her pregnant just now. Well, of course he hadn't. Any fool—even this fool called Helen Pascalis—could tell when a man was being ruled by his desires and not his intelligence.

Take note, darling Vanessa, she thought grimly. This man wanted me so badly that he couldn't stop himself from having me without the protection he stops to apply with you in bed. Now he sleeps on *my* bed with *my* kisses still moist on his skin and wearing the scents of *my* body on his warm golden flesh.

You're out, Vanessa, and I am most definitely in and with no intention of ever letting go. What I have right here, this time I keep.

It had taken her a whole year to recognise and understand that she had to fight for what she wanted instead of hiding away like some distant shadow waiting for Xander to remem-ber that she lived.

Well, now she had him and she had no intention of letting

him go. A man who could tremble in her arms the way Xander had trembled was hooked and she knew it with every single fibre of her female being. And if she had to learn sensual wiles that were probably going to set her hair on end only to imagine them, then she was willing to use them to keep her man.

Before too long, Xander was going to find himself chained so tightly to her that he wasn't going to be able to take in a breath without her knowing about it. Instinctively her hand went to her cover her abdomen, inside which the seed of her lover was busily performing its potent magic—or if not yet it would be before too long.

A baby. Their baby. The next Pascalis heir. Eat your heart out, Vanessa, because this is one thing you will never have, she thought with grim satisfaction.

Ex-lover, she then corrected as she moved quietly towards the bed with a new deeply felt sensual pulse to her movements as she began to remove the bathrobe to begin her very first seduction of any man.

A sound coming from beyond the shutters diverted her attention; dropping the bathrobe to the floor, she crossed to the window to press a gap between two wooden slats and glanced down to see that Yannis was carrying out one of his daily duties and cleaning the pool.

Something else caught her attention. For a few short seconds she stood frowning, trying to decide what was different out there. Then her eyes alighted on Xander's helicopter where it stood anchored to its concrete deck—and alone.

A strangled gasp broke from her. She suddenly remembered the swirling, whipping noises as she'd lain in Xander's arms. Those sounds were not the sounds of the whirring, pulsating heat of their loving—they had been the sounds of his mother's helicopter leaving the island!

'Oh!' A blast of mortification at the way they'd left Gabriela kicking her heels downstairs while they made love up here had her whirling round to run to the bed.

'Xander...' It was necessary to put a knee on the mattress so she could reach his shoulder to give it an urgent shake.

'Wake up!' she insisted. 'Your mother has gone! You have to call her up and bring her back here. You—'

The snaking hook of a long, muscled arm toppled her onto him. 'Mmm,' he murmured sleepily. 'I was dreaming about you.'

'Will you listen?' she insisted, trying to fight him off and not to respond to the seeking warm brush of his mouth. 'I said your mother has gone!'

'I know.' The arm curved her closer. 'I heard her leave—didn't you?'

Nell flushed at what she'd believed the helicopter noise had been. 'You have to go and invite her back,' she said anxiously. 'She must be terribly offended to just go off like that.'

'You cannot offend my mother.' He was kissing her shoulder, the tip of his tongue gliding a sensual pathway towards her throat. 'Beneath the perfect gloss beats a heart of pure steel.'

Like the son; Nell frowned at the cool way he'd said that. 'Don't be cruel…'

'You taste of fresh water and soap.'

'I showered,' Nell mumbled distractedly.

'And removed my scent from your skin. Now I will have to put it back again.'

'But you need—'

'You,' he said. 'Again,' he added on a lusty growl as he leaned over to claim her mouth.

'Mmm,' Nell mumbled out a dizzy protest. 'Don't do that. Your mother. We have to—*What are you doing?*' she choked as his hand made a shockingly intimate dive between her legs.

'Making sure that you don't disappoint,' he returned smoothly, then laughed when her eyes widened in shock that he'd dared to actually admit it. 'A deal is a deal,' he said smoothly and flattened her to the bed.

Nell was caught in her own trap and she knew it.

When Xander had come back to the island to stake his claim on his bride, he did it by unleashing the full power of his sensual repertoire upon her that by far outstripped any ideas her naïve imagination she could have come up with.

He was amazing.

Any attempt to get him to talk about anything serious was thoroughly quashed by—sex. The kind of sex that could mercilessly slay her senses even when she was only thinking about it. He just had to look at her and she wanted him. He just had to say, 'Come here', in that rough-toned, desiring voice and she went like an eager lamb to the slaughter of her own common sense.

They played together, in the pool or in the ocean. He showed her how to reach the top of the rock flanking the little cove so they could dive into crystal-clear water beneath. He taught her how to fish from the selfsame rock then laughed himself breathless as she screamed in horror when she actually caught a fish.

And of course they made love—all the time, anywhere. Xander could not get enough of her and in truth Nell learned to use the newfound power over him with a feline ruthlessness that kept him forever and delightfully on his guard.

'I knew you would be dangerous once you discovered how to do this to me,' he complained late one afternoon after she'd spent the whole day taunting him with teases and half-promises and now rode him with slow and sinuous moves with her body that kept him pitched right on the edge, fighting not to give in because giving in before she did would fill her green eyes with so much triumph.

His skin was bathed in sweat and his hands were clamped to her supple hipbones. When she leant down to capture his mouth a whole new set of sensual muscles joined the torment. She caressed his taut cheekbones, the rasping clench of his jaw. She brushed the hard tips of her breasts against him and rolled her tongue around the kiss-softened contours of his lips before whispering, 'My lover,' then drew in every sensitised, beautifully tutored muscle to send him toppling over the edge.

As role reversals went, Nell knew she had cornered the market. She had him hanging on every flirtatious word and look and gesture like a besotted slave. On the occasions he grabbed back power just to remind her that he could do if he so desired to, she became the tormented one, the hopeless, helpless, besotted slave.

One week floated in perfect harmony into two then a third. Thea watched them and smiled a lot, and began crocheting an intricately patterned gossamer-fine christening shawl with a serene complacency that made Nell blush.

This was what she'd wanted, wasn't it?

Frowning as she bent to pick up a stray piece of driftwood off the shoreline, she sent experienced fingers gliding over its undulating ocean-smoothed contours the way her mother had taught her to do, while her mind drifted elsewhere.

She suspected she was pregnant. It was very early days yet to allow the suspicion to grow too large in her head, but her regular-as-clockwork period had let her down three days ago, and if Xander's virility was as potent as the rest of him then she knew, deep down, what it meant.

It changed everything. From believing she wanted to conceive his baby she now discovered that she didn't. Not yet, not like this. Not while they still hid from the real world on this tiny island where she felt more like a very indulged mistress than she did a wife.

A sigh broke from her, sending her chin tilting up so she could stare bleakly at the blue horizon. Xander could not remain hidden here for very much longer. As it was he needed to spend more and more time in his state-of-the-art study here dealing with business.

And Nell had pressing things of her own she needed to do— if she could only get to a telephone that did not have every call made on it carefully monitored.

Marcel. She was worried about him. She needed to know how he was and what he was doing. If he was cutting himself up with guilt and remorse or too angry with her to care that she was worrying about him.

When Xander did find it necessary to leave here, did he intend to take her with him this time or was she, in effect, still his prisoner whether it be behind the gates of Rosemere or here in this beautiful place?

He evaded the question each time she asked it. He evaded any discussion about life beyond here. Their honeymoon, he called it. A time to enjoy now, not what tomorrow had to bring.

But even a honeymoon as idyllic as this one had to come to an end some time.

She released another sigh. Xander watched it leave her as he stood in the window with the phone pressed to his ear. She was wearing a blue sarong today. Beneath the sarong would be a matching-coloured bikini, and her hair was up, looped into one of those casual knots she had a way of fashioning that always tempted him to tug it free.

His fingers twitched, so did other parts as he saw himself unwrapping the beautiful package that was his sensational, warm and willing wife.

Wife. *His wife.* As soon as he thought the words a blanket of seemingly unquenchable possessive desire bathed his flesh. He wanted to be out there with her, not standing here talking business on the telephone.

'I know I have to attend,' he snapped out, sudden impatience sharpening his tongue. 'I merely asked if there was any way it could be put back a week.'

No chance. He'd known it even before he suggested it. Wishful thinking was a useless occupation out there in the real world. And that was his biggest problem. Nell and this incredible harmony they had come to share did not belong in the real world. Nell, he'd come to realise, never did. Not in his world anyway. For the last year he'd kept her safely locked up inside a pair of iron gates, waiting, he'd told himself, for her to grow up before he attempted to redress the mess their marriage had become. In his arrogant self-confidence, he had not seen that she'd done the growing seething inside with resentment at the way he treated her. If she had not crashed her car, she would have been long gone with her Frenchman before he'd known anything.

And the way the guy had disappeared so completely turned

his blood cold when he thought of Nell disappearing with him like that.

'What of that other business?' he clipped into the telephone.

His frown deepened when an unsatisfactory reply came back.

'A man cannot drop from the face of the earth without leaving some trace, Luke,' he rasped out in frustration. 'I need you to find him. I need you to interrogate him. I need to know what his true intentions had been towards my wife!'

'And if it was a subtle form of kidnap?' he lanced back at whatever Luke Morell said. 'I will continue to think of her as in danger until I have answers... No, I will not leave her safety to the hands of bodyguards again. What use was Hugo Vance? Helen is my wife, my responsibility... Then let an empire crumble.'

Grimly he slammed down the phone, knowing he was being unfair, unwise—irrational. But how the hell else could he behave around a woman as unpredictable as Nell?

He'd spent three weeks in her constant company—had sunk himself into her more times than he cared to count! But did he know what made her tick? No more than he did a year ago when he'd wrongly believed he had her tagged and labelled— my beautiful, besotted wife.

She'd turned the tables on him that time. Then she'd done it yet again when she'd tried to leave him for her elusive Frenchman. OK, so this time he had managed to breach the damn citadel of her physical defences, but with Nell he could not afford to let the sex count for anything. He did not trust her, or that strange, glinting look he'd glimpsed in her eyes now and then. The little witch still had her own agenda, he was damn sure of it. She might love what he could make her feel, but did she love him...?

When you've had your fingers burned by complacency not once but twice, unless you are a complete fool you do not take chances on it happening again.

And what was she doing with that piece of driftwood? he questioned suddenly. The way she was caressing it was almost erotic. Was she imagining it was him—or someone else?

Jealousy. Uncertainty. He did not like feeling like this! With a grim clenching of every bone in him he spun away from the window, wondering what the hell he was going to do. He had to go to London. He did not want to take Nell with him. But was she going to accept that?

Not a chance in hell, he thought as he began gathering together papers that littered the top of his desk. Papers that were important to running an empire—yet all he wanted to do was hide away here with his wife!

A black scowl darkened his face as he strode into the hallway. Seeing Nell stashing the piece of driftwood by the open door, he pulled to a stop as he made one of those clean-cut, uncompromising decisions that usually made him feel better about himself.

'We need to talk,' he announced brusquely.

'We do?' Surprise lit her tone as she walked towards him, a sensational, wand-slender, Titian-haired woman wearing a halo of sunlight all around her. 'Well that makes a change,' she drawled teasingly.

He was wearing white, Nell noted. Xander liked to wear white, white, loose, fine muslin shirts that allowed the gorgeously tight, bronzed shape of his body show through, and white linen trousers that fastened with a tie cord low on his lean waist. One tug at the cord and she would reveal the real man, she thought temptingly, felt the hot secretion of desire sting her senses and wished she had more control over herself.

But she didn't and her mouth quirked into a rueful smile that acknowledged her weakness as she came to a halt in front of him and lifted her face for a kiss.

It didn't arrive. She focused her eyes on his hard, handsome face. He was cross, she realised. Her smile died.

'What was the smile for?' he demanded suspiciously.

'Well, it was for you but I've taken it back. What's the scowl for?' she countered.

He made an impatient flick with a long-fingered hand. 'I have to go to London today,' he told her abruptly.

London. Her eyes lit up. 'OK,' she said. 'So you don't have to sound so cross about it. I'll go and pack and we can—'

'No.' Xander used the refusal as if it were a landmine he was setting down in the small space between them. 'You will stay here.'

Nell's chin shot up again, green eyes making full contact with grimly uncompromising brown, then for the space of ten taut seconds she gave no response. Not with her steady gaze or her closed, perfectly formed mouth—or any other part of her, yet some inner body language had to be speaking to him because Xander tensed every muscle he had.

'It's business,' he clipped out as if that justified everything. 'I can be back here in two days. No need for both of us to uproot.'

'Do you want sex before you leave?'

It was not an invitation. In fact it was more like a cold slap in the face. The provocative witch, Xander thought heavily. 'Not if you are going to turn it into a punishment,' he returned drily, then grimaced because he was aware by the tingling of his flesh that he'd take the punishment if it was all that he was going to get.

'Goodbye, then,' she said and abruptly turned about.

She was going to walk away! Shock lanced through him. Didn't she care one way or another if he took her with him or not?

'Nell…' He rasped out her name not sure if it was said in anger or appeal. Then he took a step forward to catch her arm and the explosion erupted. She swung back, green eyes alive now and flashing with rage and biting contempt.

'What do you want from me, Xander?' she lashed out at him. 'Do you expect me to smile happily as I wave you off? Do you think I *like* knowing I'm a prisoner here, that I can only leave this island at your behest?'

'It's for your own safety.' He frowned darkly.

'For your peace of mind, you mean.'

'I have enemies! How do I know that your Frenchman isn't one of them until I locate him so that I can find out?'

'You mean—you're actually looking for him?' Her eyes went wide with shock.

His hooded. 'My people are.' He made yet another terse gesture with a hand. 'Your fate lies in what he has to say for himself.'

But his people hadn't found Marcel yet, Nell surmised from that and could not keep the relief from showing on her face.

Xander saw it. His own face hardened. 'You know where he is!'

She went to turn away again but his grip on her arm spun her back round. Defiance roared through her system. 'Don't manhandle me,' she protested angrily.

'Tell me where he is,' Xander hissed.

'Where's Vanessa?' she retaliated.

'This is not about Vanessa!'

'Well, I'm making it about her!' she flashed. 'Tit for tat, Xander,' she tossed back. 'You tell me all about your mistress and I'll tell you about my—'

'He was never your lover,' he derided before she'd even got the final word out.

But he wasn't denying that Vanessa was his! 'Not physically,' she conceded. 'But emotionally? How would you know if I love him? You wouldn't know about emotional love if it jumped up and bit you!'

The scorn in her voice had him tugging her towards him. Even as she landed hard up against his chest she was registering that something inside him had snapped. With ruthless intent he caught hold of the silken knot holding her hair up and used it to tug her head back then capture her angry mouth.

Titian silk crackled when it tumbled over his fingers as they strained against each other right there in the hall. Thin cotton beachwear was no barrier to hide what was happening to him but Nell was determined she was not going to give in to it. He was equally determined that she would.

A sound somewhere close intruded on the struggle. With an angry growl Xander scooped her up and swung her into his study, kicked the door shut behind them as he strode across the room to drop her on the soft leather sofa then followed her with his weight.

There the struggle continued. She plucked at his skin through his thin clothes with angry fingers, he forged a path with urgent fingers between her thighs.

'Stop it,' she gasped as his touch set her sobbing because she could feel herself responding even though she hated herself for it.

'Why?' he breathed tensely. 'This is not emotional enough? You think I go crazy like this for anyone? You think that you would feel hot and as willing as this for your Frenchman's touch?'

That he did not want an answer showed in the way he crushed her mouth open and plundered its sensitive interior. He was jealous of Marcel. He was doing this from the burning depths of a jealous rage. If she didn't stop him he was going to take her like this with none of the preliminaries then hate himself for it afterwards.

Closing her fingers in his hair, she pulled his head back to free her burning mouth. 'I think I'm pregnant,' she told him shakily, and watched as shock totally froze him, the colour draining out of his face.

In the pin-drop silence that followed neither of them took a single pounding breath, then Nell's mouth gave a vulnerable little quiver and he jackknifed away from her, landing on his feet by the sofa with his back towards her, muscles flexing all over him as he came to terms with what he had just been about to do.

Nothing like a good shock to turn the heat down, Nell thought bitterly and sat up, shaking fingers pulling her sarong back into place.

'Sorry to spoil your farewell,' she heard herself add with the slicing cut of embitterment.

His dark head jerked as if she'd hit him. In many ways Nell wished that she had. She had never felt so shocked and shaken. Without saying a word he just walked from the room.

Nell couldn't move. She thought he'd taught her everything

there was to know about making love but now she knew differently. A soulless slaking of lust that he dared to call emotion had not shown up in his repertoire before.

Nor had it prevented her from almost toppling into its cold, murky, thick depths. She started to shiver she was so cold suddenly, hating herself—despising him.

On the other side of the door Xander had frozen again, eyes closed, face locked into a taut mask of self-contempt. He did not want to believe that he had just done that. He did not want to remember the pained look on her face when she'd said what she said.

Pregnant. He flinched. What had he done here? How had he allowed three weeks of damn near perfection sink as low as this?

Marcel Dubois. The name arrived in his head like a black taunt.

No excuse, he dismissed. No damned excuse for doing what he had. The hand he used to scrape through his hair was trembling. Grimly he made for the stairs with a sudden dire need to wash the shame from his skin.

Nell was just trying to find the strength to stand up when the telephone on Xander's desk began to ring. She thought about ignoring it but something stronger than good sense pulled her like a magnet towards it and had her lifting the receiver off its rest.

When your life shatters, it really shatters, she thought blankly as a soft, slightly husky female voice murmured, 'Xander, darling? Is it all right for us to speak?'

The receiver clattered as it landed back on its rest. Pale as a ghost, Nell turned and walked to the door and out of the room then out of the house.

The piece of driftwood stood where she'd left it. Why she picked it up she hadn't a single clue but she hugged it to her front as she walked around the side of the house and took the path that would take her up the hill.

CHAPTER EIGHT

Two hours later, dressed for his trip to London in tailored black trousers and a crisp white business shirt, Xander gave up trying to locate Nell on foot and decided to take to the air instead. His mouth was tense, his lean face set and severe. He left an anxious-looking Thea standing by the pool, wringing her hands.

'Why did you have to fight with her?' she'd scolded him earlier. 'She's a good girl, Alexander. A trip to London to see her *papa* would not have put you out.'

The 'good girl' part was still cutting into him. The fact that Thea had overheard just enough of their fight to draw her own conclusions did not help his riddling feelings of guilt as the helicopter blades wound up, disturbing the hot morning as he took to the air.

Sat huddled on a rock hidden beneath the deep shade of a tree close to the spot from the one they usually dived from, Nell listened as the helicopter flew overhead.

He was going—leaving her here despite everything. Why she thought he might have a change of mind now he knew her suspicions about the baby she didn't know—but she had thought it.

Her eyes flooded with hot, helpless tears.

Vanessa. She shivered, feeling cold despite the fierce heat of the day. Perhaps his urgent business in London was really urgent Vanessa business. No wonder he'd become so angry when she wanted to go with him. What man wanted a wife along when he was looking forward to enjoying his long-standing mistress?

She hated him for treating her like this. She hated herself for falling so totally under his spell when she had known—

110

known that Vanessa was always there, hovering like the black plague in the background. A sudden husky, tear-thickened laugh broke from her aching throat. Face it, Nell, she told herself. You are the one he hides away like a mistress while Vanessa gets to play the very public wife!

Sweeping around the rocky headland, with deft use of the controls Xander swung the helicopter round to face the island then began to search the tiny cove.

She had to be here somewhere, he told himself grimly. Where the hell else could she go?

Dark glasses shading the brightness of the sun from his eyes, he checked the water first for sight of her but there was no sign of a Titian-haired mermaid swimming alone down there.

Teeth flashing white on a hiss of relief because if she was feeling anywhere near as bad as he was feeling she was in no fit state to swim alone, he switched his attention to the shore. He'd already checked the other side of the island, checked the paths through the trees without a single sighting of her. A viscous curse aimed at himself for introducing her to his boyhood collection of hiding places had led him on a wild-goose chase on foot. From up here it was like looking for a butterfly in a forest. If he did not spot her soon then he was going to panic. He could already feel it clawing at the inner tissues of tension racked across his chest.

What if she had decided to swim? What if she had been crazy enough to strike a direct line right out to sea? He swung the craft around, eyes scanning the glistening blue ocean for a sign of one wilful idiot with a desire to drown herself just to make him feel worse.

Don't be stupid, he then told himself. *Nell* isn't that stupid. And he uttered another curse as he swung the helicopter back to face the island then set it crabbing along the shoreline. She might hate him right now but not enough to risk killing herself—and their unborn child.

Their unborn child. A baby! He was still struggling to come to terms with the shock. His beautiful Helen was going to have his baby and he had never felt so wretched about anything in his entire life!

What had he done? *Why* had he done it? Jealousy was not an emotion he was used to. Women were jealously possessive of him, not the other way round!

Women, he repeated and let out a scornful huff of a laugh. *Woman* in the singular, he corrected. One tough, teasing, exquisite creature that fell apart in his arms on a regular basis yet still protected her bloody Frenchman!

What was he doing out there? Nell wondered as she watched him hover then move and hover again. Then enlightenment dawned. Why it took so long to sink in that he was looking for her she had no idea but, hugging the piece of driftwood to her, she lowered her head over it and squeezed her eyes tight shut and willed him to go away.

As if her wish was his command she heard him move further along the coast and for some totally indefensible reason the tears flooded again. She wouldn't cry—she wouldn't! she told herself forcefully as she listened to the dying whoosh of the rotor blades until only stillness filled the air.

Tomorrow she left here, she decided. She could do it and she knew exactly how. All it required was for her to feign illness and frighten poor Thea Sophia into calling in the air ambulance. She knew it could be done because she'd witnessed it happening when one of the maids had been taken ill suddenly during her first week here. The air ambulance had swooped in with a full complement of medical crew and efficiently carried the maid away.

Once she was away from this island she would disappear as thoroughly as Marcel had apparently done and to hell with Xander. She never wanted to lay eyes on him again.

Then, without warning, the helicopter was back and suddenly so close that her chin scraped the driftwood as her head shot up. By then Xander had inched the machine in so close to the edge of the ledge that for a horrible moment she truly believed he was going to crash!

Leaping to her feet, she ran to the edge on some crazy idea that she could make him stop!

For a hellish kind of moment Xander thought she was going to take to the water. Icy dread bathed his flesh as he looked down at the sea where the ebbing tide had uncovered the razor jutting peaks of some lethal rocks.

'Get back, you fool!' he heard himself bellow at the top of his ragged voice, almost lost control of the helicopter and, by the time he'd wrestled with it and looked back at her, she was already teetering on the edge and caught up in a whirlwind of dry, stinging dust and flying debris, her slender frame cowering as she stared at him in abject horror.

Teeth lashed together, he pushed in closer, herding her backwards step by unsteady step until she was safely back from the edge. Then he stayed there, hovering so dangerously close that if he didn't harness nerves of steel he had a feeling it would be him tumbling to his death.

Shaken, severely shaken when she realised what Xander was doing, Nell began to back away, so terrified for him she took the stinging whip of dust full in the face while she screamed at him to move back!

The whole mad, nerve-slaughtering incident could only have used a few seconds but by the time she saw him begin his retreat she was close to fainting with relief.

Xander kept his jaw locked tight as he swung the machine away. If he could he would land on the damn beach so he could run up there and strangle life out of her for being so stupid, but there were too many overhanging branches covering the narrow crescent of sand to make it a safe place to land.

Biting out a thick curse, he flew back round the island to land by the house. Having settled the machine down, he then just sat there, bathed in sweat and shaking too badly to move. What if she'd jumped? What if the rotor blades' fierce downdraft had toppled her over the edge?

He climbed out of the cockpit. His legs felt hollow as he walked. The sun was hot but his skin wore the chill of stark, mind-blowing fear.

What next? What now…?

He knew what now, he told himself grimly as he set his feet walking in the direction of the pathway that would take him up the hill.

Nell saw the helicopter was safely back on its pad as soon as she crested the peak of the hill and her footsteps stilled. She'd thought Xander had gone. She'd *hoped* he had gone. Now she could see that he hadn't, her instincts were telling her to flee back into the woods and find a new place to hide from him.

Then the man himself appeared, rounding a bend in the path below, sunlight filtering through the trees to dapple his long frame dressed in smooth black trousers and a crisp white business shirt with a slender dark tie knotted at his brown throat. When he saw her he pulled to a stop.

He looked every inch the lean, dark Greek tycoon, Nell thought sinkingly. Hewn from rock, and twice as hard.

Lowering her eyes, she hugged the piece of driftwood even tighter to her chest then took some short, shallow breaths to help her feet to move.

He waited, watching her from behind the shade of his silver-framed sunglasses, the rest of his face caught by a stillness that worried her more than if he'd come charging like a bull up the hill. She'd always known that Xander could be tough, cold, ruthless. She'd always been aware of that streak of danger lurking inside him that was sensible to be wary of. But even on those few occasions when she'd sensed the danger had been threatening to spill over she'd never really expected him to give in to it. Now he had—twice in as many hours. First back at the villa then up there on the rock ledge when he'd driven the helicopter right at her without a care for his own safety.

Now she did not know what to expect from him—didn't want to know. If she possessed the luxury of choice she would not even want to be even this close to him again.

As it was her feet kept her moving down the path until she drew to a halt about six feet away from him. Tension sparked in the sun-dappled silence, and kept her eyes focused on a point to the right of his wide, white-shirted chest.

Xander felt the muscle around his heart tighten when he saw the chalky pallor pasting her cheeks. He knew he'd frightened her with the helicopter manoeuvre. Hell, he'd frightened himself! *She'd* frightened him. Now all he wanted to do was gather her into his arms and just hold her close, but what had come before the fright on the rocky ledge had lost him the right to do that.

'I thought you'd gone.' She spoke first, her voice distant and cool.

'No.' He, on the other hand, sounded raw and husky. 'Are you OK?'

She gave no reply as if the answer spoke for itself. She was not OK. Looking into those carefully lowered, beautiful eyes set in that beautiful face, he thought it was as if a light had gone out. He'd switched it off. Now he didn't know what to do or say that would switch it on again.

Dragging off his sunglasses, he pushed them into his trouser pocket then gripped them in a strangling clinch. 'What's with the piece of driftwood?' he asked out of a need to say something, however inane.

The bewildered way she glanced down at the piece of sun-bleached wood hugged close to her chest, he had a suspicion that she'd forgotten it was there.

'N-nothing,' she mumbled. 'I—like it.'

She liked it…

This was crazy! They'd almost killed each other not ten minutes ago; now here they were, standing halfway up a hill discussing bloody driftwood when they should be—

'Shall we go down?' he suggested on a thick, driven rasp.

She nodded, lowered her eyes all the way to the ground and pushed her feet into movement again. When she drew level with him he fell into step beside her and the tension inside him pounded in his chest as they walked side by side without uttering another damn word.

When they reached the house, Thea was standing anxiously in the doorway.

'Oh, there you are!' She hurried forward to close Nell's pale face between gnarled fingers in a gesture of relief. 'Alexander was so worried when he could not find you. The foolish boy went crazy, upsetting everyone by turning the whole house up-side down and searching the wood before he jumped in his helicopter to look for you from the air.'

The *foolish boy* stood by in grim silence while Nell quietly soothed the old lady's anxious nerves. 'I was walking on the other side of the island,' she said gently.

'This explains why you did not hear us calling to you.' Thea nodded. 'Now you must hurry and change out of those beach clothes or he will grow truly impatient and go without you.'

Nell started frowning. 'Go where?' she asked.

'With Alexander to London, of course!' Thea exclaimed in beaming triumph. She turned to her great-nephew. 'Did you not tell her that you have changed your mind?' Then before he could answer she was hustling Nell inside. 'Come—come. Your case has been packed for you. All you need to do is choose something to wear to travel in, then we…'

Nell was glancing back over her shoulder, a puzzled frown on her face. Xander was saying nothing—nothing, and his grim, dark stance did not encourage questions.

What was going on? Why had he changed his mind? 'Xander—'

'Do as Thea says,' he cut in. 'We must leave in ten minutes if we are to make our air slot out of Athens.'

With that he spun and strode away.

Bewildered and confused, Nell allowed herself to be hurried upstairs. Xander had to have decided to take her with him be-fore he started looking for her but—why?

'You must not get so upset when he lets off the anger, *pethi mou*,' the old lady murmured beside her. 'He loves you. That makes him jealous and possessive. All Pascalis men are the same. He worries that you might meet some other fine young man in London and leave him—as if you would be so cruel…'

Nell felt a blush stain her cheeks at Thea's faith in Nell's loyalty to her great-nephew, because she knew that she could be so cruel—*would* be so cruel if she was given the opportunity.

This marriage was over as far as she was concerned.

The flight to Athens airport was quick and smooth and trouble-free. As they flew across the island before heading towards the mainland, Nell didn't even bother to glance down.

She'd come to love that little island but she would not be coming back to it. And her only regret at leaving it behind was having to leave a tearful Thea behind too.

'You will come and see me soon,' the old lady made her promise. Nell didn't have the heart to say no, never again.

Landing in Athens was like being dropped from heaven into hell. The moment they began the transfer from helicopter to waiting plane, people stopped to stand and stare. Xander didn't seem to notice. Nell had a feeling he didn't see anything beyond his next target, which in this case was his private plane waiting on the tarmac.

With only a few minutes to spare to hit their slot, they boarded the plane and were taxiing towards the runway only moments after they'd strapped themselves into their seats.

And the whole shift from island to plane had been achieved in an empty hollow of perfect silence. It was awful. Neither spoke, neither attempted to, neither looked at the other. Body language did it all for them. Dressed in a razor-sharp business suit, he was grim, tight-lipped and supremely contained within himself.

Nell, on the other hand, had nothing she wanted to say. She was wearing the same clothes she'd travelled to Greece in—mainly because they were hanging in the closet and she hadn't cared what she wore so long as she got back down the stairs within the allotted time. The only difference being that her hair had been left loose because she didn't dare waste time in braiding it in case he left the island without her. As she'd walked out into the sunshine where Xander was waiting for her, he'd taken one look at her from behind those miserable sunglasses, his mouth had compressed then he'd just turned and stridden away.

She'd suffered his help into the helicopter without flinching and kept her gaze fixed directly ahead as he settled himself in his seat. Tension had fizzed all around them throughout the short hop to Athens Airport—making it almost impossible to breathe.

Now they sat surrounded by the kind of luxury travel most people only read about, yet they could have been two strangers on a packed package flight, the way they sat across the aisle from each other, ignoring the other's presence. As soon as the plane levelled out Xander was climbing to his feet. The sunglasses had gone but it made no difference; his long, glossy eyelashes had taken their place and Nell refused to look up at him anyway.

He disappeared into his custom-built office area towards the back of the plane and a smiling Greek stewardess brought Nell refreshment—at Xander's instruction, she presumed, because no one had asked her if she wanted anything.

Still, the freshly brewed tea was like manna from heaven after her having drunk nothing for hours. And she even managed to nibble at the selection of freshly made sandwiches before she gave up and pushed the tray away. After that she spent some time flipping through a couple of magazines without focusing on a single page. Then, in the end, because she felt so utterly dragged down and exhausted by all the emotional stresses, she rested her head back against the seat and went to sleep.

When she eventually opened her eyes again she found Xander standing over her. Her nerve-ends leapt on edge, her defences shooting back into place so violently that what she'd gained by managing to fall asleep was lost in that instant.

A nerve ticked in his jaw as she glanced warily up at him. He quickly flicked his eyes away. 'We will be landing at Heathrow in twenty minutes,' he informed her then strode away, his body language still speaking loud and clear.

The walk through Heathrow was like being placed beneath a microscope. As had happened in Athens, people stopped in their droves and stared. Nell wanted to curl into a tight chrysalis and just—disappear. With a trio of tough-faced bodyguards hustling around them, they must look like one of those celebrity couples you saw splashed across the tabloids. She hated it and kept her eyes lowered and was actually grateful for the protective arm Xander placed around her as he paced beside her like a sleek, prowling cat that wanted to leap off and savage a couple of those staring faces—keeping up appearances, she thought again with a tiny grimace. And wondered curiously why she hadn't been treated to this kind of walk down the concourse when they'd left London for Greece. But didn't ask; neither the man nor the moment nor the throat-clutching pump of her heartbeat encouraged speech.

Rico was waiting outside with the Bentley, its rear door held open wide. She was hustled inside the car's luxury interior, Xander followed, the door shut, silence clattered around them with the same ear-twisting quality of a full string orchestra tuning their instruments.

They sped away with all the smooth efficiency Xander clearly took for granted. Nell would have smiled if she'd had the will to but she didn't. She had never felt as cold and unhappy or as isolated—and that was saying something, she mused as she stared out of the car window.

'Do you actually like living like this?' The words were out before she could stop them.

'I beg your pardon?' That she had surprised him with real speech showed in the huskiness of his voice.

'Like you're a beast living in a zoo,' she enlightened and watched him stiffen. 'Or maybe you're the star in the quintessential TV reality show,' she went on, wishing she'd kept quiet, but unable to stop herself from going on. 'Everything you do, wherever you are in the world, is watched and discussed and pored over. The Press love you. Those people back there love you. Paths appear in thick crowds so you can pass through unhindered while they stand and goggle and gasp.'

She dared to flick a look at him then wished she hadn't. He was sitting like a block of rock, no reaction whatsoever. It infuriated her; she didn't know why but it did.

'Is there a weekly vote on who gets kicked out of your life next?' she prodded recklessly. 'Do big companies fall to a million or two phone calls? Mistresses get dumped—bodyguards that don't fit the tough-guy bill?'

'Shut up, Nell,' he advised very quietly.

She wished she could but she was on a roll here. 'If I don't please the masses, do I get to go too? Vote out the nagging little wife so our wonderful hero does not have to listen to her any more!'

She saw his hands curl into two fists on his lap. 'You are going nowhere, so don't build your hopes up.'

'Because I might be pregnant?' she flashed at him with acid bite. 'Well, that event should boost the ratings. Do we produce your son and heir in front of a blaze of cameras and maybe have your mistress watching from the sidelines just to add a bit of spice?'

The snakelike twist of his body came without warning. For such a big man he struck with stunning, lithe grace. Before she even knew what was happening he had her trapped in the corner of the seat with a hand at her nape and the other clamped across her reckless mouth.

'Now listen…' he hissed out in thin warning.

Nell stared at him over the top of his clamping hand—really stared, and for the first time took in his pallor, the tension cutting deep grooves around his wide, sensual mouth. But it was his eyes that held her, eyes like black crystal that pierced her so sharply they hurt.

'I give you the right to mock me and my lifestyle,' he bit out tautly. 'I will even admit that I probably deserve to feel the acid whip of your tongue. But you will not mock yourself in the same manner and you will *not* degrade our unborn child!'

Is that what she'd done? Oh, yes, that was what she had done, Nell acknowledged. Her lips trembled beneath his hand.

'And don't cry,' he added on a driven mutter. 'I have enough torment to contend with without you adding your tears!'

Her breasts heaved on a tightly suppressed and tremulous shudder. Some of that torment he'd admitted to flashed across his eyes. He bit out a couple of thick foreign curses then, with the same unpredicted lithe movement, let go of her and snaked back into his own seat.

'You have no idea what you do to me,' he said then in rough-toned fury while Nell just sat there and trembled. 'You have no idea of your own damn power to draw breathless gasps from the masses!'

Shocked by that, she blinked at him in bewilderment. Turning his dark head, he caught the surprised blink and his lean face hardened into cynicism.

'You have the wild, waving hair of a fantasy mermaid, the face of an angel and the body of a natural sensualist!' he ripped out as if in contempt. 'Your sensational legs are so slender and long there isn't a man alive that would not have hot dreams about them wrapped around him. Other women look at you and *wish* they possessed a small fraction of what you've got! *I* wish I'd never set eyes on you, then I would not be sitting here feeling hard and hot and bloody frustratingly impotent to do anything about it!'

'Trust you to drag it all down to your lower-body level,' Nell responded, too shaken by what he'd thrown at her to care that her voice quivered with the onset of fresh tears. '*I* wish you'd never set eyes on me too, then I would not have spent the last year being shipped from one luxury prison to another by a money-motivated brute with sex on the brain!'

'So what would you rather have been doing?' he questioned curiously.

'Getting on with my life!'

'Life with the Frenchman perhaps?'

Turning a tight-lipped profile to him, she refused to answer. Let him think what he liked about Marcel, she thought mutinously—especially if it annoyed the hell out of him!

'Tell me, Nell, because I'm genuinely curious. Did the elusive pimpernel have the fifty million to bail your father out?'

'Marcel is not motivated by money,' she stated haughtily.

'Ah, so he's dirt poor with a sensitive heart but no balls,' he said crudely.

Nell flashed him a disgusted look. 'You know nothing about him so don't pretend that you do.'

'Are you so sure about that?'

'Yes!' she insisted. 'Or you would have had him beaten up by your mob and be throwing it at me by now.'

'Clever girl,' he drawled.

'Shut up.' She hated him.

'Are you going to tell me where he is?' he persisted.

'You must be joking,' she scoffed.

'No,' he denied. 'In fact I have never been more serious. Where is he, Nell?' he repeated levelly. 'And before you answer me with some whipping comment I think I should warn you that your freedom will continue to be restricted until you do tell me…'

Nell sizzled on a seething breath of air. 'I wish I'd never married you.'

'As if your choices were crowding at your father's begging door,' he mocked. 'As far as I am aware, it was either me or some short, ugly guy in his forties with fat lips and three pairs of hands.'

Stung, she flicked him a sharp glance. 'What's that supposed to mean?'

'Nothing—forget I said it.' Frowning, he leant forward to press a button, which brought a miniature drinks bar shooting out of the car's central bulkhead.

Feeling a bit as though she was about to be slaughtered where she sat, Nell watched him select a bottle of whisky then pour himself a measure into a squat crystal glass. He relaxed back into the seat, downing some of the whisky as he went, his lean face turned to stone again with just the merest hint of self-contempt.

Nell's upper lip trembled as she parted it from her stiff lower lip. 'Xander, y-you—'

'Don't ask,' he clipped out.

But it was too late. He had not pulled that nasty remark out of a bag at random just to get at her. There had been hard meaning behind every deriding word.

'I n-need to know what you meant.'

'You married me, therefore it meant nothing.' He stared grimly into his glass.

'Tell me!' she cried.

A burning blast of annoyance racked his face. 'Your father had overstretched his resources. He was sinking very fast. He needed bailing out but there are not many people out there with fifty million pounds sterling to spare on a very bad risk. I was one such person willing to take the risk—for a price.'

Julian Garrett's daughter and his risky investment protected as much as it could be with the production of a son and heir from the union who would claim the daughter's inheritance!

'You already know all of this, so why drag it all out again?' Xander flicked harshly into the strumming tension holding Nell pale and still.

Because he was still missing out one vital detail—the man with the fat lips. The weekend before Xander came to stay at her father's house, Clive Benson had come to stay—short, overweight, constantly smiling. At first she'd suffered his over-friendly attitude towards her out of good manners and because she thought he was just doing it in a fatherly way—until he'd become just a bit too friendly, and dared to touch her thigh. She'd taken refuge by spending as much time as she could outside with the dogs, aware that her father had some heavy business going with the man—aware that she could not afford to offend.

'You're trying to imply that my father put me up for auction,' she whispered.

'You will please make note that I am trying hard *not* to say those ugly words, *agape mou*,' he returned.

But they were there—they were there!

'My father wouldn't do such a h-horrible thing to me.'

Silence. All Xander did was toss the rest of his whisky to the back of his throat. Nell felt the churning surge of nausea in her stomach.

'I w-wouldn't have Clive Benson touch me w-with a barge-pole.'

'I am so relieved that I did not encourage such feelings of objection,' Xander drawled. 'But take a moment to consider what you would have done if I had not offered a rescue package. Without me or—someone else to bail him out, your father's company, his employees and countless other subsidiaries would have gone under and sunk without a trace. He would have been in debt to his eye-teeth. His bullish pride would have been shattered. His home would have gone and his beautiful daughter would have found herself tossed out on the street. Suddenly wealthy men like Clive Benson don't look so bad, hmm?'

'Stop the car,' Nell breathed thickly.

He looked utterly incredulous. 'We are travelling on the motorway!' he laughed, then he saw her milky pallor and his voice roughened. 'For goodness' sake, Nell, it's too late for you to run away from—'

'Stop the car!' she all but shrieked at him just before her hand jerked up to cover her mouth.

To give him his due, when he realised what was about to happen he moved like lightning, wrenching forward to snatch up the internal telephone and snapping out the order to Rico. Nell all but fell out of the car, staggering on wobbly legs across the hard shoulder of the motorway before she was thoroughly and violently sick onto the grass verge.

The arms that came to take her weight and keep her hair back at the same time were a godsend. She didn't even care that he had to stand there watching her bring up the full contents of her heaving stomach. She'd never felt so wretched—or so distressed. Everything he'd said and *not* said was pulsing and throbbing inside her.

When it was over she folded at the knees. In grim silence

Xander picked her up and resettled her on the back seat of the Bentley with her feet still out on the tarmac. He began snapping out orders while Nell desperately wanted to gulp in some deep lungfuls of fresh air but didn't dare do it in case she set the nausea off again. She was shaking like crazy. Even when Xander squatted down in front of her and gently urged her to sip the cool water that had appeared from nowhere, she still couldn't stop shaking like a leaf.

'My bag,' she managed to push out thickly.

He didn't question the request, just reached inside and found her bag where she'd placed it on the car floor and silently laid it on her lap. Her trembling fingers fumbled with the catch as she tried to open it. She could *feel* Xander wanting to take it and do the clasp for her but he didn't give in to the urge. Maybe he knew that even a small thing like that was going to tip this awful situation right over the edge.

The clasp sprang open; fingers scrambling inside, she found the little plastic envelope of damp freshen-ups she always carried, and managed to peel one away from the rest. Her hair was hanging all over her face and she was glad to have it hide the ravages she knew were there. I will never look at him again, she vowed sickly as she used the damp tissue to wipe her face, then she took the cool glass of water from him and began sipping sparingly while he continued to squat there with his hands clenched in fists between his spread thighs.

'OK?' he questioned her huskily after a few more minutes.

She nodded, offering the glass back to him, but didn't attempt to lift her head. Other things began to impinge on her consciousness, like the sound of other cars roaring past them on the motorway and the other car pulled up bumper to bumper with theirs. The three tough bodyguards had positioned themselves at a discreet but protective distance around the car.

She couldn't even be spared the dignity of privacy while she was sick.

'Nell, I'm sorry. I didn't say all of that to—' One of his hands was lifting towards her.

'Don't touch me.' She withdrew from him like a tortoise retracting into its shell.

Swivelling her legs into the car, she just sat motionless while he remained squatting there, the pull on the air so taut it felt as if it could wrench her in two.

He stayed like that for a few more seconds then rose to his full height. The car door closed, Nell used the few seconds it took him to stride around the car to comb her hair away from her face with trembling fingers. He arrived in the seat beside her, Nell turned her face to the side-window. The bodyguards dispersed. Car engines fired and the journey towards London continued in perfect—perfect—silence.

She must have dozed off, though she didn't remember doing it, but the next thing she knew the car had pulled to a stop outside a row of London townhouses sporting polished brass plates on the walls by the doors.

'Where are we?' she questioned. But Xander was already climbing out of the car. By the time he opened her door for her then stood there in grim silence waiting for her to get out, Nell had worked out exactly where they were.

'I don't need a doctor,' she protested.

The hand that took a grip on her arm said everything as he all but lifted her with it out of the car. He walked her up the steps and in through a doorway, where she glimpsed the word 'Gynaecologist' on one of the plaques with a sinking heart.

'It's too soon to consult anyone about...'

Half an hour later, with her grim-faced companion's hand like an electric charge to the hollow of her back, she was walking out again feeling washed-out and wasted and close to tears.

It was confirmed. She was pregnant. About three weeks along, at a considered guess. Potent didn't even cover it. He'd managed to achieve his goal at first try, knowing him, she thought bitterly.

'Mission accomplished,' she said in a voice that dripped ice, then stepped away from that proprietary hand and walked alone to the waiting car.

CHAPTER NINE

XANDER sat beside her as the car swept them onwards and wished to hell that he knew what to do to break this bloody grip guilt had on his conscience. In one short day he had managed to obliterate three weeks of total heaven.

He didn't want to feel like this!

He didn't want to look at her only to see that pained expression she'd worn on her pale face when the doctor had confirmed her pregnancy. He'd seen the same expression once already today when she'd been forced to tell him her suspicions about their baby because she knew it was the only way she would have stopped him taking her like a rutting beast!

In a zoo.

Theos. She had never spoken a truer word to him. How do you approach a woman who saw you like that?

How did you look her in the face when you'd just bludgeoned her with the ugly truth about her father?

You don't, came the tough but true answer. You back right off if you have a drop left of civilised blood. You put your stupid, juvenile burn of jealousy over the bloody Frenchman back under wraps, then take up the happy task of slowly and painfully trying to rebuild trust.

He turned his face to the side-window. Everything inside him felt as if it was carved in stone. One minute more of this God-awful silence and he was going to explode!

Relief arrived when he saw the front of his super-modern smoked-glass office building loom up beside the car. Rico got out and opened his door for him. Xander climbed out then moved round the car with the *civilised* intention of assisting Nell to alight, but she did that on her own.

He said nothing, took her arm, she flinched then settled. In

127

a strained way he thanked her for that, and kept his own flinching contained inside. As they walked together through the smoked-glass doors into the vaulted foyer he saw the zoo analogy come up and hit him in the face like a bloody great tank.

Glass everywhere, cold tungsten steel. People—*employees*, for God's sake—stopping what they should be doing to turn and stare. He felt Nell quiver, his fingers twitched on her slender arm. Behind his grim lips his teeth were biting together so tightly they hurt as he walked her across the foyer and into the executive lift. The doors closed. They were transported upwards with ultimate speed. She stared at the floor, he stared at the wall half an inch to the side of her head.

And the hell of it was that he was willing her to look at him, *willing* her to make that slow, sensual journey up from his polished shoes to his face.

It didn't happen. He'd never felt so bloody bereft.

The doors swished open. Nell had to steel herself to accept the return of his hand on her arm. Inherent Greek manners demanded that he hold her like this but she wished he were walking ten feet away.

She had never been inside this building before, definitely never been up here in his spacious and plush executive domain. More glass and steel met her gaze, interspersed now with panels of rich walnut and yet more curious faces that kept her eyes glued to her shoes.

The murmured greetings delivered with respect echoed the length of the long walk down the corridor. Xander said nothing. He was like a mechanical machine delivering a package.

Then his hand moved from her arm to the centre of her back as he leant forward to open a pair of huge walnut doors. She felt his fingers slide into the weight of her hair and for a moment—a brief, sense-grabbing moment—his fingertips curled then straightened on a sharply compulsive sensual stroke.

Her breathing froze. She looked up at him. She hadn't wanted to do it but now it was too late and he was looking down. Everything stopped—*everything*! The door, only half pushed out of its housing, the sea of faces they'd left in their wake. He stood at least six inches taller than her and she wished—wished—*wished* she hated that handsome dark face!

Her eyes began to blur with stupid tears, her mouth started to quiver.

'Nell, don't,' he murmured thickly then turned like a whip on the sea of faces. 'Have you nothing better to do than to watch me make love to my wife?'

Shocked by the sudden outburst, Nell drew in a sharp breath. Muffled sounds erupted behind them. Xander bit out a curse then pushed the door wide and propelled her inside.

She found herself standing in a huge walnut-panelled office with a wall of glass, a steel-legged desk and a vast expanse of polished floor. The door shut with a controlled thud. As soon as it happened Nell spun around.

'What made you shout that out?' she demanded shrilly.

'Even zoo animals get sick of being stared at,' he rasped.

He had a grip on her hand now and was trailing her behind him across the room towards another set of double doors while, in a near-dizzy state of too many shocks in a single day, Nell found herself struggling with pangs of remorse.

'Look, I'm sorry I said that,' she said stiffly.

'It was only the truth. I do live in a zoo.'

A telephone started ringing somewhere. In a state of complete disorientation, Nell found herself being trailed in a different direction, towards the desk, where whole rows of paperwork stood lined up in thick, neat stacks. In amongst the stacks was the ringing telephone. Xander hooked it up with his free hand and began a clipped conversation in Greek.

She tried to slip her hand free but he refused to let go of it. The moment he replaced the receiver it started ringing again. Keeping her firmly anchored to him, Xander embarked on a series of conversations as one call led to another then another.

As one call stopped and before another started, Nell drew in a deep breath. 'Look, you're busy. And I need...' to lie down, she had been going to say but changed her mind because lying down meant a bed, and she didn't want to think about beds. 'If you'll let me use the limo, I'll go down to Rose—'

'You stay with me.' It was not up for argument. 'We are not—'

The phone shrilled out its demand for his attention. On a growl of annoyance Xander snatched it up. 'Hold the calls until I say otherwise!' he instructed, the bark of his voice rattling the windows.

Nell winced. 'I *hate* bullies.'

'Tough.' She was being trailed across the floor again. 'The vote's still out on your fate, so you stay.'

It took Nell a few seconds to get his meaning. 'Will you stop throwing my words back in my face?'

By then he'd taken them through that other pair of doors and her attention was seized, because this was no office but some kind of beautiful sitting room decorated and furnished to Xander's impeccable high standards and luxurious good taste.

'What is this place?' she asked curiously.

'My apartment.'

'You mean *this* is your City place?' She sounded so surprised that he sent her a wry look.

'What did you expect—some purple and red velvet-lined pad in atmospheric Soho specifically designed for bedding my women?'

The bedding-of-his-women bit brought the lovely Vanessa right into full focus. Instantly her face turned to paste.

He saw it and bit out a sigh. 'When I'm in town I work, I crash out here, I work,' he enunciated abruptly. 'I also keep a place in the country but have never got to sleep there yet.'

His sarcasm was really on a roll, Nell noted heavily, and was suddenly fighting yet another battle with tears... The next thing she knew she was being engulfed by a pair of arms, her face pressed to his chest.

'Idiot...'

The husky tone of his voice rumbled right through her. She wasn't sure who was the idiot, her or him, but she did know she wanted to be right where she was right now, and that had to make her a complete idiot.

The small haven of comfort didn't last long though. 'Come on,' he said gruffly, and turned her beneath the crook of his arm to guide her through yet another set of doors into a— bedroom with a huge, smooth coffee and cream covered bed on which he urged her to sit down on the edge.

'Now listen,' he said, coming to squat down in front of her. 'It's been a hell of a day and you're exhausted. The wise doctor advised rest so you will obey him and rest—alone *agape mou*,' he added severely at the protest he'd already predicted was about to shoot from her lips. 'I have work to do, consisting of a mountain of paperwork to plough through before I chair a meeting in…' glancing at his watch '…less than an hour.' Grimacing, he sprang lithely to his feet. 'There is a bathroom through that door,' he indicated. 'And a kitchen adjoining the other room if you feel the need for sustenance…'

He was already over at the window and drawing the curtains, so disgustingly invigorated by the prospect of work, while all Nell wanted to do was crawl into this bed and sleep.

'If you need me for anything,' he said as he walked back to her, 'there is a telephone in every room. All you have to do is hit the one button and you will reach me. OK?'

Locating the telephone on the bedside cabinet, Nell looked at it wistfully. 'Can I ring out on it?'

'No, you cannot!' He was suddenly in front of her and taking her shoulders to pull her upright. 'Now, listen, you aggravating bundle of controversy. I am in no mood to fight with you any more today, but if you attempt to contact your ex-lover I'll fight hard and dirty—got that?' He gave her a gentle shake.

'Yes,' she said.

He let go of her with an impatient hiss. 'Go to bed, get some rest and stop wishing for miracles.'

With that he strode out of the room with his dark head held high and his wide shoulders straight, leaving Nell wilting wearily back onto the bed.

Less than ten minutes later, stripped to her underwear, she crawled between the cool Egyptian cotton sheets. Feeling utterly bulldozed, she simply closed her eyes and dropped into sleep.

Pregnant, was her last memorable thought. I really am pregnant...

Pregnant, Xander was thinking as he stood in the doorway, following the streaming cascade of Titian hair spread out on the pillow until his gaze settled on her pale, pinched, sleeping face.

Was he pleased?

Hell, he didn't know. He wanted to be pleased. He wanted to shout it from the rooftops. But when he looked upon the face of this—impossible woman, he had a sinking suspicion that the cost he was going to pay for the pleasure of impregnating her was going to be much too high.

Smothering a sigh, he eased himself away from the doorframe and stepped back into the sitting room, pulling the door quietly shut.

Time to stop playing the lovelorn idiot, he told himself, and time to play the hard-hitting, go-getting business tycoon.

A role he was much more familiar with. A role he wished he felt an ounce of enthusiasm for right now but he didn't, which did not go down with his proud Greek ego very well.

Greek tycoon slain by a Titian-haired witch, he mentally wrote his own tabloid headline. Grimaced then braced his shoulders and went into his office, firmly closing that door behind him too.

Nell came drifting awake to the sound of rattling crockery. It reminded her so much of Thea Sophia that she lay there in smiling contentment, imagining herself to be on the island—until a lazy voice said, 'I hope that smile means you're dreaming about me.'

She opened her eyes to find Xander standing over her, looking lean and mean in his sharp business suit, and reality came crashing in. 'Oh,' she said. 'We're in London, aren't we?'

Yawned and stretched then looked back at him. 'What time is it?'

'Refreshment time,' he said lightly, turning away then turning back again with a tray in his hands.

Nell slithered up the pillows, dragged the sheet up to cover her breasts then yawned again, rubbed her eyes then swept her tumbled hair back from her face.

'Didn't know you did Room Service,' she quipped as a tray arrived across her lap.

'Anything for you, my love,' he responded in the same light vein as he sat down on the bed and removed the cover from a plate of fluffy scrambled eggs piled on a bed of hot toast.

Nell glanced at the half-light seeping through the drawn curtains. 'Is it morning already?' she asked in surprise.

Xander smiled. 'Not quite.' He handed her a glass of freshly squeezed orange juice. 'You've been asleep for hours while I've been chairing the meeting from hell. If the world were flat I would be taking great pleasure in pushing one half of a room of ten off the end of it. Is that OK?' he added questioningly as she sipped at the juice.

Nell nodded. 'Lovely.'

He sent her another smile then forked up some scrambled egg. 'Here, try this and tell me what you think.'

'It's only scrambled eggs,' she derided as she took the forkful into her mouth.

'Yes, but very special scrambled eggs, since they were prepared by my own gifted hands.'

'You?' Nell almost choked. 'I didn't think you knew what an egg looked like in its shell.'

'Shame on you.' He forked up another heap. 'I am very self-proficient when I have to be. Drink some more juice.'

Nell frowned. 'Why did you feel the need to be proficient at this particular moment?'

'Because I decided to leave the ten squabbling in my boardroom and came in here to see you. You were out for the count. I noticed that you must not have woken up to get yourself something to eat and, since you haven't had anything since you threw up on the motorway, I decided that it was time that you did. You can go back to sleep when you've eaten this...'

Another forkful was offered to her. Nell looked at his smooth, lean, totally implacable, super-relaxed face, said nothing and took the fork from him so that she could feed herself. For several minutes neither spoke while Nell ate and he seemed content to watch.

Then it came, the real reason he was sitting there looking at her like that. 'Nell—what I said about your father—'

'Is he still in Australia?'

'Yes,' he frowned. 'You knew he'd committed himself to overseeing the whole project,' he reminded her.

'Yes.' Her sigh was wistful and rather sad.

'I want you to know that I gave you the wrong impression about your father's involvement in our—'

'Oh, I don't think so,' she said as she laid down the fork. 'I think you made your point perfectly. You took me as assurance for your investment. We even have a contract that says so. You also saved me from a fate worse than death.'

A frown pulled his eyebrows together across the bridge of his nose. 'I'll rip the contract up if it will make you feel better.'

'It's so sweet of you to offer,' she mocked him. 'But the gesture would only have some weight behind it if you'd offered to do that *before* I got pregnant.'

'I did offer once before, if you recall.'

'On my birthday?' She looked up at him. 'Before my father had managed to scoop the Australian deal and put his business back on track? Bad timing, Xander,' she said. '*Not* what you're renowned for. You could have been asking to renegotiate yourself right out of the whole deal for all I knew. Still know,' she added when he opened his mouth to deny it.

The fact that he was going to have to pull rabbits out of the proverbial hat to make her believe otherwise now held him silent while he took that on board.

Nell hunted around for something trite to say to fill in the gap.

But what came out was miles away from trite. 'There,' she said. 'Plate cleaned. Baby adequately fed.'

'I did it for you, not the baby!' he snapped.

That she didn't believe him showed. He uttered a sigh, his indulgent manner disappearing without a trace. 'Does it actually matter what motivated me?' he posed curtly. 'Am I not allowed to be concerned for you both?'

He glanced at his watch then and stood up to remove the tray. 'I have a meeting to return to. I'll see you later.'

With that punishing slice of ice, he left. Nell threw herself back against the pillows and wished she knew how she should feel about him, but she didn't. Everything she had come to love and trust about him over the last three weeks had been shattered by a day-long series of hard knocks.

The telephone call from Vanessa being the hardest knock.

Restless now, she got up, feeling an instant chill on her skin because of the difference between a hot Greek summer and a cooler English one. Rubbing at her bare arms, she wandered around the bedroom, aimlessly picking things up, putting them down again, and would have gone and done the same in the sitting room but she couldn't be absolutely sure that someone might not come in from the office and catch her half-naked, and Xander seemed to have forgotten to have her suitcase brought up.

In the end she escaped to the bathroom and decided to indulge in a long, hot soak in the invitingly huge bath. A few carefully placed candles would have been nice to help her relax, but she had to make do with selecting a couple of soft downlighters. She found no sign of any female soapy things hanging around, which mollified her restless mood somewhat.

So Xander didn't indulge his women here, she mused as she lay submerged in hot, steamy water liberally laced with Xander-scented bath oil. Maybe he did have a purple and red velvet-lined pad in Soho. With a mirrored bed and flying cupids embroidered on the velvet, she extended with a soft laugh.

'Cheered up at last?'

'Oh!' She flicked her eyes open to find him casually propping up the doorframe. Sheer surprise had her slithering into a sitting position, causing a minor tidal wave to slosh around the bath. 'You were quick,' she said disconcertedly.

'I didn't like the company,' he drawled, dark eyes glossed by silky eyelashes as he looked her over from loose topknot to water-slicked breasts being caressed by steam.

It was stupid to feel shy after spending three weeks mostly naked around him, but telling herself that did not stop the blush from mounting her skin. Nell tried to make it look casual when she drew her knees up and looped her arms around them. The action did not change that look she knew so well on his lean, dark face.

He'd lost his jacket and his tie, she noticed. His shirt collar was undone and the shirt cuffs too. And if ever a man knew how to lounge sexily in a doorway then Xander had the pose down to a finely tuned art. Long legs relaxed, hands loosely looped in his trouser pockets, silk dark hair finger-ruffled just enough to add that extra brooding appeal.

Her body responded, breasts growing heavy, nipples peaking where she crushed them against her thighs. Even her lips felt as if they were filling and pulsing.

'You forgot my suitcase.' To Nell, it was an inspired stab at the prosaic.

It didn't alter his hungry look one iota. 'Stashed in the sitting room five minutes after we arrived,' he said. 'Didn't you bother to look?'

'No.' She added a grimace. 'Maybe you could get it for me?'

'Why?'

'So I can put something clean on?' she suggested ever so sarcastically to what she thought a stupid question to ask.

Xander clearly didn't. He straightened up and began approaching the bath. 'You can wear me instead,' he murmured huskily and began to undo the rest of the buttons on his shirt.

'Don't you dare try to get in here!' she cried, causing a floor-sloshing wave as she shifted up the bath. 'I'm still angry with you! I don't even like you any more! I will *not* be your sex slave just because you need—'

'Watch it...' His hand darted out, capturing her hair just before it tumbled out of the topknot into the bath.

Shaken by panic, utter confusion and a rotten desire to finish the job with his shirt, she glared at his hair-roughened breast-plate while he re-knotted her hair with an infuriating finesse.

'There,' he said. 'Now you won't have to spend half an hour drying it before we get to bed.'

'I'm not sleeping with you ever again.'

'Did I mention sleep?'

Nell tried to calculate if she had enough room to make a run for it while he was busy stripping off his clothes.

'Not a cat in hell's chance,' he teethed out, reading her like an open book.

Stark, blinding, beautiful naked, he stepped into the bath.

'We are not going to let this war continue,' he informed her as he came down on his knees to straddle her. 'You are my wife and you are having my baby.' His hands took possession of her warm, wet, slippery breasts with their tightly distended, lush pink nipples. 'As these beautiful things tell me you want me, *agape*, and as I am so majestically displaying I most certainly want you, why fight it?'

Why indeed? Nell thought helplessly as she, like a captured rabbit, watched him lower his head. It was like being over-whelmed by Poseidon again she likened helplessly as he took charge of her mouth, her body and the rest.

A few minutes later and she was slithering beneath him into the water with her arms clinging to his neck. They'd made love in a bath many times but for some reason this hot and steamy, oil-slicked occasion that was permeated with his scent tapped into another dimension. Water sloshed as they touched and ca-ressed each other, she was so receptive to everything about him that she found she didn't care if her face sank beneath the surface and she drowned like this.

His arms stopped it from happening. The way he was smoothing small, soft, tender kisses over her face kept her breathing slow and deep. His eyes kept capturing hers and fill-ing her with dark liquid promise, when he slipped a hand between her thighs she arched her body in pleasure and captured his mouth.

They kissed long and deep, they moved against each other slowly and sensuously. When with a lithe grace he changed his position, stretching out above her and murmured huskily, 'Open your legs,' she even made the move with a slow erotic invitation that set him trembling as she clasped his face in her hands so she could pull his mouth back to hers as he entered her with a long, smooth, silken thrust.

And the whole thing continued to a slow, deep, pulsing rhythm. His supporting arms stopped her from drowning in the water, while inside she drowned in a different way. When she fell apart she even did this slowly and deeply and the pulses of pleasure just went on and on and on.

When he lifted her out of the bath she clung to him weakly. Even when he dried them both she didn't let go. She was lost, existing in a place without bones or muscles; the only solid thing was him and the thickly pumping beat of his heart beneath her resting cheek.

'If you *ever* let another man see you like this you won't live,' he rasped out suddenly.

Nell just smiled and pressed a silky kiss to his hair-roughened, satin-tight chest. 'Take me to bed,' she breathed.

With a muffled groan Xander lifted her up and carried her into the bedroom, still clinging. She was still clinging when he settled them both in the bed. She fell asleep like that—clinging. Xander lay beside her wondering how long he should wait before he woke her up again.

He used up the time recalling the looks on the faces of the ten men in his boardroom when only half an hour after battle recommenced he'd stood up and brought the whole thing to an abrupt end.

'When you are ready to negotiate like adults let me know. Until then this meeting is over.' He smiled as he saw himself making that announcement because—there he was, being the hard-hitting, cool-headed, totally focused, ruthless dictator. Wouldn't they like to know that beneath the incisive veneer he'd brought that meeting to a close because he'd been aching so badly for this...

His wife. This sensational woman with a silken thigh lying across his legs and her slender arms still looped around his neck. On a sigh because he knew he should not give in yet, he reached up to claim one of her hands then carried it down his body to close it gently around the steel-hard jut of his sex.

'You're insatiable,' she murmured, letting him know that she was already awake.

'For you,' he agreed. She stroked him gently and the whole deep, drugging experience began all over again.

Afterwards he went off to raid the fridge and came back with a bottle of champagne and two glasses, one of which he handed to Nell—already filled.

'What's this?' she demanded, frowning into the glass when it became obvious it wasn't champagne because he was only now easing the cork from the bottle.

'Sparkling water,' he supplied. 'Pregnant women don't drink alcohol.'

'What would you know?' she protested.

About to take a sip at the water, since it was all that was on offer, she found her eyes pinned instead to the way he'd suddenly turned into a concrete block. The lean face, the black eyes—nothing moved.

'What have I said?' she gasped in surprise.

'I just remembered something I needed to do.' He seemed to need to give himself a mental shake before he could bring himself to pour out his champagne. 'Here,' stretching out beside her, he offered his glass up to her lips, 'a sip can't hurt, and a baby is something to celebrate...'

The odd little moment slid by.

Maybe she shouldn't have let it. Maybe Nell should have listened to the little voice inside her head that told her he was hiding something. If she had done then what happened the next morning would not have come as such a crushing blow.

Xander was already in his office and working at his desk by the time Nell sauntered out of the bathroom wrapped in a fluffy white towel. She was aching a little because Xander had been so unquenchable last night. Gentle though, she recalled with a soft smile, unbelievably gentle, as if his knowing about the baby had brought out in him a whole new level of tenderness.

Her inner muscles quivered, her expression taking on a far-away look as she allowed herself the luxury of reliving some of those long, deep, drugging kisses they'd shared, the fine tremor of his body and the look in his dark eyes just before he'd allowed her to take him inside.

If that look didn't speak of love then she'd been dreaming it, she thought as she went over to her suitcase, which Xander had thoughtfully placed open on a low cabinet by the window.

There again it could be just that, having forced herself to accept that since she did not have the power to resist him she might as well stop trying to fight him, maybe she was justifying that by misreading the look.

Oh, shut up, she told that cynical side of her nature. Do you want to spoil it? They were man and wife in every which way you wanted to look at it now that they'd conceived a baby between them, which in turn meant that they were now so deeply committed to this marriage that the Vanessas of this world could take a hike, because no other woman would ever have what Nell now had of Xander.

His first child growing inside her. A child that Xander had spent the rest of the night protecting with the gentle spread of his hand. Did it matter if this had all started out three weeks ago with him determined to achieve that goal?

At least she did not disappoint, she mocked with a grimace. And turned her attention to sifting through the clothes one of the maids on the island had packed for her. One day, she thought ruefully, she might get to pack her own suitcase; then she might find something she wanted to wear.

They'd awoken to a cold, grey day this morning. Even with the temperature in here maintained by an air-conditioning system with climate control, her skin was wearing a distinct chill. The suitcase contained a choice of lightweight short white cotton skirts and a couple of white strapless tops or the turquoise dress.

On a sigh she selected some underwear, dropped the towel and slipped into bra and panties followed by the turquoise dress, then looked around her for something to cover her chilly shoulders and goose-pimpled arms. The suit she had travelled here in lay across the back of a bedside chair but the thought of putting on the travel-limp jacket did not appeal.

On impulse she walked over to the wide walnut-faced wardrobe and opened the doors. Xander's clothes hung in clear plastic from their hangers. Business suits, dinner suits, shirts, ties. Nothing there she could borrow that would keep her warm, she thought ruefully and flipped her search towards the column of deep drawers built into the wardrobe. She found socks, men's undershorts, even a neatly stacked drawer of plain white T-shirts. A foray into the final drawer offered up a better prospect of neatly folded sweaters made out of the finest cashmere. It was probably going to drown her but as she dipped down to near the bottom of the pile to remove a black one she'd spied there, she decided that beggars couldn't be choosers and at least she would be adequately covered.

Then her fingertips came up against the sharp corners of something. On a softly yelped, 'Ouch!' she withdrew her fingers, checked she hadn't managed to draw blood, then frowningly began carefully lifting out the sweaters layer by layer until she'd uncovered the guilty object.

After that she seemed to lose touch with reality. The stack of soft sweaters she held in the crook of her arm fell unnoticed to the floor. She didn't even attempt to pick up the silver-framed photograph she'd uncovered but just stared into Vanessa's beautiful smiling face then at the miniature-sized version of Xander standing laughing in front of her then finally—most painfully—she read the hand-scrawled inscription. 'To Papa Xander,' it said. 'Love from your Alex.'

His son even had his name...

CHAPTER TEN

GLANCING up as Luke Morell stepped into the office carrying a manila file, Xander took one look at his PA's sober expression and sat back in his seat with a smile.

'Did you have to mop blood up off the floor last night after I left?' he quizzed drily.

'You know as well as I do that your shock tactic sent all ten into freefall.'

'Good. Let us hope they learned what it feels like to lose their only parachute.'

Managing a small grimace at the quickness of his employer's wit, 'They want another meeting today,' Luke informed him. 'Perhaps you could try to be a little more—tolerant?'

'For what purpose?' Xander asked. 'I am not into salving other people's egos.' Losing all hint of his own smile, he sat forward again. 'They would not want to meet with me at all if they had done their own jobs better so don't ask me to feel sorry for them. What's with the folder?' he prompted. 'Yet another set of impossible proposals from them?'

'This has nothing to do with the takeover.' Luke walked towards him, his grim expression more keenly in place. 'I suppose I should add that you are not going to like this, so I suggest you take a deep breath before you take a look inside.'

Curiosity piqued, Xander was about to accept the file when a quiet knock sounded at the door through to his private apartment. As he was about to flick his attention from the file to the door he saw Luke stiffen jerkily and his eyes narrowed and remained riveted where they were. He didn't like that telling bit of body language. He didn't like the way his assistant's face had closed up tight. A sudden warning prickle shot across the back of his neck, the kind his instincts had taught him never to ignore.

Then the door-handle began to turn and he was forced to shift his attention to Nell as she stepped into the room. He frowned when he saw that she was wearing the blue suit she had travelled in yesterday, and her hair had been contained in that braid he didn't like. But it was her face that held him. She wasn't smiling, her vulnerably kissable upper lip stuck in a downward curve to its fuller lush partner, and even the light layer of make-up she was wearing could not disguise her odd pallor beneath.

'What's wrong?' he asked instantly, springing to his feet. 'Do you feel ill again?'

He was already striding out from behind his desk as Nell fluttered an unhappy glance at Luke then quickly away again.

'Y-yes—n-no,' she replied in confusion, clearly disconcerted to find Luke Morrell standing there.

'Well, which is it?' Xander demanded, coming to a halt directly in front of her then frowning down at her when she hooked in an unsteady breath of air before focusing her eyes on a point between his tie knot and his chin. 'Nell...?' he prompted huskily when she still didn't speak.

'I'm—fine,' she told him. Then her gaze made another sliding glide towards the very still Luke.

Xander took the hint. With a twist of his long body sent an impatient glance at the other man. 'Later, Luke,' he dismissed him.

Luke hovered, seeming undecided as to whether to walk out with the file or place it on the desk before he left.

'Leave it.' Xander made the decision for him. And after another moment's hesitation, the file was relinquished and Luke was letting himself back out of the room.

'OK.' Xander swung back to Nell the moment they were alone again. 'Now tell me.'

He'd barely got the command out when one of those wretched telephones on his desk started to ring. On an impatient apology he spun away and strode back to the desk, leaving

Nell standing there feeling dazed and dizzy, hating him so much yet hurting badly at the same time.

'Xander—'

He snatched the phone up, cutting short what she had been going to say as he snapped his name into the mouthpiece.

It was like a replay of the day before, Nell thought as she stared at the long, lean length of his dark-suited figure standing in profile against a backcloth of an unrelieved grey English sky.

Beautiful, she observed helplessly, and with an almost masochistic need to feed the ache throbbing inside her began absorbing every elegant inch of him from handmade shoes to the breadth of his wide, muscular shoulders dressed in the best silk tailoring money could buy.

The man with everything, she thought, and had never felt so bitter than she did at that moment. The sensation crawled along her flesh like icy fingers and she knew suddenly that she had to get away—from him, from this raw feeling of utter betrayal, from the sound of his deep velvet voice that was twisting her up inside because she loved that sound even while she hated him.

'I'm going out,' she announced in a breath-shaking whisper and headed jerkily for the outer office door, not caring if he'd heard her, not caring if he would have the usual objections ready to voice at her going anywhere without his say-so.

The telephone crashed with a slam. He moved so fast she'd barely taken two steps before he was catching hold of her wrist and swinging her round. The whole quick manoeuvre brought back memories of the way he'd done the same thing on the island only yesterday.

Her face paled, lips trembling as she released her breath. 'Don't manhandle me.' She yanked her wrist from him.

That he was totally taken aback by the venom in her voice showed in his shock-tautened face. 'What's the *matter* with you?' he bit out.

'I am not some object you can push and tug around as your mood takes you,' she hit back.

He stiffened up. 'I never meant—'

'Yes, you did,' she cut in. 'You think you own me right down to my next thought. Well, you don't.'

'This is crazy,' he breathed in total bewilderment. 'I left a beautiful, warm and contented woman only an hour ago, now the shrew is back.'

Nell deigned not to answer that. She had been warm and contented. She had been nicely, carefully, *patiently* seduced into being that pathetic creature again. She despised herself for that.

'And why are you wearing the same clothes you had on yesterday?'

The sudden flip in subject sent her vision oddly blank as she stared down at the summer-blue suit. It took a really agonised effort to make herself reply without flinging the *why* at him. But she didn't want to tell him. She did not want him to start explaining and excusing his rights over her rights.

'It's all I've got to wear unless you want me to wander around in the turquoise dress,' she said. 'Whoever packed for me at the island packed for the Greek climate, not this one. So I am going out—to shop.'

It was thrown down like a challenge. Xander's dark head went back as he took that challenge right on his cleft chin. He knew what she was saying. He knew which particular gauntlet was being handed out this time. As the tension built and he fought to hold back the instinctive denial that was lodged in his throat, Nell stared fixedly at nothing in particular and hoped to goodness that the fine tremors attacking the inner layers of her skin were not showing on the outside.

'Wait for me,' he said, cleverly couching that denial in a husky dark plea that, in spite of everything, touched a tingling weak spot. 'We will go together. Just give me a couple of hours to free myself up and we can—'

The telephone began to ring. His dark head twisted to send the contraption a look of angry frustration but his fingers twitched by his sides and Nell almost managed a mocking laugh because she knew he was itching to answer that call. His priorities were at war. She twisted back to the door. Behind her she heard Xander hiss out a curse about irritating women.

'Have you any money?' he sighed out then, work winning over his marriage, though to be fair to him he didn't know that—yet.

'I have credit cards.' A dozen of them linked to his accounts.

'Nell…!' he ground out as her hand caught the door-handle. She turned her head to find him already back at the desk with his hand covering the shrilling phone. 'Don't be long,' he husked.

She nodded, lips pressed together to stop them wobbling, then she let herself out of the room. As she braced herself for the walk down the long corridor towards the lift, she said a silent goodbye to him.

Back in his office, Xander was ignoring the ringing phone and snatching up his mobile phone instead. He hit fast dial. 'My wife is just leaving. See that she's protected,' he instructed.

Then he was stepping to the window, hands dug into his pockets, fingers tightly clenched into fists while he grimly waited for Nell to appear on the street below while the telephone continued to ring off its rest.

He did not understand any of that, he decided tightly. He'd thought last night that they'd called a pretty effective truce. Suddenly she was back to sniping at him and evading eye contact. He missed the eye contact. He didn't like the tingling feeling that was attacking the back of his neck.

He saw her step out onto the busy pavement, continued to watch as she paused and looked around as if she had no idea where she wanted to go. His heart gave him a tug, yanking at his gut and contracting it because even from way up here she looked so—lost!

As she seemed to come to a decision and struck out to the left Xander watched Jake Mather slip into step behind her. He remained where he was with his eyes fixed on the top of her shining head until she had disappeared out of sight with her bodyguard safely in tow. Then he turned away from the window and stood grim and tense, feeling unfathomably like a man who'd just made the biggest error of judgement he was ever likely to make.

The phone had finally given up though, he noted, and, straightening his wide shoulders, he stepped up to the desk, hovered on another few seconds of inner restlessness, then the manila file Luke had brought in caught his eye.

Recalling his PA's grim words of warning did not ease the tension singing inside him as he sat down, picked up the file then drew in the advised deep breath.

A breath that froze even as he opened the front flap. A breath that he did not release for the several long minutes it took him to scan the pages set in front of him. By the time he'd finished he felt as cold as death.

She was away for three hours and in that time Xander was in touch with every step that she took. Grim, cold—face stretched taut by the burning pulse of anger he was keeping tamped down inside.

Work had ceased. *Life* had ceased, he mused harshly. Beyond the four walls of his office a series of instructions was being carried out to the letter while he sat in grim isolation, telephones, people, everything shut out but for his mobile link to Jake Mather.

If she bolted she would not get five paces before Jake would have her in his grasp. If she was foolishly letting herself believe that safety lay in the heaving crowds she was trying to lose herself in then she was in for a hard knock of truth. Jake had been joined by his other men, one of which was in the process of tracing the call she had just made from a public call box. Xander had not enquired as to how this could be done. He did not want to know. But behind the cold mask he was wearing on his face he knew that the name Marcel Dubois was about to be quoted at him.

It was.

'Where is she now?' he scythed at Jake Mather.

'To be truthful, boss, I think she's on her way back to you.'

To be truthful, Xander mimicked acidly, he knew that Nell must know by now that she did not have another choice.

She thought he lived in a zoo? Well, now she knew what it felt like, having been swarmed all over by his security people since she'd stepped onto Oxford Street.

Though he now had to accept that he was going to be disappointed that she did not require bundling into the back of the limo that was loitering in a side-street, ready and prepared to receive its protesting package.

Satisfaction coiled around his tense chest muscles when Jake's voice arrived in his ear with, 'Turning into the street now...'

He was out of the chair and swinging to the window before the final word left his security guard's lips. Something hard hit him in the chest as he caught sight of her head with all of its glorious, bright Titian hair shimmering around her face and shoulders instead of being neatly contained in the braid she'd left with.

Xander found himself gritting his teeth as he absorbed her purposeful stride. She was angry. Good, because so was he. If she wanted all-out war he was ready for it.

She was carrying the distinctive yellow and black bags from her wild buying spree in Selfridges. She'd changed her clothes too. The summer-blue suit had gone and in its place tight designer jeans that moulded her long, sensational legs and a soft brown suede jacket that hung loose across a creamy coloured top.

If she'd deliberately chosen the clothes to make him sit up and take notice then she could not have done a better job, because he was seeing her exactly as he had first seen her when she'd walked through her father's front door, wild and windswept. As she turned to walk up the grey marble steps to his building she paused and looked up and, as if she knew he was watching her from up here, her green eyes suddenly sparked and tossed up bolts of burning fire.

'Well, come on up, my fiery witch,' he invited beneath his breath.

Turning, he broke the connection with Jake Mather then reached out to flip a key on his computer keyboard to bring his glass and steel foyer up on to the screen. As he watched his wife stride purposefully across the foyer via the in-house CCTV system he was lifting his jacket from the back of the chair and smoothly shrugging it on. Her barely concealed patience as she rode alone inside the steel-cased lift held his attention while his fingers dealt with his shirt-collar button and straightened his tie. By the time she began the long walk down the corridor towards his office, his finger-ravaged hair had been neatly smoothed and he was ready for her.

Nell pushed open the door and stepped into the room, green eyes flashing like emerald storms. The door slammed back into its housing and she dropped the bags then speared those eyes on Xander, who was casually swinging in his chair behind the desk, looking as crisp and as sharp as he'd looked when she left him—and of course he was holding a telephone to his ear.

Her fury hit boiling point. 'Would you like to explain to me where the heck you get the stone-cold arrogance to believe that you own my life?' she shrilled.

Without so much as a flicker in response from those long dark eyelashes, he murmured some very sexy Italian into the phone's mouthpiece, then gently replaced it on its rest.

'If you have a yen to argue the finer points of ownership then by all means do so,' he invited. 'But before you begin you will explain to me please why you needed to spend thirty minutes in the ladies' room in Selfridges. Were you feeling ill again?'

Oh, so casually asked. Nell felt a sudden trickle of ice run right down her spine. 'How many men did you have following me?' she gasped.

'Seven,' he supplied. 'Including Jake Mather, whom I presume you spotted quite quickly—mainly because he was not instructed to hide,' he seemed compelled to add.

'He tried to stop me using a public telephone,' she said tightly.

With the calmness of a coiled snake, he reached out and

picked up the phone then offered it to her. 'Try this one. All calls are free.'

The green eyes sent him a withering look. 'Don't be so obnoxious,' she condemned. 'You have no right to have me tagged, tailed and guarded like some—'

'Animal in a zoo?' he suggested when words failed her. 'Or, more appropriately in this case,' he then added thinly, 'like an untrustworthy wife!'

'*I* can't be trusted?' Nell launched back at him. 'That's rich coming from the most twisted and devious—*Machiavellian* swine it was ever my misfortune to meet!'

'Oh, you met a worse one, *cara*,' Xander drawled.

'What's that supposed to mean?'

Without any warning he lost his relaxed posture to shoot to his feet. 'You were leaving me for him—again!'

With the backcloth of grey Nell could not see his face but she could feel the anger bouncing off him.

'On the first opportunity you were presented with you rang *him*!' he all but snarled.

'You traced that call?' she gasped out in disbelief.

'You make me sick,' Xander announced, then gave a contemptuous flick of a long-fingered hand when Nell just gaped. 'I don't even want to look at you.'

On that damning indictment he swung away to the window, leaving Nell standing there shaking and quivering—not with hurt but in disbelief!

'How dare you speak like that to me?' she shook out furiously.

'Easily.' Twisting back, he picked up a manila file from his desk, brandished it at her then dropped it again. 'The police report on your accident,' he incised. 'You may read it if you wish.'

But Nell did not wish. Nell was already striding across the office and pushing open the doors to his apartment.

'You were not driving that car!' he flung after her. 'The angle of your seat belt burns proves it! You were sitting in the left seat, not the right—and if I drove myself more frequently in England I would have realised that as soon as I clapped eyes on your bruises and you would have been dead!'

Her face white, her lips clamped together in a flat line of disgust that was ripping her apart inside, without a pause in her stride she threw open the next set of doors, aware that Xander was tracking right behind her. Aware that in one small, satisfied way she had taken him by surprise by walking away.

'You are so in love with the guy that you told nobody that salient fact!' he rasped out from the bedroom doorway. 'You have been protecting him from taking any blame even though the lily-livered coward slunk away from the scene, leaving you lying there badly injured and in need of help!'

All the time he was tossing his accusations at her Nell was throwing the doors open wide on his wardrobe and dragging open his sweater drawer. The soft cashmere garments landed in a discarded scatter. If Xander had been in a more sensible state of mind he might have been forewarned as to what was about to hit him.

As it was he strode forward, gripping the manila file as if it was some kind of weapon. Now she spun on him and it was so *nice* to watch his breathing still when he saw the expression of icy distaste on her face.

'He did not slink away. I sent him away,' she corrected. 'As you say, I protected him from you and your lynch mob and what you might do to him.'

'Because you love him.' He sounded hoarse.

Nell nodded. Why deny it? 'In the same way you have been protecting your family—because you love them?'

The sarcastic tilt in her questioning tone floated right by him. 'You are my family,' he ground out.

'No—here is your family, Xander,' Nell said quietly, and placed the framed photograph down on the bed. 'Goodness knows why you didn't marry Vanessa and give her and that— little boy who looks like he loves you very m-much the right to use your name.' She sucked in a dreadful, choked breath. 'But don't ever dare refer to me as your family again because

I'm not—they are. I think it's time that you got your priorities right and owned up to that.'

He seemed to be having difficulty taking it all in. Nell stared up at his blank, taut face and waited for some kind of response. But all she did see was his eyes shifting from her white face to the sweaters scattered on the floor before slowly, almost unseeingly moving to the bed. As understanding did begin to dawn she watched his face slowly leech of its rich golden colour then his eyes turned black.

'I can explain this—'

'No.' Nell shook her head. 'Explain to *them* why you dared to marry *me!*'

'But this is crazy!' He suddenly exploded back to life again. 'I *can* explain this—!' he insisted.

'But I don't want to hear!' she all but screamed at him.

His eyes flashing black with rage now, he stepped round the bed, slamming the manila file down as he came towards her. The file landed right on top of the framed photograph, Nell saw in dismay.

'You did that on purpose,' she shook out accusingly.

He didn't even bother to deny it. 'I would love to know,' he gritted, 'how you've managed to turn this into a fight about them instead of one about your bloody lover!'

'I h-hate you for that.' Nell wasn't listening. 'How could you do that to that poor little boy?'

Taking hold of her shoulders, he gave them a small shake then pulled her hard up against his chest. 'Listen to me when I speak,' he ground out. 'They are not important. You—your Frenchman is!'

'He isn't French, he's Canadian,' Nell mumbled, still staring at the way he'd covered the photograph as if he'd committed some mortal sin. 'He's also my—'

'Canadian…' Xander repeated as if a whole load of pennies had just dropped into place. 'You stupid fool, Pascalis,' he growled furiously at himself. Then those expressive black eyes flared Nell a look of blistering contempt. 'What did the two of you do—make love on a mountain while your mother lay dying in her bed—?'

The crack of her hand landing against the side of his face made a whiplashing echo around the room. Nell stood locked within his iron-hard grip, panting, breasts heaving as she watched her finger marks rise on his cheek. There was a horrible moment while she stared into those black eyes when she thought he was going to retaliate.

Then he let go, his fingers unclipping from her shoulders before he took a step back. The moment he did Nell began to shiver. Pale as death now and still shocked by her own act of violence, a cold chill shook her, bringing her arms up to hug her body, tense fingers clutching at the soft suede sleeves of her jacket.

She took in a slow breath. 'As I was about to say before you said w-what you said, Marcel is not my—'

'Well, I know he did not taste the main treat, *yenika*,' he drawled insolently. 'But there is more to sex than a—'

'He's my *brother*, you filthy-minded beast!' Nell flung at him.

It was as if someone had plugged him into an electric socket, the whole of his posture racked up with a jerk. '*Theos*,' he husked. 'That was a joke—yes?' Then as he stared into her angry face, '*Theos*,' he breathed again. 'You are serious.'

'H-half-brother,' she extended in a trembling voice.

Violently, he twisted his back to her, lifted up a long-fingered hand and grabbed the back of his neck. Blistering tension was scored into every bone and sinew.

'You should have told me.'

'Why?' Nell quavered.

'*Why...?*' He swung round to spear her with a piercing glare. 'I did not know you even had a brother! Don't you think such a thing warranted a mention some time in the last year?'

'If you'd cared enough about me to want to *know* about me you would have found it out!' she shrilled. 'And anyway...' she pulled in a deep breath '...I enjoyed watching you squirm. It made a pleasant change from squirming myself.'

'What is that supposed to mean?' he demanded stiffly.

Nell felt the sudden threat of wounded tears. 'I was in love with you when you asked me to marry you. I don't think you even noticed or cared!'

'I cared,' he grunted.

'So much that you were with your mistress a week before you married me! Now I find out that she has your child!'

White-faced now, 'No,' he said. 'Listen to me...' He took a step towards her, one hand reaching out, but Nell backed away.

'I w-was going to leave you today.' She shook out the confession. 'If it hadn't been for your men dogging my every step I would have disappeared and you would not have found me.'

The way his jawline gave a tense twitch made her wonder if he was biting back the desire to argue with her about that.

'You play with people, Xander. You like to be in control and when you're not you react as if we have no right to pull on your strings! I've seen you do it with your mother. You did it with those ten men last night. You're *always* doing it with me. You did it today when you set your hounds on me—'

'You said it yourself you were going to disappear—'

'That was my choice!' she launched at him, felt the tears start to come and had to tug her fingers up to cover her quivering mouth. At the same time her other hand went to her stomach because it was beginning to feel strange, kind of achy and quivery and anxious.

'Nell...'

One hand covering her mouth, the other her stomach, Nell was already spinning away. She made a dash for the bathroom with no idea that Xander was right behind her, so he took the full force of the door slamming shut in his face.

CHAPTER ELEVEN

FOR a few blinded seconds Xander just stood there with that solid wall of wood a mere hair's breadth from his face and the whole of his front vibrating from the force with which the door had shut.

Still reeling from the stuff that Nell had thrown at him, he spun to face the other way.

Her half-brother.

'Hell,' he muttered thickly.

His eyes went to the bed and the manila file and he went over there and snatched it up with some deep-ridden desire to toss that damn thing across the room—only he saw the photo frame he'd uncovered and he froze as he stared down at the lovely smiling Vanessa and a laughing Alex.

'To Papa Xander, love from your Alex', he read and the oddest kind of laugh broke from his throat.

Then the sound of retching filtered out through the bathroom door and he was dropping the file again to stride back the way he had come. Even as he pushed open the bathroom door and saw her hanging over the toilet bowl guilt was dealing him a well-deserved punch to his gut because he had allowed himself to forget her delicate condition while they'd been fighting like cat and dog.

Nell heard him arrive just as she was shuddering into stillness. 'Go away,' she whimpered, only to discover that talking was enough to set the whole thing off again.

Two seconds later he was taking control of the situation with the same grim, silent efficiency he had used on the motorway the day before. When eventually it was over and she'd rinsed her mouth out with a mouthwash, he lifted her limp, wasted and hot body into his arms and she discovered she had no strength left to fight him off.

'I hate you,' she whispered instead.

'*Ne,*' he agreed, carrying her into the bedroom.

'I wish you'd never set eyes on me.'

'*Ne,*' he agreed again, reaching down to toss back the covers before bringing her gently down on the edge of the bed.

'My feeling like this is your fault.'

'Entirely,' he admitted. 'Relax your arms from my neck so I can remove your jacket...'

It was the most humiliating part of it all to realise how she was clinging to him. Her arms dropped heavily to her sides. He removed the jacket while she watched his totally expressionless face. No man should be that good-looking, she thought bitterly. It gave him unfair advantage in the jaws of a fight because she wanted so desperately to reach out and kiss him that she felt dizzy all over again.

Her new flat shoes came next, landing with a clunk on the floor. His sensual mouth set straight, eyes hooded by those glossy black eyelashes, he then laid her back against the pillows with extreme care before shifting down her body to unzip her new jeans; a second later and the denim was sliding off her legs with a deft expertise. As the cool air hit her clammy flesh she began to shiver and, with his lips now pinched back against his set teeth, he covered her with the duvet then stepped back and proceeded to yank off his jacket followed by his tie.

'Don't you dare!' she gasped in quivering horror.

'Don't be stupid,' he growled back. 'I might be a control freak but I am not a sadist.'

The next thing his shoes had been heeled off and he was stretching out beside her and tugging both Nell and the duvet into his arms. She curled herself right into him then burst into tears. It was like throwing open a floodgate; she just couldn't control it. With the top of her head pressed into his chest she sobbed her heart out while he lay there and held her and said absolutely nothing.

It was as if every hurtful thing he'd ever done to her came

out for an airing in those tears. The way he'd made her fall in love with him then asked her to marry him in that cool, grim tone she only noticed much later when it was too late. The way he'd stood over her while she signed his rotten pre-nuptial without batting an eyelid because she loved him and trusted him then discovered the painful way that love *was* blind! If Marcel hadn't emailed her urgently with a link to the gossip pages of an American tabloid, she would have sailed down the church aisle to him in a besotted haze.

'I h-had to marry you,' she sobbed into his shirt front, un-aware that he hadn't been in on her first wave of grievances. 'I was scared you'd pull out of the deal with my father.'

'Shh,' he said, tangling his fingers in her hair and pressing her closer.

'I f-felt like a child-bride in a regency m-melodrama—s-sold to the unprincipled rake then dropped like a hot potato w-when he got more than he bargained f-for.'

She'd spent the next year pining for what might have been and wishing she'd stayed blind.

'Marcel wanted to come and get me then but I wouldn't let him. I *played* the child-bride in a regency melodrama, h-hoping you were going to turn up one day and realise you were head over heels in love with me but you didn't.'

'You saw me as a self-obsessed rat and I probably was then but you were so innocent and naïve you didn't have a clue what was happening around you. I was trying to protect you until you—'

'Enter the hero stage left,' she mocked thickly, rolling away from him and reaching out for the box of tissues that sat on the table by the bed. Fingers trembling, she plucked a tissue free and sniffed into it. 'Right in the knick of time he saves the innocent twit of a girl from the ugly guy with the f-fat lips.'

There was a shimmer of movement behind her that made her twist sharply to look at him. But if he was laughing at her it wasn't showing on his face. The tears clogged in her throat because it wasn't fair that he should have such liquid, dark,

serious eyes that seemed to be trying to tug her right inside him.

'Nothing to say?' she challenged.

'I will not answer these charges while you're so distressed,'
he said flatly, then on a sigh when fresh tears welled he moved
to pull her back to him again. 'Tell me about your half-brother,'
he prompted huskily.

'He's the son my father wanted from my mother but never
got.'

'So he's younger than you?'

She nodded. 'Nineteen. My mother was already pregnant
with him when she left us. He lives with his father in Banff.'

'You were miserable being married to me. You needed a
shoulder to cry on so you rang him up.'

'Someone I knew loved me.' She gave another nod, thereby
missing Xander's infinitesimal wince. 'I didn't expect him to
climb on the next plane to England to come and sort you out.
He had no idea who he was dealing with. It was almost a relief
when Hugo Vance refused him access to the house.'

'Why did he do that? If he's your brother of course he's
welcome in our home!'

'Marcel wasn't on your very short accepted list.' Nell sat up
and used the crumpled tissue to dab her eyes again. 'And he
might only be nineteen but looks a lot older because he's big—
six feet three already and built to suit—a heck of a sportsman;
can white-water raft like you would not believe.'

'You're proud of him.'

'Mmm.' It was that simple and neat. 'I think Hugo Vance
felt threatened by him.'

'How is it that you or your father have never so much as
spoken his name to me?'

'My father refuses to have his name mentioned because he
blames Marcel for stealing his wife away. He's still hurting.
I've just got used to never mentioning him because that's the
way it's always been. And anyway, you and I didn't have the
kind of relationship that encouraged sharing secrets.'

A small silence followed while Nell dabbed at her eyes and

Xander lost himself in deep thought. Then he hissed out a sigh. 'The irony of it,' he muttered.

Nell didn't find anything ironical in what had been said.

'Why was he driving your car?' he asked suddenly.

She gave a small shift with her hunched shoulders. 'Because I let him,' seemed excuse enough because the hell if she was going to admit that once she'd escaped Rosemere she then had a stupid change of heart and got so upset about it, Marcel had to drive because she wasn't fit to.

'OK...' said with such slow patience Nell knew that he knew she was fobbing him off. 'Explain to me, then, if he's so into playing your hero, why he ran away from the accident scene.'

'He didn't—and don't you *dare* speak of Marcel in that nasty tone!' She swung on him angrily.

'Now I know why I'm jealous,' Xander said bluntly.

Nell looked away again, refusing point blank to take up that comment. 'He wasn't licensed to drive here,' she admitted grudgingly. 'He wasn't used to our narrow, winding lanes,' and he wasn't used to driving such a small but very powerful car. 'When he lost control on the bend I thought we were both going to die...'

A hand arrived at the base of her spine, long fingers rubbing in a strangely painful, comforting stroke. 'But you didn't...' he said gruffly.

Nell shook her head. 'Marcel wasn't wearing his seat belt.' It was just another thing she'd felt guilty about. She'd been so stupidly upset she hadn't noticed he hadn't belted himself in. 'If you want irony,' she mumbled, 'when he was thrown out of the car he suffered barely a scratch.' She grimaced into the tissue. 'When I realised how bad things were for me I was scared for him. I convinced him to lift me into the driver's seat then begged him to leave. He wouldn't go. He was upset, angry with himself, scared for me—and I've never seen him look so young and helpless...' The hand at her spine rubbed again, she quivered on a sigh and swallowed fresh tears. 'He used my mobile phone to call an ambulance then stayed beside me until we heard it arrive then he hid in the woods until I was safely inside the ambulance. I was so worried about him, I got a nurse in A&E to call his mobile and reassure him I was absolutely fine.'

'I didn't know that.'

'Don't sound so surprised,' Nell flung out. 'You might be the control freak around here but I know how to get my own way when I need to. I picked a young student nurse with her romantic ideals still intact. She thought she was calling up my lover—she adored being a part of my wicked tryst.'

'You amaze me sometimes,' he laughed though it wasn't really a laugh. 'I truly believed you were the most open and honest person I know but you can lie with the best of them!'

Her shrug told him she couldn't care less what he thought or believed.

'Where was he staying?' he bit out next. 'I had every hotel and pub for miles around carefully combed for him without getting back a single damn clue!'

'He was backpacking. He camped out in a farmer's field.'

'Enterprising of him.'

'He's very self-sufficient.'

'Matinée-idol material.' His hand left her back.

He really was jealous. Nell smiled into the now crumpled tissue. Then he uttered another one of those sighs and tried to pull her back down to him but Nell refused to go.

'I want to go to Rosemere,' she announced.

'I want you here with me.'

Just like that, quietly spoken but deadly serious. Nell turned to look at him and found those jet-glossed eyes roaming over her with blatant messages.

It wasn't fair. She looked away again as a whole gamut of weak sensations went sweeping through her. 'I'll stay married to you until the baby comes.'

'Thank you,' he said.

'But afterwards we get a divorce.'

'You need another tissue, *agape mou*. That one is just about done.'

'I'm being serious!'

'So am I. You are about to start weeping again and that tissue has mopped up too many tears as it is.'

And those tears just returned all the harder. 'I can't seem to switch them off,' she sobbed.

'Come here.' This time he refused to take no for an answer so she landed in the crook of his arm. 'You are just in need of some tender loving care right now.'

'Not from you.'

'Yes, from me. Who else have you got?'

It was so brutally frank that she winced.

'Tell me why the call you made to Marcel today was traced to Paris.'

'He's been staying with the French side of his family. I knew he was flying back to Banff today so I wanted to catch him and doubly reassure him that I was OK before he left.'

'Was he reassured?'

Nell nodded but kept her mouth clamped tightly shut as to how she had given that reassurance.

'I would like to have listened in on that call,' Xander drawled with lazy amusement.

He knew, the beast. He knew she'd convinced Marcel that she was gloriously, happily in love with her husband.

'I thought you had meetings to attend,' she prompted.

'I am attending to you.'

'Well, I can—'

'Remain right where you are.' Tightening the hold he had on her, he rose up until he had her pinned to the bed. 'I am the control freak,' he murmured huskily. 'Be controlled or watch me get upset.'

Green eyes searched gently mocking dark ones. He was gorgeous—irresistible. He kissed her—lightly on both corners of her vulnerable mouth, on the warm, soft, tear-swollen bottom lip then tracked a whole line of soft kisses along her jaw until he reached that sensitive spot by her ear. Things she did not want to happen started to happen. Nell quivered out a sigh of discontent. He caught it, tasted it with his tongue and she felt the blunt jut of his desire thicken against her thigh.

'No,' she said. 'I don't want—'

To do this, she was going to say but the moment she opened her mouth to speak the gentle dart of his tongue stole the rest away. With the arrival of his fingers across her cheekbones he deepened that kiss, making love to her mouth with a slow tenderness that had her shifting restlessly beneath his weight. Each time he paused he looked deep into the conflict taking place in her eyes, if she tried to say anything he returned to the kiss until eventually she forgot what it was she wanted to protest about. Her fingers shifted, relaxing out of the tense fists she had them clenched in to begin a slow foray across the leanness of his taut hips to his waist and eventually with a slow, shuddering sigh over warm flesh covered by cool white shirting to his shoulders, his neck and with a final convulsive move buried them in his hair.

She was lost, his for the taking. The duvet was pushed aside. The only time he allowed her to think was those few too brief seconds he required to remove the rest of her clothes and even then the moment she showed signs of protesting he was back again, smothering out everything but him and what he was doing and how he was making her feel.

His own clothes disappeared by degrees, she didn't even notice until the manoeuvre was over and she was being overwhelmed by the fully naked male. He made love to her breasts, so acutely receptive that she stretched into a lithe, sensual arch, toes and fingers curling in drowning pleasure that earned her yet another deep kiss to her mouth. And he was trembling, she liked that. Her restless hands crowded each muscular flex and quiver until, 'Touch me,' he groaned and she did, closing her fingers around smooth silk on steel and felt him throb and thicken then lost touch with her breathing when his long fingers tested the wetness between her thighs.

Bright rainbows of colour began to dance on her senses, and he answered them with a thick, hoarse growl. His heart was pounding, hers was pounding, as he eased his weight between her spread thighs then made that smooth drive into her, and she opened her eyes to look at his harsh look of hungry passion etched on his face.

'I don't want to love you this badly,' she confided on a sad little whisper.

He lost control. She'd never known him do it so thoroughly before so the difference between smooth, slick, sophisticated lover and a man lost in the wild, throbbing beat of his desire was startling. All she could do was hang on for dear life as he drove the two of them to the edge then over it in a wild, hot charge that threw him into a paroxysm of gasps and shudders that just seemed to go on and on.

Afterwards, exhausted, she thought she might have actually lost consciousness. She certainly didn't remember another thing until she awoke much later to find herself alone in the bed with the cringe-making knowledge that once again she had allowed him to whittle away at what bit of pride she had left by letting him make love to her.

And not only make love—which was bad enough—but she'd also let him twist her into such knots by getting her to confess her crimes to him while he got away without confessing a thing about his mistress and his son!

His son. The tears began to sting. Throwing herself onto her back, she stared fiercely at the ceiling in an effort to stem the threatening flood. How could she let him do this to her? How could she *go on* letting him do this to her? She had to get away from him, she knew that now, because she couldn't fight this sexual empowerment he had over her and each time she gave in to it she lost a bit more of herself.

She brought an arm up with the intention of covering her stupid watery eyes—but as she moved the backs of her fingers touched something and, turning, she saw a folded slip of paper lying on the empty pillow beside her head. With her heart lodged in her aching throat, she lifted the piece of paper up then lay there just staring at it.

She was afraid to read it. Really scared because he had never done anything like this before and all she could think was it had to have something to do with Vanessa and that little boy.

Mouth—fingers trembling, she made herself open it out.

'I love you', it said. That was all, nothing fancy, no hearts and flowers, or trumpeting fanfares, just those three words scrawled in bold black pen.

She curled into a tight ball beneath the duvet and cried her eyes out with the note pressed against her breasts.

Getting showered and dressed was an effort. She throbbed and ached and trembled too much to be efficient at anything. Back in the jeans and the cream top and her hair brushed, she pushed open the bedroom door with the intention of going to the kitchen and making herself a fortifying drink before she had to face him again—but it wasn't to be.

One of the doors through to his office had been left spread wide open and the first thing to hit her was the sound of Xander's voice tearing into someone in cut-throat Italian. As her feet drew her unwillingly towards that open door the next thing to hit her was Xander himself wearing one of his dark business suits and looking as razor-sharp as the sound of his voice.

The sun had come out since she'd last seen him standing behind his desk like this, and sunrays were playing across his jet silk hair and the deep bronze sheen of his skin. Angry as he was, he looked magnificent, all-powerful, all-masculine, all hard, dark lines of lean musculature. Animal, sexual, so utterly magnetic that her breathing feathered in her chest and brought her feet to a halt as a wave of helpless, hopeless love swept through her on a shimmering wave of anguished defeat.

Why him? she asked herself painfully. Why did I have to fall for a man like him? Why did he have to leave a note on her pillow spelling out words he had never once said to her face? Guilt? Remorse? Damage control? She couldn't believe those words. How could she believe them when Vanessa and that poor little boy stood in the way?

She went to turn, needing to slip out of sight before he saw her because she just wasn't ready to face him, but as she went to move another voice spoke angrily and her heart sank.

She'd thought he was talking on the telephone. He was *al-*

ways on the telephone! Maybe she uttered the strained little laugh she could feel clogging up her throat because Xander's dark head whipped round.

'Nell…' the hard, husky rasp of his voice scored a shudder right down her spine as still she tried to escape from this.

'No, don't go…' He was already striding round the desk while she hovered reluctantly, several feet into the sitting room. The sound of his swift footsteps sounded in her head then his hand caught her arm just above her elbow. He tried to turn her but when she dug in her heels he stepped around her and reached for her other arm, holding her still in front of him. She could feel his tension, the hot simmer of his anger as his harsh breath scoured the top of her head.

'Look at me,' he husked.

But there was no way she was going to look at him. She stared at the knot in his silk tie instead.

His fingers flexed then began to slide upwards, they reached her shoulders and used them to tug her closer, then moved on to bury themselves in her hair at the defensive curve of her nape. It only took the light stroke of his thumbs beneath her chin to have it lifting.

Once again her breathing feathered as she found herself flickering a dancing glance over his face. Tension packed it, strain, the simmering anger glinting in his eyes. As she fluttered her eyes downwards again she was suddenly caught by the difference in his mouth. Held tight though it was, the fuller bottom lip still protruded more than it should. It looked darker—swollen; a hot tug deep inside her abdomen reminded her how urgently she'd sucked and bitten that swollen bottom lip—clung to it in the wild throes of—

A tense hiss of air left his throat. 'I know what you're thinking but I don't want you to think,' he said fiercely. 'I want you to stay calm and for both our sakes trust me, *agape mou*. I can explain myself—'

'With little notes left on pillows?' It was out before she could stop it.

'Little notes left on pillows can be read and reread,' he

pointed out. 'If I said those words out loud they would be swallowed up by too many conflicts rattling around in your head right now.'

Well, he was oh, so right about that. 'I can't do this any more,' she told his shirt front. 'You play games with me, Xander. You make me feel like your stooge.'

'You are not the stooge around here, *cara*. I am—someone else's stooge. But it is going to stop.' It sounded more like a threat than a promise. 'All I need from you is your patience. I *can* explain this.'

'Will you stop saying that? And don't you dare kiss me!' she protested when he started to lower his head. 'You think you can just kiss away every objection I put up against you but you can't. I—'

'If you two are going to start that again I may as well leave you to it...'

As if in a daze, Nell looked around, saw her mother-in-law— dressed goddess-style in wine-red silk—appear in view. She blinked, stunned that she could have so easily forgotten that Gabriela was even there! Then she became aware of other things, like the way she and Xander were standing in the door-way, almost wedged there by his rock-solid, unyielding stance. Her hands were on his chest, palms flat, fingers splayed. His still curved her slender neck. But worst of all her hips were resting against his hips. They didn't need to be pressing that close to him but they were as if they couldn't help themselves.

A rush of colour burned into her cheeks. As if he knew why it did, Xander slid his hands down her tense back to her hips and crushed her even closer, then did what she'd told him not to do and kissed her on the mouth.

'Don't so much as move another foot near that door, Madre,' he murmured with cool threat as he lifted his head again. 'It is judgement day, and you will not get out of this building until you have paid your dues to my wife.'

Judgement day? Pay her dues? Nell stared up at him with a mind gone blank.

He ignored the look, and suddenly he was all sharp and businesslike again. 'In here, I think.'

Looping an arm around Nell's shoulders, he turned her into the apartment then led her over to a chair then pressed her down into it.

'Don't tremble so much,' he scolded quietly.

'I...'

He kissed her fiercely—again.

'Oh, stop it, *caro*,' his mother snapped out impatiently as she appeared on the threshold of the apartment. 'Can't you keep your hands off her for five minutes? Helen is not going anywhere, as apparently I am not. *Dio*, Helen,' she added with a small shiver. 'How can you stay in this soulless place? I always hated it. Demitri never managed to get me to stay here once.'

'Did he ever get you to do anything you didn't want to do?' her son shot back at her.

'Oh, that's so unfair!' Gabriela protested. 'And so typical of you, Alexander, to always take your father's side!'

'You made him miserable—'

'I made him happy!' his mother angrily declared. 'How dare you, with your own marriage hanging in the balance by what I choose to reveal here, stand there and judge mine?'

They were suddenly back to fighting across the width of the sitting room, and doing it in English this time so Nell could at least understand the words if not the reasons for them. Looking from one face to the other, she couldn't decide which of them was going to catch light first. Xander was a proud Greek by birth but a hot-tempered Italian by nature, and she wondered if he had a clue as to how much like his mother he was?

'I can judge because I had to live with it.'

'Poor little rich boy, so badly treated,' his mother mocked. 'Helen, what is that top you are wearing?' Gabriela turned her attention away from her angry son to toss some derision her daughter-in-law's way instead.

'Leave Nell out of this,' her son hissed as Nell cringed into the chair feeling like a rag doll suddenly.

'I think she's already very much *in* it.'

The fact that her dry point hit home showed in the way Xander stiffened his elegant shoulders.

'Maybe you're right.' He took in a deep breath, then next thing Nell knew he had moved to stand behind her chair and his hands were settling on her shoulders in a possessive act no one could mistake. 'Congratulate us, Madre,' he then murmured dulcetly. 'Nell and I are going to have a baby, which means that you are going to be a grandmother…'

CHAPTER TWELVE

GABRIELA went so white that Nell thought she was going to faint on them and tried to rise to her feet to go to her.

'Remain where you are.' Xander's hands kept her seated. 'She will recover in a moment.'

'How can you be so heartless?' she gasped.

'I find it remarkably easy,' he answered coolly.

'But she's in shock—'

Gabriela gave a slow—slow blink of her beautiful eyes.

'I am all right.' Her pale mouth even managed to stretch into a wry little smile though her usual grace was missing as she walked to the nearest chair and slowly, carefully sat herself down. 'A *bambino*...' she whispered dazedly. 'Now, that, *mia caro*, was quite a blow even from you,' she admitted.

'As you can tell, my mother is not very enamoured with babies, *agape mou*,' Xander drawled lethally to Nell.

'It is not the *bambino* part that repels me but the *nonna* part,' Gabriela inserted surprisingly. 'Now I understand your desire to have me explain about Vanessa and her—son.'

Nell immediately began to stiffen. 'The desire for you to explain has always been there.' Xander's hands tightened on her shoulders in a gentle but determined squeeze. 'You simply chose to ignore it.'

'Until now...'

'Until now,' he agreed. 'So start talking or so help me, Madre, I will publicly denounce you as my mother and acknowledge them!'

Nell was beginning to feel sick, very sick. A hand went up to press against her mouth. Gabriela saw it and a look of what could have been remorse crossed her beautiful face.

'Our apologies, Helen,' she sighed. 'You have no idea what

169

we are talking about and therefore are thinking the very worst. Alexander, Helen needs a glass of water,' she concluded quietly.

With a soft curse he took his hands from her shoulders, his angry steps took him into the kitchen then seconds later brought him back again, then the man himself appeared in Nell's vision, squatting down in front of her to offer her a glass of cool water at the same time that he touched a concerned hand to her warm brow then was lifting her fingers from her mouth and carrying them to his lips.

'Sorry,' he said gruffly. 'This was not supposed to turn into a battle in front of you. I hoped that you would sleep a little longer so we could get this part out of the way before you needed to hear.'

'Hear what?' Nell tugged her hand free. 'That you have another family out there that is more important to you than your own mother—or me, come to that?'

'That just is not true.'

'You know about Vanessa and the boy?' Gabriela murmured in surprise.

Stupid fresh tears sprang into Nell's eyes as she sipped at the water. Robbed of her hand, Xander brought his to rest against one of her pale cheeks.

'Start talking, Madre,' he rasped out.

Gabriela flinched at the serrated edge to his voice. 'I had an affair with a man half my age,' she confessed in a reluctant rush.

'And broke my father's heart—'

'He broke mine too! Vanessa is only a few years older than Helen! He should have been shot for taking such a child to his bed!'

Vanessa? Nell's attention picked up. She glanced at Xander to find his gaze fixed on her, narrowed and intent.

'Both you and your father had an affair with Vanessa?' she breathed in stricken horror.

Anger reshaped his mouth. 'No, we did not,' he denied and

sprang up and spun away, angry tension racked across his shoulders.

Gabriela sighed. 'You are such a fool, Alexander,' she informed him. 'Have you never learned how to get your priorities right?'

'Like my father did?' he lashed back.

'Sì!' Gabriela cried. 'As we both did!' she impressed. 'You cannot pick between the two of us when you look for faults, Alexander. It just is not fair!'

'You took another lover before he did,' her son dismissed that line of defence.

'And he had his revenge.' Gabriela took in a deep breath and returned her attention to Nell. 'You cannot begin to know about middle age until you reach it, Helen. No one can—not even the great Alexander, who apparently has never put a foot wrong in his life!'

As a dig at his marriage to Nell, it hit the mark.

'Middle age eats away at your heart and your belief in yourself. You see lines where only smoothness had once been and a sagging figure where once everything had been tight. You see younger women receiving the admiring looks you used to receive.'

'You break my heart.'

'Be quiet!' his mother responded. 'You're a man,' she said in disgust. 'You do not fade like an ageing rose, you improve year by year! Your father did this! He improved and improved in his physical stature *and* he admired these younger women while assuring me I looked *nice*. Have you any conception at all how badly *nice* can hurt?' She swung on Nell again. 'If my son ever uses that word on you, *cara*, then take my lead and find yourself another man, preferably one a lot younger than he is—'

'You're careering from the point,' Xander incised.

'Feeling the vulnerability of your age difference to Helen's, *caro*?' Gabriela incised back. 'When you hit your fifties she will still be in her thirties—the absolute prime of a woman's life!'

'Get to the point!' The tension in him was close to snapping. Nell blinked at the sight of darkness scoring the rigid line of his cheeks.

'At least you chose the child for your wife, not your mistress,' his mother continued with the same cutting scorn. 'I am the same age as your father. I *felt* it deeply when his interest began to stray. You are built in his image—a true Pascalis male who will not lose his good looks and his sex appeal as he grows older.'

'So you jumped on the first man that showed you some admiration.'

'I did not jump, I *dived*,' his mother declared without conscience. 'I lost myself completely in the glorious flood!'

'You have no shame.'

Nell stood up. 'I think I should leave you two to finish this on your—'

'Sit down again!' Xander thundered.

Her chin came up. 'Don't speak to me like that.'

With a flare of rage he stepped up to her and forcibly made her sit. She'd never seen him like this, so controlled by his emotions that he was almost fizzing. She opened her mouth to protest. He covered it—hard. Yet even though it began as an angry way to subdue her, the kiss did not conclude that way and she could feel the effort it took for him to drag his mouth from hers.

'Listen to what she has yet to say—please,' he begged, and when she could only nod, he claimed her mouth again, soft with gratitude—then moved away.

Having watched the little interplay with interest, oddly, Gabriela went quite pale. 'My son loves you—'

'The point, Madre,' Xander curtly prompted.

'He made me come here because he said you would not believe a word he says about this—thing with Vanessa DeFriess.'

'Liars lose the right to be believed,' Xander inserted.

'I still don't understand why you felt you needed to lie!' his mother cried. 'What man with a beautiful wife to love would want to lay claim to that—*puttana*? Unless, of course, you were... Ah,' she said when he all but threw himself over to the window.

'Stop trying to outguess me and spit it out,' Xander gritted.

'Well, he was lying.' She turned back to Nell again, and then took in a deep breath. 'It was *my* husband who had the affair with Vanessa,' she spelled it out at last. 'Demitri took that woman to his bed to get his revenge on me. When the madness was over for both of us and we decided we could not live without each other, we made a promise that neither affair would ever be spoken about again.' She paused to take in a breath. 'All was well for several months. Indeed, we enjoyed the bliss of a second honeymoon.' Her beautiful dark eyes took on a wistful glaze. 'Then Vanessa came to Demitri and told him she was pregnant with his child. Everything fell apart in that moment. After Alexander was born and I discovered I was unable have more children Demitri had assured me that it did not matter...'

'I didn't know that,' Xander murmured gruffly.

'No.' His mother looked at him. 'You believed I was a fashion plate with a thin figure to protect. And you are now thinking of your own lonely childhood when I was not a very good mother to the one child I did have,' she tagged on to his hard expression. 'Which I suppose does give you every right to look upon me with such cynicism. I *admit* that I am not the maternal kind.'

It was like listening to some bizarre rehash of her and Marcel's story, Nell thought as she listened, while her mind stung her with disbelief. Coincidences like this just didn't happen. It was reality gone berserk. She looked up at Xander to find his fierce gaze was fixed on her.

'I know,' he said tensely, reading what she was thinking. 'This is why I knew you would not believe me if I told you this myself.'

His mother looked from one to the other. 'What are you talking about?' She frowned.

'Nothing,' Xander said. 'Please continue.'

'Continue.' Gabriela laughed stiffly. 'What is there left to say? There was your father, about to become a father again and he could not disguise his delight. I was going to lose him again and I was so terrified I—took an overdose and had to be flown to hospital. By the time I was out of danger Demitri was a different man. I begged him to never see Vanessa and her baby and, to his word, they were never mentioned again.'

'How much more proof could he offer that he loved you?' her son put in. 'He handed responsibility for Vanessa and his unborn child to me with the instruction that I never speak of them because he would not have you distressed like that again.'

'And you never forgave me for being so spineless.'

'The child has rights,' Xander said. 'You gave him none. The mother had the right to be treated with respect if nothing else. You denied her that right. She was gagged so quickly by my father's lawyers that she was left without a single leg to stand upon.'

'For money,' Gabriela pointed out. 'Don't forget the millions you take care of for her. Or the huge trust set up in the boy's name.'

'Or the hours of emotional support both Vanessa and her son required once Alex was born. I became a father without taking part in the act of conception and I do not recall you ever feeling sorry for my plight.'

'You didn't have to take duty to such extremes—'

'He's my half-brother!' Xander expelled in hoarse-voiced fury. 'Half my own flesh and blood!'

'I know I am a very selfish woman,' his mother said shakenly. 'I know you see me as a spoiled, vain, useless waste of space. But it is happening again, isn't it?' She looked helpless suddenly. 'You are willing to sacrifice me for them just as your father was willing to do the same thing.'

'No,' Xander uttered gruffly.

'You already threatened it, Alexander,' she wearily reminded him. 'Your father did the same.'

'Hence the dramatic overdose aimed to pull him back into line again?' Xander said hardly. 'If that isn't extreme then I don't know what is, Madre. Now I've made you talk about this, am I to wait with bated breath for you to use the same emotional blackmail on me?'

His mother went white. On a gasp of horror at his cruelty Nell shot to her feet. 'Xan—'

But Gabriela got in first. 'I have my regrets, Alexander,' she told him stiffly. 'And I can now feel the cutting pangs of remorse for denying your father the right to know his other son. But if you believe I have not been punished very adequately for my sins then you're wrong. When Demitri died I lost a major part of myself. I still miss him so much…'

'You know,' Xander drawled, 'I would respond kindly to that blatant attempt to play on my sympathies if it was not for the fact that only minutes before Nell came in you were still refusing to sacrifice your ego for the sake of our marriage.'

Gabriela accepted this final indictment with a wry little smile. 'Ah, that sin called ego,' she drily mocked herself then turned to go.

'No—don't go,' Nell begged huskily. 'You both need to resolve this…'

Gabriela looked into her daughter-in-law's anxious face then at Xander's rock-like stance and offered up a grimace. 'You are a sweet person, Helen. You will make a good mother to my grandchild. Let us hope that my son will be a good father, for I think he forgets that I was not the only parent to leave him for another love.'

Then she walked away, leaving Nell staring helplessly after her while Xander continued to stand there like a cold, hard, *stubborn* fool!

'Go after her.' She swung on him urgently. 'She's your mother, for goodness' sake. You love her, you know you do— faults and sins alike!' When he still didn't move from his stiff stance, 'If you let her go now you will never see her again because the *both* of you are too stuffed full of pride to give a solitary inch! I thought you were bigger than this! Xander, please…!' she begged painfully.

But she didn't need to add the last part because with a tight, angry growl of blistering frustration he spun and strode after her, leaving Nell staring after him feeling very much as if she'd just been run over by a pair of trucks.

She watched his hands reach out to grasp Gabriela's narrow shoulders, watched through a deepening glaze of tears as he turned her into his chest. She caught the tones of thick, gruff, husky Italian, felt her heart quiver as the proud Gabriela broke her control on a muffled sob.

Then she turned away and began to shake like a leaf, still too befuddled by what she had been told to even attempt to sort it out in her head.

She made for the kitchen, leaving mother and son alone to mend their differences while she attempted to do something really normal like setting about making coffee but feeling so at odds with herself and with Xander that she didn't hear him arrive at the door.

'OK?' The husky question came from behind her.

Stiffening her spine, she pressed her lips together and nodded, not sure she wanted to look at him until she'd made up her mind if she hated him for putting his mother through that ordeal, or loved him for doing it for her.

'No more nausea?' he questioned when it became clear she wasn't going to speak.

'I'm fine,' she managed, fingers fiddling with the slender white china cup she'd set out ready for her coffee. 'Would you like a drink?'

'Not if you're planning to poison it,' he said drily, then hissed out a weary sigh. 'Nell, we need to—'

'Your telephone's ringing.'

And it was. They both listened to it for a few fraught seconds, Nell with her eyes squeezed tightly shut on a tense prayer that he would just go and answer the damn thing. Xander, she was sure because she could feel it, piercing the vulnerable tilt of her neck with grim intent in his gaze, wanted her to turn and look at him.

'Easy on the belladonna,' he instructed heavily after a moment and went back to his office, leaving her wilting though she didn't really know why.

A few minutes later she was bracing her shoulders and carrying two cups of freshly made coffee into his office. Xander was still on the phone with his dark head resting back against the chair's leather upholstery, and his eyes were closed. He looked tired, she noticed, dragged down and fed up. As she walked across the expanse of floor towards the desk she saw his lashes give a flicker and quickly looked away.

'Efharisto,' he murmured as she put one of the cups of coffee down in front of him.

She managed a brief upward glance at his face before turning away again.

'Stay,' he husked, showering her in tingling tremors. 'Sit down, relax, drink your coffee. I will be only a few more moments here.'

Sit down, relax, drink your coffee, Nell repeated silently and sank into the chair by his desk and wondered why she was still feeling so at odds with him when everything had been explained—hadn't it?

He was talking in Greek, she noticed, sitting up now and swinging his chair slightly with his eyes lowered to where a set of long fingers hit intermittently at the computer keyboard lying on the desk. His deep voice was quiet, asking low key questions with no hint of sharp command evident, as if someone had switched off his normal incisiveness.

The phone went quietly back on its rest. Strumming silence followed. Nell felt it so deeply inside that she tensed.

He picked up his coffee cup and looked down into it. 'How much belladonna?'

'Two spoonfuls,' she answered.

'Still not forgiven, then.' He grimaced a wry smile at her then lifted the cup to his lips and drank. The way that he did it was so much like a man willing to take his poison that she shot like a bullet to her feet.

'Stop it,' she stabbed at him.

'Stop what?' He looked at her.

'Making a joke of it.'

'Of what?'

'All of that—stuff we've got through today.'

'Are we through it?'

She frowned at the question, her tightening nerve-ends forcing her to discard her coffee-cup before she spilled it down herself. 'Y-your mother is your mother.'

'Is that supposed to make some sense to me?'

'Sh-she is what she is and you have to accept that.'

'I do—as much as I can do,' he reminded her. 'Next problem.'

The way he said it as if she was in a business meeting made her start to seethe. She jerked round to face the other way. 'I don't like you.' That was a problem, she thought. 'Sometimes…' she then added grudgingly because it was crazy to deny that she liked him in bed—*loved* him in bed.

Loved him all the time, she extended unhappily, but loving didn't have anything to do with liking, did it?

'You hurt people and don't seem to care when you're doing it.'

'Are we still discussing my mother?'

'No—me,' she said huskily.

Silence met that announcement. Nell folded her arms beneath her breasts and stared down at her feet.

'You should have told me the truth about Vanessa.'

'You should have told me the truth about Marcel.'

'That was different.'

'Why?'

'Because he wasn't an issue when you married me. Vanessa was and once you knew it you should have told me the truth straight away instead of letting me spend the next twelve months imagining you in her arms instead of mine!'

A sigh sounded behind her. The next sound was the creaking of his chair as he came to his feet. Her chin hit her chest when he came to stand right in front of her. Without saying a word he clamped his hands to her waist and lifted her up to sit on the desk. Next her thighs were summarily pushed apart and he

was wedging himself between them, then her arms were firmly
unfolded and lifted round his neck.

'OK,' he said. 'Now that we are more comfortable I will
explain... I fell in love with you within about two seconds of
you walking through your father's front door...'

Her chin shot up, green eyes wide with shock and disbelief.

'Got your full attention now?' he mocked. 'Ready to hang
on my every word with bated breath?'

'You never did love me then, or you would not have left me
on our wedding night believing what I did.'

'You are referring to that memorable time when you stood
there in your bridal gown, shouting at me and looking so heartbreakingly beautiful, hurt and *young*?' He uttered a sigh. 'It
was either leave you there or toss you on the bed and ravish
you and—trust me, *agape*—you would not have survived the
kind of ravishing I had in mind right then. I was mad with you
for believing that trash—mad with myself for not seeing it
coming. Do you think that Vanessa is the only skeleton a man
like me has lurking in his closet? I've had women trying to
foist their babies on to me and women trying to blackmail me.
I've had them sneaking into my bed in the dead of night and
crawling through windows in an effort to get to me.'

'Oh, don't be modest; do tell the rest,' Nell drawled acidly.

'You think I like being every greedy gold-digger's dream
catch? Why do you think my security is so tight? Would you
like a ballpark figure on how much it has cost me to keep such
stories out of the Press over the years? Give any one of those
grasping women a glimpse at more money and they would be
singing to the Press today. Vanessa was the exception. She was
not my skeleton, which made those computer printouts you
showered at me all the more annoying because I did not feel I
had the right to break the promise of silence and protection I
had made to my father on his death bed.'

'Not even to me?'

'Don't look so hurt,' he chided. 'Do you think it didn't hurt
me to realise that you were not equipped with the necessary
defences to live my life? I already knew I'd been unforgivably

selfish, crowding you into marriage so young. I saw in a single miserable flash of enlightenment as I watched you enact that little tragedy just how selfish I had been. I saw how every jealous woman out there was going to have a story to whisper in your ear. It would have been like leading a lamb into a slaughterhouse then standing back to watch it be skinned.'

'So you walked away.' Her soft mouth wobbled.

'Yes.' He kissed the wobble then sighed. 'When I left you at Rosemere I did it determined to set you free—but I could not. I kept on putting it off. Kept coming to see you, couldn't stay away! Kept trying to convince myself that while you seemed content with what you had then you were OK. The night I offered to renegotiate our contract was the one time I was ready to rip the damn thing up and let you go. I've never felt happier when you turned the offer down without even hearing me out. I was off the hook for another few months until my conscience got to me again. Then that second photo of me with Vanessa appeared and you crashed your car. I've never felt so bloody lousy in my entire life!'

'Good,' she said. 'It's nice to know that I wasn't the only one feeling like that.'

'Ah, but that was before I knew about the new man in your life.' He smiled. 'I switched from feeling lousy with remorse to a thirty-four-year-old lusty, cradle-snatching lecher in a single blink of an eye. You think you were jealous of Vanessa? You barely scratched the surface of jealousy, *agape mou*. But I did. I scratched it right down to its bloody, primitive raw.'

'I love it when you're primitive.' She moved a little closer in an effort to capture his mouth.

His head went back. 'I'm being serious!'

'So what do you want me to say—get away from me, you uncivilised beast? Shall I get your pack of bodyguards to string you up to a tree and tar and feather you for wanting me too much to let me go?'

'Loving you too much,' he corrected softly.

'And aren't you the lucky one that I loved you too much to drive away…?'

'What's that supposed to mean?' He frowned at her.

Nell gave a little idle shrug. 'Only that Marcel was driving me *back* to Rosemere when we crashed. I thought your police report would have told you that.'

'If it did, I never got to read that far,' he murmured dazedly. 'I just read the bit about you being in the passenger seat and went berserk.'

'I noticed,' she murmured feelingly.

'Forgive me for what I said?'

Nell shook her head.

Xander uttered a sigh then changed tactics. He lifted her up until she straddled him then strode across the room.

'Where are we going?' she asked innocently.

'Guess,' he drawled. 'If I am to pay a penance then I will do it in comfort.'

And he did.

The island was trapped in the sultry heat of the late afternoon when the helicopters began to arrive. From her place at the nursery window Nell watched as Marcel jumped down onto the ground then walked towards the glinting pool. He looked so absolutely gorgeous that Nell uttered a small sigh of sisterly pride. A sudden cry of delight went up, then a young boy in swimming shorts was racing to meet him. Marcel grinned lazily as he accepted this show of pure hero worship from the much younger Alex.

'My hero status has been eclipsed by the matinée idol,' Xander murmured with a regretful sigh.

'Never mind, your real son worships you,' Nell consoled. 'And look at your mother and my father watching them to-gether. They're actually smiling. That has to be a first for both of them.'

'It's called bowing to fate,' Xander said. 'They either accept our family as a whole or they miss out.'

'And who'd have thought Gabriela would be so besotted?'

'Why should she not,' Gabriela's son defended loyally, 'when my son looks exactly like me?'

'Too like you,' Nell complained, turning away from the window to go and lean over the cot, where Demitri Pascalis lay kicking contentedly. 'Now, you know I love you,' she informed the wide-eyed baby. 'But I still don't think it's fair that you didn't even elect to have my green eyes.'

The baby let out a shriek of delighted laughter. He didn't care that he looked the absolute spit of his dark-eyed *papa*.

'Cruel,' she scolded. 'But I will get my own back,' she warned him.

'And how do you intend to do that?' Xander asked.

Straightening up to find herself slipping easily beneath his waiting arm, Nell smiled one of those wait-and-see threats at him as she let him lead her away.

'I see,' Xander murmured fatalistically. 'The wicked witch is mixing spells again.'

As they left the baby's room Thea Sophia slipped quietly into it, and took the comfortable chair placed by the cot. Out came her lacework and her gnarled fingers got busy while the baby chatted away to her. He would fall asleep in a few minutes, bailing out with a blink of an eye, but until that happened he had his ever-attentive *thea* to entertain.

Walking Nell into their sunny bedroom, Xander turned her to face him. He was dressed in one of his loose white shirts and casual trousers, but soon they would have to start getting dressed up for the party that was to take place tonight—which was a shame, in Nell's opinion, because she preferred to keep him in clothes she could strip off quickly.

'Mmm,' she said as she pressed her lips to the triangle of hair-roughened flesh exposed by the open neck of his shirt. 'You taste of sun and salt and sexy masculinity.'

'And you have a one-track mind,' he sighed.

'It's my birthday. I'm allowed a treat.'

'Several treats.'

'OK,' she shrugged, not arguing the point because it was oh, so much more interesting to discover how smoothly the shirt fell open to her lightest touch. She ran her fingernails down his front and watched taut muscles flex.

'You're so gorgeous,' she murmured helplessly—and received her reward with the hungry clamp of his mouth.

It didn't take much longer for them to be lost. Xander's muttered, 'We don't have time for this,' was ruined by the urgency with which he stripped her blue T-shirt dress off her and tumbled her onto the bed. They made hot, frenzied love while the rest of the family chatted by the poolside.

When they came downstairs two hours later you would be forgiven for thinking that Nell had spent the whole afternoon achieving that gloriously chic look she'd donned in a short half-hour. She was wearing aquamarine silk, smooth and slinky, a perfect set of blue diamonds sparkling at her creamy throat.

Her hair was up to show them off because Xander had given her them for her birthday. And if anyone wondered at the rueful grimace he offered when his mother congratulated his wife on how two hours' pampering could put such a wonderful glow to her daughter-in-law, no one would have thought to question whether he knew something that they did not. He looked far too smooth and sophisticated to be recalling what they'd been doing in the shower only half an hour ago.

They separated, they danced and circulated amongst their fifty-strong guests as goods hosts did. They laughed and teased and flirted and came together on the terrace to snatch a private moment or two gazing at the moon.

'Happy?' Xander asked, holding her in front of him.

'Mmm,' Nell murmured uncertainly.

'Something missing from your perfect day?'

'Mmm,' she nodded.

'You would like me to toss you into the pool perhaps?'

'Not tonight, thank you,' she answered primly, then took hold of one of his hands and slid it over her abdomen. 'I'm afraid it's tender loving care time again,' she softly confided.

Xander immediately stiffened like a man in shock. 'I hope you are teasing me!' he grated.

'No,' Nell sighed.

He swung her around, a dark glitter in his eyes. 'You mean you really are pregnant? But our son is only ten months old!'

'I want a red-haired, green-eyed girl child this time,' she told him. 'And you really are lousy at birth control.'

'Ah, so I am to get the blame again.'

'Of course,' she said then wound her arms around his neck and leaned provocatively into him. 'But then you never, ever disappoint…'

The Spanish
Billionaire's Mistress

SUSAN STEPHENS

Susan Stephens was a professional singer before meeting her husband on the tiny Mediterranean island of Malta. In true Mills & Boon® Modern™ style they met on Monday, became engaged on Friday and were married three months after that. Almost thirty years and three children later, they are still in love. (Susan does not advise her children to return home one day with a similar story, as she may not take the news with the same fortitude as her own mother!)

For all my long-suffering friends. You know who you are. I couldn't do it without you.

CHAPTER ONE

'COME here—come closer so we can see you,' the male voice commanded.

Cursing softly under her breath, Zoë Chapman slithered down to the ground and straightened up. Uncomfortable but invisible, or so she'd thought, she had been wedged into a smooth crevice between two giant rocks, discreetly observing the activity around the campfire.

She had located the flamenco camp and chosen her hiding place before anyone arrived. Her unique and popular cookery shows depended upon the co-operation of special interest groups, but the fact that she worked on a TV programme didn't make her welcome everywhere. She had wanted to observe the dancing before she introduced herself, just to make sure it was as good as was rumoured in the village.

The man speaking now had arrived shortly after she had. Back turned, he had stood gazing out across the valley. She had seen nothing more than an aggressively tall male figure, a shock of inky black hair and a wide sweep of shoulders—in fact, everything she had vowed to avoid since gaining her freedom.

As more people had joined him, she'd realised he was the leader of the group. Why hadn't she been surprised? She had wondered who he was, wondered about the quivers running through her as she stared at him. It had made her angry to think she had learned nothing since her divorce. She was still drawn to dangerous men.

Now, walking up to him, she saw he was everything she had expected: strikingly handsome, arrogant, and angry that

5

she was here uninvited. If this hadn't been work she would have done the sensible thing, and left.

During the course of her television series she searched out interesting people from all walks of life. Local people in whichever country she chose to film were the seasoning in her shows, the magic ingredient that lifted her above the competition.

Generally she enjoyed the research. This time she had to put her personal feelings to one side and hope the dancing started soon. She couldn't let some local brigand put her off. Forget the man! This was her target group. The only thing that mattered was persuading someone to perform flamenco on her programme.

Dance was Zoë's passion outside of work. She knew she would never make a professional, but part of her climb-back after the divorce had been to join a jazz dance exercise group. It had proved the best therapy she could have chosen—though right now it looked as if all her good work was being undone.

She could not have prepared for this, Zoë reminded herself. She had not expected to run up against such a strong character again quite so soon.

'Well, what are you waiting for?'

He beckoned her forward with a short, angry gesture, and his voice was cold. It brought back memories she didn't need, but she was like a terrier with a bone when it came to work, and she focused her concentration easily. They were attracting a lot of attention. Perhaps one of the people around the mountain hut would agree to audition for her programme?

The man held up his hand to stop her coming any closer. It was close enough for Zoë, too. He was quite something. Along with the aura of power and brute strength, she had to admit he had style. Why did she have to find such a man irresistible when she knew he had danger carved into the stone where his heart should be?

Somewhere between thirty and thirty-five, he was around

six feet two or three, and his build was every bit as impressive as she had thought from some distance away. Everything about him was dark: his eyes, his hair...his expression.

'Why have you come here?' he demanded.

'I heard this is where flamenco enthusiasts gather, and I want to learn more about flamenco.'

'So you can go home to England and show off to your friends?' He made a derisive sound and clicked his fingers, mimicking the worst of the shows she had seen down on the coast.

'No, of course not. I...' His steely gaze remained fixed on her face, but she couldn't let that get to her. 'I am genuinely interested in flamenco.'

'Are you alone?'

'I am at the moment—'

He cut her off. 'At the moment?'

'I know this looks bad—'

'What do you mean, you're alone at the moment?'

'I'm working with a television crew. They're not here right now.'

Could his expression darken any more? She tried to explain, but her voice came out as a croak. Unconsciously, her hand flew to her throat. She should have brought some water with her. She had been at the mercy of the sun all afternoon, and now she was desperate for a drink.

'Do you think I could have some water?' She gazed around.

'What do you think this is? A café?'

But people were drinking all around her. 'I'm sorry, I—'

'Did you think this was one of those cheap tourist places where you get a free drink along with your *paella* and chips?'

'No!' She calmed herself. 'No, of course not—'

He straightened up and moved a menacing pace towards her, and all her courage drained away. Lurching backwards, she nearly stumbled. She was only saved by the sheer bulk of a man behind her. He was carrying a stone flagon and some pottery beakers. He didn't understand when she started to apologise, and poured her a drink.

She didn't want it. She just wanted to get away—back down the mountain to safety, to where people barely looked at her, where no one knew who she was or where she had come from.

But the man with the flagon was still smiling at her, and the situation was bad enough already. *'Gracias, señor.'*

Keeping watch on the brigand, Zoë took the beaker from the older man and gratefully drank from it.

It was delicious, and tasted harmless—like fruit juice and honey laced with some spice she couldn't name. The beaker felt cool, and she was so thirsty she didn't protest when he offered her more. The golden liquid gleamed in the light as it flowed from the flagon, and the elderly man filled her beaker to the brim.

'Salud!'

The alpha male's voice was harsh and unfriendly. Handing the beaker back to the man with the flagon, Zoë raised her chin. She felt better now, bolder. 'Delicious,' she said defiantly, staring her unwilling host in the eyes. 'What was that drink?'

'A local speciality, brewed here in the village.'

'It's very good. You should market it.'

'On your recommendation I'll certainly consider it.'

His sarcasm needled Zoë, but it also renewed her determination to go nowhere until she got the feature for her programme. At any cost?

At the cost of a little charm, at least. 'I really should introduce myself.'

'You really should.'

Brushing a strand of titian hair from her face, Zoë stared up and tried to focus. She hadn't realised the drink was so strong. On an empty stomach, she was suddenly discovering, it was lethal. She was in no state to object when he reached forward to steady her.

His grip on her arm was light, but even through an alcohol-induced haze she could feel the shock waves radiating out from his fingertips until every part of her was throbbing. He led her away out of earshot, to where a wooden hut cast some shade.

'So, who are you?'

'Zoë—Zoë Chapman. Could I have a glass of water, please?'

Rico thought he recognised the name, then brushed it aside. It hardly mattered. She had damned herself already out of her own mouth: a television crew! He might have known. He grimaced, catching hold of her again when she stumbled.

'I think you'd better sit down.' He steered her towards a bench, and once she was safely planted turned and called to two youths. 'José! Fernando! *Por favor, café solo—rápido!*' Then, turning to her again, he said, 'Welcome to the Confradias Cazulas flamenco camp, Zoë Chapman. Now you're here, what do you want?'

'It's good to meet you too—'

'Don't give me all this nonsense about flamenco. What do you really want? Why have you come here? Are you spying on me?'

'Flamenco isn't nonsense.' She reeled back to stare at him. 'And I'm not spying on you. I'm researching.'

'Oh, of course. I see,' he said sarcastically.

No, he didn't, Zoë thought, shading her eyes with her hand as she tried to focus on his face. Her head felt so heavy. It bounced instead of simply moving. Squeezing her eyes together, she struggled to follow his movements—he seemed to be swaying back and forth. 'So, who are you, then?' Her tongue was tied up in knots.

'Rico. Rico Cortes.'

They were attracting attention, Zoë noticed again. Peering

round him, she gave a smile and a little wave. He moved in closer, shielding her from his companions. 'I'm very pleased to meet you, Rico.' As she put her hand out to shake his, it somehow connected with a coffee cup. Raising the cup to her lips, she drank the coffee down fast. The hot, bitter liquid scalded her throat, but it couldn't be helped. She had to pull round from this fast. The last couple of programmes based around flamenco were supposed to be the crowning feature of her series.

'Here, drink some more.'

His voice was sharp, and then he made a signal to the boy with the coffee pot to fill her mug again.

'Leave it here, José, *por favor.*'

He sounded different, warmer when he spoke to the youth, Zoë registered fuzzily.

'We're going to need every drop,' he added.

And he was back to contempt when he turned to look at her! It wasn't the best start she'd ever had to a programme.

This time, once she'd drained the strong black coffee, it was Zoë who asked for more. The second she had finished, the questions started.

'If you're with a television crew I take it you're after an exclusive. I'm right, aren't I? That's why you were spying on us, sneaking about.'

Thanking the boy, Zoë gave him back her empty cup. Her head was clearing. She felt better, much more focused. She might still be a little under par, but she had no intention of being bullied by Rico Cortes—by anyone.

'I'm here to see if flamenco will make a suitable item for my television series. Nothing more.'

'*Your* television series?'

'It's my programme. I have full editorial control. I own the company that produces the programme.'

'So, it's you.'

'Me?'

'Staying at the Castillo Cazulas.'

'Yes, my company has taken a short-term lease on the castle—'

'And it's there you're going to create your masterpiece?'

'I beg your pardon?' She couldn't keep the chill out of her voice now. Could he have been more disparaging? She had worked long and hard to raise her programme above the rest, to make it different and special. She had brought a great team together, and she was proud of what they had achieved.

'Flamenco for Spain, opera in Italy, fashion when you shoot a programme in France—is that how it goes? Skimming over the surface of a country, using the name of art just to make money?'

'I make money. I won't deny it. How would I stay in business, pay the wages of the people who work with me, otherwise? But as for your other assumptions—frankly, they stink.'

'They do?'

His voice was faintly amused now, and he was looking at her in a whole different way. She wasn't sure if she liked it any better. Her thundering heart told her it was dangerous. 'Look, Rico, if you're not the person I should be speaking to about the dancing, then perhaps you could find me someone who will listen to what I have to say.'

'And allow you to trample over my privacy? I don't think so.'

'*Your* privacy? I wasn't aware that my programme was going to be made around you.'

His look was cynical. 'It's time you went back to your film crew, Ms Chapman.'

'Are you asking me to leave?'

'It's getting dark—I'd hate for you to lose your way.'

'Don't worry, I'll go. Just as soon as I finish my business here.'

'You *have* finished your business here.'

'Why are you so touchy about my being here? I'm not doing you any harm!'

'People have a right to space.'

'And this is yours?' Zoë gestured around.

'If you like. I don't have to explain myself to you.'

'Correct,' Zoë said, standing up to face him. 'But I wasn't aware that there were any private estates up here in the mountains. I've got as much right to be here as you have. And, for your information, I have never had a single complaint from a guest on my show. I treat everyone with respect.'

He shifted position and smiled. It was not a friendly smile. It was a 'don't mess with me' smile.

'I give you my word,' Zoë insisted. 'Nothing in my programme will invade your privacy—'

His short bark of laughter ran right through her, and his derision made her cheeks flame red.

'You really believe that?'

'Yes, of course I do.'

'Then you're dreaming.'

'Perhaps if you'd allow me to explain how everything works—'

'You still couldn't come up with anything to reassure me.'

This was her most challenging project yet. But she had never failed before. Not once. No one had ever refused to take part in one of her programmes, and she wasn't going to let Rico Cortes start a trend.

'Have the effects of that drink worn off yet?'

He couldn't wait to get rid of her, Zoë guessed. 'Yes, they have.' Hard luck. She was firing on all cylinders now.

He turned away. Evidently as far as Rico was concerned their discussion had come to an end. He couldn't have cared less about her programme—he just didn't want her blood on his hands when she tumbled over a cliff after drinking the local hooch at his precious flamenco camp. 'We haven't finished talking yet!' she shouted after him.

'I have.'

As he turned to stare at her Zoë wondered if he could sense the heat building up in her. His slow smile answered that question, and she wasn't sure if she was relieved or not when he walked back towards her. 'Please, let me reassure you. I don't pose a threat to you or to anyone else here. I'm just trying to—'

'Find out more about flamenco?'

'That's right.'

As their eyes met and locked Zoë shivered inwardly. Rico was exactly the type of man she had vowed to avoid. 'It's getting late.' She looked hopefully at the sky. 'Perhaps you are right. This isn't the time—'

'Don't let me drive you away,' he sneered.

She was painfully aware of his physical strength, but then something distracted her. A broken chord was played with great skill on a guitar, so soft it was barely discernible above the laughter and chatter—but this was what she had come for. Silence fell, and everyone turned towards a small wooden stage. Lit by torchlight, it had been erected on the edge of the cliff, where it could catch the slightest breeze from the valley.

'Since you're here, I suppose you might as well stay for the performance.'

Rico's invitation held little grace, but she wasn't about to turn it down.

He cut a path through the crowd, and Zoë followed him towards the front of the stage. She could see the man with the guitar now, seated on a stool at one corner of the stage, his head bowed in concentration as he embraced the guitar like a lover. Then an older woman walked out of the audience and went to join him. Resting her hands on her knees to help her make the steep ascent up the wooden steps to the stage, she looked her age, but when she straightened up Zoë saw an incredible transformation take place.

Giving the audience an imperious stare, the woman

snatched up her long black skirt in one hand and, raising the other towards the sky, she stamped her foot once, hard.

A fierce energy filled the air as the woman began her performance. Zoë had no idea that Rico was watching her. She was aware of nothing outside the dance.

'Did you feel it?' he murmured, close to her face, as the woman finished and the crowd went wild.

'Did I feel what?' she said, moving closer so he could hear.

'*Duende.*'

As he murmured the word she looked at his mouth. '*Duende.*' Zoë tasted the word on her own lips. It sounded earthy and forbidden, like Rico Cortes. She sensed that both had something primal and very dangerous at their core.

'You wanted real flamenco,' he said, drawing Zoë back to the purpose of her visit. 'Well, *this* is real flamenco. This is wild, impassioned art at its most extreme. Are you ready for that, Zoë Chapman?'

She heard the doubt in his voice. Perhaps he saw her as a dried-up husk, incapable of feeling passion of any sort—and why not? He wouldn't be the first man to think that. 'I'm just really grateful to have this chance to see flamenco at its best.'

'You don't see flamenco. You feel it.'

'I know that now.' He thought of her as a tourist out for a cheap thrill, Zoë realised. But she was a long way from the tourist trail here. She was a long way from her old life too—the old Zoë Chapman would have backed off without a fight, but there was no chance of that now. She knew what she could achieve, with or without a man at her side. And she hadn't come to Spain to be insulted. She had come to make a programme, a good programme. She wasn't going to let Rico Cortes distract her from that goal. 'Can you explain this word *duende* to me?'

'You'll know it when you feel it.'

'What—like an itch?'

'Like an orgasm.'

Zoë's mouth fell open. Not many things shocked her. OK, so she'd been less than reverent in response to his cutting remarks, but it had been a serious question. She had been right about him. Rico Cortes was a man of extremes—a man who was looking at her now with a brooding expression on his face, no doubt wondering if his shock tactics had been sufficient to scare her off.

'An emotional orgasm, you mean?' She was pleased with her composure under fire.

'That's right.'

There was a spark of admiration in his eyes. It gave her a rush—maybe because there was passion in the air long after the woman's performance had ended. Vibrations from the flamenco seemed to have mixed with his maleness, taking her as close to *duende* as she would ever get. She held his gaze briefly, to prove that she could, and found it dark and disconcerting. Her body was trembling with awareness, as if an electric current had run through her.

'So, you have taken a summer lease on Castillo Cazulas,' he said, staring down at her as if he knew what she was feeling. 'And you want to make a programme about flamenco. Why here, of all places? Hardly anyone outside the village knows about the Confradias Cazulas flamenco camp.'

'People who know about flamenco do. And I enjoyed the walk.'

'But how will you find your way back again? It's almost dark.'

He was right, but she was prepared. 'I have this.' Digging in her pocket, Zoë pulled out her flashlight. Suddenly it didn't seem adequate. She should have remembered how fast daylight disappeared in Spain. It was as if the sun, having blazed so vigorously all day, had worn itself out, and dropped like a stone below the horizon in minutes.

They both turned as some more dancers took the stage. They were all talented, but none possessed the fire of the first woman. She had already found her guest artist, Zoë realised, but she would still need an introduction.

Glancing up, she knew that Rico was her best chance. But there were man waves coming off him in torrents, and he smelled so good—like pine trees and wood smoke. His sexual heat was curling round her senses like a blanket. *And lowering her guard!* She hadn't come to Spain to indulge in an adolescent fantasy over some arrogant stud. Her interest in flamenco was purely professional. Work was all she cared about; a new man figured nowhere in her plans.

By the time the stage had cleared again it was pitch-dark, with no moon. Quite a few people had come by car, parking in a clearing not too far away. Zoë watched with apprehension as their headlights glowed briefly before disappearing into the night.

'You really think that little light of yours is going to be enough?' Rico said, as if reading her mind.

Zoë glanced at him. 'It will have to be.' Shoving her hands in the pockets of her track suit, she tilted her chin towards the stage. 'Was that the last performance for tonight?'

'You want more?'

'How much would it cost to hire someone like that first performer—the older woman?'

She saw an immediate change in his manner.

'All the money on earth couldn't buy talent like that. *You* certainly couldn't afford it.'

Zoë bit back the angry retort that flew to her lips. This was no time for temperament: everyone was leaving—the woman too, if she didn't act fast. Their gazes locked; his eyes were gleaming in the darkness. This man frightened her, and she knew she should turn away. But she couldn't afford to lose the opportunity.

'I'm sorry—that was clumsy of me. But you can't blame me for being carried away by that woman's performance—'

'Maria.' His voice was sharp.

'Maria,' Zoë amended. She felt as if she was treading on eggshells, but his co-operation was crucial. She generally made a very convincing case for appearing on the show. Right now, she felt like a rank amateur. There was something about Rico Cortes that made her do and say the wrong thing every time. 'Maria's performance was incredible. Do you think she would dance for me?'

'Why on earth would she want to dance for *you*?'

'Not for me, for my show. Do you think Maria would agree to dance on my programme?'

'You'd have to ask her yourself.'

'I will. I just wanted to know what you thought about it first.' Zoë suspected nothing happened in Cazulas without Rico's say-so.

'It depends on what you can offer Maria in return.'

'I would pay her, of course—'

'I'm not talking about money.'

'What, then?'

A muscle worked in his jaw. 'You would have to win her respect.'

Did he have to look so sceptical? 'And what do you think would be the best way to do that?'

They were causing some comment, Zoë noticed, amongst the few people remaining, with this exchange, conducted tensely head to head. It couldn't be helped. She had to close the deal. She wasn't about to stop now she had him at least talking about the possibility of Maria appearing on the show.

'You'd have to bargain with her.'

An opening! Maybe not a door, but a window—she'd climb through it. 'What do you suggest I bargain with?' She smiled, hoping to appeal to his better nature.

'Are *you* good at anything?' Rico demanded.

Apart, that was, from joining the hordes who spied on him and the idiots who thought an important part of his heritage had the same value as the cheap tourist tat along the coast.

She had manoeuvred him into starting negotiations with her, though. She was sharper than most. He should have got rid of her right away, but his brain had slipped below his belt.

He shouldn't have stayed away from Cazulas for so long. He should have kept a tighter hold on who was allowed into the village. But he had trusted such things to a management company. He wouldn't be doing that again.

'I don't just make programmes,' she said, reclaiming his attention. 'I present them.'

'I apologise.' He exaggerated the politeness. 'Apart from your ability to make programmes and present them, what do you have to bargain with that might possibly interest Maria?'

'I cook.'

Removing her hands from her pockets, she planted them on her hips. She smiled—or rather her lips tugged up at an appealing angle while her eyes blazed defiance at him. Her manner amused him, and attracted him too. 'You cook?'

'Is there something wrong with that?'

'No, nothing at all—it's just unexpected.'

'Well, I don't know what you were expecting.'

Just as well. He had been running over a few things that would definitely make it to the top of his wish list, and cooking wasn't one of them. Outsiders were practically non-existent in the mountains. It was a rugged, difficult terrain, and yet Zoë Chapman, with her direct blue-green gaze and her wild mop of titian hair, had come alone and on foot, with a flashlight as her only companion, to find—what had she expected to find?

Rico's eyes narrowed with suspicion. In his experience, women made careful plans; they didn't just turn up on the off chance. 'We'll discuss this some other time. I'll have someone see you home.'

'When I've spoken to Maria.'

Her mouth was set in a stubborn line. He liked her lips. He liked her eyes too—when they weren't spitting fire at him.

She was about five-five, lightly built—but strong, judging from her handshake. The rest was a mystery beneath her shapeless grey track suit. Maybe it was better that way. There were very few surprises left in life.

But this was one mystery parcel he had no intention of unwrapping. The gutter press could use subtle tactics to succeed. Zoë Chapman might be working for anyone—how did he know? The television company, even the programme she was supposed to be making, could all be a front. Cazulas was special—the one place he could get some space, some recreation—and no one was going to spoil that for him.

'So, you'll introduce me to Maria?'

She was still here? Still baiting him? Rico's jaw firmed as he stared at Zoë. The sensible thing to do would be to cut her, blank her out, forget about her. But she intrigued him too much for that. 'It's not convenient right now—'

'Who says so?'

'Maria!' Rico turned with surprise. 'I didn't hear you coming.'

'That is obvious.' The older woman's eyes were bright and keen as she stared curiously at Zoë. 'But now I am here why don't you introduce us, Rico?'

'She won't be staying—'

'I will!'

Maria viewed them both with amusement.

'I didn't think you would be interested in what Ms Chapman had to say,' Rico said with a dismissive shrug.

'So now you are thinking for me, Rico?'

There was a moment when the two of them stared at each other, unblinking, and then Rico pulled back. 'Maria Cassavantes—allow me to present Zoë Chapman to you.'

'Zoë,' Maria repeated, imbuing Zoë's name with new colour. 'I have heard rumours about your television programmes and I would like to talk to you. Forget Rico for a moment. Perhaps we can come to some arrangement?'

It was everything Zoë had hoped for—but forget about Rico? That was asking a bit too much. She saw him tense and she couldn't resist a quick glance of triumph.

Rico was seething. What was Maria thinking of? They knew nothing about this Zoë Chapman—nothing at all. What set her apart from all the other female sharks, with their bleached teeth and avaricious natures? Maria hadn't a clue what she was letting herself in for—she was playing with fire...

'We should know more about your cookery programme before Maria agrees to do anything.' He took a step forward, deliberately putting himself between them. 'I don't see how flamenco could possibly be relevant.'

'If you'd only let me explain—'

'How can I be sure you're not wasting Maria's time?'

'I said I don't mind this, Rico.' Maria put a restraining hand on his arm. 'I would like to talk to Zoë and hear what she's got to say—'

'I promise you, Maria,' Zoë cut in, 'I'm not in the habit of wasting anyone's time, least of all my own. And if you need me to prove it to you—'

'I really do.' It was Rico's turn to butt in.

Maria was forgotten as they glared at each other. Then Zoë broke eye contact, allowing him a brief moment of satisfaction.

'I'll make everyone in the village a meal,' she declared, gesturing extravagantly around the clearing. 'How does that suit you, Rico?'

Now he was surprised. 'That's quite an offer.' There was just enough doubt in his voice to provoke her, to brighten her green eyes to emerald and make her cheeks flare red.

'I mean it.'

'Fine.' He lifted up his hands in mock surrender, then dipped his head, glad of the opportunity to conceal the laughter brewing behind his eyes. Somehow he didn't think Ms

Chapman would appreciate humour right now. But there were about one hundred and sixty souls in the village. She would never pull it off.

Ms Chapman. Who knew what was behind a name?

Rico's gaze flew to Zoë's hands. Clean, blunt fingernails, cut short, but no ring, no jewellery at all. He drew an easing breath. That was all he needed to know. It gave him the freedom to overlook his vow never to court trouble on his own doorstep again. 'I shall look forward to it, Ms Chapman.'

'Rico,' Maria scolded him, 'why don't you call our new friend Zoë, as we're going to be working together?'

'So we *are* going to be working together, Maria?'

She sounded so excited. Rico ground his jaw and watched with concern as the two women hugged each other. Zoë Chapman wouldn't win *him* round so easily.

'I have never appeared on television,' Maria exclaimed.

'I'm going to make it special for you, Maria.'

Zoë's promise grated on him. If she let Maria down—

'I think we'll make a good team.' Maria looked at him and raised her eyebrows, as if daring him to disagree.

For now it seemed he had no choice in the matter. Zoë Chapman had won this round, but he would be waiting if she stepped out of line. Maria might have been taken in, but he wasn't so easily convinced. The thought of an artist of Maria's calibre appearing on some trivial holiday programme with a few recipes thrown in made him sick to his stomach.

As far as he was concerned, *Ms* Chapman had identified her quarry and had stopped at nothing until she got her own way. She was no innocent abroad. She had all the grit and determination of the paparazzi. That wary look he had detected in her eyes when she looked at him didn't fool him for a minute. It was all an act. She was as guilty as hell. But Maria was right. He wouldn't presume to make decisions for Maria Cassavantes, though in his experience third-rate television companies only dealt in plastic people; treasures like Maria were out of their league.

If he had to, he would step in to protect her from Zoë Chapman. But for now he was sufficiently intrigued to give Ms Chapman enough rope to hang herself. He would watch her like a hawk, and the first time she tried to cheapen or trivialise what Maria Cassavantes stood for both she and her television cameras would be thrown out of Spain.

CHAPTER TWO

'CAN we talk business now, Maria?'

'That sounds very formal,' Rico cut in.

He was suspicious of her motives. She had to curb her enthusiasm, take it slowly, Zoë reminded herself. She usually got to know people first, before talking business. Building confidence was crucial. Contrary to popular opinion, not everyone wanted to appear on television. Usually she was good at choosing the right moment, but having Rico in the picture was making her edgy, making her rush things.

'I know it's late—I won't keep you long.' She glanced at Rico. 'Perhaps if Maria and I could talk alone?'

'It's all right, Rico,' Maria said soothingly.

'I'd rather stay.'

Zoë looked up at him. 'It's really not necessary.'

'Nevertheless.' He folded his arms.

For Maria's sake Zoë tried to bite back her impatience, but she was tired and stressed and the words just kept tumbling out. 'Really, Rico, I can't see any reason why you should stay. Maria and I are quite capable of sorting this out between us—'

'It's better if I stay.'

She could see he was adamant. 'Are you Maria's manager?'

'They call him El Paladín,' Maria cut in, interposing her not inconsiderable body between them.

'El Paladín?' Zoë repeated. 'Doesn't that mean The Champion?' She only had a very basic knowledge of conversational Spanish to call upon. 'What's that for, Rico? Winning every argument?'

23

'Rico is everyone's champion,' Maria said fondly, patting his arm.

That seemed highly unlikely—especially where she was concerned, Zoë thought. 'Champion of what?' she pressed.

'Zoë likes her questions,' Rico observed sardonically, 'but she's not too keen on giving answers about why she's really here in Cazulas—'

'And Zoë's right about you,' Maria cut in. 'You don't like losing arguments, Rico.'

'I like to win,' he agreed softly.

Lose? Win? Where was all this leading? Zoë wondered, suppressing a shiver as she broke eye contact with Rico. 'We're never going to win Rico's approval, Maria, but I believe we can make great television together.'

'What have you been telling this young woman, *malvado*?' Maria demanded, turning her powerful stare on him.

'Nothing. If you want to dance and she wants to cook, that's fine by me. Only problem is, we know *you* can dance.'

'Rico!' Maria frowned at him.

'My third television series says I can cook!'

'There—you see, Rico,' Maria said, smiling at Zoë.

'And the connection between dancing and cooking is what, exactly?' He raised his shoulders in a shrug as he stared at Zoë.

He would never go for her idea, but at least she had Maria's support. She had to forget Rico's insults and build on what she had. But he was one complication she could do without. He probably crooked his finger and every woman around came running. Well, not this woman.

Turning to Maria, Zoë deliberately cut him out. 'This is the connection, Maria: the people around me inspire the food I cook on television. In this part of Spain the influence of flamenco is everywhere.'

'So cooking isn't just a hobby for you?' Rico said.

Zoë stared up at him. He refused to be cut out. 'No, Rico, it's a full-time career for me.'

'Along with your television company.'

Maria stepped between them again. 'So you would like me to dance on your television programme to add some local interest to the dishes you prepare? Is that right, Zoë?'

'Exactly.' Zoë's face was confident as she flashed a glance at Rico. 'I'll cook, you'll dance, and together we'll make a great team.'

'*Bueno,*' Maria said approvingly. 'I like the sound of this programme of yours. Of course, any payment must be donated to the village funds.'

'Absolutely,' Zoë agreed. 'Whatever you like.'

Maria smiled. 'Well, that all sounds quite satisfactory to me.'

But not to Rico, Zoë thought. At least he was silent for now. 'I have never seen anyone dance like you, Maria. You are fantastic.'

'*Gracias*, Zoë. And you are very kind.'

'Not kind, Maria, just honest.' Zoë stopped, hearing Rico's scornful snort in the background. What did she have to do to convince him?

She turned to look at him coldly. There were a couple of buttons undone at the neck of his dark linen shirt, showing just how tanned and firm he was. She turned back quickly to Maria. 'When you appear, I just know the programme will come to life…' Zoë's voice faded. She could feel Rico's sexual interest lapping over her in waves.

'Don't worry, Zoë,' Maria assured her, filling the awkward silence. 'It will be fine—just you wait and see.'

Zoë wasn't so sure, and she was glad of Maria's arm linked through her own as the older woman drew her away from Rico, towards the bright circle of light around the campfire.

'Have you offered Zoë a drink?' Maria said, turning back to him.

'She's had more than enough to drink already.'

'Surely you didn't let her drink the village liquor?'

'It's all right, Maria,' Zoë said hastily. She could see the hard-won progress she had made winning Maria's trust vanishing in the heat of a very Latin exchange. 'Thank you for the kind offer, but I've already had some coffee.'

Rico was staring at her almost as if he was trying to remember why she made him so uneasy. But they couldn't have met before. And he couldn't know about her past; she was anonymous in the mountains. Television reception was practically non-existent, and there were no tabloid papers on sale at the kiosk in the village.

'So, Zoë, when do I dance for you?' Maria said, reclaiming Zoë's attention.

'How about Tuesday?' Zoë said, turning back to thoughts of work with relief. 'That gives us both time to prepare.'

'Tuesday is good for me.' Maria smiled broadly as she broke away. 'On Tuesday you cook, and I dance.'

'Are you sure you know what you're taking on, Zoë?'

Rico's words put a damper on their enthusiasm.

'Why? Don't you think I'm up to it?'

'It's *what* you're up to that I'm more interested in.'

'Then you're going to have a very dull time of it,' Zoë assured him. 'I'm going to cook and Maria is going to dance. I don't know what you're imagining, but it really is as simple as that.'

'In my experience, nothing is ever that simple.'

Zoë's gaze strayed to his lips: firm, sensuous lips that never grew tired of mocking her.

'Today is Saturday—no, Sunday already,' Maria said with surprise, staring at her wristwatch. 'It is well past midnight. I have kept you far too long, Zoë.'

'That's not important,' Zoë assured Maria, turning to her with relief. 'All that matters is that you're happy—you're the most important person now. I want to make sure you have everything you need on the night of your performance.'

'Such as?' Maria said.

'Well—would you like to eat before or after you dance?'

'Both. I need to build up my strength.' She winked at Zoë. 'Some people don't need to build up strength, of course.' She shot a glance at Rico. 'But you had better feed him anyway. I'm sure he'd like that.'

'I'm sure he would.' Zoë's gaze veered coolly in Rico's direction. She might find him a few sour grapes.

'Don't take me for granted, Zoë,' he said, 'I might not even be there.'

'Don't worry, Rico. Where you're concerned I won't take anything for granted. I'll expect you at the castle around nine?' she confirmed warmly with Maria.

'And I will dance for your cameras at midnight.'

Zoë felt a rush of pleasure not even Rico could spoil. She had accomplished her mission successfully, and there was a bonus—she had made a new friend in Maria. She just knew Maria would have what they called 'screen magic', and the programme in which she featured would be unique.

'Rico, would you make sure that everyone in the village knows they are welcome to come and eat at Castillo Cazulas and celebrate Maria's performance on Tuesday night?' Zoë said, turning to him.

For a moment he was amazed she had included him in her arrangements. He had to admit he admired her guts—even if she did annoy the hell out of him. He should be there, just to keep an eye on her.

In fact, he could take a look around right now if he drove her back to the castle. Time to turn on the charm.

'Don't worry, no one loves a party more than we do in Cazulas—isn't that right, Maria?' He looked at Zoë. 'You'll be calling in extra help, I imagine?'

There was something in Rico's eyes Zoë didn't like.

Something that unnerved her. 'There's no need. I'm not alone at the castle, Rico. I have my team with me—and don't forget that cooking is what I do for a living.'

Turning away from him, she said her goodbyes to Maria, all the time conscious of Rico's gaze boring into her back. He might as well have gripped her arms, yanked her round, and demanded she give him her life history. She could only think that having a woman set both the rules and the timetable was something entirely new to him.

'How are you going to get home tonight, Zoë?' Maria said.

'I'll drive her back.'

'I'll walk.'

Maria frowned, looking from Rico to Zoë and back again. 'Of course you will drive Zoë home, Rico.' She put her arm around Zoë's shoulder. 'It is too dangerous for you to walk, Zoë, and you will be quite safe with Rico—I promise you.'

There was something in Maria's eyes that made Zoë want to believe her. But as she walked away Zoë could have kicked herself. Why hadn't she just asked if she could take a lift with Maria?

'Are you ready to go?' Rico said.

'I thought we'd already been through this.' Digging in her pocket, Zoë pulled out her flashlight again.

'Oh, that's right. I had forgotten you were an intrepid explorer.'

'I'll only be retracing my steps—'

'In the dark.'

'Well, I'd better get going, then.'

She moved away, and for one crazy moment hoped he would come after her. When he did she changed her mind. 'I'll be fine, Rico. Really.'

'What are you afraid of, Zoë? Is there something at the castle you don't want me to see?'

'Is that what you think?' She ran her hand through her hair

as she looked at him. 'I can assure you I have nothing to hide. Come around and check up on me if you don't believe me.'

'How about now?'

'I'd rather walk.'

'Well, I'm sorry, Maria's right. I can't let you do that. It's far too dangerous.'

Maria hadn't left yet. Her friend's truck was still parked in the clearing. She might just catch them. But Maria moved as fast as she had on the stage. Climbing into the cab, she slammed the door and waved, leaving Zoë standing there as the truck swung onto the dirt road leading down to the village and accelerated away.

'Don't look so worried.'

Don't look so worried? I'm stuck at the top of a mountain in the middle of the night with a flashlight and the local brigand—who happens to have a chip on his shoulder labelled 'media-types/female'—and I shouldn't worry?

'Like I said, I'll drive you back.'

'No way!'

'You can cut the bravado, Zoë—there's no moon, hardly any path, and this stupid little light won't save you when you're plunging down a precipice.'

'Give that back to me now.' Zoë made a swipe for her flashlight, but Rico was too quick for her.

'It's no trouble for me to drop you at the castle.'

'Thank you, I'll walk.'

She got as far as the rock-strewn trail leading down to the valley before he caught hold of her arm and swung her around.

'You are not going down there on your own.'

'Oh, really?'

'Yes, really.'

Their faces were too close. As their breath mingled Zoë closed her eyes. 'Let go of me, Rico.'

'So you can mess up a rock? So you can cause me a whole

lot of trouble in the morning when I have to come looking for your mangled body? I don't think so, lady.'

'Your concern is overwhelming, but I really don't need it! I know these mountains—'

'Like the back of your hand? And you've been here how long?'

'Nearly a month, as a matter of fact.' That silenced him, Zoë noted with satisfaction.

As long as that? Rico ground his jaw. Another reason to curse the fact he had stayed away too long. He couldn't let her go—he didn't want to let her go—and he wanted to find out what she was hiding. 'You don't know these mountains at night. This path is dangerous. There's a lot of loose stone, and plenty of sheer drops.'

'I'll take my chances.'

'The road isn't half bad.'

Somehow he managed to grace his last words with a smile.

She stopped struggling and looked at him, her bright green eyes full of suspicion.

'Come on, Zoë, you know you don't really want to walk.' Charm again? New ground for him, admittedly, but well worth it if she agreed. If he took her back he could take a look around. He knew her name from somewhere—and not just from the television. But how did she affect him? Was she a threat? 'It's only a short drive in the Jeep.'

'OK,' Zoë said at last.

She was relieved she didn't have to walk back in the dark. But as Rico dug for his keys in the back pocket of his jeans she wondered if she was quite sane. If it hadn't been for Maria's reassurances she would never have agreed to anything so foolish. She didn't know a thing about Rico Cortes, and the day her divorce came through she had promised herself no more tough guys, no more being pushed around, mentally or physically.

'Don't look so worried. You'll be a lot safer going down

the mountain in the Jeep with me. Are you coming or not?' he said when she still hesitated. 'I've got work tomorrow.'

'Tomorrow's Sunday.'

'That's right—and I have things to get ready for Monday morning.'

'What things?' Maybe he *was* the local brigand, and Monday was his day for mustering the troops. And she had agreed to take a lift home with him...

Zoë frowned as he opened the passenger door for her. Rico Cortes was as much a mystery now as ever, and it wasn't like her. She was an expert at winkling out information. It was the secret of her success—or had been in the past.

The moment he swung into the driver's seat beside her she fired off another question. 'What keeps you in this part of Spain?' He was larger than life, which went with the dramatic scenery, but he didn't fit into the small-town scene at all.

'I have many interests.'

'Such as?'

He didn't answer as he gunned the engine into life. The noise was supposed to distract her, she guessed. He was dodging her questions like an expert—almost as if he was used to dealing with the media.

Local reporter, maybe?

No way! And better not to ask—better not to get involved. She had only just won her freedom from an unhappy marriage. Divorce had come at a high price, even if the break had been like a cleansing torrent that washed most of her insecurities away. And she didn't want them back again. Ever. So why had she agreed to take a lift back to the castle with a man she didn't know? The only answer was that Maria liked him, and she liked Maria.

Was that enough? It had to be, Zoë realised as they pulled away.

Maria had said he was a fighter. El Paladín. Was fighting

his profession? Zoë felt a quiver of apprehension run down her spine as she flashed a glance at him.

No, it couldn't be. Not unless he was the luckiest pugilist alive. He was built like a fighter but his face was unmarked, and his hands, as she had already noticed, were smooth. And in spite of his casual clothes, and his life up in this remote mountainous region, he had polish. But then quite a few boxers did too...

'Seen enough, Zoë?'

'I'm sorry, was I staring? I'm so tired I hardly know what I'm doing.'

Rico could feel the sexual tension between them rising fast. Any other time, any other woman, he might have swung off the road and fixed it for them both. But he had to know more about a woman before he got involved. He wasn't about to commit some reckless indiscretion Zoë Chapman could broadcast to the world.

He had learned not to court disaster on his own doorstep. She was luscious, but she would keep, and she backed off every time he looked at her. If she had kept her legs crossed all this time she would wait a little longer.

What if she was innocent? It seemed unlikely, but— No. Life wasn't like that. Fate never dealt him an easy hand.

Guilty, innocent—it hardly mattered which. He would still go slow until he'd worked out what made her tick... Go slow? So he *was* going somewhere with her?

Rico smiled. He could feel Zoë looking at him. Life got too easy at the top of the mountain. He hadn't had anything approaching a real challenge to deal with in quite some time.

Normally Zoë was a confident passenger, but Rico Cortes scared the hell out of her driving back down the steep track. He really did know the mountains like the back of his hand. And the speed he took the road, it was just as well—because the only faster way would have been over a cliff.

She was relieved to arrive back in one piece at the castle,

and even more relieved when she talked him out of staying. He'd wanted to look around, but he couldn't argue when she pointed out how late it was and that they would wake everyone up. But he would be back on Tuesday for the party—he made that clear.

This mess had to be sorted out before then.

Zoë groaned as she looked round the set. She had discussed the layout with her chief designer. But, according to the note she'd found propped up on the kitchen table, Carla had been called home to attend a family emergency and her young assistant had stepped in.

Zoë couldn't be angry with him; she could see he had tried. But he had fallen a long way short of achieving the authentic look she had decided on with Carla. How could she expect Maria to take part in a show that featured a fake Spanish kitchen decorated with imitation fruit? It might look real enough through a camera lens, but it would never pass close scrutiny, and it would only reinforce Rico's misconceptions about her work.

Why should he barge into her thoughts? She had more important things to consider—like rescuing the programme from disaster! Men like Rico Cortes were no good—great to drool over, maybe, but worse than lousy in real life.

Planting her hands on her hips, Zoë looked round again, but things didn't improve on closer inspection.

Posters brashly proclaiming the title of her latest bestselling cookery book were tacked up everywhere, while garish bunting was strung overhead. The exquisite marble-tiled floor had been hidden beneath a hideous orange carpet, and in the centre of the shag-pile the open-fronted area where she would be filmed sat in all its plywood and plastic glory. Hardly any attempt had been made to mask the fact that it was blatantly fake. There was lurid fake greenery draped around the top, with plastic fruit tacked in clumps to the backdrop.

It would all have to come down, but it could wait until the

morning. She couldn't concentrate while she was so tired. She couldn't concentrate while her thoughts kept straying back to Rico Cortes. A good night's sleep would help her get over him, and then she would get down to work.

As soon as it was light Zoë leapt out of bed. The crew were due on set at nine for a technical rehearsal. That was when the lights, camera angles and sound levels would be decided upon. The best she could hope for was that they would sleep in. She didn't have much time to strip the set and redress it, but it was important she had an authentic set in place for the rehearsal so there would be little or no change when she recorded the programme. She didn't like surprises when the red light went on.

Half an hour later she had picked fruit straight from the trees and brought in a basket full of greenery from the shady part of the castle gardens. Each time she'd visited the market in Cazulas Zoë hadn't been able to resist buying another piece of the local hand-painted pottery, and she now laid out her hoard on a working table along with the fresh produce.

She stared up at the plastic bunting.

Balancing halfway up a ladder wasn't easy, but, working quickly, she got the bunting down, then moved to the 'fishing net' on the back wall of the set to flip out some more tacks. Then she still had to tackle the plastic castanets pinned up with the plastic fruit on the same wall. Proper wooden castanets were miniature works of art. They came alive in the hands of an artist like Maria. These plastic efforts were about as Spanish as chop suey!

Sticking the screwdriver she had found in a kitchen drawer into the back pocket of her jeans, Zoë glanced at her wristwatch and made a swift calculation. If she could get the rest of them down without too much trouble, she might just finish in time.

'Talk about a relief!'

'Are you speaking to me?'

'Rico!' Zoë nearly fell off her ladder with shock. 'What are you doing here?' Her knuckles turned white as she gripped on tight. She watched transfixed as he swooped on the clutch of castanets she had just dropped to the floor.

'Very nice,' he said, examining them. 'Which region of Spain do these represent?'

'Bargain basement,' Zoë tried lightly, trying to regulate her breathing at the same time. How could any man look so good so early in the morning after hardly any sleep? It just wasn't human. 'How did you get in?' she said, as it suddenly struck her that she would never have gone to bed and left the front door wide open.

He ignored her question—and her attempted humour. 'What is all this rubbish?'

Coming down the ladder as quickly as she could in safety, Zoë faced him. 'The set for my television show.' Her appreciative mood was evaporating rapidly. She had never seen such scorn on anyone's face.

'I gathered that.' He stared around with disapproval.

OK, so it was a mess—but it was her mess, and she would sort it out. Zoë could feel her temper rising. According to the lease, at this moment Castillo Cazulas belonged to her. She could do with it what she liked. And if plastic castanets were her style, Señor Testosterone would just have to put up with it.

Reaching out, she took them from him. 'Thank you.' His hands felt warm and dry. They felt great. 'Can I help you with anything?' Her voice was cool, but she was trembling inside.

'Yes, you can. You can get all this trash out of here.'

'Trash?'

'You heard me. I want it all removed.'

'Oh, you do?' Zoë said, meeting his stare. 'And what business is it of yours, exactly?'

Ignoring her question, Rico paced the length of the set, shoulders hunched, looking like a cold-eyed panther stalking its prey. 'You can't seriously expect an artist of Maria's calibre to perform in this *theme park*?'

'No, of course I don't—'

'Then get all this down! Get rid of it! Do whatever you have to do to put it right—just don't let me see it the next time I'm here.'

'Next time? There doesn't have to be a next time, Rico,' Zoë assured him with a short, humourless laugh.

'Oh, forgive me.' He came closer. 'I thought you invited me here for Tuesday.'

'If you feel so bad about all this—' Zoë opened her arms wide '—there's an easy solution.'

'Oh?'

'I'll just withdraw my invitation, and then you won't have to suffer another moment's distress.'

'That would be too easy for you.'

'Easy?' Zoë rested one hand on her head and stared at him incredulously. What the hell was easy about any of this? As far as she was concerned, nothing had been easy since she'd run up against Rico Cortes.

'If you want Maria to dance, I'll be here.'

'Oh, I see,' Zoë said sarcastically. 'You own Maria. You make all her decisions for her—'

'Don't be so ridiculous.'

'So what do you think is going to happen here, Rico? As far as I know we'll be making a television programme. I'll be cooking, Maria will dance, and everyone in the village will have a great time at the party. Is that so terrible?'

He made a contemptuous sound. 'You make it sound so straightforward.'

'Because it is!' What was he getting at? Why didn't he trust her?

They glared at each other without blinking, and then Rico

broke away to stare around. His expression hardened. 'You don't seriously expect me to allow my friends to come to a place like this on Tuesday night.'

'Oh, so now you own the whole village? I didn't realise the feudal system was alive and well in Cazulas. I suppose it's never occurred to you that my neighbours might be capable of thinking for themselves?'

'Your neighbours don't know what you plan to do here.'

'What *do* I plan to do, exactly?'

'You don't respect them.'

'How do you know that?'

'You don't respect their culture.'

'How dare you say that?'

'How dare I?' Rico's voice was contemptuous as he glared down at her.

He was close enough for her to touch—or attack—but she would never lower herself to that. She wasn't about to lose control, like every man she had ever known, and let Rico add that to her long list of shortcomings.

'You come here to Cazulas—Cazulas, of all the flamenco villages in Spain! And you try to tell me it's just a coincidence? And then you bring Maria into it. Another coincidence? I don't think so.'

She'd had enough. She wasn't going to stand by and let him rant. 'You're right, Rico. Bringing Maria into my plans was no coincidence. The reason I asked her to appear on my programme is because she is easily the best dancer I have ever seen. She is certainly the best performer in Cazulas. That's no coincidence; it's a fact.' Zoë couldn't be sure if Rico had heard her or not. He was so tense, so angry—like a wound-up spring on the point of release.

'You come here with your television cameras and your questions.' He gazed around the half-finished set contemptuously. 'You throw together some cheap items and pass it off as a Spanish setting. You really think that's going to convince me that you're putting together some worthy programme about cultural influences on Spanish cooking? You must think I'm stupid.'

'You're certainly mistaken.' But she could see that he might think she was putting up the plastic rubbish, rather than taking it down.

He was so still, so keyed up, he reminded her of a big cat before it pounced. Zoë was beginning to ache with holding herself so stiffly. She sagged with relief when he pulled away from her with a jerk.

'I'll be back to check up on you later. If this rubbish isn't removed by then you can forget Tuesday. Maria will not be dancing for you.'

'Doesn't Maria have a mind of her own?'

Rico was already striding towards the door. He stopped dead. He couldn't believe that she would still dare to challenge him. 'Yes, of course Maria has a mind of her own. She will take one look at this mess and refuse to dance.'

'Oh, get out!'

As he wheeled around he saw the local produce—fresh fruit, greenery, even some attractive pieces of hand-painted pottery. His lips curled in a sneer of contempt. Someone had planned to do something classy for the programme, something appropriate to the area. What a shame Zoë Chapman didn't have any taste.

She really was no better than the rest. Even if she didn't work at the gutter end of television, he would not stand by and see her discard Maria the moment her usefulness was at an end. Maria was too soft-hearted for her own good. It was up to him to protect her from people like Zoë Chapman.

Zoë jumped as the door slammed. Contempt for the disastrous set was about where her dial was pointing, too. But that didn't give Rico Cortes the right to come storming in, ordering her about.

Snatching a plastic parrot down from his perch, she tossed

it into the bin bag with the rest of the rubbish. She hated being caught on the back foot, hated leaving Rico Cortes with the impression that this was all her doing. Most of all she hated the fact that he was coming back to check up on her later. Who the hell did he think he was?

But it would have been far worse still if he hadn't planned to come back at all.

CHAPTER THREE

IT WAS all Rico could do to stay away from the castle. It was
barely noon. He had planned to return around late afternoon,
but every moment since leaving the castle had been torture.

He had never witnessed such desecration in his life. That
was the only reason he was pressing his heel to the floor now.
He ground his jaw with satisfaction as the Jeep surged forward. Zoë wouldn't expect him until later, and a surprise visit
always revealed more than a planned return. With any luck
he would catch her unawares.

Maybe she wasn't the type of tabloid journalist he loathed,
but she was still as shallow as the rest, still ignorant of the
precious heritage Maria carried forward in the village.

Before he'd left the castle that morning he'd found a member of the television crew, who had assured him they would
still be in rehearsal at midday. The youth had also confessed
that he was responsible for the set design.

What type of television company used boys fresh out of
college for such responsible work? If she owned a decent
television company, why didn't she have a proper set designer? Plastic parrots! What the hell did she think she was
filming? *Treasure Island?* And what kind of programme had
sets dressed with garish rubbish? He could think of a few
cable channels that might have gone down that route, and
none of them was respectable.

He'd seen Zoë up a ladder dressed in figure-hugging jeans
and a skimpy top, instead of her shapeless track suit—and
he'd heard her harangue him. He knew now she could play
angel or vamp with equal zest.

Glancing at his watch, Rico smiled grimly. He had timed

it just right. The rehearsal should have started. He would check out what line of entertainment Zoë Chapman was really in. Anticipation surged through him. Even through the red mist of his rage this morning she'd looked sensational. Pin-thin women weren't his style, and there was nothing pin-like about Ms Chapman. What would she wear to play her plastic castanets? She had curves that would have done credit to a Rubens.

Slowing the Jeep as he approached the ancient stonework, Rico picked up speed as he hit the long main drive. Accelerating down the avenue of cypress trees, he gave a final spin of the wheel and turned into the familiar cobbled court-yard.

Leaning back with his arms folded against a door at the far end of the Great Hall, he didn't announce his presence, just stood watching in silence. No one noticed him in the shadows. All the focus was on Zoë, in front of the camera.

Even he had to admit the transformation to the set was marked. In place of the fairground bunting and fake castanets there was a plain wooden butcher's block upon which she appeared to be chopping a mountain of herbs. She had a collection of wine bottles at her side, and from their shape he recognised a couple as coming from pretty decent cellars.

Rico began to feel increasingly uncomfortable as he watched Zoë working—and he never felt uncomfortable. But then, he had never misjudged anyone quite so badly before.

She couldn't possibly have thrown all this together in a few minutes. It had to be how she always worked—she was too familiar with everything around her for it to be a sham. Brass pots gleamed brightly on the cooking range, and the implements suspended from an overhead rail were all steel, with not a single gimmick in sight. There were wooden bowls close to hand on the counter where she was working, as well as several white porcelain saucers—bearing a selection of spices, he supposed. Next to them a large, shallow blue and white ceramic bowl overflowed with fresh vegetables. Maybe there were a lot of other things he couldn't trust about her, but this was real enough. He had to give her credit for that.

Zoë worked quickly and deftly, her small hands moving instinctively about the necessary tasks as she addressed herself cheerfully to camera. She had charisma as well as beauty, Rico thought, and he felt a sudden longing to harness her smiles and turn them in his own direction.

But how was he supposed to believe she had turned up in Cazulas by chance? If he could talk her into having dinner with him, maybe he could find out. But it wouldn't be easy after their ill-tempered exchange that morning... Easing away from the door, he decided to go. He had seen all he needed to see.

In between takes, Zoë's glance kept straying to the door. Half of her wanted to see Rico again, while the other half dreaded him walking in unannounced. But she needn't have worried because her director, Philip, had just wrapped the day's filming and there was still no sign of Rico. Empty threats, Zoë presumed. Rico's Spanish pride had taken a hit when she'd stood up to him. Or maybe she was just beneath contempt. That was probably it. His face when he'd seen the apprentice set designer's attempts to recreate a 'typical' Spanish setting had said it all. He'd thought she meant to trivialise everything he held dear.

And what was the point of trying to explain when he never listened? But he might have let her know if the others still planned to come on Tuesday night. If he had put them off... She would have to make sure he hadn't talked Maria out of appearing on the programme or she would be facing disaster. Perhaps she should go back to the mountains and find out what was happening?

Zoë was still frowning when one of the girls in the crew asked if she would like to eat with them in the local café that evening. 'I'd really love to come with you,' she said honestly, 'but there's something else I have to do first.'

Was all this totally necessary for a trek into the mountains? Zoë asked herself wryly as she craned her neck to check her rear view in the elegant console mirror. Of course she could always take off the snug-fitting jeans and replace them with a dirndl skirt… *No way!* And what about the blouse: ever so slightly see-through, with just one too many buttons left undone? OK, so maybe that was going a step too far. She fastened it almost to the neck. Reaching for a lightweight cotton sweater from the chair, she checked her hair one last time and then added a slick of lipgloss and a spritz of perfume.

Her eyes were glittering like aquamarine in a face that seemed unusually pale, Zoë noticed—apart from two smudges of red, high on each cheekbone. That was thanks to excitement at finally bringing the programme together. It was the culmination of a year of hard work. It had nothing at all to do with the fact that she might be seeing Rico Cortes again.

She had come to him. Rico subdued the rush of triumph before it had time to register on his face. 'Ms Chapman,' he said coolly. 'To what do we owe this pleasure?'

Leaning back against a gnarled tree trunk, arms folded, he watched Zoë's approach through narrowed eyes. Her unaffected grace was so like that of the dancers she admired, and she looked great in casual clothes. She wore little make-up, and her skin was honey-gold from her time in the sun. She was beautiful—very different from the glamorous women he was used to outside Cazulas, but all the more beautiful for that. The light was slipping away fast, and the sky behind the snow-capped mountains was more dramatic than any he had seen for a while: a radiant banner of violet and tangerine— the perfect backdrop for their latest encounter. The night breeze was kicking up, rustling through the leaves above his head as she walked up to him.

'You said you would come back to the castle.'

Her blunt statement took him by surprise—a pleasant one. 'I did come back, but you were working.'

That rather took the wind out of her sails, Zoë thought, but her heart was still thumping so violently she felt sure Rico would be able to hear it. 'I see.' She was relieved to sound so cool. 'I trust the changes I made met with your exacting standards?'

He gave a short laugh and relaxed. 'You did a great job, Zoë. Can I get you a drink?'

'Nothing stronger than orange juice!'

'Fine by me.'

He gestured that she should follow him, and his impressive rear view led her to silently praise the inventor of close-fitting jeans.

It was too early for the campfire to be lit, but there were still quite a lot of people around. Most of them were waiting for the children to finish their dance class. This meeting place served a number of functions, Zoë realised. There was the social side, and the performance opportunities, as well as the very valuable teaching that went on to preserve tradition.

She could see the youngsters now, tense with excitement and anticipation as they clustered around their dance teacher, listening to what she had to say. In another area a couple of the boys were sitting at the feet of the guitarist who had played for Maria, watching engrossed as his agile fingers rippled across the strings.

Pouring them both some juice from a covered jug that had been left for the children on a trestle table, Rico handed a glass to Zoë and then took her to sit with him on a flat rock out of the way. Crossing one leg over the other, he rested his chin on his hand as he listened to the music.

The low, insistent rhythm of the solo guitar was the perfect soundtrack for Rico Cortes, Zoë thought, glancing at him surreptitiously as she sipped her drink. Dressed in simple black jeans and a black top, he made her heart judder, he looked so good. The close-fitting top defined every muscle and sinew across the wide spread of his shoulders, and the jeans moulded thighs powerful enough to control a wild stallion, or a woman…

'You're far too early to see any of the adult performers dance, you know,' he said, his gaze lingering on Zoë's face as the guitarist picked out a particularly plangent arpeggio.

'I haven't come to see them,' she said, meeting his gaze steadily.

'Oh?' A crooked smile tugged at one corner of his mouth.

'Or you,' she said immediately. 'I hoped I might find Maria.'

'Well, you will—but you can't talk to her yet. So you might just as well settle back and enjoy the children rehearsing for our fiesta.'

'Fiesta? That must be fun.' Zoë turned to watch them. 'Does everyone take part in the fiesta?'

'Why don't you come along and see for yourself?'

She wanted to. She really wanted to feel part of Cazulas. Since the moment she'd arrived in the village she had felt an affinity with the area, and with the people. Rico made it sound so easy for her to become part of their way of life, but she wouldn't be staying that long.

'When will everyone else arrive?' Zoë looked around. There were a few cars parked already, notably Rico's rugged black Jeep.

'Most people take a long, lazy siesta in the afternoon, when the weather gets hot.'

'So Maria's still in bed?' Zoë could feel the blood rushing to her cheeks. Where was she going with *this* line of questioning?

'Many people are still in bed—but Maria is not one of

them.' Standing up, he beckoned to Zoë to follow him, and, walking ahead of her, he made for the stage where the children were still learning their steps.

Once again, he reminded Zoë of a big black panther. He had the same grace and stealth of a big cat, and made her feel very small by comparison. It was impossible not to imagine how it might feel to be enclosed in his arms and held safe. Or to be pinned down by those long, hard-muscled legs, and— *Stop it! Stop it now!* This was dangerous.

'Zoë?'

'Maria!' Zoë exclaimed, throwing her brain into gear. 'I'm sorry, I was daydreaming. I didn't realise it was you dancing with the children. It's good to see you again.'

'Why have you come here? Not to see the children, I think,' Maria said, tapping the side of her nose.

'No—no, of course not,' Zoë said, recovering fast. 'I came to see you.'

'Ah,' Maria said, staring at her keenly.

'I wanted to make sure you hadn't changed your mind.'

'Changed my mind? About dancing on Tuesday, you mean?' Maria said. 'Why would I?'

'Oh, I don't know,' Zoë said, suddenly embarrassed at the weakness of her supposed mission. She was conscious of Rico watching them, arms folded, with the same brooding look that made her quiver. 'I just wanted to be sure no one had put you off the idea.' She stopped, thinking frantically for something to explain her visit. 'After all, you don't know me—'

'Stop worrying,' Maria insisted. 'I will be there for you on Tuesday, Zoë. Your television programme will be made, and everything will turn out for the best in the end.'

Would it? Zoë wondered. There were moments when she wished she had never come to Spain. A fresh start was supposed to be just that—not a rerun with a matching set of characters that just happened to have different names.

Was she overreacting? She really hoped so. Men like Rico

had always been her downfall: big, powerful men like her ex-husband. Men who oozed testosterone through every pore; men who made her believe she could be desirable and might even find sexual fulfilment with them.

Unconsciously, Zoë made a small sound of despair. She was a sexual oddity—and likely to remain so. She was frightened of sex, it always hurt, and she wasn't sure how to improve the situation. Her husband had grown tired of her excuses. She had made him hate her. Small wonder they had divorced.

But that was behind her now. She had rebuilt her life. She couldn't allow anyone, especially Rico Cortes, to fan her past insecurities into flame...

'Zoë?' Maria asked softly. 'What is the matter?'

'Nothing.' Collecting herself, Zoë spoke firmly and smiled. 'Now,' she added quickly, before Maria could probe any deeper, 'I'd like to discuss my outline plan for the programme in which you're to appear. I want to be quite sure you're happy with everything.'

'*Bueno,*' Maria murmured softly, frowning a little as she allowed Zoë to lead her away from Rico.

The two women remained deep in conversation for some time. They were both on the same wavelength, Zoë realised. Maria was only too pleased to have the opportunity to bring genuine Spanish culture to a wider audience, and Zoë liked to present her food in context, rather than offering individual, unconnected recipes. This was her definition of lifestyle TV— a show that was genuine in every single respect—and now she had control over the content of her own programmes it was exactly what she delivered.

It was going to be really good, she realised with a sudden rush of excitement. Maria's talent would imbue the show with her own special quality. Rico had correctly identified it as something that no amount of money could buy.

Glancing around, Zoë looked for him. But he must have left while she was talking to Maria.

'Don't look so sad,' Maria insisted, chucking her under the chin. 'I know what we will do,' she added, getting to her feet.

Once again Zoë was struck by the difference in mobility between the Maria who had been sitting next to her and the Maria who performed on the stage—the one so fluid and graceful, the other showing definite, if gracious, signs of her age. 'What will we do, Maria?'

'We will dance together.'

'Oh, no, I can't—'

'You can walk, you can run, and you can jump?'

'Well, yes, of course—'

'Then you can dance,' Maria told her sternly. 'But first we must find you some clothes. Those will not do,' she said, eyeing Zoë's slim-fitting jeans and top. 'You look like a boy. I want to make you look like a woman.'

Zoë's eyes widened. She was too polite to argue. And far too curious to see what Maria meant to refuse.

Now she knew the secret of the wooden mountain house around which people congregated. It was packed to the rafters with the most spectacular clothes: rows of shoes, boxes of hair ornaments, cascading fringed shawls, and dresses by the score in every colour under the rainbow.

'You're so lucky to take performing under the stars for granted.' Zoë peered out of one of the small windows at the darkening sky. Someone had lit the campfire, and flames were just beginning to take hold. It was such a romantic scene, like something out of an old musical film. The children were still rehearsing—not because they had to now, but because they wanted to. Their heads were held high, faces rapt, their backs were arched and their hands expressive. 'The children are a credit to you, Maria.'

Maria paused as she sorted through the dresses packed tight

on the rail. 'They are a credit to themselves and to each other,' she corrected Zoë gently. 'And if they can do it, so can you.'

'Oh, no, really—I can't—' Her dancing was confined to her classes.

'Who said you can't? Here, try these on.'

Maria brought her an armful of clothes and Zoë's face broke into a smile. Maria was like a gust of fresh spring air behind a heavy rain cloud. It was impossible to be hooked by the past when she was around.

'The colour of this dress will look good on you.'

Zoë exclaimed with pleasure as she gazed at the beautiful lilac dress. Maria's confidence was infectious.

'You can put the dress on over there.' Maria pointed across the room. 'That's where the children get changed—behind that screen. When you have it on, come out and choose some shoes to fit you from this row here. Don't worry—I will help you to finish fastening the dress, and then I will do your hair.'

For once it was a pleasure to do as she was told. Zoë knew she would dance, because Maria would give her the confidence to do so. She was excited at the prospect of trying something new, especially now Rico had gone. She wouldn't have wanted to make a show of herself if he'd still been around.

Maria was right; the low-cut lilac dress did look good against her titian hair. It moulded her figure like a glove down to her hips, where it flared out, and then was longer at one side than the other. She was showing quite a bit of leg, Zoë saw in the mirror, raising the skirt with a flourish. Just wearing the dress made her stand straight and proud, made her want to toss back her hair with the same defiant move she had seen Maria perform on stage.

Dipping her chin, Zoë tried out her expression, staring fiercely into the mirror through a fringe of long lashes. A poster on the wall behind her caught her attention. The dark-haired young woman was incredibly beautiful. Passion blazed from her eyes as she glared straight into the camera. She had the sinuous frame of a top model, though was more striking than any model Zoë had ever seen. Her full lips were slightly parted and a strand of her long ebony hair had caught across them, giving her flamenco pose a sense of movement. There was a single word stretched across the top of the fiery background: Beba.

'*Bueno!*' Maria said with approval when Zoë finally emerged from behind the screen. 'That dress really suits you. I knew it would. Let me just finish the hooks and eyes at the back for you. They are hard for you to reach.'

'I feel different. It's ridiculous, but—'

'It's flamenco.' Maria laughed happily and stood back to look at Zoë. 'Now you feel proud and confident, like a woman should. Come, I will arrange your hair for you. And then we dance!'

Taka taka taka tak tak tak…taka taka taka tak… She was doing it! They had practised for about an hour on the dusty ground, and now Maria had deemed Zoë ready for the stage where, working together, the heels of their shoes made a crisp, satisfying sound on the hard wooden floor.

Breathing hard, her face fierce with concentration, Zoë thrust her head back as Maria had directed. One arm sweeping behind her back, she raised the other hand stiff, in a defiant pose, as if calling up some invisible energy…

'*Olé!*'

'Rico!'

'Don't stop now,' Maria ordered sharply.

But Zoë suddenly felt exposed and foolish. 'I'd much rather watch you,' she said, moving to the back of the stage. 'You haven't danced a solo yet.'

'I'm saving myself,' Maria said sardonically. 'Whereas you, Zoë, are hiding yourself.'

'That's not true…'

'Isn't it?' Maria demanded as Rico approached the stage.

'Why did you stop?' He stared up at Zoë.

'I'm very much a beginner—I'm not ready to perform in public.' Her heart lurched at his assessing look.

'But from what I have seen you have potential—don't you agree, Maria?'

'*Mucho* potential,' Maria agreed, but she made a disapproving sound with her tongue against the roof of her mouth when she looked at Rico, as if she sensed some double meaning behind his words.

'So, will you dance for me, Zoë?'

Rico's question had an alarming effect on Zoë's senses. It was like every seduction technique imaginable condensed into a few short words. She would love nothing more than to dance for him, with this new and abandoned feeling rushing through her. Just the thought of being so uninhibited in his presence was tempting. She felt strong, and in control, and highly sexual—as if the dance had enabled her to plunge head first into a world of sensuality for the first time in her life. Sucking in a deep, shuddering breath, Zoë realised she loved the feeling. It was intoxicating—and extremely dangerous.

'I'm waiting for your answer,' Rico reminded her.

Zoë glanced around, but Maria had melted away, lost in the crowds already gathering for that night's performance.

'Come down from there.'

She looked at him and hesitated.

'Please, Zoë?'

She was surprised. His voice had gentled.

'I don't bite, and—'

'Are you apologising to me?' Zoë said, cocking her head to one side as she looked at him.

'Me?' Rico half smiled at her as he touched one hand to his chest.

His eyes were different now, she noticed. Darker, still a

little guarded, but warmer—definitely warmer. 'Yes, you. Who else has doubted my motives in Cazulas, Rico?'

And he still doubted her motives. But he could handle it. He could handle her too. 'So, you're too timid to dance for me?'

'I don't do private exhibitions.'

'That's a pity.'

'Is it? Would you really think more of me if I made a habit of dancing for men? I don't think so. You've already shown your contempt for me—I can just imagine what you would make of that.'

'I admit we've got off to a bad start—'

'That's putting it mildly.'

'So, here's our chance to start again.'

'Should I want to?'

She saw his mouth quirk at one corner, as if he wanted to smile.

'I hoped you might.'

Zoë half turned away, lifting her chin as she considered his words. 'I'm not so sure,' she said, turning back to him again with a frown. 'Why should I? I don't need the aggravation.'

'Who said anything about aggravation, Zoë? Come on— come down from there and let's talk.'

She couldn't stand up on the stage all night. People were beginning to stare at her. She would have to do something soon—dance a solo or get off the stage. Picking up her skirt, she walked briskly down the steps.

'Zoë, please.'

She looked down at Rico's hand on her arm. 'This had better be good.'

'I hope you think so.'

She gasped when he drew her in front of him. 'Rico, what—?'

'I think I've behaved rather badly.'

'Yes, you have.' It was harder than she had thought to meet his gaze this close up.

'I can understand why you don't feel like trusting me now.'

'Can you?' She didn't trust herself either when he was around.

'Will you let me make amends? Have dinner with me.'

Zoë stared at him. Was he serious?

'Zoë?'

She had to get herself out of this somehow. 'I've got an idea.'

'Which is?'

He seemed amused. But hopefully this would get her off the hook. It was the only challenge she could think of that Rico wouldn't want to take up. 'If you cook for me, I'll dance for you.'

'*Bueno.*' He didn't waste any time over his answer. 'Shall we say later tonight?'

'Tonight?' All the breath seemed suddenly to have been sucked out of her lungs.

'We eat late in Spain.' Rico was quite matter-of-fact about it. Did he think her hesitation was due to ignorance of local customs? 'Shall we say ten o'clock?'

'Ten o'clock?' Zoë repeated, staring up at him blankly.

'Yes, let's say ten. That will give you enough time to prepare.'

To prepare what? She bit her lip. Unaccountably, her brain stalled, and not a single word of refusal made it to her lips.

'Then it's agreed,' Rico said with satisfaction. 'We will meet again, later tonight, at Castillo Cazulas.'

CHAPTER FOUR

THIS was the last thing she had expected to be doing, Zoë thought, as she tested the small four-wheel drive she had just hired to its limits. Rico had said he would follow her back to the castle later, to cook the meal and watch her dancing. She could only hope he was joking. The idea of dancing for him already seemed ridiculous.

Glancing in the driver's mirror, she saw the bundle of clothes Maria had insisted she take with her, assuring her that she would feel more comfortable dancing in them than jeans. More comfortable? Maybe—until Rico saw her wearing the flimsy low-necked blouse and ultra-feminine practice skirt!

She knew she was playing with fire, but where Rico Cortes was concerned it seemed she couldn't resist courting danger. Fortunately the film crew would be out partying until late, so no one would even know what she planned to do—or what kind of fool she made of herself.

As she pulled into the courtyard she thought about cancelling. But she didn't know how to get hold of Rico—and why should she pull out? She was more likely to dance than he was to cook. It was an opportunity to redress the balance between them...he would never doubt her will again.

The heavy iron knocker echoed ominously through the long stone passages as Zoë hurried to open the front door. Prompt at ten o'clock, Rico had said, and he was bang on time, she saw, glancing up at the tall grandfather clock on the turn of the stairs.

She was shivering all over with excitement and apprehension, and, reaching the hallway, she made herself slow down. She didn't want to appear too keen.

But as she walked her hips swayed beneath the ankle-length skirt, and as the swathes of fabric brushed her naked legs she knew the clothes Maria had given her to wear made her move quite differently. Even the simple peasant blouse was enough to make her want to throw her head back and walk tall. No wonder the women of Spain looked so magnificent when they stepped onto a stage when all their clothes were designed to make the most of the female form.

'Zoë.'

She could feel her face heating up as Rico stared at her. She tried for cool and unconcerned as she stood aside to let him pass. 'Welcome. How nice to see you.'

Nice! Zoë felt as if a furnace had just roared into flame somewhere inside her. She felt weak, she felt strong, and her legs were trembling uncontrollably beneath her skirt. She registered the flash of a dark, imperious gaze, and then he was gone, walking past her towards the kitchen.

He seemed to know his way—but then he would. Who knew how long he had been hanging around the castle earlier that morning? And so far he seemed to be keeping his side of the bargain: he had a box of provisions, as well as a guitar case slung over his shoulder.

'That was absolutely delicious,' she said, some time later.

'You seem surprised.'

She was, Zoë realised. Not only had Rico kept to his part of their bargain, he was an excellent cook. 'I am.'

'Because I can cook?'

Zoë smiled. It was hard to concentrate on anything apart from Rico's face as he stared at her. It wiped her mind clean, made her long to know him better. Physically, he was everything she knew to avoid. But they were alone together, and she wondered if she had misjudged him. He was still proud, male and alpha, but he had a sense of humour too—something she hadn't anticipated. 'I'm not surprised you can cook. I'm just surprised that you can cook so well.'

'Is there any reason why I should be incapable of feeding myself?'

'Of course not. It's just that most men—'

'Most men?'

She loved the way one of his eyebrows tilted a fraction when he asked a question. She'd been thinking of her ex, sitting at the table waiting for his meal after they had both put in a long day at work. He'd only commented on her food when it hadn't been to his liking. She had never received a compliment from him for her cooking.

'Most men wouldn't know their way around a warm barbecued vegetable salad with anchovies.'

'Escalivada amb anxoves?' Rico translated for her. 'It's a great dish, isn't it? My mother is a fabulous cook, and she taught all her children how to prepare food. It is no big deal.' He got to his feet to collect their plates.

'Your mother?' Instantly Zoë was curious. Either Rico ignored her interest, or he didn't notice. But she noticed the fact that he was clearing up after them. He wouldn't even allow her to help, just pushed her gently back down in her chair again.

'Save your strength for the dancing.'

His eyes were glinting with humour again. Not mockery, humour—humour shared between them. Feeling her confidence returning, Zoë smiled back. 'You know your way round a dishwasher too. I'm impressed.'

'You must have known some very strange men in your time, Zoë.'

Zoë smiled faintly. *You don't want to know how strange.*

Rico insisted on doing everything—even wiping down the surfaces and clearing the condiments from the table. Only when the kitchen had been returned to its former pristine condition did he turn to her.

'Now it is time for you to dance, Zoë.'

His eyes, she noticed, were already dancing—with laughter and with challenge. But somehow it gave her courage. He gave her courage.

'I'm ready. After that meal I've got a lot to live up to, so I'd better limber up before I begin. I would hate to disappoint you.'

'I will tune my guitar while you prepare.'

How long would that take? she wondered. Not long enough for her to be ready to dance for him, that was for sure!

As fast as Zoë's courage had returned, it vanished again. She wanted to impress Rico, and doubted she could. She wanted his gaze to linger on her, to bathe her in his admiration. She wanted him to want her as much as she wanted him.

She wanted to know more about his mother, Zoë corrected herself fiercely.

'Why don't we have pudding first, and talk a little longer?'

'You can't put it off all night. Are you having second thoughts, Zoë?'

'Not at all.'

'Then no more delaying tactics,' Rico said, reaching for his guitar. 'Sweet things come later, when we have earned them.'

How good his command of English was! His few words had set her on fire. She hadn't given a moment's thought to *later*, but clearly Rico had.

Subduing a rush of apprehension, Zoë led the way into the Great Hall. Rico sat on the stool she had placed there for him, and began adjusting the strings of his guitar.

'You have a beautiful guitar.' Under Rico's hands it had come to life, producing sounds that were rich and lovely.

'It's a flamenco guitar, made of spruce and cypress.'

'So it really does represent the music of the region?'

'Absolutely,' he murmured.

Zoë looked away first.

While Rico strummed some chords, testing them for clarity and tuning, Zoë centred herself, bending and stretching before the dance began.

Rico seemed to sense when she was ready to begin, and turned his head. With a brief nod, she walked to the centre of her improvised performance space in the centre of the vast square hall.

At first she was stiff and self-conscious, but Rico second-guessed her every move. She had never danced with such a sympathetic accompanist before—in fact she'd never danced with a real live accompanist before, and certainly not one who made her thrill even more than the music.

Rico made no allowances for the fact that she was new to flamenco, and in truth she didn't want him to; after just a short time she didn't need him to. Their partnership was as tight as Zoë could have wished, and after a few minutes all her tension disappeared.

There were some large ornate mirrors in this part of the hall, which was why she had chosen it. She could see Rico sitting cross-legged on his stool. He appeared lost in the music, but then looked up and Zoë was lost in his eyes.

Instead of hesitating, Rico picked up the pace, his gaze boring into her as he drew rhythms hotter and more powerful than Zoë had ever thought possible from his guitar. His fingers moved at speed across the fretboard, producing an earthy sound that throbbed insistently through her. She could feel herself growing more abandoned with every step, until she was whirling in time to a rhythm of Rico's choosing. Then, abruptly, he slowed the tempo so that it rose and fell in waves of sound that dropped at last to a low and insistent rumble.

The sound was so faint Zoë could barely hear it. She might not have known he was still playing had it not been for the fact that she could still feel the music in every fibre of her being.

'That's enough for tonight,' he said suddenly, damping the strings with his hand.

She had been so absorbed in the dance, so lost in the sound he was creating, it took her a moment to come round and realise that Rico had stopped playing. She watched him prop his guitar against the wall, and was still in a sort of trance when he walked across the floor to her.

And then she came to with a bump, realising she was so aroused that her nipples were pressing tautly against the fine lawn top. Instinctively she lifted her hands to cover herself, but she could do nothing about the insistent pulse down low in her belly.

'I think you enjoyed that, Ms Chapman…and you're very good.' He stopped a few feet away, and made no attempt to close the gap.

Zoë licked her lips. Rico knew she was aroused. She could feel his response to that arousal enveloping her. He might as well have undone the ties on her blouse and exposed her erect nipples. Or lifted her skirt high above her waist and seen her there… He could arouse her as easily as that—without even touching her. And now she didn't want him to stop or turn away. This could be her one and only chance to push past arousal and see if she could handle the next stage…

'I think it's time for our dessert, Zoë.'

Zoë tried to hide her disappointment when Rico held out his hand to her. Her face was on fire at the thought she had made such a fool of herself. 'Dessert? Yes, of course.'

'Spanish-style.'

She saw the look in his eyes and felt a rush of heat flood through her as she realised that the last thing on Rico's mind was a return visit to the kitchen. *Oh.*

Her gaze fixed on his hand. He was waiting for her to clasp it. Was this what she wanted? Could she go ahead with it? Wasn't it better to stop now, before she proved to herself as well as Rico that as far as sex went she was one big disaster area? She didn't want to spoil the evening—which was what would happen if she allowed things to go any further.

For some reason the young flamenco dancer on the poster in the mountain hut flew into Zoë's mind. Beba was a proper woman, a sexual woman... But then Rico's arms closed around her and it was too late.

Zoë shuddered with desire as his mouth brushed her lips. She felt so small, so dainty—and desired. This far was fine—it was as far as she could ever go: a kiss, a light caress... She closed her eyes as he applied a little more pressure, his firm lips moving over her mouth until she softened against him.

Could so much pleasure come from a simple kiss? But there was nothing uncomplicated where Rico was concerned.

He felt her tense, and stroked her back with long, light strokes until she eased into him again. He tugged lightly with his teeth on her bottom lip until the tremors rippling through her reached her womb. She whimpered, wanting more, and, teasing her lips apart, he deepened the kiss.

Zoë accepted the pace Rico set just as she had accepted the music he had played for her—music that had begun so gently, so calmly... It was like that now. He was so strong she could sense the powerhouse contained beneath his tracing fingers and wonderfully caressing hands. His touch was as light as the softest chord on the guitar, and as if she was his instrument now the vibrations through her body went on and on.

As their kisses grew more heated she was swept up in the need to rub against him, to feel the hard bristle on his face scoring her cheeks, rasping her neck. Their breathing was hectic and there were sounds welling from deep inside their throats as the pace quickened like the fiery rhythms of flamenco. Need was overwhelming them. They were as rough now, and as mindlessly passionate, as the final furious torrent of demanding chords.

Then a flash of reality intruded, brutal and strong. She didn't know if she could stop him. He frightened her. She frightened herself. Things were getting out of control. What the hell was she doing?

Zoë tensed as the floodgates of the past gave way beneath the weight of ugly memories. 'No, no! Stop it! I can't—' She tried desperately to push him away.

'What do you mean, you can't?' Rico said sharply, holding her fast as he stared intently into her eyes.

'I just can't,' Zoë said, snatching her face away from his as she struggled to break free.

But he wouldn't let her go, and, cupping her chin, brought her back to face him again. 'What can't you do, Zoë? Answer me.'

She knew he sensed her fear.

'Tell me, please.'

His voice was gentle, and when she looked up at him their faces were almost touching.

'Tell me what's wrong, Zoë. Is there someone else?'

'I can't tell you what's wrong.' Zoë pressed her lips together. That was true. How could she? Where were the words to explain how some giant switch had simply turned off inside her, so that all she felt now with him was fear and apprehension?

'Has someone hurt you? Or do you already have a man? Did he do something to you? Did he hurt you?'

'No!' Zoë covered her ears with her hands, protecting herself against the barrage of questions, trying to shut out the ugly scenes replaying in her mind. She wasn't ready for this. Would she ever be ready?

But none of it was Rico's fault. Her gaze flew to his face, and she knew he saw the answer in her eyes.

'Zoë...Zoë.' He brought her close. 'Why didn't you tell me?'

'We don't know each other.' Her voice was muffled against his chest.

'I'd like to change that.'

She wanted to believe him. She wanted desperately to believe him, to think he might be different. But her past kept on insisting she was wrong. 'Can we change the subject?' She straightened her hair. 'What about if I make the pudding?'

'Zoë—'

'I don't mind.'

'Stop it, Zoë.' Pulling back, Rico held her in front of him.

'It won't take me long.' She couldn't look at him.

'Not tonight.'

There was a sharp note in his voice that drew her gaze, and she saw his face was serious and troubled.

'All right, you make the pudding,' she said.

She was determined to stick to the mundane, Rico realised. That way she could pretend it had never happened. He stared at her, wishing she would tell him everything, knowing that would never happen. 'OK. I did promise to cook for you tonight.'

He could feel the relief radiating from her, but the easy atmosphere they'd shared earlier had gone; they both knew it. He had opened an old wound, and he shuddered to think what that wound might be.

Rico occupied Zoë's mind throughout most of that night. She couldn't sleep and she couldn't think about anything apart from him. She had gone cold and he had gone—no surprises there. His bright golden fritters dressed with fresh lemon juice and vanilla sugar had been a surprise. They'd been truly unforgettable—as had his swift departure the moment he had bolted them down!

He hadn't been able to get away fast enough. She couldn't blame him. They had shared one lovely evening, thanks to Maria. And now, with The Kiss out of the way, at least he knew she wasn't interested in that sort of thing.

She had laid her cards out in front of him. She couldn't be like other women—women who took their right to enjoy physical love for granted. Women like the flamenco dancer on the poster. It was better Rico knew that.

Her ex had been right. She was frigid. And it wasn't that she didn't try—she felt sexy, and she hoped she looked at least a little bit appealing, but as soon as things turned hot she went cold. That was what had happened tonight. No one could change what she was—not even Rico. Thumping her pillows into submission, Zoë settled down to sleep.

Zoë's hands flew to her face. The stinging slap had jolted her whole frame. She could never beg; that was her problem. She could never ask for forgiveness, for understanding, when she didn't know what she had done wrong.

She backed away, stumbling in the darkness, feeling for the furniture to guide her. Finally there was nowhere else to go. She was pressed back against the cold, hard door. She could only stand now, and wait for her punishment. There was no escape. The door was locked. She knew that too, without trying the handle. She knew it just as surely as she knew what was coming next.

She looked at him then, but his face was shadowed and she couldn't be sure who it was. She searched her mind desperately, trying to think of something that would make him change his mind, make him listen to her. But he was already taking off his belt.

This was always the worst part—the waiting. She could hear herself whimpering as she held up her hands to shield her face…

'Oh!' Zoë lurched up into a sitting position, reeling with shock. It took her a few minutes to get her bearings and realise she was safe in her bed at the castle.

Steadying her breathing, she looked around. Of course there was nothing unpleasant in the room. It was quite empty. The castle was completely still. She had heard several doors slamming when the film crew came back from their evening at the café, but it was the middle of the night now; everyone was sound asleep.

Glancing at her wristwatch on the bedside table, she saw that it was three o'clock in the morning. Slipping out of bed, she pulled back one side of the heavy curtains and gazed out to where the castle walls were tipped with silver in the moonlight. Where was Rico now? Where was he sleeping? Was he alone? He had never told her where he lived, and she had never asked. Did he live with anyone? Was he married?

A bolt of shame cut through her. She would never hurt anyone as she had been hurt—yet she knew none of the answers to these questions. She had let Rico kiss her without knowing anything about him, and then she had gone on to betray her innermost fears to him.

Zoë pulled away from the window. Unwelcome details of the nightmare were slithering back through the unguarded passages in her mind. She couldn't shut them out. She had tried that before, but they always, always came back. Rico didn't know anything about her, about her past. How would she bear the shame when he found out? His rejection tonight would be nothing compared to the scorn and contempt he would feel for her then.

In her mind's eye Zoë could already see his face; it was cold and unforgiving. But even that was better than revisiting the dark side of her memories. She could only be grateful that by filling her mind with Rico Cortes she had finally found a way to blot the worst of them out.

Was this how it was always going to be—her ex-husband haunting her for ever?

Yes—if she allowed him to, Zoë realised.

Opening the window as far as she could, she leaned out, drinking in the healing beauty of the mountains.

The moonlight was like a blessing on her face. Closing her eyes, she inhaled deeply. There was a faint scent of blossom on the air.

CHAPTER FIVE

ZOË was up shortly after dawn on Monday. She was skilled at putting the dark shadows behind her, and, though she was tired after her disturbed night, her mind was full of the party the following day. She was determined to have everything ready in good time.

The local producers took a well-earned rest over the weekend, and Monday was the only day the market opened late. That played into her hands, giving her a chance to draw up a schedule and get organised before she went shopping for ingredients. She enjoyed supervising everything—even down to which flowers she would have on the tables.

Taking a glass of freshly squeezed orange juice with her onto the veranda, she perched on a seat overlooking the cypress grove to make her list. It was still cool, and she had taken the precaution of wearing a cosy sweater over her pyjamas. Her hair was still sleep-tangled round her shoulders and for a while she just sat idly, soaking up the view. The air was quite still, apart from the occasional flurry of early-morning breeze, and there were few sounds to disturb her tranquil state other than the birds chorusing their approval of another bright new day.

Closing her eyes, Zoë relished the touch of the sun on her freshly washed face. She breathed deeply and smiled as she inhaled the same scent she had enjoyed the previous night. The cicadas were just kicking off with a rumba. The perfume of the blossom was overlaid with the warm, spicy aroma of Spain. She couldn't have been anywhere else. She didn't want to be anywhere else. Feeling a sudden rush of joy, she

65

stretched out her arms towards the sun—then another sound intruded.

Opening her eyes, she straightened up and looked around, and saw a horse and rider coming towards her at speed. Shading her eyes against the low, slanting rays of the sun, she could just make out the shape of a man crouched low over the neck of his horse. He was galloping flat out towards her, down the tree-lined grove, using the mile-long stretch like his own private racecourse.

'Rico?' Zoë murmured, getting to her feet. Her heart was pounding, and for a moment she panicked. Only an emergency could have brought him to the castle at such a pace.

But then he slowed abruptly, when he was still some yards from the entrance to the courtyard.

Almost as if he knew he was close to water, the horse pricked up his ears and pranced towards the trough located right beneath the veranda where Zoë was standing. The sound of his hooves on the cobbles made her smile. Did everyone dance to the rhythm of flamenco in Cazulas?

The black stallion and his rider were a magnificent sight. Rico was so much a part of his mount it was difficult to tell who made the decisions, and Zoë smiled again in admiration as she raised her hand in greeting. She could ride—but not like that.

Reining in beneath the veranda, Rico smiled up at her.

Zoë was surprised he looked pleased to see her. Had he forgotten what had happened between them the previous night? She had made a fool of herself. So why was he here? What had he come for?

'Buenos días, señorita!' Rico bowed low over the withers of his horse. 'I trust I find you well this morning?'

His uncomplicated greeting bolstered Zoë's determination not to slip back into her old ways. He wasn't being scornful or cruel, he was just saying good morning.

'Buenos días, señor.' Planting her hands on the veranda rail, she smiled down at him.

'You look tired,' Rico observed as he sprang down to the ground. Swinging the reins over the horse's head, he tethered him to a pole.

'Do I?' Zoë put a hand to her cheek. She had no intention of telling him why. 'I haven't had a chance to put my make-up on. That must be it.' Then she remembered her shabby old pyjama bottoms, flapping in the breeze beneath her rumpled sweater.

'You don't need make-up.' He took the steps two, three at a time. 'But you do look tired.' Pulling off his soft calfskin riding gloves, he slapped them together in the palm of one hand. 'That juice looks good.'

'It is. I'm sorry, would you like one?'

'Thank you, that would be nice.'

The jug of juice was in the refrigerator in the kitchen. And he would need a glass. She would have the chance to slip out and change into a respectable outfit. 'Please, sit down. I'll go and get the juice for you.'

'I'll come with you.'

'No, that's—' Pointless arguing with him, Zoë thought wryly, leading the way inside.

Every tiny hair rose on the back of her neck at knowing Rico was behind her, and as he held the door for her she could picture his muscles flexing beneath the close-fitting riding breeches, the turn of his calf beneath the long leather riding boots. And that was before she considered the wide spread of his shoulders, the powerful forearms shaded with dark hair, the inky black waves caressing high-chiselled cheekbones, slightly flushed beneath his tan after the exertions of his ride.

She could picture everything about him—his mouth, his lips—she could feel the scrape of his bristle on her cheeks, and she could remember all too clearly that she had pushed him away when he had wanted to kiss her.

Because she was frigid.

It was no use, Zoë realised as they walked into the kitchen. She would never be able to relax with a man like Rico. She would never know what it felt like to be properly kissed by him. But that didn't stop her wanting to.

'The work for this meal isn't proving too much for you?' He looked around when she had given him a glass of fresh juice. 'You seem to have made enough for an army already.'

'I'm never happier then when I'm cooking.' She stared at him as he went to wash out his empty glass at the sink. She was so used to clearing up after people she knew she would never get used to this.

When he had finished, Rico turned back to her. He slipped one thumb into his belt-loop, and before she knew what she was doing Zoë had followed the movement. Feeling her face flame red, she redirected her gaze into his eyes.

'It all smells wonderful.' Rico smiled.

'Thank you.' Zoë's throat seemed to have closed up. The riding breeches moulded him precisely, revealingly—terrifyingly. 'Why are you here?' Her voice sounded faint, and she was glad there was a table between them.

'It's such a beautiful morning I thought you might like to ride out with me—if you're not too busy…'

She could hardly pretend to be when she had been lazing on the veranda when he arrived. 'I've thought about riding lots of times since I got here, but—'

'But?'

'Well, I can't ride like you.'

'There are plenty of quieter mounts than mine to choose from in the stables.'

'I'd really like that.' Zoë frowned. 'But I'd have to change.'

'Go right ahead. I'll wait for you.'

'All right, then.'

Closing the door behind her, Zoë leaned against it for a moment to catch her breath. What was she doing? She closed her eyes. She couldn't let her old life get in the way. She had fought her way out; she wasn't going to slip back now. There was nothing wrong in riding with Rico. She could do with the exercise. The rest of the day was for shopping and cooking, so an hour's recreation would be perfect. In fact, it was just what she needed.

Zoë changed her clothes quickly, putting on jeans and a shirt. When she returned to the kitchen Rico was gazing around at the changes she had made.

'I trust you approve?' Zoë hoped she didn't sound too defensive. He put the pottery dish he had been examining back on the shelf. The changes were small, but it made the place feel like home—and that was no easy task in a castle.

She spent so much time in the kitchen it had to feel right. It was where she prepared everything, painstakingly testing each dish any number of different ways long before the cameras rolled on set. So she had hung some new blinds at the windows to control the flow of light while she worked, and there was a row of fresh herbs lined up in terracotta pots along the window-sill. She loved the local pottery. It was precious in a world where everything was growing more and more alike.

'Wouldn't it have been easier to do the filming in here?'

'Yes, but my director felt there was more space in the hall, so I gave in to him on that point.'

'Your director? He works for you?'

'For my production company.'

'I'm impressed.'

'No need to be. It's not unknown in the television world for people to take the independent route.'

'So whose fault was the set dressing?'

'Mine,' Zoë said quickly. 'I own the company. The buck stops here.'

Rico's lips pressed together as he stared at her, then curved as if he was amused. 'Are you ready to go?' He glanced towards the door.

As he held it open for her, and she walked past him, Zoë felt a tingle race down the length of her spine. The heady scent of saddle soap and leather laced with warm, clean man was overwhelmingly attractive, and her thoughts turned wilfully to what was beneath Rico's breeches. She had never indulged in erotic thoughts before, always dreading where they might lead. But there was something about Rico Cortes that made it impossible to think about anything else.

Daydreaming was a dangerous game...

Once they were outside in the fresh air Zoë knew that at least for the next hour or so she was going to put every negative thought from the past out of her mind.

They stood on the veranda side by side for a few moments, enjoying the view. They were standing very close, close enough to brush against each other, but then Rico's stallion scented his master's presence and squealed with impatience.

'I think he's trying to tell us that he's been kept waiting long enough,' Zoë said.

'We had better go down,' Rico agreed, 'before he pulls that post out of the ground.'

She followed him down the steps.

'We should find you a horse.' Rico tipped his chin towards the stables. 'Before Rondeno breaks free.'

'Rondeno?'

'A native of Ronda. My stallion is named after the most famous of all the White Towns in Andalucia. Ronda is surrounded by rugged mountains that once sheltered bandits and brigands.'

'How very romantic.' And how perfectly suited to Rico, Zoë thought, looking up at him. He would have made a very good pirate, with his swarthy, dangerous looks. Had Rico's career taken a similar path to her own, she could see him as a leading man, breaking hearts on the small screen as well as the large. There was always a hunger for new talent. 'Have you ever thought of acting as a career?'

'Never.' He slanted her a look. 'I prefer reality to fantasy every time.'

'Flamenco, cooking, riding…' She smiled. 'Is there no end to your talent?'

'You haven't even begun to scratch the surface yet.' He laughed. 'Come on, let's get you that horse.'

At a gentle canter, and with the warm wind lifting her hair, Zoë began to wonder if she had ever felt so carefree before. The countryside was bathed in a soft, golden light, and the sky was as clear a blue as she had ever seen.

In this part of Spain the ground was well fed by a fast-flowing river, but now it was approaching the hottest months of the year the water was little more than a sluggish trickle. The pastures in the shadow of the mountains, however, were still green, and provided the perfect ground for riding over.

'We'll stop over there by the bridge.' Rico had brought his stallion alongside her horse, and was keeping pace at an easy canter. 'There should just be enough water for the horses to drink.'

As she cantered ahead of him, Zoë couldn't believe she hadn't ridden one of the horses stabled at the castle before. She had assumed they were in livery for any number of local riders, and therefore not included in her lease. Not so, Rico had explained. They all belonged to the same person—someone he knew, presumably. He knew the horses, and had chosen a quiet gelding for her to ride, saying Punto was perfect for her.

And he was, Zoë thought, patting the horse's dappled neck. Punto was just the type of horse she liked: he was kind, and willing, and wore an American-style high saddle, which was a lot more comfortable than the English saddle she was used to.

Rico's stallion moved ahead as he scented water. Urging her own horse forward, Zoë caught him up by the slow-moving stream. She allowed the reins to fall loosely on Punto's neck and gazed around. Apart from the gurgle of water and the sound of the two horses drinking there was utter silence. Lifting her face to the sun, Zoë closed her eyes, allowing the light to bathe her in its warmth.

'It's so beautiful here.'

'I agree,' she heard Rico murmur.

She longed for him to lean over in his saddle then, and kiss her as he had kissed her before. This time she wouldn't pull back. No bad feelings could intrude here, on such a beautiful day.

But Rico didn't kiss her. He didn't even try to touch her. He just sat patiently, waiting for their horses to finish drinking.

Of course he wouldn't kiss her. Men couldn't stand women who pulled away at the last minute. It was every man's idea of a turn-off. *There were only so many knocks to his pride a real man could take.* Wasn't that what her ex-husband had told her? He was right, and this was the proof.

She collected up the reins. 'I'd better get back to the castle. There's still so much to do. I have to get to the market before all the best produce is sold.' She turned Punto away from the water.

'You don't have to do that,' Rico insisted. 'Why don't I get someone to collect what you need?'

The breeze flipped Zoë's hair from her face as she turned to him. 'That's very kind of you, Rico, but I prefer to choose everything myself.'

'Force of habit?'

'That's right.'

They began to trot, and then the horses broke into a canter.

'So, are you still coming tomorrow?' She had to yell to make him hear.

'Try and keep me away. Shall we race back to the castle?'

The challenge excited her. Urging Punto on, Zoë loved feeling the wind in her hair and hearing the sound of Rondeno's hooves pounding after her. She knew Rico had to be holding back, and, snatching a glance over her shoulder, she laughed with exhilaration. Rondeno was far more powerful than her own mount, but she could almost believe Punto was enjoying this as much as she was.

The control Rico exercised over his mighty stallion was the biggest turn-on of all, and Zoë's heart was thundering louder than the combined sound of both horses' hooves. The friction of the saddle as she brushed back and forth was something new to her. She had never taken notice of it before, but now she was intensely and electrifyingly aroused. Leaning low over Punto's neck, she begged the horse to speed up and carry her away from Rico—and away from temptation.

He had to dig his heels into Rondeno's side to catch up with her. His laugh of pleasure and surprise was carried away on the wind because they were moving so fast. She was quite a woman. He liked her spirit. In fact he liked Zoë Chapman—a lot, Rico realised, easing up so they were galloping alongside each other.

Her lips were parted to drag in air, and there was a faint line of pink along the top of her cheekbones that had not been put there by the wind. Her lips were moist where she had licked them, and when she flashed him a glance he saw that her exquisite eyes had darkened to the point where only a faint rim of turquoise remained.

She was not leading him on even a little bit—she was sexually unawakened. The realisation sent arousal streaking through him like a bolt of lightning. So much sexuality packed into one woman with everything to learn about the art of love. Even if he'd cared nothing for her, he would still have had to find that a turn-on. But after Zoë's fearful response to him sorting her out in the sex department was starting to feel more like a crusade. Her frustration was obvious—something had to give. And he wanted to be around when that happened.

As they approached the castle they both reined in, but Zoë kept the lead. She laughed, and smiled across at him in triumph.

The change in her was striking. Where was the cool professional businesswoman now? Where was the frightened girl who had pushed him away? Right now she radiated confidence. The grey cloud that sometimes hung over her had vanished; he hoped it stayed that way.

She wanted to feel this good for ever, Zoë thought as she sprang down from the saddle. 'Thank you.' She turned to Rico, smiling. 'That was the best time I've had for—'

'Ever?' he suggested.

'I should definitely try to ride more frequently. Perhaps I will, now I know I can take one of the horses from the stables here.'

'The groom will always pick one out for you, or just tell him you prefer to ride Punto.'

'I will.' Zoë rested her cheek against Punto's neck for a moment. 'He's the best—aren't you, Punto?'

'Don't ride unaccompanied until you know the lie of the land better.'

Zoë's pulse began to race as she gazed up at Rico. 'I won't.' It was such an easy promise to make. With Rico riding next to her she would be in the saddle every spare moment that came her way.

'The groom will ride with you if you ask him.'

Somehow she kept the smile fixed to her face. 'That would be great.'

'*Adios*, Zoë!'

'*Adios*, Rico.' He was too busy holding his black stallion

in check to note her sudden lack of enthusiasm, Zoë saw thankfully. 'I appreciate you taking me out.'

'Don't mention it.' He wheeled Rondeno away.

I wouldn't dream of mentioning it, Zoë thought, smiling to herself as Rico cantered away.

Turning, she viewed the elderly bow-legged groom with wry amusement. Riding was definitely crossed off her 'must-do' list for now.

CHAPTER SIX

TUESDAY was almost too busy for Zoë to give much thought to anything apart from cooking—cooking and Rico. Now she knew for sure he was coming, everything had gained an extra impetus. She wanted to make Maria feel she was part of something special, something that gave the exceptional flamenco dancer the recognition Zoë believed she deserved.

She was in the kitchen by nine, having been up at dawn to go to market to find the freshest ingredients for those dishes that could not be made in advance. On her return she had laid everything out on the counter to make one last check. But, however many times she looked at them, she couldn't get past the feeling that there was still something missing.

She had decided upon a menu of clams *à la marinara*, in a sauce of garlic, paprika and *fino* sherry, with an alternative of *zoque*, the popular gazpacho soup made with red peppers and tomatoes. But for the main course she had called upon her secret weapon—a wise old man from the village who seemed to be everyone's *tio*, or uncle. Zoë had been debating over the best recipe for *paella*, and the *tio* was the only person who could advise her properly, according to Maria, who had unexpectedly appeared at her side at the market.

Thanks to the introduction from Maria, the elderly expert uncle had approved Zoë's choice of ingredients, after turning them over and sniffing for freshness. He had even demanded a heavy discount from the stallholders, reminding them, as Zoë would never have dreamed of doing, that they would be eating the food they had just sold to her when they came to the castle for the party that night.

'Locals care more about the rice than the rest of the meal,' the *tio* had said, patting his nose with one finger just as Zoë had seen Maria do. 'It must be well washed if you want the grains to separate, and then the rice must be cooked in fish stock—never water—water is for soup. You must have *caldo*—sorry, broth—for your rice. And the yellow colour of *paella* comes as much from the *noras*—you would call them peppers—as it does from the strands of saffron you add to the broth. Did you enjoy your ride?'

Cooking methods and Rico in the same breath! Zoë knew her astonishment must have shown on her face.

'It's a very small village,' the *tio* had explained with a smile, tapping his nose once again.

So it was, Zoë had thought, as she thanked him for his kindness.

Armed with quite a lot more local knowledge than she had bargained for, she had returned to the castle to prepare the main dish.

Balancing a cheap pan the size of a bicycle wheel on the counter, Zoë laid out pieces of chicken and squid, clams, scampi and *rojas*—large red prawns—with all the precision of a stained-glass window on top of a bed of rice, onion, garlic and peppers. Finally she added three types of beans and then some seasoning. Now the dish was almost ready for the oven.

She paused, inhaling the faint salty tang of the sea rising from the cool, fresh ingredients, her mind straying back to the earlier events of the day. How had the *tio* known she had been riding with Rico? Did everyone in the village know? Was it coincidence that Maria had found her at the market?

Suddenly Zoë wasn't sure of anything. Had she imagined she could ride out with Rico, bathe in his glamour, and get away with it? Frowning, she turned back to her cooking. She had already made some rich fish stock laced with strands of deep red saffron, and she poured that over the raw ingredients. Standing back, she had to admit she was delighted with the finished product.

The *tio's* last piece of advice had been to wrap the *paella* in newspaper once it was cooked. Then the finished dish should be left for ten minutes for the rice grains to separate. But wouldn't the newsprint spoil the striking colours?

Newsprint. Banner headlines. Zoë actually flinched as she turned away.

The icy fingers of the past were with her again, clutching at her heart. *Star Sells Sex.* Three words that damned her for ever in her own mind, even though they were lies. As far as the world at large was concerned, the story had brought her to wider public notice, and, in the topsy-turvy way of celebrity, had actually boosted her career. Going along with public perception had actually helped her to get through things. Keeping a smile fixed to her face had become such a habit that gradually the reality that lay behind the headline had been consigned to the back of her mind like a sleeping monster.

The Zoë Chapman who didn't appear on the television screen or at book signings was careful never to wake that monster—but she knew it would stir if she allowed herself to feel anything too deeply again. The shame, the failure, the brutality that lay behind it—all of that would rise up and slap her down into the gutter, where her ex-husband thought she belonged. So far she had frustrated his attempts to see her eat dirt, but it had been a long road back.

But she *had* made it back, Zoë reminded herself, and that was all that mattered. Every time the past intruded she pictured herself as a cork being held down in the water—she *always* broke free; she *always* bobbed up again. It was only men with brutally strong characters she had a problem with now. Men like Rico Cortes.

She had to get over this—get over him. She had to force her thoughts back on track. Perhaps she would wrap the *paella* in one of her huge, freshly laundered cloths when she removed it from the heat, and allow it to settle that way...

* * *

She could relax at last. The *paella* looked great on camera. It had been filmed at each stage of its preparation, and she had been sorry for the film crew, who had had to carry the loaded pan back and forth between the set in the Great Hall and the kitchen, where she was working.

Philip, her director, was demanding, but he was the best—which was why she had hired him. She trusted his judgement, and his decision to do things this way had kept everyone out from under her feet. Her own 'to camera' shots would be added later, when make-up and wardrobe had been let loose on her. It wasn't easy to cook and appear as cool as a cucumber at the same time.

Now she had finished the *paella*, Zoë's thoughts turned to pudding, which was her favourite part of any meal. She planned to serve a chocolate and almond ice cream, garnished with her own *guirlache*, which was crushed and toasted almonds coated with a sugar and lemon juice toffee. And there would be hot orange puffs dusted with sugar, as well as *figuritas de marzapan*, marzipan shaped into mice and rabbits for the children.

She concentrated hard, loving every moment of the preparation. Cooking was an oasis in her life that offered periods of calm as essential as they were soothing. She counted herself fortunate that her love of food had brought her success.

Resisting the temptation to sample one of everything she had made, Zoë finally stood back, sighing with contentment. It all looked absolutely delicious.

Someone else thought so too—before she knew what she was doing Zoë had automatically slapped Rico's hand away as he reached for a marzipan rabbit.

'Rico!' She clutched her chest with surprise. 'I thought it was one of the crew! I didn't realise it was you...' And then all she could think was that her chef's jacket was stained and her face had to be tomato red from the heat in the kitchen. 'I didn't expect you until tonight.'

'It is tonight.' He gazed past her through the open window. 'I must have got carried away. What time is it?'

'Don't worry. Not time to panic yet.'

Not time to panic? So why was her heart thundering off the chart? Zoë tried to wipe her face on her sleeve without Rico noticing. 'What brings you here so early?'

'I thought you might need some help. It looks like I was right.'

'I'm doing fine.'

'I brought drinks.'

'Drinks… *Drinks!* That was what was missing!' She turned to him. 'I've made some lemonade to pour over crushed ice for the children, and for anyone who doesn't drink…'

'That's fine, but you should have plenty of choice. It's going to be a long night.' Going to the kitchen door, he held it open and a line of men filed in. They were loaded down with crates of beer, boxes of wine and spirits, and soft drinks.

'*Cava*, brandy, sherry, and the local liquor…' Rico ticked them off, shooting an amused glance at Zoë as a man bearing a huge earthenware flagon marched in.

'Oh, no—not that!'

'You don't have to drink it,' he pointed out, smiling when he saw her expression.

'You're far too generous. Of course my company will pay for everything—'

'We'll worry about that later.'

'The crew will drink everything in sight, given half a chance.'

'Not tonight. Just worry about getting the white wine and *cava* chilled.'

'What do you mean, not tonight? Once they've filmed Maria, and taken a couple of crowd shots, the crew will join in the party—'

'Haven't I told you not to worry?' Rico slipped the lead man some banknotes to share around as tips.

'You don't know the crew like I do. I don't want to spoil it for them, but, bluntly, with all this drink around—I just can't face the mess in the morning.'

'Let me assure you that your crew are going to be far too busy to get into any mischief. You have my word on it.'

'Rico, what are you talking about?'

'Your director has arranged for another feature to be filmed tonight. Hasn't he told you yet?'

'No...' Zoë frowned. How could that happen when they always discussed everything in advance?

'He is very enthusiastic.'

'That's why I hired him.' She resigned herself. It had to be something good. She couldn't imagine the man who was the mainstay of her team asking everyone to work late unless it was really worthwhile...

'He's got everyone's agreement to work overtime,' Rico added.

'Can you read my mind?'

'From time to time.'

Zoë looked at Rico, looked at his lips, then dragged her gaze away. 'It must be an excellent feature.'

'Last minute.'

'Yes, I guessed that.' She couldn't be angry with Philip, though she was curious. She welcomed suggestions from anyone in the team. The strength of her company was that they worked together, with no one person riding roughshod over another. She knew from bitter experience that those tactics never worked. 'Do you know what it is?'

'A typical sport of this region.'

'A sport?' Zoë looked doubtful.

'Something colourful and authentic for your programme.'

'Don't tease me, Rico. Tell me what it is.'

'I'm going to get some extra glasses out of the Jeep.' Before Zoë could question him further he added, 'And by the way, *señorita*, your *figuritas* are delicious.'

So what was this surprise feature? Zoë flashed a glance at the door. Rico should have told her. He made her mad, and he made her melt too—a dangerous combination, and not something she should be looking for in a man. She wasn't looking for a man, Zoë reminded herself firmly.

'Tell me about this sport,' she insisted, the moment Rico came back.

Putting the case of glasses down on the counter, he turned to look at her. Zoë tried not to notice the figure-hugging black trousers and close-fitting black shirt moulding his impressive torso, or the fact that there was something wild and untamed about him. It lay just beneath the sleek packaging, telling her he would never settle down. Men like Rico Cortes never did.

'Wrestling.'

'Wrestling!' And then it all fell into place: El Paladín!

She shuddered inwardly. 'Will you be taking part?'

'Perhaps.' He shrugged. 'I've arranged for people to come and wash these glasses for you, and to serve tonight, so that after you finish filming you can have fun too. My people will clear up after the crew. You don't have a thing to worry about. You should kick back a little, enjoy yourself for a change.'

'Thank you,' Zoë murmured, her good manners functioning on automatic pilot. Her brain was working on two levels: the first accepted the fact that she needed help on the practical side because she had promised the crew they could join the party after work; the second level was dragging her down to a place she didn't want to go. Anything that smacked of violence, even a sport, made her feel queasy.

'Wrestling is hugely popular in this part of Spain. When your director asked me about it, I knew I could help him.'

'El Paladín?' Zoë's voice came out like a whisper, and she tried very hard not to sound accusing. It *would* make a good feature. If the programme was to reflect the area properly, it was just the type of thing she would normally want to include.

'I'm always looking for authentic items to bring the programmes to life...'

'It doesn't get more authentic than this.' Rico smiled at her on his way out of the door. 'See you later, Zoë.'

Zoë watched with mixed feelings as the raised square wrestling ring was erected in the middle of the courtyard. A beautiful day had mellowed into a balmy evening, and there was scarcely the suggestion of a breeze. Wrapping her arms around her waist she knew she had to pull herself together and stop fretting. Half-naked men would definitely be a bonus for her viewers. She could do this. She had to do this. How hard could it be?

The ring was almost finished, and people were starting to arrive. Soon it would be showtime. Surely it couldn't be that bad? She wouldn't have to watch it all—though she would have to be in shot for at least some of the time.

Firming her jaw, Zoë took a final look through the ropes at the empty ring. She still had to take a shower and prepare for the programme. Turning back to the castle, she hurried inside.

By the time she returned to the courtyard it was packed. Men had come from all over the region to test their strength. She guessed it was something of a marriage market too, judging by the flirtatious glances several groups of girls were giving their favourites.

The thought of Rico stripping off and stepping half naked into the ring was enough to make anyone shiver. Zoë tried hard not to react when she spotted him at the opposite side of the courtyard, surrounded by a group of supporters. At first she thought he was just greeting friends and she relaxed, but then he stepped away from the others and she saw he was naked from the waist up. Maria and the wise old *tio* from the village were standing with him; it seemed every soul in

Cazulas had come to support him. They were a good-natured group, and cheered him on as he strode to the ringside.

Zoë turned away, but then she guessed Rico must have vaulted over the top rope, because the applause around her was suddenly deafening. She looked up. She couldn't help herself. She had to see him for herself.

He was everything she found attractive in a man—and everything that terrified her too. It was impossible to believe that any of the other men had a physique to equal Rico's, or could match the fierce, determined look in his eyes. He was, after all, the champion. Rico Cortes was El Paladín.

Zoë fought down the panic struggling to take control of her mind. He was about to become a guest on her programme—no one said she had to sleep with him. She shivered, feeling fear and excitement in equal measure as she watched him flex his muscles in the ring. The woman standing next to her shouted something in Spanish, and then grabbed hold of her arm in her enthusiasm.

All the women wanted Rico, Zoë saw when she glanced around. For one crazy moment she felt like climbing into the ring and laying claim to him herself. And then the television lights flared on and she was working.

Smiling for the viewers, Zoë looked properly for the first time at the ring. She had to observe everything carefully so she could provide an appropriate voiceover for the film.

Clinging to her responsibilities certainly helped her through. But how to describe how she really felt at the sight of Rico's smooth, bronzed torso without turning her cookery programme into something for late-night viewing?

His belly was hard and flat, and banded across with muscle, whilst the spread of his shoulders seemed immense from where she was standing. And she couldn't stop her gaze tracking down to where his sinfully revealing wrestling shorts proved that it wasn't just the spread of his shoulders that was huge.

She wanted to look anywhere but at the ring—but how could she when she knew the camera would constantly switch between her and El Paladín? She had to stare up at Rico Cortes, and she had to applaud enthusiastically along with the rest of the crowd.

As the evening wore on the temperature began to rise. Rico was red-hot.

She would see it through because she had to. It was only a sport, after all, Zoë told herself. But by the time the bell rang and the first bout was over she was shaking convulsively from head to foot.

Making her excuses over the microphone to Philip, she eased her way through the crowd and went back into the castle, where she hurried up the stairs to her bedroom. Sinking onto the chair in front of the dressing-table, she buried her face in her hands.

How could she go back? Lifting her head, Zoë stared at her reflection in the mirror. She was pallid beneath her tan, and her hands were still shaking. She tried to apply some fresh lipgloss, and gave up. She couldn't risk a smudge of red across her face. And why was she trying to make herself look appealing? Did she want to attract trouble? Was she *asking for it* again, as she had done in the past?

When the shuddering grew worse, Zoë sat with her head bowed until she'd managed to bring herself back under control. She had to go back outside again eventually. She couldn't let everyone down—not Maria, not the *tio* who had helped her so generously, nor the film crew. And, most of all, she couldn't let herself down. She had fought hard to get her life back. She had to get over this.

There was a soft knock on the door. Marnie, the girl in charge of Wardrobe, had brought her a fresh top to change into. It was identical to the one she was wearing—low-cut and sexy—and the brash cerise looked good with her jeans. It was meant to stand out on camera when she was in a crowd.

It certainly did that, Zoë thought as she viewed herself critically in the mirror. The colour was identical to the skintight flamenco dress the girl named Beba wore on the poster at the mountain hut.

'I'm going to change.' She started tugging off the top.

'You can't, Zoë. What about continuity?'

'I don't care. I'm going to put on a shirt. If we have to reshoot, so be it.' Zoë saw Marnie's expression, but nothing was going to change her mind.

'Do you need me for anything else?'

'Marnie, I'm really sorry. This isn't your fault. Just tell Philip I insisted.'

'Well, it's your programme,' Marnie pointed out.

'Before you go, could you redo my lips?'

'Sure.' Marnie smiled at her.

Marnie applied the lipgloss expertly, with a steady hand. Zoë knew it was more than she could have done. She checked in the mirror. 'That's great. Thank you. I'm sorry to have dragged you up here just for that.'

'As long as I'm back in time to see Rico Cortes in action—' Marnie winked at her '—I'll forgive you.'

Zoë felt a chill strike through her composure, but forced a laugh as Marnie left the room.

She looked fine for the camera. The ice-blue of the shirt looked good against her tan, and complemented her red-blonde hair. She looked far more businesslike. She didn't look sexy at all. It was much, much better.

The shots on set inside the castle went smoothly—too smoothly, Zoë thought, cursing her professionalism. They didn't need a single retake.

'The change of clothes is fine for in here,' Philip advised her. 'But of course you'll change back into that cerise top again for ringside?'

'No, Philip.' Zoë shook her head. 'I'm keeping this shirt on. We'll just say the second half of the competition took place on another day—I don't care, I'm not changing.' She could tell by his face that Philip was taken aback. It wasn't like her to be difficult or unprofessional.

The competition was in its final stages by the time Zoë returned to the courtyard. The noise, if anything, had grown louder. Philip had to cut a path for her through the crowd. Then she realised that he meant her to stand right up at the front, as close to ringside as possible.

'Is this my punishment for changing clothes without warning you?' Zoë had to grab Philip's arm and yell in his ear above the roar of the crowd. She even managed a wry smile. But the moment he left her to return to his cameras Zoë's throat dried.

Philip's voice came through on Zoë's earpiece, testing the sound levels.

'You OK, Zoë? You sound as if you're getting a cold.'

'No, I'm fine—absolutely fine.'

'Then it must be the excitement at seeing all those muscles up close. You can't kid me,' he insisted, 'I know you love it—just like all the other women.'

That was the point. She wasn't like all the other women. *She wasn't normal.*

It was surprising how well you could know people, and yet know nothing about their private lives, Zoë thought, remembering that Philip had once worked for her ex-husband. He had been surprised when she had called time on their marriage, having thought them the perfect couple.

'Do you want me in shot for the presentation of the prizes?' she said into her microphone, clinging to her professionalism like a life raft.

'I'll want a reaction shot. You should have chosen something more glamorous to wear than that shirt. You look so plain!'

Perfect, Zoë thought.

'Never mind. It's too late to do anything about it now. I'll stick to head shots.'

She felt guilty because Philip sounded so grumpy, but it couldn't be helped. She was more concerned about getting through the next few minutes.

Women on either side of her were clutching each other in excitement as they stared into the ring. One of them turned to her, gesturing excitedly, and Zoë looked up. Rico was standing centre stage.

The television lights drained everything of colour, but Rico's torso still gleamed like polished bronze. The ghosts were hovering at Zoë's shoulder as she stared at him. But he was laughing good-naturedly with one of his defeated opponents, and then, leaning over the ropes, he reached out to help the elderly *tio* of Cazulas into the ring.

Zoë frowned. She hadn't expected that. Drawing on other times, other trials of strength, she had expected a grim face, a hard mouth and cruel eyes. But those trials of strength had been no contest. How could there be a physical contest between a woman and a powerful bully of a man?

Watching her elderly friend take Rico's hand and raise it high in a victory salute, Zoë tried to piece together what the *tio* was saying with her very basic knowledge of Spanish. Finally she gave up, and asked the woman standing next to her if she could translate.

'Our *tio* is announcing the prize,' the woman explained, barely able to waste a second of her awestruck gaze on Zoë.

A heavy leather purse changed hands between Rico and the *tio*. 'What's that?' Zoë shouted as cheers rose all around them.

'A purse of gold,' the woman shouted back to her.

But now Rico was passing it back to the *tio*. 'What is he doing?' Zoë said, looking at her neighbour again.

'It is the same every year,' the woman explained, shouting above the uproar. 'El Señor Cortes always returns the purse of gold to the village.'

'And what are they saying now?' Zoë persisted, but the excitement had reached such a fever pitch she couldn't hear the woman's reply. After several failed attempts her neighbour just shrugged, and smiled to show her it was hopeless.

Rico was staring at her, Zoë saw, going hot and cold. What did he want?

Holding her gaze, he walked quickly across the floor of the ring, leaned over the ropes, and held out his hand to her.

Zoë glanced around. No one could tell her what was happening because everyone was cheering and shouting at the top of their voices.

Rico held up his hands and silence fell. Everyone was staring at *her* now, Zoë realised. She couldn't understand it, but then Rico leaned over the ropes again and her face broke into a smile. She reached out to shake his hand, to congratulate him on his win. The next thing she knew she was standing beside him, with the spotlights glaring down on them both, and the *tio* was beaming at her while the crowd cheered wildly.

Rico's mouth tugged in a grin and he held up his hands again to call for silence. After he had spoken a few words in Spanish the cheering started up again. 'I choose you,' he said, staring down at Zoë.

'Me?' Zoë touched her chest in amazement. 'What for?' Her heart was racing out of control. She couldn't think what he meant. She couldn't think—

'You will find out.' Humour warmed his voice.

Zoë laughed anxiously as she stared up at him. She could still feel the touch of his hands around her waist— Her thoughts stalled right there. She might have weighed no more than a dried leaf in his arms. Shading her eyes, she tried to read his expression, but he drew her hand down again and enclosed it in his own.

Taking her into the centre of the ring, he presented her ceremoniously to the *tio*, and Zoë forced herself to relax.

What could happen with the *tio* standing there? She found a smile. These pictures would be flashed around the world. The last thing she wanted was to cause offence to an elder of Cazulas—a man who was her friend.

The *tio* seemed delighted that Rico had 'chosen' her, and embraced her warmly.

'What's all this about, Rico?' Zoë asked the moment the *tio* released her and turned away to address the crowd. Someone handed Rico a black silk robe and she waited while he put it on.

'You're part of my prize,' he said, when he had belted it.

'I'm *what*?'

Before Rico could answer, the *tio* turned around. Television cameras were angled to capture every nuance in Zoë's expression, and she cared for the *tio's* feelings, so she forced a smile.

'Do you understand our tradition?' he said to her warmly.

'I'm not sure.' She didn't want to look to Rico for answers.

'Allow me to explain.' The *tio* made a gesture to the crowd, begging their indulgence. Then, taking Zoë's hand, he led her out of the spotlight.

'It is our tradition. Having won the competition, Rico may choose any woman he wants. He chooses you.'

Incredible! Antiquated! Totally unacceptable! But the *tio* was looking at her so warmly, so openly, and he made it sound so very simple.

'Don't I have any say in the matter?' Zoë was careful to keep her voice light.

'Don't worry—the custom is not open to the same interpretation it might have been fifty years ago, when I was a young man.'

Zoë managed a laugh. 'I'm pleased to hear it.' She smiled at him, and then glanced at Rico. The expression in his eyes suggested he would have preferred sticking to the old ways.

Waves of panic and bewilderment started threatening to engulf her.

'It is a great honour to be chosen,' the *tio* coaxed. 'Look how disappointed you've made the other women.'

Zoë gazed around to please him, but whichever way she turned she saw Rico.

'All you have to do,' the *tio* explained persuasively, 'is to spend one night with him.'

'What?'

'I mean one *evening* with him,' he corrected hastily. 'My English is…' He waved his hands in the air with frustration, making Zoë feel worse than ever.

'I'll do it for you—of course I'll do it. Please don't worry.' This wasn't about her own feelings any more, or just work. It was about showing loyalty to an old man who was only trying to uphold the traditions of his youth. 'I won't let you down.'

Zoë allowed the *tio* to lead her back into the centre of the ring. She wouldn't let him down, but she was damned if she was going to play some antiquated mating game with Rico Cortes. She smiled tensely while the official announcement was made.

'Don't worry, I'll take a shower before I come back for you,' Rico murmured, the moment the applause around them subsided.

'Let's get one thing straight, Rico,' Zoë said, turning to face him. 'I'm grateful you took me riding, and helped me out here with staff for tonight. But I don't like surprises— especially not surprises that affect my work. The television lights are off now, the *tio* has gone to join his friends, and as far as I'm concerned the show's over.'

'And?' His eyes had gone cold.

'And I have no intention of becoming another of your trophies!'

'*Bravo*, Ms Chapman,' he murmured sardonically.

'Why don't you go and take that shower now? There are plenty of bathrooms in the castle.'

Rico's expression hardened as he looked down at her—and who could blame him? Zoë hadn't meant to sound so harsh, but there was an engine blazing away inside her, and a voice in her head that said, *Drive him away.*

What had happened tonight—all the fighting, the sounds, the tension, Rico overpowering everyone... It was just too close to her nightmares. She tried telling herself that all his strength was directed into sport. She had seen him ride; now she had seen him fight. But another side of her said: This is Rico Cortes, El Paladín, the man who conquers everyone with his strength... Her mind was fogged with fear. Unreasonable fear, maybe, but she couldn't shake it off.

The only thing she could latch on to in a world that was slipping away beneath her feet was the thought that she must not let the *tio* down. She would keep her promise to him, spend the rest of the evening with Rico. But first she had to go and seek some space, some cool, quiet place where she could get her head together.

She should fix somewhere to meet up with Rico before she did that. 'When you come back, Rico, I'll be—'

'I'll find you,' he said coldly, swinging a towel around his neck.

He vaulted over the top rope, dropped to the ground, and strode away from her without a backward glance.

CHAPTER SEVEN

THE meal was everything Zoë hoped it would be. The *tio* stood up and told everyone that the *paella* was the best he had ever tasted.

Rico was sitting next to her at the top table. He turned when she sat down after accepting the enthusiastic applause. 'Congratulations, Zoë. This has been a huge success for you.'

He was polite, but then, since he'd decided to trust her he was always polite. She wanted more. 'It's all thanks to the *tio* of Cazulas—' But Rico had already turned away to continue his conversation with the young Spanish beauty seated on his other side.

Zoë's smile faded. Rico had been cool ever since they'd sat down. It was understandable after her behaviour in the ring. But she couldn't tell him why she'd felt so bad after the wrestling. The *tio* of Cazulas had embroiled her in some ancient fertility rite that had fallen flat on its face.

She had kept her part of the bargain, staying with Rico throughout the evening, though he preferred the company of the vivacious young woman sitting next to him. His back had been half turned to her for most of the time.

Zoë noticed people were still smiling at her and raising their glasses. She smiled back, raising her own glass, but it was a hollow victory. She was thrilled everyone had enjoyed themselves, but the one person whose enthusiasm really mattered to her was otherwise occupied. She had thought of changing tables, but it would only cause comment—and Maria would be dancing soon.

There were about twenty people seated around each of the long tables set at the edges of the courtyard. The tables were laden with food, as well as countless bottles of beer, still water, and jugs of wine. She had used red and white gingham tablecloths to add a splash of colour, and placed lofty arrangements of brilliantly coloured exotic flowers on every one. Strings of lights swung gently in the night breeze overhead, twinkling like tiny stars, and waves of conversation and laughter were flowing all around her.

Resting her chin on her hand, she saw Maria's guitarist place his stool in a corner of the performance area. Sitting down, he began to strum some popular tunes. It was all perfect. She had asked to sit at the end of the table so that she could get up easily to supervise the food when necessary. Her plan had worked well—brilliantly, in fact. Though she might as well have stayed in the kitchen. Why hadn't Rico chosen the ebony-haired beauty as his trophy in the first place?

Zoë was distracted from her thoughts by Maria's entrance, and sat up. Straight away it was incredible. The air was charged with energy the moment she appeared. Framed in the doorway of the castle, Maria stood with one hand pointing towards the stars, calling up whatever mysterious energy fuelled her performance. Even Rico had turned to watch, forgetting, at least for a moment, the young beauty at his side.

The guitarist picked out an arpeggio, filling each note with incredible weight and passion. Maria stood unmoving until the last vibration from the strings of the guitar had faded away, and then she stepped proudly into the full glare of the television lights. Hovering like an eagle for an instant, she suddenly moved forward with all the grace of a much younger woman, crossing the courtyard with swift, precise steps.

She came into the centre of the performance area, raised her chin, and stared at some far distant point only she could see. The expression on her face was one of defiance, great pride, and anger, but there was pain and compassion too. Sweeping her crimson skirt off the floor in one hand, she made a powerful gesture with the other, and at the same time struck the floor one sharp blow with her foot.

Philip was by Zoë's side minutes after Maria had finished her performance. 'This programme will go down in history. That woman is superb—they're saying she's even better than Beba—though she's old enough to be Beba's mother.'

'I'm sure you're right.' Zoë frowned, tuning out for a moment. She had never heard of this Beba before in her life, and now she was haunted by the woman.

Philip dashed away before she could ask him anything, and then Maria had another surprise for them. She came back into the centre of the courtyard and invited everyone to join her in a dance.

Strictly speaking, this was country dancing, the *tio* said when he came over to explain what was happening to Zoë. All Zoë knew was that Rico's seat, as well as the one next to him, was empty, and what he and his young partner were doing on the dance floor was more dirty dancing than country dancing.

'Rico is good, eh?' the *tio* said, following her interest keenly. 'But the girl is too obvious. No subtlety.'

No subtlety at all, Zoë agreed silently. The young woman was like a clinging vine, all suckers and creeping fingers.

'Why don't you dance?'

Zoë turned to smile at the *tio*. 'With you?' She started to get to her feet.

'No, not with me!' The *tio* pressed her down in the seat again. 'I mean you should dance with Rico.'

'Rico is already dancing with someone,' Zoë pointed out, trying her best to sound faintly amused and casually dismissive.

'Here, in this part of Spain,' the *tio* told her slyly, 'women do not wait to be asked.'

Zoë turned to stare at him, wondering if she'd heard correctly, but instead of explaining himself the mischievous old man drew his shoulders in a wry shrug.

There were a million reasons why she could not—should not—do as the *tio* suggested, Zoë thought as she stood up. This was insane, she told herself as she walked towards the dance floor. Rico Cortes would simply stare at her and turn away. As for his young partner—Zoë could just imagine the look of triumph on her face when Rico told her to get lost. She was about to make a fool of herself in front of the whole village—the whole world, if you took the television cameras into account. But she just went on threading her way through the crowds on the dance floor.

'*Brava, Zoë! Eso es!*'

'Maria!'

'You should have worn your performance dress,' the older woman whispered in her ear before melting back into the crowd.

Too late for that now—jeans and a tailored shirt would have to do. She couldn't stop to think about it, Zoë realised as she reached her goal. She tapped the young Spanish beauty lightly on the shoulder. 'Excuse me. I'm cutting in.'

'*Qué?*'

The girl couldn't have looked more shocked. Zoë almost felt sorry for her. Almost. She didn't have a chance to see the expression on Rico's face; the next thing she knew she was in his arms.

'Well, this is a surprise.'

She could feel his breath warm against her hair. 'A pleasant one, I hope?'

'Unexpected, certainly.'

He had changed into casual clothes for the party: blue jeans, shirt with the sleeves rolled up and the collar open at the neck. He smelt divine, and he felt...

Zoë shivered as the music slowed to a sensuous rumba rhythm, as if responding to her mood. She saw that the young girl had quickly moved away to dance with some people of her own age, and didn't seem too upset—though right at this moment Zoë had decided to be selfish. She only cared how *she* felt. And she felt wonderful.

Having so many people around them gave Zoë the confidence to relax in Rico's arms. As they brushed past people smiled with approval. Whether that was to show their appreciation of the party or because she was in Rico's arms, Zoë didn't know, and right now it didn't matter. Even with the difference in their size they fitted together perfectly. They were dancing as one, as if they had always danced like this, and the planes and curves of his body invited her to mould against him.

Rico had an innate sense of rhythm, and Zoë could only be grateful that Maria had given her the courage to dance in a way that made her feel seductive and desirable. Nothing existed in her universe outside of Rico as they danced on to the haunting music, and Zoë barely noticed when one of his powerful thighs slipped between her legs, bringing her closer still. She only knew that it felt right, essential to the dance, and now they were one—moving as one, breathing as one, and dancing as one...

He let her go when the melody turned to something lively. Zoë realised that they had been the centre of attention, and that now couples were turning to their own pleasures again. It was true, she had been so deeply and sensually aware of Rico she had forgotten for the space of their dance that they were not alone.

She trembled as Rico stared down at her. The tempo of the music had increased, but they were both oblivious to it. Nothing existed outside the ambit of his gaze, and as she watched his lips tug up in a smile Zoë realised she was hoping for something more.

'Shall we?' He tipped his chin in the direction of their empty places at the table.

She dropped back into the real world. Of course Rico didn't want to dance with her all night. People were staring. The music had stopped again, and she was still standing on the dance floor like a fool.

'I'll...go and see if there's any pudding left. Someone might be hungry.'

Rico didn't try to stop her as she struggled to make her way through the whirling couples, but then she realised he was beside her, shielding her with his arm. When he stopped to talk to an old acquaintance she slipped away, making for the door to the kitchen. But she hadn't even had a chance to close it when Rico came in behind her.

'What's wrong with you, Zoë? Why are you running away from me?' He leaned back against the door, and she got the impression he wasn't going anywhere until she explained.

'Nothing.'

'Nothing?' His voice was flat, disbelieving. 'I think it's time you told me what all this is about, don't you? You were fine when we were out riding together, and then tonight you turn on the ice.'

'You haven't spoken to me all night!'

'Do you blame me?'

Truthfully, she didn't.

'Then you come up to me and want to dance. And then you run away again.' Rico made a sound of exasperation as he spread his arms wide. 'Are you going to tell me what all this is about?'

'I can't—'

'You can't?' He shook his head. 'Why not, Zoë? You've never been short of opinions in the past.'

'I can't explain because you'll just think I'm being ridiculous.'

'Try me.'

She met his gaze, and this time neither of them looked away.

'Violence frightens me.' Her voice was just a whisper.

'Violence?' Rico frowned and straightened up.

'Of any kind. I know how that must sound to you—and I do know wrestling's just a sport—'

'Are you saying I'm a violent man?' His eyes narrowed, and she could see she had offended him deeply.

'No—not you…' Zoë's voice dried. She looked away.

'Are you saying I remind you of someone who was violent in your past?' He looked stricken. 'That's it—isn't it, Zoë?'

'I can't help it.' She made a weak gesture with her hands.

'Do you have any idea how insulting that is?'

She saw his hand tighten on the door handle until his knuckles turned white, and took a step towards him. 'I'm sorry, Rico. I haven't even congratulated you—'

He made an angry gesture, cutting her off. 'I don't know what shocks me the most—the fact that you can mention violence in your past as if it were nothing, or the thought that you could possibly confuse me with some snivelling bully who preys on women and others who are weaker than himself.'

'I just don't want tonight to be all about me. This is your night too, Rico.'

'What you've just said overrides anything else.'

'We can't talk about it now. I can't just abandon my guests.'

'Forget the damned party!'

'How can I?' Zoë said, moving towards the door. 'It's wrong of me to keep you so long like this, Rico. Your young companion—'

'Will do perfectly well without me.' He caught hold of her arm as she tried to move past him. 'You can't leave it like this, Zoë. If you are protecting someone—someone who's hurt you—'

'I'm not,' she said steadily, meeting his eyes. 'I promise you, Rico, it's all over now.'

'Is it?'

'Yes,' she said, holding his gaze. 'Yes, it is.'

He shook his head, and his eyes were full of concern. 'Know this, Zoë: I am not and never have been a violent man. I have never raised my hand in anger to anyone. When you have great strength the very first thing you must learn is control. Strength has not been given to me to use against a weaker person, or some helpless creature. It has been given to me to help other people when I can, and for me to enjoy. Nothing more.'

And before she could say another word, he added in a fierce undertone, 'And don't you ever confuse me with some other man again.'

Rico opened the door for her and stood aside to let her pass, and the happy noise and bustle of the courtyard claimed her.

'Señorita?'

Zoë looked round to see that he had followed her out. It took her a moment of recovery after their highly charged exchange for her to realise what he meant to do.

Sweeping her a formal half-bow, he offered her his arm. 'May I escort you back to the party, Señorita Chapman?'

The rest of the night passed in a blur of laughter and dancing for Zoë. By the time people started drifting away her feet were aching. She had joined in every traditional dance of the region—men, women and children, all on their feet, colourful skirts flying and proud hands clapping the irresistible syncopated rhythms.

Now she was exhausted, and more grateful than ever to Rico's efficient staff, who had cleared away absolutely everything from the hall, leaving her with nothing to do there.

'Why are you back in the kitchen?'

'Rico—you caught me.' Zoë turned, embarrassed that he had seen her stealing her own *figuritas*. Now it was her turn to get her hand slapped—the only difference was, Rico's slap was more of a caress, and then he raised her hand to his lips. 'You have earned a break, Zoë.' He looked around. 'My people are only too happy to clear up—I told them they could take anything that was left home with them.'

'Oh, I'm sorry.'

'Don't be. I'm sure they can spare you one marzipan mouse.'

'Why are you frowning?'

'I just don't have the knack of dismissing the things you told me—as you seem to have.'

'Have I spoiled the party for you?'

'Don't trivialise what you said, Zoë. You can't keep everything locked inside you for ever.'

Why not? She'd been doing a pretty good job up to now. 'Let's not talk about it tonight,' she said, forcing a bright note into her voice. 'We're both tired—'

'Are we?'

Heat flared up from Zoë's toes to scorch her cheeks. 'Is it a deal? Can we just leave all the other stuff for another time?'

Pressing his lips together, he frowned. He didn't look keen. 'If that's what you want. I don't want to spoil the night for you.'

'You could never do that.'

The suggestion of a smile tugged at his lips.

They broke eye contact at a knock on the door. She couldn't have given a better cue herself, Zoë realised as Rico's helpers trooped in. It was impossible to talk about the past now. 'Shall we go back to the party?'

'Not for too long.'

There was something in the way he said it that made Zoë blush. 'Why?' She looked up at him, and immediately wished she hadn't.

Dipping his head close as he opened the door for her, he

whispered in her ear: 'I'm tired of playing games, Zoë. Can't you see how much I want you?'

It was so unexpected. She couldn't imagine anyone other than Rico even saying the words. No man had ever admitted to wanting her—he was the first. She didn't know how to answer him. She didn't know what was expected of her. 'I don't want to talk about—'

'Who said anything about talking? And you have my word I won't make you do anything you don't want to do.'

Rico drew her out of the bustling kitchen through a door that led into the silent hall. 'That's better,' he murmured, pulling her close to drop a kiss on her brow. 'I like to see you smile. I don't want to see you tense and unhappy ever again.' Nudging her hair aside, he planted a second tender kiss on the very sensitive place below her ear.

When he rasped the stubble on his chin against her neck Zoë gasped, and allowed him to draw her closer still. It was so easy to slip beneath Rico's seductive spell. She could have broken away at any time; but his hold on her was so light there was no reason to try.

She parted her lips, welcoming the invasion of his tongue, but he teased her gently, pulling away until she locked her hands behind his neck and brought him back again. And then their mouths collided hungrily, and it was Rico's turn to groan as she moulded into him.

She was in a dream state as Rico led her swiftly by the hand through the castle. Every part of her was aching for his touch. His hand was firm and warm, and she went with him willingly through the archway that led to the luxury spa.

'I haven't been down here before,' Zoë admitted as Rico let go of her for a moment to close the door. She couldn't bear the loss, and reached for him.

'Not yet,' he warned, his fingertips caressing her cheek.

'Why not?'

'Because it's better this way.'

She followed him down a short flight of marble steps.

'Are you sure you have never been down here before?' Rico stopped at the bottom and turned to look at her.

'Never.'

'Then you're about to get a very pleasant surprise.'

Zoë watched Rico punch a series of numbers onto a panel on the wall. A door slid behind them. 'What are you doing?'

'I've changed the code so we won't be disturbed. Zoë?' Rico touched her face with one fingertip when he saw the expression on her face. 'The code is twenty-one, twelve—my birthday. Don't look so worried. You can leave any time you want.'

'I just thought if there was an emergency—and I needed to get out in a hurry—'

'An emergency?' Rico smiled. 'What? You mean something like this?'

And then somehow she was in his arms again, and he was kissing her so tenderly, so thoroughly, Zoë wondered how she remained standing. Heat flooded through her veins, and when his tongue tangled with her own a soft moan came from somewhere deep in her chest, showing him how much she wanted him to kiss her.

When he pulled back, she reached up, wrapping her arms around his neck to mesh her fingers through his hair and draw him close again. When Rico kissed her she felt no fear. She wanted him to know how she felt, that she was ready for him: moist, swollen, hot. But then she remembered...

'First ice, and now fire?' Rico murmured, looking down at her.

He was so tender, so caring—but how could she be sure he wouldn't be shocked or disappointed when she experienced the painful spasm that had always made fully penetrative sex impossible for her? She had to be sure she wouldn't stop, Zoë thought as her hand strayed to his belt buckle...

Rico moved her hand away, bringing her fingers to his lips

to kiss each tip in turn. Zoë's eyes filled with hot tears of failure.

'You need to slow down, Zoë.'

Glancing up uncertainly, she saw his lips were curving in a smile. She started to try and say something, to explain herself, but, putting one firm finger over her lips, Rico stopped her.

'I'm going to find you something to wear in the hot tub.' He broke away. 'And then I'll order some refreshments for us from the kitchen.'

Something to wear? Food from the kitchen? She was so naïve! She had expected to be naked, feeding on him.

'And then we'll sample the hot tub together.'

Better.

She gazed around. The ancient walls had been sandblasted in this part of the castle until they were pale yellow. The floor was a mellow golden marble, and all the tiles and fittings had been selected with a view to nothing startling to the eye or the senses. The temperature was perfect, the silence complete.

Rico reached inside a beautiful old oak chest and brought out some fluffy caramel-coloured towels, then black swimming trunks for himself and a swimming costume the same shade as her eyes.

'That's a lucky find.'

'Or good planning,' Rico said.

'You know your way around here pretty well.'

'I should. The castle belongs to a very good friend of mine. Do you want to go and change now? Music?' he added, handing her the costume.

'Why not? Something gentle and soothing would be nice.'

'I'll see if I can accommodate you.' His voice was ironic as he moved to select a CD.

A sinuous melody started weaving its spell around Zoë as Rico took hold of her hand again, and she went with him, deeper into the spa.

The hot tub in the centre of the floor was illuminated by hundreds of flickering candles. Zoë gasped. 'How—?'

'You ask too many questions. Just accept you're going to be pampered for a change.'

There were a million questions she would have liked to ask him, but for once in her life she bit them back.

They changed in beech-lined changing cabins, and she covered her costume with one of the white towelling robes hanging on the back of each door.

'To think I didn't even realise this place existed!'

'The hot tub is kept locked up for most of the time.'

'Your friend must like you a lot to let you use it.'

Loosening the belt on his robe, Rico let it drop to the floor. Zoë kept her gaze strictly confined to his face, but to her relief saw the black bathing trunks in her peripheral vision.

'Aren't you going to take your robe off?'

'Yes…yes, of course I am.'

Zoë waited until she was up the steps of the hot tub and had one leg in the water before slipping off the robe. Then she was in like a flash, submerged beneath the water before Rico had even climbed in.

There were tiny lights above her head, winking on and off in a deep blue ceiling decorated with puffs of smoky cloud to give it the appearance of a night sky. 'This is unbelievable.' Zoë sighed, stretching out her arms along the top of the tub to keep her balance in the swirling water. She leaned her head back, and closed her eyes.

'I prefer an open-air bathroom.'

She looked up again. Rico had settled himself across from her. 'You mean the sea?'

A door opened before he could reply to her, and a waiter came in with a tray of refreshments for them.

'Thank you,' Rico said, glancing round at the man. 'You can leave them here.'

Zoë blinked. There was champagne on ice, two tall crystal

flutes, a bowl of sweet wild strawberries, some whipped cream and a bowl of chocolate sauce on the tray. 'Now I have seen everything.' She shook her head incredulously.

'You really think so?'

Rico's voice was challenging, and soft. She didn't answer.

Wrapped in fluffy towels, and stretched out on a recliner next to Rico's, Zoë sipped champagne while Rico lay back watching her through half-closed eyes.

'If this is the Cazulas way of thanking people for giving a party, I may have to stay a lot longer than I planned.' Putting her glass down, she relaxed back against the soft bank of cushions and stretched out her limbs in languorous appreciation.

Selecting a plump strawberry, Rico dipped it in rich chocolate sauce. 'Open your mouth.'

He touched it to her lips, and she could smell the warm chocolate sauce. She wasn't quick enough, and it started escaping in runnels down her chin. Leaning over her, Rico licked it off, and then he was kissing her—kissing her deeply.

It was the taste of Zoë that made him greedy. It made him want more, a lot more of her. It made him want everything. But he knew better than that. He knew he had to wait. Pulling back, Rico saw that her eyes were still closed, her lips still slightly parted as she sucked in breath, and there were smudges of chocolate all round her mouth.

'Don't be mean,' she whispered, opening her mouth wider. 'I want more.'

Smiling wryly, Rico began to feed her again. He kept on until she was begging him for mercy as she laughed; until she couldn't keep up with the chocolate sauce and the cream, and it dripped onto her breasts, and slipped between them. Her lips were stained red with strawberry juice and her eyes were almost as dark as the chocolate. And then he couldn't help himself. He was kissing her again, and she was clinging to him, not caring that her towel had fallen away.

Zoë gasped as Rico's tongue began to lave between her breasts. She had sunk lower and lower onto the recliner, wanting him to continue until every scrap of chocolate had disappeared. Her breasts were streaked with juice and cream, and there was a coating of chocolate on each painfully extended nipple. His tongue was deliciously warm, and rasped against her sensitive skin in a way that was unbearably good.

She wanted more. But Rico was heavily into foreplay—something she had never experienced before. He knew how to tease and torment her; he knew every erogenous zone on her body. Her flesh sang with pleasure as she writhed beneath him, and she could no longer make any pretence at shyness. How could she, with his warm breath invading her ears? She cried out to him, shuddering uncontrollably, but just as she did so he pulled back.

Short of grabbing him by the hair and forcing him to suckle her breasts, she had no idea what to do next. She was getting desperate. 'Shall I feed you now?'

Holding himself up on his fists, Rico looked down at her. 'What did you have in mind?'

There was such a wicked smile tugging at his lips, Zoë couldn't resist it. 'Just this.' Cupping her breasts, she held them out to him.

CHAPTER EIGHT

RICO stared at Zoë's breasts. They were magnificent—a fact he had been trying hard to ignore from the moment he had seen her in a tight top pulling plastic oranges down from the walls. His control had never undergone such a painful test—especially now, when she was warm, soft, and more lovely than ever. But was she ready for this?

He couldn't stop looking at her tight, extended nipples, currently reaching out to him in the most irresistible invitation.

'Wrong colour?' she teased him softly.

'Perfect.' And they were—the most delectable shade of shell-pink.

'Wrong size for you?'

She was still smiling, waiting, her eyebrows arched in enquiry as she stared at him.

'Zoë—' Rolling off his recliner, he hunkered down by her side. 'What would you like me to do, Señorita Chapman?'

'Eat me.'

'Eat you?' He pretended surprise. 'That's very forward of you...'

'Yes, isn't it?'

Taking matters into her own hands, she sat up and locked her hands around his neck to bring him down to her.

Swearing softly in his own language, he pulled back, drawing her with him, staring into her face as he unlocked her hands. Laying her back down on the narrow couch, he took a long, lazy look down the whole lovely, naked length of her. 'Wild cat!' he murmured approvingly.

There was barely an inch of Zoë's body that had been spared the chocolate, the cream, or the sweet red strawberry juice. He applied himself first to the task of cleaning her breasts, using long greedy strokes of his tongue. With each caress she cried out—he might have been inside her, so intense was her response.

Had she never experienced foreplay in her life? He thought not. When he suckled her nipples she moaned rhythmically in time with his actions until he knew he had to stop. He had never known anything like it before; he had never been so aroused before. His senses were on fire and his anticipation of his final possession of her was overwhelming in its intensity. But before he realised what she meant to do she had surprised him.

Scooping up some sticky chocolate sauce, she smeared a handful over his chest. When she began to lick it off, he knew he was in danger of losing control for the first time in his life. Capturing her in his arms, he rolled with her onto a soft rug on the floor, straddling her, and pinning her arms down above her head. Trying to keep her still while she wriggled beneath him was almost impossible. She was moving her head from side to side, laughing and threatening him in the same breath. Finally securing her wrists in one strong fist, he reached for the cream jug with his free hand, and emptied the contents all over her.

Shrieking with surprise, and laughing at the same time, she tried to break away, but when he started lapping at her belly she changed her mind. Meshing her fingers through his hair, she was all compliance, all sensation, as she told him she wanted more. And when he moved lower, nudging her thighs apart, she whimpered with pleasure and angled herself shamelessly towards him.

He stopped just short of where she wanted him to be, making her cry out with disappointment. Before she had a chance to complain any more, he sprang to his feet and swept her into his arms.

The moment had come, Zoë thought, laying her head on

Rico's shoulder. As he carried her across the relaxation room she knew she trusted him completely. By the time they reached the wet room she was shaking with anticipation. She had never been so aroused. This time Rico would make everything right.

Zoë shrieked as she landed with a splash in the hot tub. Moments later Rico was in with her, holding her safe above the water. Reaching for a sponge, he began soaping her down until all the chocolate and cream had disappeared.

He had never been called upon to exert so much control in his life, Rico realised when they'd got out and he had reclaimed his sanity beneath an icy cold drench shower. And he had never had so much fun with a woman.

Wrapping a towel around his waist, he stared at Zoë drying her lush red-gold hair. She looked more beautiful than ever. Her cheeks were still flushed from their seductive play-fight, and her eyes were gleaming as if her zest for life had suddenly increased. She was starting to trust him, Rico knew, and they could never make love until she did. He only had to touch her, to kiss her, to look at her, to know how inexperienced she was. And it troubled him to think what might have happened to her in the past.

She was humming softly to herself, staring clear-eyed into the mirror as she arranged her hair like a shimmering cape around her shoulders. When he walked up to her, and she looked at him, he could feel his heart pounding so hard in his chest it actually hurt.

It seemed that whatever ghosts there were in her past, or in his, they had no power when they were together. He felt a great swell of happiness inside him. It was a dangerous development, and one that made him feel unusually vulnerable.

Dropping a kiss on Zoë's shoulder, he went to get his clothes. He felt a lot more than lust for her. Her innocence had touched him deeply. Was this love?

When he was almost dressed she came to him. Standing

close behind him, she placed her hands on his shoulders. He felt her rest her face trustingly against his back. And in that moment he knew the whole world and everything in it was his.

He wouldn't have agreed to spending the night in separate rooms at the castle for anyone but Zoë, Rico realised, calling a halt to his pacing. She might be a successful career woman, but beneath the gloss of achievement he knew she was terribly vulnerable, and it made him feel protective, even responsible for her.

It was unusual—no, unique—to find someone so tender and pure. Gold-diggers disgusted him, and there were so many of them around. He had closed his mind years ago to the possibility of ever finding someone who cared for him, and not for his money. Zoë didn't need his money, but even if she had, he knew she would have been as sickened as he at the thought of using a person's wealth as a measure for their worth. It warmed him just to be thinking about her. This was special. She was special.

Going to the open window, he planted his fists on the sill and leaned out. A silver-pink dawn was creeping up the sides of the snow-capped mountains, and the sight bewitched him. Zoë would be sleeping now. He smiled to think of her curled up in bed, sleeping the deep, untroubled sleep of the innocent.

Gazing along the balcony they shared, Rico noticed that her window was open. Her career absorbed her completely. She had to be exhausted.

He turned to look at the computer screen. There was nothing yet.

Natural caution made him investigate everyone who threatened his privacy. He knew already that Zoë was no self-seeking adventuress, but his night-owl investigator had been on the case since she'd arrived in Cazulas. It was a juggernaut he couldn't stop now. He had keyed in his password, and expected an e-mail at any time. Once his mind was set at ease, he would go and wake Zoë in a way he knew she would enjoy.

Just the thought of rousing her from sleep, all warm and tousled, and kissing her into the new day had been enough to keep him from his bed. He was eager to be with her. Throwing back his head, Rico let out a long ragged sigh of frustration. It was hard to believe that here, in one of the remotest regions of Spain, fate had put him on a collision course with someone as honest and forthright as Zoë. He was tempted to go to her right now, without waiting for reassurance.

He tensed abruptly, all senses on full alert. Pushing back from the balcony, he strode quickly to the door. He stood outside his room, in the corridor, and listened intently. He thought he had heard a cry. But there was nothing. He turned, knowing everyone in the castle was asleep. Some nocturnal animal must have disturbed him.

Going back into his temporary study bedroom, Rico closed the heavy door carefully. That was it! He cursed himself for not thinking of it sooner. The doors in the castle were so heavy no sound could possibly penetrate them.

Walking onto the balcony, he quietened his breathing and listened outside Zoë's window. At first there was nothing aside from the soft swish of fabric as the fine voile curtains billowed in the early-morning breeze. Then he heard her cry out again, and, reaching through the window, he turned the key in the double doors and stepped into her room.

She was just awake, and clearly confused.

'Zoë—what is it?' He knelt down at her side. She was as beautiful as he had imagined, still warm from sleep and more lovely than any woman had a right to be if a man was to remain sane.

'Rico.' She pressed her hands against his chest. 'Rico, I'm fine. I'm really sorry if I woke you—'

'You didn't wake me. I'm still dressed,' he pointed out. 'But as for your being fine—I'm sick of that word. You're not fine.'

'All right. I had a nightmare.'

'A nightmare?' He turned away. 'You cried out, and I was worried about you—'

Her face went bright red, as if it was she who was in the wrong.

'You don't need to worry about me.'

He was amazed to see how quickly she could recover her composure. Then he remembered that she was used to covering up the truth.

'As I told you, Rico. There's really nothing to worry about.'

'How long are you going to lie to me about this, Zoë?'

There was a long silence, and then she said, 'I don't know what makes you say that.'

'I heard you this time. I heard you cry out. And then, as I came into your room, I heard what you said.'

She covered her face with her hands, but he couldn't let it rest now. 'Don't,' he said softly. Gently taking hold of her hands, he lifted them away. 'You were in the throes of something much worse than a nightmare, Zoë. You were crying out, begging—'

'No!' She shouted it at him, and he waited until she grew calm again, holding her hands firmly between his own.

'Begging?' She forced out a laugh. 'You're mistaken, Rico—'

'I am not mistaken. And I'd like to know what made you call out—"Please, don't hit me again."'

'I've told you, you're wrong. I would never say something like that. Why should I?'

'That's what I'm trying to find out.'

She shook her head, and her eyes wore a wounded expression. 'Is that why you were so gentle with me, Rico? Is that why you won't make love to me? Is that why you agreed to stay over in a separate room? You feel sorry for me—'

'Don't be so ridiculous!' He raked his hair in sheer exasperation. 'I don't spend time with women because I feel sorry for them.'

'How many women?'

'Why are you doing this to yourself, Zoë?'

'I tell you, Rico, you're wrong about me.' She scrambled upright with the sheet firmly clutched in her hand. 'You don't need to feel pity for me. It was just a nightmare. Nothing more.' She shook her head, seeing the disbelief in his eyes. 'I'm really grateful you came in to make sure I was all right. You're kind—very kind—and thank you—'

'Don't!' His voice was sharp as he put his hand up. He regretted it immediately, seeing her flinch. 'I would never hurt you.' His voice was just a whisper, but she had already gathered herself into a ball and pulled the sheet up to her chin. 'Don't ever thank me for being kind to you, Zoë. It's the very least one human being can expect from another.' He was consumed with relief when she lifted her head and looked at him.

'Who hurt you, Zoë?'

'No one…'

Her voice was tiny, like a child's, and it hurt him more than anything he had ever heard. 'Is that why you were crying out?' he pressed gently. 'Were you remembering what had happened to you?'

'Rico, please.'

He could feel the anger pumping through him. His hands, balled into fists at his sides, ached with tension. Who could ever hurt her? It was inconceivable to him that anyone could wish to harm one hair on her head. He wanted to protect her—but how could he when she insisted on pushing him away? 'Won't you trust me enough to tell me, Zoë?'

'I can't. I just can't.'

'Please, don't shut me out. I want to help you, but I have to know the truth—'

'The truth?' Zoë made a short incredulous sound. She hated herself as it was for her weakness. How could she know she would cry out when she was sleeping? 'Do *you* always tell the truth, Rico? Do you?'

He couldn't answer her. How could he when he had been staring at a computer screen half the night? They were both victims of the past in their own way. Suspicion was branded on his heart, but Zoë was damaged too, and her wounds had been carved far deeper and more cruelly than his.

Standing up, he moved away from the bed, carrying the image of Zoë in his mind. Her hair was like skeins of silk, gleaming in the moonlight, and her skin was so soft and warm. The room was filled with the scent of the orange blossom she always wore. As he turned, she turned too, and their eyes locked. He longed to tell her everything. He wanted nothing more in all the world than to take her in his arms and keep her safe for ever. But he could not. Instead, he would go back to his own room and maintain his vigil until the information he had asked for came through.

'Goodnight, Zoë.' He walked onto the veranda, closing the doors softly behind him.

Throwing his head back, with his eyes tightly shut, he let out a heavy sigh. For the first time in his life the price he had to pay for being Rico Cortes was far too high.

CHAPTER NINE

CLUTCHING the receiver between neck and shoulder while she scooped up her discarded nightwear from the floor, Zoë listened patiently. There was an opportunity to do a live interview with a national television show—a roving reporter had just arrived with a camera crew. Could she make it in time?

She looked like hell after her disturbed night. She felt like it too, especially remembering what had happened with Rico. But this was work, and there was nothing on her face that make-up couldn't fix. Her heart was another matter, but that would have to wait.

She was curious, and she was tempted too. The publicity would be great for the series—and she was interested to find out why someone from such a well-known show had come all the way to Cazulas to speak to her. Of course the last series had been a big success, and it had generated a lot of media interest. That had to be it.

'Of course I'll do it,' she said, decision made. 'Half an hour suit you? OK, fifteen minutes,' she conceded. 'But get Marnie and the girls up here right away with the war paint.'

Philip had told her there would be a chance for a run-through first, so there would be no surprises and nothing for her to worry about. It was just what she needed to take her mind off Rico... He must have gone by now. There wasn't much to keep him at the castle. But she still had her career. The thrill of the places it took her to, and the amazement that she had made something of herself after all, in spite of her ex's assurances that she never would, had not diminished. She hoped they never would.

She had to stand under a cold shower to try and put Rico

out of her mind. Finally, reasonably focused on work and totally frozen, she rubbed herself down vigorously with a towel.

There was a bad feeling niggling away inside her, Zoë realised as she dressed. It made no sense. She had done this sort of thing lots of times before, and knew that nothing was left to chance. It might all appear impromptu at home, but the groundwork had already been covered so that none of the questions came out of the blue. And yet…

'To hell with it,' she murmured, spritzing on some perfume. She was a seasoned campaigner and there was nothing to worry about.

Seasoned campaigner or not, she hadn't factored quite such a bubbly young presenter into the equation. The latest in a long line of glamorous young women with an incisive mind, she was the type of person that Zoë found wearing, but fun in short bursts. They talked through the questions, and decided on the best strategy to adopt to promote the show. Zoë was confident she could keep things moving forward smoothly. They were going to film outside, with a backdrop of mountains behind them, and went on air almost immediately.

'So, Zoë, how does it feel to be here in such a fabulous location, as opposed to being stuck in an overheated studio?' The girl fanned herself extravagantly and smiled, as if this made them comrades in adversity.

Her openness made Zoë laugh. 'It feels great, Lisa—but it's hot outside here, as well as under the lights. Don't forget this is Spain—'

'You've got quite a glow going on there, Zoë.' The girl cut across her, facing the camera to address the viewers. 'Could this be something more than a suntan? I hear the Spanish men around here are quite something. Or *man*, rather,' she added as Zoë stared at her. 'Come on, you can tell us—we won't tell a soul, will we?' she exclaimed, turning again to include several million viewers.

'Let's talk about the programme first.' *And last,* Zoë thought, keeping a smile on her face while her mind raced. They hadn't planned to touch on anything other than her new television series. In fact she had made a point of insisting there would be no delving into her personal life. The past was just that—behind her. That was what she and the young reporter had agreed on.

'You're right, Zoë. Let's talk about your programme. That's what we're here for.'

Zoë stalled. The look on the girl's face was open, inviting… Inviting what? There was just enough guile in her eyes to churn Zoë's stomach. 'I think this series is going to be my best yet—'

'You only *think*? Don't tell me Zoë Chapman's become a shrinking violet?'

'Sorry?'

'You're not going to turn coy on us now, Zoë, are you? Disappoint the viewers?' The girl turned to camera and made a moue, but there was a shrewd gleam in her eyes when she looked back. 'After spending the night as the prize of a wealthy man?'

She had just managed to leave out the word *again,* Zoë thought, feeling the blood drain from her face.

'That's right, isn't it, Zoë?' The girl's lips pressed down as she shrugged and managed to look ingenuous for the camera. 'I've seen the footage.' Her eyes opened really wide and she stared around, as if seeking confirmation that her reportage was absolutely accurate from some unseen source.

Zoë's gaze iced over as she waited for the bombshell to fall. After all, the camera never lied…

'Half-naked men wrestling beneath the stars in this sultry Mediterranean climate—and the champion, El Paladín, also known as Alarico Cortes, claiming you as his prize for the night.' She stretched, showing off her taut young belly as if she had all the time in the world to deliver her *coup de grâce*. 'Mmm, sounds pretty hot to me. *He's* pretty hot!'

'That was just an item.' Zoë tried to laugh it off and put on a good-humoured smile for the camera. Inwardly she was seething. The girl's agenda was obvious. This wasn't about her series. There was still mileage in the old scandal.

'Just an item!' The girl cut her off with a short, incredulous laugh. 'OK, Zoë, let's cut to the chase. You bagged Alarico Cortes for one glorious night. I'm only quoting the age-old tradition here in Cazulas, Zo—no need to look at me like that. Alarico Cortes, if you don't know of him at home, is only *the* most eligible bachelor in Spain—a billionaire, and a good friend of the Spanish royal family. So, what was it like? How does it feel, mingling with the aristocracy? And were you really just a prize for the night? Or is this love?'

Alarico Cortes? Aristocracy? Billionaire? Zoë was stunned. If what the young reporter said was true... The last way she would have wanted to hear it was like this.

'I was lucky enough to be invited to take part in a traditional celebration that has been upheld here in Cazulas for centuries. It was great fun—nothing more than that. I'm really sorry to disappoint you.' She finished with a good-natured shrug towards the camera. Game, set, and match, she thought, seeing the girl's face turn sulky.

'Well, you heard it here first, folks.' The reporter quickly recovered. 'The most beautiful celebrity chef on the circuit has something really special in the pipeline for all of us. Don't miss Zoë's new series, or you'll miss those yummy men— and we're talking drop-dead gorgeous in the case of Alarico Cortes, girls. Thank you, Zoë, for sparing us these few precious minutes away from your show.'

'My pleasure,' Zoë said, with a last cheery smile to the viewers. 'Thank you all for your time.'

She even thanked the girl again when the cameras had stopped rolling. They both knew who had come out on top, and Zoë was determined to remain professional to the last. But she couldn't quite believe she had allowed herself to be set up. It had been two years since the scandal broke. Two years to learn caution. She'd thought she was too wary to be trapped like this—but apparently not.

And Rico Cortes, all round good-guy and local one-man protection agency, had been lying to her all along: his *friend's* castle, his *friend's* horses, the down-homey camaraderie of the flamenco camp—and he was a Spanish grandee. Why wasn't she surprised? It all made sense now. He had been lying to her ever since that first meeting, pulling the wool over her eyes, confusing her with his sweet talk and worthy notions. And wasn't she a chump to have thought him any better than her ex? Rico Cortes was one smart operator.

'Great job, Zoë!'

Zoë looked at Philip blankly as he clapped her on the back.

'Our ratings will soar if you keep this up.'

'That's fantastic.' She was already running towards the castle. She had no idea if Rico would still be there. Inside the castle—*his* castle!

Pausing for a moment in the middle of the courtyard, she looked around. Rico's castle. His village, his horses, his spa, his kitchen, his bed, his office. Shading her eyes, she stared up at the balcony they had shared, and in that moment she hated him.

Zoë walked straight into the study bedroom where Rico had been sleeping. At least now he was gone she could use the computer to let her far-flung family members know the interview would be repeated on breakfast television throughout the morning.

'Rico!' Zoë's heart lurched as she saw him, and her eyes filled with tears as he moved away from the computer screen. 'I thought you would have gone by now.'

'I came back.'

'What are you doing?'

'Don't you knock before you enter a room?'

The situation had an element of farce. He was looking at her with a face full of mistrust and anger when *she* was the one who had been wronged. Rico had been lying to her all along—misleading her, pretending to be a local man when he was... She didn't even know who he was.

'I still hold the lease on the castle. Technically this is my room, Rico.'

Tension stretched between them. Whatever he had on the screen, he didn't want her to see it, Zoë realised. 'I'd like to use the computer now, if you don't mind.'

'There's some data on here I can't afford to lose.'

'So save it. My mails are urgent too.'

'Is something wrong?'

'Plenty. But right now I want to contact my family, because I've just done an interview for TV—' She stopped as he made a contemptuous sound. 'What's wrong with you?'

'An interview?' The look he threw her was full of disdain.

'Yes, an interview, Rico—for my new cookery series. Now, if you don't mind—'

'Nothing else?'

Zoë looked at him. 'What are you getting at? Are you worried I might have talked about you, Rico? Let the world know I bagged myself a really rich man—a billionaire? A real live Spanish grandee and good friend of the King?'

When he said nothing, it was Zoë's turn to make a low, angry sound. 'Have you finished with the computer yet?' she demanded, planting her hands on her hips.

'Help yourself,' he said, moving away from the screen.

She didn't need to read the tall, bold letters on the monitor. They had been branded on her mind two years ago. They were lies. Everyone who knew her, who cared about her, knew that. Facing up to them was the only way she knew to snuff out their power.

Star Sells Sex.

Turning to look at Rico, Zoë could read his mind. He had believed the truth about her, and now he believed the lies. And his pride wouldn't allow him to accept that he had been so wrong about her. He believed she had sold herself for money. The thought turned Zoë cold, drained her of feeling. As Rico thought so little of her, perhaps he had her pegged as a gold-digger, after his money, all the time. Perhaps he had even set up the interview to shame her in public... He couldn't believe he had been so mistaken about someone. Neither could she, Zoë realised sadly.

'Are you expecting a reaction from me, Rico? Heated denials—hysterics, possibly?' She could see he was surprised she was so calm. 'This all happened a long, time ago.'

'Two years ago, to be precise.'

'Well, it feels like a lifetime to me.'

Time flew, Zoë reflected. Two years since her ex-husband had tried to destroy her career. She had been so set on rebuilding her life she had hardly noticed how quickly the time had passed. She could still remember the burn of shame when she'd first read the headline. How could she have known then that the old adage would prove true? There was no such thing as bad publicity; this morning's interview had only proved it yet again.

It was two years since her notoriety in the 'Star Sells Sex' scandal had put her name on everyone's lips. Almost immediately her cookery programme had begun to break every ratings record. Her next step had been to form her own company, and that had led to even greater success.

These days the headline was hardly ever mentioned, and on the few occasions when it was people laughed with her, as if it had all been nothing more than a rather clever publicity stunt. She knew the truth behind the headline, and it couldn't hurt her now. Only Rico could do that, if he believed the lies.

'So you've nothing to say in your defence?' he said. 'No explanation to offer me at all?'

'Am I supposed to ask for your forgiveness?'

'The whole scandal blew over quite quickly.' He shrugged. 'That's why I couldn't place you at first.'

'True.' Zoë smiled sadly at him. 'Did you hope I was hiding something, Rico—so that you and I could be quits?'

A muscle worked in his jaw; other than that there was nothing, until he said, 'Do you blame me for being defensive?'

A short sound of incredulity leapt from Zoë's throat.

'If I had told you who I was from the first moment we met—'

'I wouldn't have thought any more or any less of you.'

They stared at each other in silence for a moment, and then, leaning in front of Zoë, Rico clicked the mouse and cleared the screen.

Straightening up, he gazed at her. 'My full name is Alarico Cortes de Aragon. I have many business interests, but flamenco is my passion, and Castillo Cazulas, as I'm sure you have already worked out, belongs to me.'

'When were you going to tell me, Rico? After we'd slept together?'

'Don't speak like that, Zoë. You must understand I have to protect my position.'

'*Your* position? And I have nothing worth protecting—is that it? I was nothing more than an entertaining diversion while you toured your estates in Cazulas?'

'Zoë.' Rico reached out to her, and then drew back. 'Try to understand what it's like for me. I have to know who I'm dealing with.'

'What are you trying to say, Rico?' Zoë said softly. 'A man as important, as rich and influential as you, has to be cautious about the type of woman he takes to bed?'

'It's a lot more than that, Zoë, and you know it.'

'Do I?' She smiled faintly. 'I'm afraid I must have missed something.'

'Can you imagine my shock when I read this headline?'

'It must have been terrible for you.'

'Don't be sarcastic.'

'How do you expect me to be? You tell me you have to protect yourself from me as if I'm some piece of dirt that might tarnish your lustre.'

'Don't say that. I asked for this information before I knew you, Zoë.'

'And now you do know me,' Zoë said bitterly, glancing at the screen. 'You must be glad that you took that precaution.'

'You don't know me very well.'

'I don't know you at all.'

The coldness in her voice, the bitterness in her eyes cut right through him. He wasn't sure about anything any more, Rico realised. He had spent most of his adult life protecting himself from the gutter press. It was ironic to think that it was their common bond. He focused on her face as she spoke again, and was shocked to see the pain in her eyes when she gazed unwaveringly at him.

'I don't have anything concrete like a headline to shake the foundations of my belief in you,' she said. 'All I have are candles, a romantic night in a beautiful luxury spa, and the horrible suspicion that maybe you arranged all that because you wondered if you had what it took to seduce a frigid woman.'

'How can you say that?'

'You seem shocked, Rico. Why is that? Because I'm getting too close to the truth?'

'No!' The word shot out of him on a gust of loathing that she could even think such a thing. 'It isn't true. I don't know what's happened to you in the past, but you're not frigid. And I don't need the sort of reassurance you seem to think I do!'

'You lied to me.' Her voice was low, and cruelly bitter. 'You made assumptions about me, Rico. You invaded my privacy—that same privacy that's so precious to *you*, El Señor Alarico Cortes de Aragon! *You had me investigated.*' She ground out each word with incredulity, and then gazed up at the sky to give a short, half-sobbing laugh. 'And while that was going on you tried to get me into bed. And then—' She held up her hand, silencing his attempt to protest. 'Then you sold me out to the tabloids for some type of sick revenge.'

'Zoë, please—'

'I haven't finished yet!' She shouted the words at him in a hoarse, agonised voice, leaning forward stiffly to confront him, her face white with fury. 'To cap it all, you turn all self-righteous on me—pretending it matters to you that someone else hurt me, used me as a punch-bag—as if you care any more than he did!'

'You've gone too far!' He couldn't hold back any longer. 'How dare you compare me with that—that—'

'What's the matter, Rico? You think of him and you see yourself? Even you can't bring yourself to admit what you are.'

'And just what am I?'

'A deceitful, lying user!'

'User?' He threw his hands up. 'Who's using who here, Zoë?'

'That's right—stay up in your ivory tower, where you're safe from all the gold-diggers, why don't you, Rico? Only I don't want your money—I never did. I can manage quite well on my own!'

'And that's what you want, is it, Zoë—to be on your own?'

'What do you think?' she said bitterly.

'Then I'd better leave.'

'That would be good.'

'You signed the lease on the castle. You can stay until it runs out. Do whatever the hell you want to do! I'll see myself out.'

CHAPTER TEN

HE'D been thrown out of his own castle. That was a first. Rico looked neither left nor right as he strode purposefully across the courtyard towards his Jeep. Throwing himself into the driver's seat, he slammed the door, breathing like a bull. The knuckles on his hands turned white on the steering-wheel.

They wanted each other like a bushfire wanted fuel to sustain it. They were burning so hot they were burning out—burning each other out in the process. He had seen her muscles bunched up tight across her shoulders. And she wanted to believe him—that was the tragedy of the situation. They wanted each other, they wanted to believe in each other, to be with each other and only each other—but they were tearing each other apart. They needed each other—but she didn't need him enough to tell him the truth. She didn't trust him. Maybe she would never trust him. Could he live with that?

The answer was no, Rico realised as he gunned the engine into life. Some of it he'd worked out for himself—the rest he could find out. But that wasn't what he wanted. He wanted her to tell him. She *had* to tell him if there was anything left between them at all. If she was the victim, not the architect, of that newspaper headline, why the hell didn't she just come out and say so? Maybe there was a grain of truth in it—maybe that was why she couldn't bring herself to explain.

Her accusers were guilty of making a profit out of the scandal—but newspapers were in business to make money, not friends. He had been shocked when he'd read the torrid revelations, but he had to admire her. She was a fighter, like him. But was she fighting to clear her name or to put up a smoke-screen? Would he ever know?

Trouble was, he cared—he really cared—and it made him mad to think that all the money in the world couldn't buy him the whole truth. Only Zoë could give him that.

Rico's eyes narrowed and his mouth firmed into a flat, hard line. Thrusting the Jeep into gear, he powered away. She was entitled to stay on at the castle—he had no quarrel with that. He had always rattled round the place. Though it was certainly a lot more lively these days, he reflected cynically, flooring the accelerator pedal.

He eased the neck of his collar with one thumb. He was restless, frustrated—even a little guilty that he hadn't stayed to fight it out with her. He shouldn't have left with so much bitterness flying between them. He should have finished it or sorted it. But how could he when she had made such vicious accusations? The very idea of losing control to the extent that he'd hurt anyone, let alone a woman, revolted him. And then to accuse him of setting up that interview. He made a sound of disbelief. Didn't she know how deep his resentment of trash journalism went?

Rico frowned, gripping the wheel, forcing himself to breathe steadily and wait until he had calmed down. Gradually the truth behind the furious row came to him, as if a mist was slowly lifting before his eyes. He could see that the level of Zoë's passion was connected to the level of pain she had inside her. The legacy of her past had just played out between them. Instead of being hurt and offended by her accusations, he should be relieved that she had finally been able to vent her feelings, and that she had chosen to do it in front of him.

She was right. They both needed space, time to think. When he was with her his mind was clouded with all sorts of things that left no room for reason. He had never felt such a longing for anything or anyone in his life. Just the thought that some-one—some man—some brute—had hurt her made him phys-ically sick. So why wouldn't she let him in? Couldn't she see that he would take on the world to make things right for her again? Why wouldn't she trust him?

Swinging onto the main road, Rico channelled his frustration into thoughts of exposing all the bullies in the world to public ridicule. It would be too easy to use strength against them; strength of mind was more his speciality, and a far better tool to drag Zoë back from the edge of the precipice that led straight back to her past.

As he settled into his driving he suffered another surge of impatience. It was so hard to be patient where Zoë was concerned. He had to remind himself that she was worth all the time in the world, and that he hadn't made his fortune by acting on impulse. And, yes, she was right. He had expected an emotional response from her when she saw the screen full of huge letters, each one of them condemning her. He respected that. The headline was more than two years old, but he couldn't believe she had ever reacted to it in any other way. It took real courage to handle it so well.

But he had seen her lose control later. Was it his betrayal that had forced her over the edge even when she could keep her cool under fire from the tabloid press? If so, did that mean there was something really worth fighting for growing between them?

Quite suddenly the newspaper article seemed ridiculous. Zoë had forged a successful career for herself; she had no need to sell anything other than her talent. But where sex was concerned she was seriously repressed. He had firsthand experience to back that up…

Remembering, Rico grimaced. He felt like hell. What had he done? What had he done to Zoë? He should have been there for her. He should have made allowances. He should have proved to her, as well as to himself, that he understood how complex she was. She wasn't like other women, she had been right about that—but not in the way she thought. Her past had left her damaged, and instead of trying to help he had trampled her trust into the ground. There wasn't a brazen bone in her body, and if he had to delve deeper into her past to find out the truth and make things right for her, then he would.

Why was it so important to her that Rico Cortes knew the truth? Zoë wondered as she closed the door on the study bedroom after sending her e-mails. She had been so sure she wouldn't care, so certain she would brazen it out if he looked at her with scorn and contempt. He had done neither, but still the matter wasn't resolved in her head. She had to see him at least once more to sort it out. She had thought she could treat him like anyone else—if he believed the lies, so be it; if he didn't, so much the better. But now she knew she wouldn't rest until he knew the truth.

Her ex had planted the headline—though Rico couldn't know that. He had taken his revenge when she'd left him after years of abuse. She had refused to accept the public humiliation two years ago, and she wasn't about to let it get to her now.

What hurt her far more was the fact that Rico Cortes was a man she might have loved, and that he had deceived her into believing he was nothing more than a local flamenco enthusiast. She could accept his need for caution; Rico was a very rich man indeed—and an aristocrat, according to the search engine on the computer. But he was a self-made man for all that; he had started with nothing but a title.

As she pushed open the kitchen door and walked inside Zoë made a sharp, wounded sound. She was just Zoë Chapman, marital survivor and cook—hardly an appropriate match for a billionaire aristocrat.

She had allowed herself to develop feelings for a man she could never have. Right now she wished she'd never come to Spain, had never met El Señor Alarico Cortes de Aragon, because then he couldn't have broken her heart.

*   *   *

Arriving back at his beach house, Rico tossed the keys of the Jeep onto the hall table and smiled a greeting at his butler.

'A package arrived for you, sir, while you were out.'

'Thank you, Rodrigo.' Rico scanned the details on the well-stuffed padded bag as he carried it through to his study.

Before opening it he pulled back the window shutters so that brilliant sunlight spilled into the room. His whole vision was filled with the shimmering Mediterranean, and he drew the tang of ozone deep into his lungs. Simple things gave him the greatest pleasure. These were the real rewards of extreme wealth: the rush of waves upon the sand, the seabirds soaring in front of his windows, and the matchless tranquillity.

Opening the package, he tipped the contents onto his desk. There was a log of Zoë's everyday life back in England, along with diaries, tapes, transcripts of interviews, photographs, press-cuttings… Rico's hand hovered over the disarray, and then he pushed it all away.

He didn't want to read what someone else had to say about Zoë. He didn't care to acknowledge the fact that his pride and his suspicion had demanded such an invasion of her privacy. He felt dirty, and disgusted with himself, as if the contents of the package somehow contaminated him.

If he cared to look, he knew that whatever he found in the newspaper cuttings would be a sensationalised account. Even the most respected broadsheet had to succumb to such tactics in a marketplace where fresh news was available at the click of a mouse.

Coffee was served to him, and taken away again without being touched. The crisp green leaves of a delicious-looking salad had wilted by the time he absent-mindedly forked some up.

Pushing the plate away to join the rest of the detritus on his desk, he stood up and stretched. Walking over to the window, he was not surprised to see how low the sun had dipped in the sky. The colours outside the window were spectacular, far richer than before, as if the day wanted to leave behind a strong impression before it gave way to the night.

He would not let Zoë go. He could not. If she told him to go again, then he would still let her stay on at the castle as long as it suited her. It was a hollow, unlovely place without her.

After a quick shower and a change of clothes, he didn't wait for the Jeep to be brought round to the front. Sprinting down the steps, he jogged down the drive towards the garage block and, climbing in, switched on and powered away.

He found her in the kitchen, eating with the crew. They were relaxing in the way only good friends could relax—some with their feet up on the opposite chair, men with their shirts undone, sleeves rolled back, and girls with hardly any make-up, and real tangles rather than carefully tousled hair. The table was littered with the debris of a put-together meal, and when he walked in a silence fell that was so complete it left the walls ringing. There was the sound of chairs scraping the floor as everyone stiffened and straightened up. He could sense them closing in around Zoë like a protective net.

Her lips parted with surprise as she stared at him. She was wearing nightclothes—faded pyjamas—with her hair left in damp disarray around her shoulders. She looked to him as if the day had been too much for her and she couldn't wait to get it over with and go to sleep. Someone at the table must have talked her into joining them for a light meal.

It was the enemy camp, all right. Every gaze except for Zoë's was trained on his face. These were the people who had stood by her, who had stayed with her when she'd made the break from the television company run by her ex-husband. That much he'd learned from the Internet. These were the people who had put their livelihoods on the line for Zoë Chapman.

He waited by the door, and she half stood. But the girl sitting next to her put a hand on Zoë's arm.

'You don't have to go, Zo.'

'No, no… I'll be all right.' She pushed her chair back from the table and looked at him. 'I have to get this sorted out.'

He went outside, and she followed him. 'Will you come with me?' He glanced towards the Jeep.

'I'm not dressed.'

If that was the only reason, he'd solve the problem for her. Striding quickly back into the castle, he plucked a shawl down from a peg. As he came out again he threw it round her shoulders. 'You'll be warm enough now.'

'It's not that, Rico. I'm not sure I want to come with you.'

She took a step away from him. Folding the shawl carefully, she hung it over her arm, as if she wanted time to put her thoughts back in order.

'Please.' He wasn't good at this, Rico realised. He could negotiate his way in or out of anything to do with business. But feelings—needs—they were foreign to him, an emotional bank accessed by other people. He was a man of purpose, not dreams—but quite suddenly he realised that purpose and dreams had become hopelessly intertwined. 'Just give me an hour of your time. Please, Zoë. That's all I ask.'

'Will you wait in the Jeep while I get changed?'

He would have waited at the gateway to hell if she had asked him to.

Rico's knuckles were white with tension by the time Zoë emerged from the castle. She hadn't kept him waiting long, and now he drank her in like a thirsty man at a watering hole in the desert. She was wearing her uniform of choice: jeans and a plain top. She looked great. She was so fresh, so clean, and so lovely, with her red-gold hair caught up high on the top of her head in a band so that the thick fall brushed her shoulders as she walked towards him.

'Are you sure we can't talk here—or in the garden?'

'I'd like to show you something,' he said, opening the passenger door for her.

After a moment's hesitation she climbed in. He felt as if he had just closed the biggest business deal of his life. Only this was better—much, much better.

'What a fabulous place,' she said, when they turned in the gates at the beach house. 'Whose is it?'

Her voice tailed off at the end of the question, and he knew she had already guessed. Sweeping through the towering gates, Rico slowed as they approached the mansion. Even he could see it was stunning now he saw it through Zoë's eyes.

'It's all very beautiful,' Zoë said, when they were inside.

He watched her trail her fingers lightly over the creamy soft furnishings as they walked through the main reception room. Everything looked better to him too now she was here. He could see how well the cream walls looked, with smoky blue highlights provided by cushions and rugs, and the occasional touch of tobacco-brown. The walls had been left plain to show off his modern art collection.

'Chagall?' She turned to him in amazement.

He felt ashamed that he took such things for granted. Not for him the colourful poster prints that had adorned his mother's home and made it so cheerful. He liked the real thing, and he could afford it now—Hockney and Chagall were just two of his favourites. He envied the expression on Zoë's face. He wanted to recapture that feeling. He wanted to remember how it had felt to attend his first fine art auction sale, where he had vowed one day he would be bidding.

Zoë turned back to the picture again. She had never seen anything like it outside a museum. The picture showed a handsome man embracing a woman with long titian hair. They were both suspended in an azure sky, with the head of a good-natured horse sketched into the background. A happy sun shone out of the canvas, turning the land beneath it to gold.

'It's genuine, isn't it? This isn't a print?'

'That's right.' He felt shame again. Such things were meant to be shared. When was the last time he had brought anyone into his home?

'I saw a Chagall in Las Vegas—a man and woman, head to head—' Zoë stopped talking, realising they were standing head to head too, and that Rico was smiling down at her.

'You know what I mean.' She waved her hand and moved away, going to stand by an open window. 'Rico, why am I here?' she said, still with her back turned to him.

'I know everything about you.'

'Oh, do you?' she said, managing to sound as unconcerned as if they had been discussing a new style of drapes.

'Zoë, please, can't we talk about it?'

'Why should we? What purpose would it serve?' She turned round to stare at him.

'Will you come with me?' he said.

Something in his expression made her walk towards him.

This must be his study, Zoë realised. It was a pleasant, airy room, but small on the scale of other rooms in the mansion. It was cosy, even a little cluttered. This was the hub around which the rest of his life revolved, she guessed.

'Please sit down,' he said, holding out a chair for her across from his own at the desk.

'I'd rather stand.'

'Please.'

She didn't want to make a fuss.

'Why didn't you tell me?' Rico said, sitting across from her.

'Tell you what?'

'That all that nonsense in the newspaper was a pack of lies?'

'Because I don't feel the need to defend myself.'

'Nor should you.'

Glancing down at the desk, Zoë realised that all the papers

she had thought were Rico's were, in fact, her own history in print. 'So now you know.'

'I only wish I'd known about it sooner. Why didn't you tell me?'

'Because it's none of your business. And because I don't want, or need, anyone's misplaced sympathy.'

'Misplaced?' Rico sprang to his feet and planted his fists on the desk, leaning so far over it their faces were almost touching. 'A man who is supposed to love you beats you up, and you call my sympathy misplaced? You build a whole new life for yourself, and a successful career, only to have that— that—' Rico stopped, the words jamming in his brain as he searched for something to properly describe what he thought of Zoë's ex-husband.

'I finally left him when he tried to sell me to someone he owed money to.'

All the emotion was gone from her voice. He wanted her to rail against her fate, to show some emotion.

'It was just a night of sex, to pay off the debt…'

'Just! Zoë, Zoë—' Rico passed his hand across his eyes, as if it would help him to make some sense of what she was telling him. Walking around the desk, he drew her to her feet. 'Come with me.' He took her to the open window. 'Look out there. Tell me what you see.'

'It's night-time—'

'It's nature, Zoë—pure, harsh, and lovely. Here at my beach house, and at the castle in Cazulas, I escape from the world when I need to. That's why I was so protective of my privacy when you arrived. Why I still am so protective—but now I want you to have the same. I don't want you to live with a nightmare stuck in the back of your mind. I can't bear to think of you trapped like that, in the past.'

Wrapping her arms around her waist, Zoë inhaled deeply, and then turned away from the window to face him. 'I got away, in case you're interested. I could see the man's heart wasn't in it. False bravado brought him to me after a few drinks with my ex-husband. I just explained it was a bad time for me—that there had to be some mistake. He didn't lose face. There was no unpleasantness. I think I handled it well.'

Handled it well? The words tumbled around Rico's head as if someone was knocking them in with a hammer. He wanted to drag her into his arms right then, tell her it would be all right from now on, that he would be there for her, to protect her from harm. He wanted to promise her that she would never have to face such a monstrous situation in her life again—but she was already walking towards the door.

'Will you take me back to the castle now?'

'I'll do anything you want me to.'

She smiled faintly at him, as if to acknowledge his understanding without necessarily accepting that it helped or changed anything for her.

The call came when Zoë had just climbed into bed, and for the second time that night she rushed to pull on her jeans. This time she tugged a sweater over the top of her tee shirt. She didn't know how long she would be, or what might be involved. She just knew she had to be prepared. A phone call from Maria in hospital was serious. Snatching up her bag and some money, along with her car keys, she hurried downstairs.

Zoë felt as if there was a tight band around her chest until the moment she reached the small private room and saw Maria sitting up in a chair beside the bed with a rug over her knees. 'Thank God you're all right,' she said, crouching down at her side. 'Is it serious?' She reached for Maria's hand. 'I've been so worried about you. Will it affect your dancing?'

Maria lifted her other arm from beneath the blanket, revealing strapping. 'Thankfully just a sprain—nothing more. The X-rays have confirmed it. I'm sorry if I frightened you, Zoë. I just couldn't stand the thought of being here all night, and I have such a thing about taxis—'

'No. You were absolutely right to call me. I'm so relieved. I don't know why, but I thought you might have injured your leg.'

'My fault. I should have explained, instead of just saying I had fallen. I can see now that my legs would be the first thing you thought of.'

'Has anyone told Rico? If he hears you are in hospital he'll be very worried.'

'I tried him first,' Maria told her. 'But he wasn't at home.'

No, he was taking me home, Zoë thought, feeling doubly guilty knowing Maria had probably rung Rico to take her to the hospital. And she had been so lost in her own thoughts on the way back to the castle she hadn't spoken a word to him.

'The main thing is that no permanent harm has been done,' Zoë said, returning to practical matters. 'Can you leave now, or must we wait for a doctor?'

'The doctor has to formally discharge me before he goes off duty for the night. But we can talk until then.' Maria stopped and viewed Zoë with concern. 'You look exhausted, Zoë, is something wrong?'

'No.' Zoë forced a bright note into her voice. 'Nothing.' Nothing apart from the fact that Rico knew the whole sordid truth about her now and she would probably never see him again. He'd been sympathetic enough, but, remembering how he had deceived her about his identity, she couldn't help wondering if his sympathy had just been an act too.

She refocused as Maria started to speak again.

'Are you sure that son of mine hasn't said something to upset you?'

'Your son?'

'Rico?' Maria prompted.

'Rico!'

Zoë turned away. Why hadn't she thought of it? Why hadn't she seen it before? Rico's defensive attitude towards

Maria when she had first wanted to approach her... She had thought it pride on his part that she, a stranger, had dared to expect such an artist to put her talent on show for commercial gain. And the attention he paid Maria, his obvious pride in his mother's cultural heritage. All this should have told her. But how could it be? He was not Rico Cortes, local flamenco enthusiast, but El Señor Alarico Cortes de Aragon, a grandee of Spain.

'I don't understand.' She turned back to Maria.

'It is very simple—'

'You don't have to tell me,' Zoë said quickly. 'It's none of my business.'

'I'm not ashamed of what I did. Rico's father was the local landowner. His wife was dead, and we loved each other. We never married, but I gave him a son.' She smiled.

'But how did Rico inherit the title and the castle?'

'There were no other heirs. His father insisted the title must be passed to Rico. They were very close. It was just the title— his money went to the village.'

'But what about you?'

'I was proud—maybe too proud.'

'But Rico was a success?'

'A huge success,' Maria agreed with a wry laugh. 'Rico has always supported me, and eventually he made enough money to buy back the castle. As his father suspected, Rico didn't need his money—he was quite capable of making his own fortune.'

'You must be very proud of him.'

'I am,' Maria assured her. 'And now Rico cares for the village just as his father used to do.'

Maria's glance darted to the door. She was growing anxious, Zoë realised. 'I'll go and find the doctor, and see if I can hurry him up.' Another thought struck her. 'Did you try Rico on his mobile?'

'Yes,' Maria said, her dark eyes brightening as she looked towards the door.

CHAPTER ELEVEN

HAD Maria planned this? Zoë wondered. She couldn't see how that was possible—unless Rico had said something to his mother, and then Maria had put in a call to both of them, using her misfortune as a mechanism to bring them together.

Her heart was hammering louder than Maria's shoes had ever thundered on a floor as Rico moved past her to draw his mother into his arms. Pulling back, he spoke to her quickly in Spanish. Having received the answer he hoped for, he smiled and kissed her cheek before turning to Zoë.

'Thank you for coming, Zoë.'

How could I not? Zoë wondered. 'I was only too pleased I could help. But now you're here I'll leave you with your mother—'

'No.' Rico touched her arm. 'It's late, Zoë. You should not be driving home alone.'

'I'll go and find the doctor before I leave, and send him in to you.'

'No.' This time he closed the door. 'I'm taking you back with us, and that's final. You've had a shock too, and the roads can be dangerous at night.'

No more dangerous than they had ever been, Zoë thought. But Rico's expression was set, and she didn't want to make a fuss in front of Maria.

They settled Maria into her cosy home in the centre of the village, and then got back in the Jeep.

'It really was good of you to go to the hospital for Maria,' Rico said as they moved off again.

'I'd do anything for her,' Zoë said honestly, resting back against the seat.

'I can see you're tired. I'll take you straight back.'

'Thank you.'

So much for Maria's machinations. If it had been a plan at all, nothing was going to come of it. And of course she was relieved...

Clambering into bed and switching off the light, Zoë sank into the pillows, shot through with exhaustion. It had been quite a day. Her body was wiped out, but her mind refused to shut down. Turning on the light again, she thought about Rico, and about Rico and Maria being mother and son. And then she ran through everything Maria had told her about Rico.

Swinging her legs out of bed, she poured herself a glass of water. Rico had set out on a mission to reclaim his inheritance, to preserve everything he believed in, just as she had. They had both succeeded. They were both proud and defensive—you had to be when you'd fought so hard for something. She always felt as if everything she had achieved might slip through her fingers if she didn't hold on tight enough.

Zoë's glance grazed the telephone sitting next to her on the bedside table. She had to decide whether to call him or not. Of course she didn't have to do anything—she could just let him slip away into the past...

Zoë was surprised when the operator found the number so easily. She had imagined Rico would have a number that would be withheld from the public. Instead a cultured voice answered her in Spanish right away. It wasn't Rico's voice, it was some other man—his butler, perhaps. She gave her name, and he asked her to wait and he would see whether it was convenient for Señor Alarico to take her call.

It felt like for ever before Rico came on the line, and then he sounded as if he had been exercising. It was a big house,

Zoë reminded herself, with acres of floor space. 'I'm sorry to trouble you.'

'It is no trouble. What can I do for you?'

'Did I disturb you? Were you sleeping?'

'Sleeping? No. I was in the pool—they had to come and get me.'

'I see. I'm sorry,' she said again.

'Don't be.'

The line went quiet as if he was waiting for her to speak. She couldn't change her mind now. 'We didn't finish our conversation earlier.'

Now it was Zoë's turn to wait, not daring to breathe in case she missed his reply.

'I'll come over tomorrow.'

It was less than she had hoped for, but more in some ways. They were speaking at least.

'Or would you prefer to come here?'

Space from the film crew would be good. They were so defensive on her behalf. She loved them for it, but it made any private discussion with Rico impossible. 'I'm going to see Maria—your mother—in the morning.' She was thinking aloud, planning her day.

'Then I'll pick you up around nine. We'll go and see her together. You can come back here for lunch afterwards…if you like?'

'I would like that.' She smiled. 'Nine o'clock, then.'

'See you tomorrow, Zoë.'

The line was cut before she could reply.

Maria couldn't have made it more obvious that she was pleased to see them. She was already up and about, and insisted on making coffee.

'I'm not an invalid,' she told Rico, brushing off his offer to help. 'And before you say a word, I am returning to teaching today.'

'I forbid it—'

'Oh, you do? Do I dance on my hands, Rico? I still have one good hand with which to direct proceedings. And,' she said, refusing to listen to his argument, 'I am to be collected in half an hour. Before I leave, I have something for you, Zoë—to make sure you never stop dancing.'

'I can't possibly take that!' Zoë looked at the lilac dress Maria was holding up. The one she had worn for her first flamenco lesson. 'It must be worth a fortune.'

'It's worth far more than that,' Maria assured her as she pressed it into Zoë's hands. 'And I want you to have it.'

'It's so beautiful,' Zoë said, resting her face against it.

'Yes, it is—and if you ever need a boost, Zoë, you just look at it and think of us.'

'I'll only need to think of you, Maria,' Zoë said, smiling as she hugged Rico's mother.

It was fortunate Zoë couldn't see his mother's imperative drawing together of her upswept black brows, or the fierce command in her eyes, Rico realised as he took the cue to go, and take Zoë with him. 'We'd better leave you now so that you can get ready for your class, Mother.'

'Yes,' Maria said firmly, clearly relieved that her silent message had been understood. 'But before you go, Rico, you can do one more thing for me.'

'What's that?' he said, pausing with his hand on the door.

'Take this with you,' she said, handing him a camera. 'I want a photograph of Zoë in that dress—to hang in the mountain lodge at the flamenco camp,' she explained to Zoë. 'Then I will be able to see the dress and you, Zoë, any time I want.'

Alongside Beba? Immediately Zoë regretted the thought. Maria just wasn't like that. 'I'm sure you don't want reminding of my pathetic efforts—'

'I most certainly do. You were very good—full of genuine passion,' Maria said firmly. 'Now, take this girl to lunch,

Rico. She looks half starved. And don't forget my photograph.'

'I won't,' he promised, sweeping her into his arms for a parting embrace.

Zoë had her hand stuck up her back when she emerged from Rico's dressing-room. He was sitting on the shady veranda at his beach house, where they had been having lunch. He stood as she approached.

'I can't seem to get the dress right—can you help me?' Maria had been on hand the last time to finish off the fastenings for her.

The setting was superb. There was an archway coated in cerise bougainvillea where she would stand for Maria's photograph, with the sea behind her and some flamenco music playing softly to put her in the mood.

Giving up on the dress, Zoë straightened up. 'Help?' she prompted softly.

'Yes, of course.'

Lunch had been a neutral, emotion-free affair, with delicious food served at a leisurely pace, prepared for them by one of Rico's excellent chefs. Zoë knew they were starting again. They were taking it slowly—each of them feeling their way, each of them strangers to love, each of them determined to put at least a toe in the water.

Rico couldn't have planned anything better than this, Zoë thought as she waited for him to finish fastening her dress. It was a treat just to eat food someone else had prepared. Before she met Rico, she had always taken charge of things in the kitchen. He was right: it was good to kick back and relax from time to time.

'Te gusta el flamenco, señorita?'

'*'Sí, señor,* I like flamenco very much,' Zoë whispered, trying not to respond to the closeness of his body or the tone of his voice as he reached around her waist to secure the fastenings. Then he murmured, 'Turn around,' and it was impossible, because the warmth of his breath was making every tiny hair on the back of her neck stand erect.

'There—that's done,' he said.

She must have turned too quickly. One silk shoulder strap slipped from her shoulder, and as she went to pull it up again their fingers tangled.

'I'm sorry.' Zoë quickly removed her hand.

'Sorry? What are you sorry for, Zoë?'

His voice was neutral, but his eyes... They were very, very close. His hands were still resting lightly on her waist. 'I didn't give you the chance to explain anything. I just poured out all my own troubles.'

'Stop.' Rico's voice was low, but firm. 'You make it sound as if what happened to you was normal. It wasn't normal, Zoë—and you must never think of it that way or you will come to accept it as normal. You were brutalised—your mind, your body—'

'But I'm all right now.'

'And I'm going to make sure you stay that way.'

'You—'

Rico didn't plan on long explanations. He kissed her so tenderly he made her cry, and he had to catch the tears on her cheeks with his fingertips.

'I feel such a fool.'

'No, you don't,' he assured her. 'You feel wonderful to me.' And, sweeping her into his arms, he walked back into the house.

'What a shame we must take this dress off again,' he said when they reached his bedroom, 'when you have only just put it on.'

He was already halfway down the fastenings as she lay in his arms on the bed. 'Maria's photograph—' Zoë tensed as the last one came free.

'Later.' Rico kissed her shoulder, moving on to nudge her hair aside and kiss her neck.

'But it will be dark later.'

'You will look beautiful by moonlight.'

And then the silk dress was hanging off, and, feeling self-conscious, she wriggled out of it.

Picking it up, Rico tossed it onto a chair by the side of the bed. She wore little underneath it—just a flimsy scrap of a lace thong, not even a bra. There was support built in to the bodice of the dress.

Rico planted kisses as he freed the buttons on his shirt. That followed the dress, and when he kissed her again, and she felt his warm, hard body against her own, Zoë whimpered; she couldn't help herself.

He rested her back against silk and satin, and the linen sheets beneath the covers were scented with lavender. Everything was contrived to please the senses—and it was so easy to slide a little deeper into pleasure beneath his touch.

As Rico looked at the small, pale hands clutching his shoulders, and heard Zoë call his name, he knew she was everything he wanted. Her breasts were so lush, so provocative, the taut nipples reaching out to him, pink and damp where he had tormented her. Her legs moved rhythmically over the bed as she groaned out her need, and now there was just the scrap of lace dissecting the golden tan of her thighs between them.

His gaze swooped up again, lingering on the dark shadow of her cleavage, so deep and lovely. He longed to lose himself in it, to bury his tongue and more besides in its warm, clinging silkiness. But it wasn't just her beauty that bewitched him. He needed her. He had never needed anyone in his life before—he'd made sure of it. But Zoë was different—*he* was different when he was with her, and perhaps that was the most important thing of all.

He watched as she freed the tiny thong and inched it down over her thighs. Had he ever been so aroused? Clamouring sensations gnawed at his control, but he held back. Her trust was too hard won to risk now. How could anyone have abused her? Her skin was as soft and as fragile as the silk upon which she lay. Her eyes were darkening with growing confidence and her lips were parted in invitation. As their eyes locked and she reaffirmed her faith in him, he knew he would defend her with his life.

'Rico…'

As she breathed his name he remembered wryly that foreplay was intended to be an aphrodisiac, not a torture.

He went to pull off the rest of his clothes, but she stopped him. He drew in a deep shuddering breath. He would stop even now if she asked him to.

Scrambling into a sitting position, she touched the belt buckle on his trousers. 'You'll have to help me—my hands are shaking.'

Taking both her hands in his, he kissed each one of her fingertips in turn and then, turning her hands over, planted a tender kiss on each palm.

When Rico finally stood naked before her, Zoë's breath caught in her throat. He was totally unabashed, his dark gaze steady on her face. A lasso of moonlight fell across him, showing the power in his forearms and the wide spread of shoulders. She saw now that his broad chest was shaded with dark hair that tapered down to a hard belly, below which…

She stared into his face, waiting for him to come to her.

Her perfume was intoxicating, drawing him towards her. He stretched his length against her on the bed, not touching her, still holding back. Inhaling deeply, he stroked her thick, silky hair, sifting it through his fingers and enjoying the texture. He loved the way she quivered beneath his touch, eyes closed, mouth slightly open, her breathing nothing more than whispery puffs.

'Rico—'

He kissed her lightly on the lips.

'Kiss me properly.'

'Properly? What do you mean?' His restraint was making her bloom beneath him like a flower that had been too long out of the sun. Her breasts, two perfect globes, were thrust towards him, and her nipples, cruelly neglected, were almost painfully erect. The soft swell of her belly led his gaze down to where she was aching for his attention. Cupping her breasts, he made her gasp. And that gasp soon turned to a whimper as he began to chafe each perfect nipple with his firm thumb pads.

The pleasure was so intense it was almost a pain. He had forgotten how exquisite she was, how sweetly scented, how tender she felt beneath his lips. As he suckled and tugged, and heard her cry out his name, he knew that all he wanted in the world was to keep her safe and love her.

CHAPTER TWELVE

IT WAS so pleasurable, so seductive and intoxicating, fear never entered her head. Zoë wanted to beg Rico to hurry when his firm touch reached her thighs. She had never been so aroused. She cried out with pleasure when his searching fingers finally moved between her legs, and then she begged him not to stop.

Reaching for him, she found she needed two hands to properly encompass him, and he groaned softly beneath her questing fingers until at last she was forced to lift her hands away. Dropping a kiss on her lips, he probed deeply with his tongue, and she pressed against him, searching for the firmer contact she needed so badly.

'Not yet—be patient, *querida…*'

Lifting Zoë's arms above her head, Rico drew her underneath him. As one powerful thigh moved between her legs she shuddered with desire.

'Open your eyes, and look at me, Zoë.'

It was the most exquisite pleasure Zoë had ever known, and the warm, insistent pressure took her to a place where she could only breathe and feel. And then he caught the tip inside her, and it was she who swarmed down the bed to take him deeper. It was so easy, so right, there wasn't a moment of fear or the hint of a painful spasm to wipe out that pleasure.

The pain she had always felt before had been caused by fear, Zoë realised. She wasn't frigid at all. She was just a normal woman who had been waiting for a normal man. And all she wanted now was that Rico took full possession of her body and filled her completely.

She loved this new sensation, the stretching, filling, pulsing.

148

They started moving together, oblivious to the hungry sounds that escaped their lips, moving firmly until Zoë's fingers bit into the firm flesh of Rico's shoulders and she gave herself up completely to pleasure.

He held her in his arms, stroking her until she was quiet again, and then turned her so that now she was on top of him, straddling him, her legs widely parted. Sweeping the curve of her buttocks with a feathery touch, he tantalised her until she squirmed with delight and longed for him to drag her to him, plunge his tongue deep into the warm secret places of her mouth. But he had more skill than that, and made her wait until she was intoxicated by the raw power burning beneath her.

Feeling the insistent pressure of Rico's erection, Zoë took him deep inside her until she was completely filled. Then she began to move slowly, backwards and forwards, until she felt him take over. Throwing back her head, she closed her eyes, losing herself in sensation while he claimed her breasts, agitating her nipples between thumb and finger until she groaned out her pleasure and begged him for more. He turned her again, bringing her beneath him and using a few firm thrusts to bring on an electrifying climax that went on endlessly until she fell back panting on the bed.

Every part of her was glowing pink in the stunning aftermath of pleasure, Zoë realised, laughing softly with happiness. She had not thought it possible that a man could give himself to a woman so unselfishly. The expression on Rico's face was a fierce mix of passion and tenderness. It made her want him more than ever. She wanted to be the only woman who could put that expression on his face. She wanted his warmth and his strength curled around her for ever. She wanted everything.

As she murmured his name and reached out to him he dragged her close. His drugging kisses, the seductive touch of his hard body was more tantalising than anything she had ever imagined. He knew how to play her, to gently tease her and build her confidence. It was as if they had all the time in the world, and he meant to devote every moment of that time to pleasing her.

His hands were skilled, the look in his eyes commanding. He could order her to new heights of pleasure and she would obey at once. As she enjoyed his warm musky scent, laced with cinnamon and juniper, she felt as if her bones had turned to molten liquid. Her legs moved restlessly on the bed, seeking a cool place and then wrapping around him so he could be in no doubt as to what she wanted.

A great pulse was throbbing between her legs, and yet still he toyed with her, teasing and tempting until she could think of nothing but his firm touch. He must thrust inside her again to the hilt, stretching her wide— 'Please, Rico!'

'So you have not had enough yet?' He sounded pleased.

'Not nearly enough.' She didn't care what he thought of her; all she knew was her need for him. 'Please.'

Rico looked at Zoë, writhing beneath him. More pleasure could be gained by testing themselves to the limit. She must wait. He moved now with an agonising lack of speed, holding away from her until at last he consented to catch just inside her.

Her eyes shot open. 'How can you tease me now?'

'Easily.' He smiled. When she gasped with delight, he slowly brushed the velvet tip against her. 'Is this what you want, Zoë?' He slipped one controlling hand beneath her buttocks.

'You know it is.'

'More than anything?' But she didn't hear him now. Her mind was closed to anything as demanding as speech. She only wanted to feel, and be lost in his arms.

It was late by the time Rico took Zoë back to the castle. He still had work to do, and so did she. The sat in the Jeep like two teenagers who had just discovered each other. They kissed and touched as if every moment might be their last.

Parting from Rico was the hardest thing she had ever had to do, Zoë realised as she climbed out of the Jeep and shut the door. She stood motionless in the courtyard until he had driven away, disappeared from sight, and she couldn't even hear the noise of the engine.

But as she turned she felt as if she was walking six feet off the ground. It was as if the world around her had suddenly come into sharp focus and she had only been viewing it through a veil before. *So this is what happiness feels like,* she thought as she turned her face up to the sky.

Hurrying inside, Zoë couldn't keep the smile off her face. She didn't try. She didn't care if the whole world knew about her and Rico. This was love.

There were five Louis Vuitton suitcases lined up neatly at the end of her bed. Frowning as she dipped down to read the labels, Zoë pulled her hand away as the door swung open behind her.

'Can I help you?'

The voice was young and supercilious. High-pitched. The slight accent suggested she was Spanish.

And very beautiful, Zoë discovered when she turned around. Dressed all in red, the young woman was slender, and shorter than Zoë. The tailoring was Chanel, Zoë guessed from the buttons on her suit jacket, and her glossy black hair was arranged high on her head in an immaculate chignon.

She made Zoë felt scruffy in comparison—scruffy and apprehensive. Her heart was thudding heavily in her chest as she tried not to let her imagination get the better of her. She hadn't a clue who the woman could be. They certainly didn't know each other. This was Rico's castle, yet she seemed perfectly at home. Her mouth was pursed with disapproval, and she was doing a good job of making Zoë feel like the intruder. Zoë was conscious of her own tangled hair, still damp from

Rico's shower. Her face had to be glowing from the aftermath of so much lovemaking, and she knew she was under close inspection.

'What are you doing here?'

'I always stay here,' the young woman said confidently. Crossing to the window, she threw it wide open. She fanned herself theatrically and inhaled deeply, as if its previous occupant had somehow polluted the room.

'I'm sorry—have we met?' Walking up to her, Zoë extended a hand in greeting.

'I'm sure we haven't.'

Dark, cold eyes bored into Zoë's. Fingertips were proffered reluctantly. They were cold too.

'Beba Longoria.'

Zoë couldn't have been more shocked, but she hid it as best she could. *The* Beba? This woman looked nothing like the voluptuous young girl in the poster at the mountain hut. Success had stripped away her bloom, replacing it with an edgy tension. Maybe that was a result of having to defend her position against a constant stream of younger rivals. Yet Maria had remained unchanged…

Zoë pulled herself round with difficulty. 'I'm Zoë Chapman.'

'Ah, so you are Zoë Chapman. I hardly recognised you. You look quite different from the way you appear on television—much older.'

Touché, Zoë thought grimly. She tensed as Beba tossed her handbag onto the bed. The sight of the shiny red pouch clipping the edge of her pillows was the last straw. 'I'm sorry you've had all your things brought in here—someone should have told you I'm using this room. But don't worry. I'll have them transferred.'

'Transferred? What are you talking about?'

'To one of the spare rooms.' Zoë smiled helpfully.

'You clearly don't know who I am.'

'I've seen your poster at the mountain hut—'

'Then Rico must have told you.'

'Rico?' Zoë's confident expression faltered. Inwardly she was in crisis. But she had to try not to jump to conclusions. Rico had brothers and sisters. Beba might be one of them. Longoria could be her married name.

'Alarico Cortes? You do know who I'm talking about?'

'Of course I know him.'

'I see.' One perfectly groomed brow lifted as Beba stared at Zoë thoughtfully, and Zoë realised her hasty response had given away too much. She was on the back foot, cheeks blazing, when it should have been Beba feeling the heat.

'There's an understanding between us.' Beba's voice had dropped to a confidential level, as if she was trying to drop a bomb lightly on Zoë's head. 'Rico and I have been together since we were children. I'm surprised he didn't mention you to me—but then I suppose he can't be expected to remember every woman he meets.'

Turning away, she checked her hair in the dressing-table mirror, picking up Zoë's hand mirror to look at the back.

Zoë could feel the hostile black eyes spying on her through the mirror. But she was determined to hold herself together. 'There's obviously been a mistake.' She shrugged, and kept it pleasant. 'You see, I have taken a lease on the castle, and I'm using this suite of rooms during my tenancy. As you haven't unpacked yet, I'll just call down and have one of the crew come up and help you move to another room—'

'That won't be necessary.'

'I don't want to cause you any inconvenience.' Zoë's anger propelled her into action. She was already freeing the handle on the top of one of Beba's suitcases when she spoke again. 'So of course you are welcome to stay at the castle until you find alternative accommodation.'

'Rico will hear about this!'

'I'm afraid he has no legal rights over the castle until my lease expires. I doubt he can help you.'

'Alarico Cortes wields more power than you could ever understand.' Beba's face was twisted in an ugly mask as she snatched up her handbag from the bed. 'When he hears that I have been insulted—'

'He'll what?'

'Throw you onto the street!'

As Beba swept out of the room Zoë sank down on the bed. Her heart was thundering, but her mind was mercifully empty. She was numb with shock. All she was aware of was the click-clack of heels rattling away down the landing towards the main staircase.

When it was silent again, Zoë found she was shuddering uncontrollably. Burying her face in her hands, she drew her feet up on the bed and curled herself into a tight, defensive ball. Had Rico known about this when they were in bed together? Would Beba have dared to march into the castle and throw her weight around unless they were an item, as she said? Rico had never mentioned another woman. But a man like Rico Cortes with no woman in his life? She really had been living in a dream world!

Was she the type of companion El Señor Alarico Cortes de Aragon would take to the court of the King of Spain? Or would he take Beba—glamorous flamenco star? It was a stark choice between a cook with red hands and wild hair, or someone perfectly groomed, someone fragrant and dainty, with long, manicured fingernails and a musical laugh. She was quite certain Beba had a musical laugh.

Zoë reached for the phone and punched in some numbers. Rico's butler told her Señor Cortes was still out on business. No, he didn't know when he would be back. When pressed, the man admitted Señor Cortes was expected to return before a dinner appointment out, later that evening.

Later that evening! She couldn't wait until later that evening. She had to see him now—speak to him right away—resolve all this. There had to be an explanation.

Rico hadn't mentioned any plans for them, Zoë realised as she cut the line. It had never crossed her mind to ask when they would see each other again—she had taken it for granted. She felt sick, faint. She wanted this to be a nightmare. Because if it wasn't, she was on her way to making a fool of herself for the second time in her life.

She couldn't do anything yet, and it was far better to be busy than to brood, Zoë thought, wheeling the last of Beba's suitcases out of her room. She was hot all over again with the effort of lugging five overweight suitcases into position. She had showered and changed into fresh clothes right after Beba left, and now she would have to shower again, and dry and brush her hair until it shone. She had no intention of wearing her heartbreak on her sleeve. Life went on, with or without Rico Cortes. She was just glad to have a job to pour her energies into, as well as people who relied on her to take the helm.

This time when Zoë left her room she locked the door—something she hadn't felt the need to do since she'd moved into the castle. Hurrying downstairs, she found the team busy working on something in the Great Hall.

Philip swung round when he heard her.

'What's going on?' Zoë could see he was in one of his excitable moods. 'Well, are you going to tell me?' she said, smiling at him as she watched him picking his way over some camera cables.

'Cazulas is one incredible place, Zoë. You won't believe who has turned up now.'

Oh, yes, she would! 'Try me.'

'Only Beba! The best flamenco dancer in all of Spain.'

'Maria is the best flamenco dancer in all of Spain.'

'You know this Beba chick?'

'I've heard of her.'

'Well, you could sound a little more excited.'

'We haven't discussed another feature, Philip,' Zoë said, frowning as she realised what he planned to do.

'What about replacing that footage we didn't like? It's too good an opportunity to miss. Come on, Zoë. We could make this the last and best show of the series.'

He was right. 'So what's the angle? We already have the best flamenco dancer in Spain. That's how we billed Maria.'

'Beba appeals to the youngsters. She's like a pop star in the Latin world. We're talking glamour, we're talking riches, we're talking one sassy lady.'

'Yes, thank you. I think I get the picture.'

'But you haven't heard it all yet. Our audience get Beba—and then you remind the viewers about Maria, the greatest flamenco dancer in Spain! She's agreed to come for the filming, by the way—the old and the new, two for the price of one! What do you say, Zoë?'

'I'd say if I was Maria I'd be pretty insulted.'

'That's where you come in to it. You write the script and make sure she isn't insulted.'

'I can see you've got it all worked out, Philip—but after I write the script what will I cook? You do remember this is a cookery series?'

'Stop worrying, Zoë. I've got it all worked out. We're going to have a café-style setting, with a fabulous selection of food.'

'I see. And where are the ingredients coming from for this fabulous selection of food? And who is going to eat it all?'

'There's a vanload of produce arriving any time now. Come on, Zoë, don't be difficult.'

The thought of having Beba under the same roof for a moment longer than necessary didn't appeal—and Zoë wasn't happy about casual arrangements for food she hadn't picked out herself. But if she agreed she would be so frantically busy there would be no time to think about her personal problems…

'The girls have been round the village already, and everyone is keen to come back and act as extras for the programme, so we have our audience.'

'I do have some stock in the deep-freeze...'

'Don't get hung up on minor details, Zoë. This is going to be a sensational programme and you know it.'

'Food is a pretty large "minor detail" on a cookery show,' Zoë pointed out dryly. But it would prove to Beba—and Rico?—that she had bounced back without causing more than a ripple in her everyday schedule if she could pull it off. 'OK, I'll do it.' And then something else occurred to her. 'Was it you who installed Beba in my bedroom?'

'No, of course not. I didn't even know she had done that.'

His shock was genuine, Zoë realised. 'Don't worry, I moved her out. But you had better see she gets a nice suite of rooms if you want her happy for the programme.'

'She'll have the best.'

'No—I've already got that,' Zoë said, savouring her one small victory. She was starting to fire with enthusiasm. She always did for a new programme. 'I'll need some quiet time to work on the script, then I can get on to the food. When are we filming?'

'Tonight.'

'Tonight!' Get over it, Zoë thought. True, it didn't give her much time. But if they were filming, and Beba was dancing, Beba couldn't be with Rico. That suited her. And if Beba could dance as well as everyone said, it would make great television...

Zoë worked on her script in the bedroom, where she knew she would be undisturbed. She had one call from Philip, to warn her that Beba had insisted on complete artistic control over her performance. Zoë was happy to give it to her. The film would be edited before it was shown. Philip also told her that Beba was now happily installed in one of the grandest suites at the castle. Zoë was relieved to hear she was keeping a low profile, and had been most co-operative. One less thing to worry about, she thought with relief, replacing the receiver.

By the time the food was ready Zoë had to admit the team had done a great job. The Great Hall looked magical. Jewel-coloured tapestries and Persian rugs glowed in the candlelight, and there were colourful floral displays everywhere.

The setting was that of an intimate cellar club, with café tables arranged in groups around a circular wooden stage. People from the village had started to arrive, and were already being shown to their places. Zoë smiled with anticipation. She couldn't help it. This tense air of anticipation for the unexpected was what had drawn her to television in the first place.

But Rico was always there in her mind.

The worry, the uncertainty about him didn't go away. There had still been no word from him. She had tried telling herself it didn't matter, but that was a lie. All she wanted was for him to walk in now, walk up to her, take her in his arms and tell her she had nothing to worry about—that Beba meant nothing to him and never had.

There was no sign of Beba either.

People smiled, and she smiled back, but concern was nagging away at her. He should have been in contact by now. He drove too fast. Surely he hadn't had an accident?

Zoë spun round as the door opened. 'Maria! I'm so pleased you agreed to come.'

'I wouldn't miss this night for the world.'

'Have you seen Rico?'

'No.' She looked at Zoë with concern.

'I'm sorry, Maria, I'm sure he'll be along later. How's your arm?'

'Sore, but mending. I don't need the sling now, and I took the bandage off.'

'That's good.' Zoë could see Maria felt her agitation. So

much for not brandishing her private concerns in public! 'You are dancing tonight? I'm sorry it's such short notice...'

As Maria touched her arm she smiled warmly into Zoë's eyes. 'Maybe I will have the chance to dance with you, Zoë?'

I hope not—for the sake of the audience, Zoë thought wryly—though even that, whether she bodged it or not, would make good television. 'Do you know Beba well?' she said, returning to the subject uppermost in her mind.

'Beba?' Maria paused. 'Yes, I know Beba.'

'Was she always so friendly with Rico?'

'You know about that?'

Zoë's heart plummeted. Time to act her socks off. But they were standing very close, and Maria was very shrewd. 'Yes, Rico told me all about it. They make a handsome couple.'

'You do know that she used to be my pupil?'

'Your pupil?' Of course. It all made sense now. 'I saw the poster at the mountain hut.'

'My most celebrated pupil.' There was an odd expression on Maria's face.

'I see.'

'No, you don't,' Maria assured her, patting Zoë's cheek.

'Is she with Rico now?'

'It would not surprise me.'

Zoë couldn't stop now. 'Have you seen them together here at the castle—tonight?'

'Stop worrying, Zoë,' Maria said gently. 'Rico will be here. He will not let you down.'

He already had, Zoë thought.

Her legs felt like lumps of lead as she showed Maria to her table at the front of the stage. She felt sick and light-headed; there were icy cramps in her stomach. She really had no idea how she was going to get through the rest of the evening. But then the floor manager beckoned to her urgently. She welcomed the distraction. Work had always proved a refuge. Quite soon Wardrobe and Make-up would want her too, and she still had to make a crucial addition to her script to explain that Beba had been Maria's star pupil. The news couldn't have come at a more useful time. As far as the show went, Zoë reflected dryly, it couldn't have worked out any better.

Half an hour later the cameras were ready to roll. The main lights had been switched off, and apart from the necessary television lights the only illumination now came from candlelight. It was the most romantic setting imaginable. But as Zoë stood waiting for her cue to introduce Beba she was sure her heart had shrivelled to the size of a nutmeg.

Her sights were firmly fixed on the single spotlight trained on the main entrance. The guitarist was already seated on his stool, and at any moment Beba would appear.

She started when the *tio* from the village touched her arm. She didn't want to offend him by pointing out that the red light would flash on at any second.

'You look worried.' He frowned.

'Always am just before we start recording,' Zoë explained in a whisper. 'Maria's saving you a seat at the front.'

Worried? Concern was eating her up inside. *Was Rico with Beba? How could Rico be with Beba?* The two thoughts were spinning in her mind until she thought she would go mad.

'You must be looking forward to seeing Beba dance?'

'She is a fine dancer.'

Zoë wondered at the *tio's* lack of enthusiasm for the local star. Maria had taught Beba to dance, so surely Beba's success reflected well on Cazulas as well as on her teacher?

A sudden sound made Zoë jump, and with another light touch to her arm the *tio* was gone. Preparing to do her voice-over, Zoë realised the sound she had heard was the rattle of castanets, played by an expert.

There was one more imperative tattoo, and then, wearing a scarlet dress so tight it might have been painted onto her naked body, Beba stepped into the spotlight—on the arm of Rico Cortes.

CHAPTER THIRTEEN

SHE couldn't break down. Not here—not with everyone to see. Zoë forced her concentration on to the small performance area and cleared her mind of everything but the music—that and her commentary between the various dances.

Beba danced with such purpose, such certainty, it made Zoë shiver. It was as if the young flamenco dancer siphoned up energy from the music and spat it out again in furious movement. Her stabbing heels beat faster than a hummingbird's wings, and there was such passion in her dance that inwardly Zoë recoiled from it. The swirling skirts of Beba's tight scarlet dress shattered the air into smothering perfumed waves.

The dance ended on a crashing chord. The proud head tilted down and Beba's fierce black stare found Zoë's face. At the same moment Zoë knew Rico was making his way discreetly around the back of the hall towards her. After a brief moment of silence the thunderous applause came. She took the chance to move away, but someone caught hold of her arm.

'Maria!' Looking round, Zoë saw the *tio* was talking to Rico. They were trying to hold a conversation above the cheers, the shouts and the stamping feet—the *tio* had his hand cupped to his ear.

'Do you hear that?' Maria whispered in her ear.

How could she not? Zoë thought, forcing a smile. The noise was deafening.

'Do you hear *duende*?' Maria persisted.

'No,' Zoë admitted. She could hear, *'Olé! Brava! Eso es!'*

She really wanted to go. She couldn't bear this any longer. What difference could one word make?

'Now you will hear *duende*!' Maria's voice was commanding as she thrust the beautiful lilac dress she had been holding over her arm into Zoë's hands.

'Are you mad?' Zoë looked down at it in amazement. 'I could never follow that.'

'I can.' Maria's eyes were twinkling again. 'Let us go now, and change into our performance clothes.'

'No!'

'Would you let me down, Zoë? Would you?' she said again, when Zoë remained silent. 'I have told your director; he knows all about this. He says it will be the perfect final sequence for your series.'

Zoë shook her head, thinking of Rico and how he would view her dancing right after Beba's spectacular display. She felt bad enough about the situation. How much humiliation could she take? 'No, Maria. I don't want to let you down, but I can't do it.'

'Yes, you can,' Maria insisted fiercely. 'Whatever happens on that stage, it will make good television.'

'Maria, please—'

'And I need you to help me into my dress. My arm, as I already told you, is still a little sore...'

Zoë made a sound of despair. She couldn't refuse. And now the *tio* had finished talking to Rico, and he was making fast progress around the hall towards her. 'All right,' she agreed tensely. 'I just hope you know what you are doing.'

'Of course I do,' Maria said firmly, pushing Zoë in front of her with her good arm.

Zoë would never know quite what happened on stage that night. She only knew that concern for Maria took her there, and the thought of how Rico had betrayed her supplied the passion.

Maria performed as she always did as if she had absorbed the emotional energy of every person in the audience and released it in breathtakingly fluid moves, and by the time the finale came Zoë hardly cared that Beba had joined them on stage.

'Do you hear it now?' Maria whispered in Zoë's ear.

Zoë listened. She had been so absorbed in her dancing she was hardly aware that it had come to an end, and that now the three of them were standing side by side, acknowledging the gratitude of the audience.

The cries of *'Duende!'* were coming from all around her, Zoë realised incredulously. She could hardly believe it, and then Rico was on stage too, and her mind was reeling as he seized her hands and raised them to his lips.

'You did it, Zoë! You did it!'

He seemed pleased…even proud. And he looked so handsome, with his seductive mouth curving into a grin. She couldn't bear it, and turned her face away. But he cupped her chin and brought her back so she had nowhere to look but into his eyes.

'You have just earned the ultimate accolade in the world of flamenco, Señorita Chapman.' Then he raised her arm and the crowd went wild.

Why didn't you tell me about Beba? Why didn't you warn me? Why did you make love to me when you knew she would be here? Was I just something to fill a gap in your schedule before you had to meet her?

All Zoë's pleasure had drained away. She was like a rag doll, limp and unresponsive. Rico hadn't noticed. He was already moving away from her to embrace his mother. Then finally he took Beba's hand, and Zoë saw the way the dancer looked at him, her dark eyes shining with adoration as he raised her arm in a victory salute.

As another great roar went up Zoë felt her eyes fill with tears. She hated herself for the weakness and could think of nothing but getting away—out of the spotlight, out of Cazulas, and out of Spain. Everyone was happy to see Rico and Beba together again—of course they were. And she was a fool if she thought El Señor Alarico Cortes would choose a cook over his very beautiful, very gifted fiancée.

She could never stand by and see the man she loved with another woman at his side. She had built a new life, won back her self-respect. Making herself available whenever Rico had an itch to scratch was not for her. Smiling brightly at the cameras for the last time, Zoë seized the chance to slip away.

When the knocking started up on her bedroom door, Zoë clutched the sheet to her chest and stayed motionless, listening.

'Zoë, it's me,' Rico called to reassure her. 'Open the door.'

She tensed. Was Beba with him? No—even Rico would not go that far. But Maria was right; the Cortes family did move in sophisticated circles. Rico might think they could make love all day, and again at night, with Beba sandwiched in between. She would not open the door, no matter how much he knocked...

But he didn't knock again. Zoë frowned. She couldn't help but be disappointed that he had given up so fast.

She turned to the window. 'Rico!'

'You should lock these doors at night,' he said, stepping into the room from the balcony.

'I always do.'

'Well, tonight you forgot.'

Instinct made her gaze past him, just to make sure he was alone.

'Who are you expecting?' he said quizzically.

'I didn't think Beba would want to be left alone.'

'Beba is never alone.' Rico laughed as he bent to switch on the light.

'Do you mind? I'm asleep.'

'No, you're not—unless you talk in your sleep.' He smiled as he sat down beside her.

'What do you think you're doing?'

'I'm taking my shoes off. I don't usually wear them in bed.'

'You're not getting into bed with me!'

'Why not?'

'Rico. I can't—'

'You can't what, Zoë?' He brushed a strand of hair back from her face. 'I thought we'd got past this.'

Even though every fibre of her being was filled with longing she pushed his hand away. 'Please—don't.'

'What's happened, Zoë?'

'Beba happened.'

'Beba?'

'You went to her after you slept with me.'

'She wanted to see me.'

'You don't even bother to deny it?' Zoë stopped. She could hear the hysteria rising in her voice.

'No. Why should I?'

This wasn't how it was supposed to be. She had intended to be brisk and to the point, to confront him with facts, hear him out, and then tell him to go. But life was never that clear-cut, or that simple. She should have known. 'I can't do this, Rico—this is never going to work for me.'

'What isn't going to work for you, Zoë? Are you afraid of me? Is that why you're pushing me away?'

She *was* afraid of him, but not in the way he thought. She didn't have what it took to sustain a relationship. A career, yes—she had proved that—but for some reason it seemed she wasn't meant to find happiness with a man. 'I can't believe you misled me again, Rico.'

'About Beba?' He stood up and looked down at her, the proud angles of his face harshly etched in the lamplight.

'She told me—'

'She told you what?'

'That you and she were an item.'

'Then she lied.'

'You never cared for each other?'

'I didn't say that.'

Zoë didn't want to hear any more; she couldn't bear to. 'If you'll excuse me,' she mumbled. Swinging her legs over the opposite side of the bed, she hurried to the bathroom. She closed the door and leaned back against it. Everything she had rebuilt before coming to Spain was in danger of collapsing, thanks to Rico.

But when she had calmed down a little she knew the answer didn't lie in hiding away from him. Grabbing her robe down from the back of the door, she threw it on, belting it tightly. She went into the bedroom again, and switched on the main light.

'Sit down, Rico.' She pointed to the elegant sofa positioned to take in the view from the balcony. 'We really need to get everything out in the open.'

'I'm all right—you sit down. You've had quite a night.'

She searched his face for irony; there was none. 'You can't have us both, Rico.' Standing stiffly, facing him, Zoë raked her hair until it stood around her head like a wild golden-red nimbus.

Rico's gaze never wavered. 'I don't want anyone but you, Zoë.'

How she wanted to believe him. How she wanted to close the small gap between them, throw her arms around his neck and tell him she would stay with him for ever, and under any circumstances. But that would only lead to bitterness and resentment in the end.

'Is there an understanding between the two of you?'

'There was.'

Spain was a traditional country; this was a very traditional part of Spain. Zoë couldn't imagine such 'understandings' were embarked upon lightly.

'I can see you must need an appropriate wife…'

Yes, he had thought that at one time, Rico remembered. When he was younger. When he'd made his first fortune he had been brim-full of arrogance—partly because he hadn't been sure what was expected of a young aristocrat with a huge amount of money in the bank. Now he realised it didn't matter how much money you had, or what your title was. The only thing that mattered was that you made your corner of the world a little better. His mother Maria had done that, without a fortune or a title, and she was his only benchmark for success.

'I don't *need* a wife at all. Do you want me to tell you what Beba's doing at the castle?'

Suddenly she wasn't sure that she did, Zoë realised. If she was going to leave Spain in one piece emotionally, she didn't want to hear another word. In fact, this was the moment she should tell Rico to get lost.

He didn't give her that option. In a couple of strides he had her arms in his grasp. 'I listened to you, Zoë, and now it's your turn to listen to me.'

Zoë tensed. Rico's gaze was frightening in its intensity.

'Or are you just too scared to risk your heart again?'

Scared? She was scared of nothing. She stopped fighting him and clenched her jaw.

'You've built walls so high around you, Zoë, you can't see what's happening outside your own stockade.'

'That's not true!'

'Isn't it? Oh, you're safe enough in there, but you're not going to have much of a life.'

'Just tell me this—are you engaged to Beba?'

'Beba was my fiancée.'

'Was?' Zoë made a short humourless sound. 'She certainly didn't give me the impression she was in the past tense. Oh, I'm glad you can smile about it!'

'I can smile where Beba's concerned—that's just the point. She doesn't change. That's why we're not together now—whatever she might think, or might have told you.'

'So what is the position between you? Did she just turn up

in Cazulas out of the blue—to help me make a television programme, perhaps?'

He ignored her sarcasm. 'Beba? Helping others? That's more in your line, Zoë. Beba was the star in my mother's dance class. We became lovers around the same time I heard I was going to inherit my father's title.'

'Do you think that was a coincidence?'

'I don't think anything is a coincidence where Beba is concerned. I was young, and I thought we were in love. I thought we loved each other. Then Beba discovered that my inheritance was just a title and nothing more—no money, no castle. She hadn't expected that. I explained that it was only a matter of time before I rebuilt the family fortune, but she couldn't wait. I can't blame her. She had talent. She could earn her own money. I was all fired up. It never occurred to me that Beba might not share my enthusiasm for the long years of poverty that lay ahead. She broke off our engagement and went to Madrid to seek her fortune.'

'Which she found,' Zoë murmured.

'I never wanted to hold her back, and I'm delighted that she has been so successful. I was equally determined that I would earn the right to be called El Señor Alarico Cortes de Aragon.'

'Which you did.'

'Yes.'

'And now Beba has returned to Cazulas for the one thing she doesn't have yet, and that's you.'

'Another trophy to add to the others.' Rico smiled wryly at her. 'I would have explained all this to you if I'd known what Beba planned to do in advance, and if my business meeting hadn't gone on for so long. When I arrived at the castle and found she was here it was already too late.'

'But you met with her?'

'I had to talk to her. I had to tell her how I feel about you.'

'About me?'

There was no such thing as dipping your toe in the water with Rico. It was total immersion or nothing. It was the sort of commitment Zoë feared above anything else. Staying safe inside her stockade, as Rico put it, had kept her sane since her divorce. The closest she had ever come to letting go was with him, and she didn't know if she had what it took to let go completely.

'It was only right to escort Beba onto the stage when she asked me to,' Rico went on. 'I knew that playing the tragic heroine suited her purpose. That sort of thing always puts her in the right mood for the dance. But I have no ambition to become an emotional punch-bag. She's just not my type of woman.'

'Are you sure about that?'

'Of course I'm sure. Didn't you notice all that anger and aggression? It has to come from somewhere, Zoë. Beba uses people. She sucks them dry and spits them out—they're just the fuel for her dance.'

'You make her sound so callous.'

'So lonely. That's why she came here to find me—to see if there was any chance of us getting together again.'

'And you refused her?'

'Of course I refused her. Beba and I don't love each other—we never did. I asked her to marry me because I thought I should, and she agreed to marry me—well, you know why. Circumstances pushed us together when we were too young to know any better, but we each had our own very different road to travel.'

'And now those roads have crossed again?'

'I want a wife who will travel the same road as me, Zoë. I don't want a woman who is trawling the world in search of the next thrill.'

'But if Beba had been different?'

Shaking his head, Rico gave a wry smile. 'Beba couldn't be different. Beba couldn't be you.'

'And Cazulas was too small to hold her?'

'The world is too small to contain Beba. She's only here now because she is in between tours. She feeds on drama. The stage, a new lover—it's all the same to her. There is no doubt in my mind at all, Zoë. It's you I want.'

Foreboding coloured everything Zoë was hearing—everything Rico was saying to her. El Señor Alarico Cortes would one day want a suitable wife—not one who travelled the world to pursue her own career. When that day arrived would she be expected to stand aside and spend the rest of her life in the shadows? Rico's father had been a Spanish grandee too. He'd given Maria the flamenco dancer a son, but hadn't married her. Was that par for the course? Was his proud, complex son now offering her his love along with the promise of future pain? Was that what she wanted? Passion with all the heat of flamenco that would burn itself out until it only existed in her memory like a few fast-fading chords?

'Won't you come downstairs to join the party?' Rico pressed, relaxing now he believed he had set everything straight. 'Maria and the *tio* are waiting to see you—to congratulate you on your success.'

It was the end of an intensive stretch of work for the crew. It was churlish of her to stay in her room. Rico didn't need to know that her mind was made up: she was leaving Cazulas for good.

Zoë actually flinched as the thought hovering in her mind became reality. Just outing it gave it clarity, gave it purpose, set it in stone. It was easier than she had imagined. She *was* leaving Cazulas for good. And not because she didn't believe Rico about Beba, but because she did. He really loved her, he really wanted her; she could see that now. But she had nothing to offer him in return. She didn't have anything left inside her. She didn't have the courage it took to risk her heart again, to risk the pain he could cause her. She had been safe feeling nothing…

'Zoë, look at me—don't shut me out.'

The look in Rico's eyes was so intense she felt dizzy, bewildered, disorientated. And then he took her hand and she felt the power he wielded, the force of his will, his strength, his passion flooding into her.

Escape for one more night. Physical pleasure so intense she could shut off the part of her that knew there must be consequences—Rico could offer her that. They could have one last night together, and then she would retreat inside that stockade he'd talked about—her stockade, where not even the memory of their affair would be able to reach her.

'If I put on the lilac dress again, would you take that photograph for Maria?'

'You know I will. Shall I wait outside while you change your clothes?'

'Do you mind?'

'Not at all.'

Zoë watched Rico until he left the room. After all the intimacy they'd shared it seemed bizarre to have such reserve spring up between them now. He respected her, and if she had been content to be his mistress without having to give her love she had no doubt he would have protected her. But it wasn't nearly enough.

When she was ready, Rico escorted Zoë downstairs again.

'I'm wearing the dress so Rico can take that photograph you wanted,' she said when they found Maria.

'You make it sound as if you're leaving us, Zoë.'

There was an expression in Maria's eyes that made Zoë look away. She could lie to herself—she had perfected the art. But she could never lie to Maria.

'Rico.' Beba came over the moment she spotted him. 'We were all wondering where you had got to.'

Her cold dark gaze lingered on Zoë's face, and Zoë was glad when Rico drew her arm through his own.

'I had some important business to attend to,' he said.

'So I see. Well, if you will excuse me…' She turned away, then swung back again. Seizing Zoë's hand, she clasped it in her own. 'I wish you luck.' She slanted a hostile glance at Rico. 'You're going to need it.'

Sour grapes? Zoë wondered. Or sound advice?

She could see the crew already starting to clear up some of the equipment. The hall was emptying fast. Once the series was in the can no one hung around; they had all been away from home too long as it was. She knew they would work through the night if necessary, just to be able to catch the first flight back. She would leave the castle shortly after them, though Rico didn't need to know that.

The arrival of Beba had shaken her. Rico had reassured her where Beba was concerned, but what happened when he wanted a wife? She couldn't give up the independence she had won at so high a price to become a rich man's mistress… But she could have one more night.

'Rico?'

Something in her voice told him what she wanted, and his eyes darkened with desire. 'Are you ready to go to bed now?'

'If you still want me.'

They said their goodnights quickly. And as their fingers intertwined Zoë could think of nothing but the next few hours as Rico led her towards the stairs.

CHAPTER FOURTEEN

Zoë's lips slipped open beneath the gentle pressure of Rico's mouth. Deepening the kiss, he stripped off the lilac dress while his tongue sought out the dark, secret places in her mouth.

It was as if they had never made love before, her hunger for him was so great. He was inside her before they reached the bed with her legs locked around his waist and her arms secured round his neck, her fingers meshed through his hair. He supported her easily, with his strong hands beneath her buttocks, and the reassurance of feeling him hard and deep inside her was almost unbearably good.

She had to remember this moment for a lifetime, Zoë thought, as Rico lowered her onto the edge of the mattress.

They made love there, with no preliminaries and with no thought of seeking the luxury of the well-sprung bed. Zoë cried out her encouragement as Rico tipped her at an angle, resting her legs over his shoulders to increase satisfaction for them both. And all the time he moved inside her he murmured her name, and told her how much he loved her, and how he wanted to be with her for ever...

This was for ever, Zoë thought. For her, at least.

Zoë stopped waving as the last van disappeared out of sight. She could feel her colleagues' hugs still imprinted on her skin, and hear their words of encouragement and good wishes ringing in her ears. None of them knew how she felt inside. They would never know.

Rico had left her at dawn. It really couldn't have worked

out any better. He had some business to attend to back at the beach house, and so she had been spared a painful parting.

She had slept fitfully in his arms all night, dreading the morning, dreading the moment when she would tell him she couldn't stay in Cazulas. Her idea of sleeping with him one last time, making love with him half the night in the hope of keeping the memory alive, had been a terrible mistake. Instead of leaving her with tender memories to carry forward when she left Spain for good, it had left her with guilt and unbearable loss.

She had learned nothing from the past. She was betraying Rico just as she had been betrayed. Her ex-husband had won the final battle now she had completed the circle of violence. There was no physical violence, of course, but she was violating Rico's trust. She had taken his love and was letting it slip through her fingers because she didn't have the guts to hang on to it. She was still scared of commitment, still scared to risk her heart. She was brave enough to take the pleasure now—just not brave enough to take the consequences.

The best thing for Rico, the best thing all round, would be if she left without a fuss. Her suitcases were already packed, and she intended to drive to the station around noon.

It was strange being alone in the castle. Even Beba had packed up and gone, and it was a quiet, lonely place now. She couldn't bear the thought of leaving her friends in the village, but she didn't belong in Cazulas any more than Beba. Her life revolved around a television programme, and it was time to return to reality.

Back in the kitchen, Zoë could hardly bring herself to look at the collection of local pottery on the table. She was taking all of it back to England. She was quite sure Rico wouldn't want any reminders of her visit. The crew had left some empty packing cases for her, and a removal van was due to arrive before she left for the station. All the heavy equipment for the show that wouldn't fit into the vans had to be shipped back to the UK, and the pottery would be delivered to her London home at the same time.

She had been packing and wrapping for some time when she heard the music. Leaving the kitchen, she hurried into the hall.

'Good morning, Zoë.'

'Rico!'

He was sitting cross-legged on a stool in the centre of the floor, one hand caressing the neck of his guitar, the other hovering over the strings. She had thought it would be possible to get used to the idea of living without him, but in that instant Zoë knew she was wrong.

Turning back to his guitar, he started to play again, as if she wasn't there. The music held her transfixed. He stopped playing quite suddenly. His slap on the side of the guitar echoed around the empty hall. Laying the guitar down carefully on the floor, he stood, reminding her how tall he was, how commanding.

'When were you going to tell me you were leaving?'

Zoë stared at him. There was nothing she could say to justify her actions.

'Don't you think you owe me an explanation?'

'I'm sorry—'

'You're *sorry*?' he said incredulously.

'I need my work—'

'And?'

Zoë's voice was barely above a whisper. It was as if she was talking to herself, trying to convince herself and not him. 'I can't let anyone take over my life again.'

'Take over your life? What the hell are you talking about, Zoë?' He made no attempt to close the distance between them.

'It's all I've got. It's what I do.'

'It's all you had,' he said fiercely.

'You don't understand, Rico. I just can't be there for you.'

He turned away, but not before she saw the hurt in his eyes. 'That's different.'

His voice was hoarse, and he didn't look at her when he spoke. They might have been standing on separate ice floes, drifting steadily apart. But this was what she wanted, wasn't it—this final break between them? She just hadn't imagined doing it face to face. In her usual cowardly way she had been going to bury her head in the sand somewhere far away from Spain.

'You can't be there for me?' he repeated bitterly. 'So what was I, Zoë? Some type of experiment? Just a random male you could use to exorcise your ghosts?'

'Don't say that, Rico.'

'Why not? Because it's true?' He laughed, and it was a hard, ugly sound. 'You should be happy.'

'Happy?' Zoë could hear incredulity approaching hysteria in her voice.

'At least you know you're not frigid now.'

'Stop it!' She covered her ears.

'No, you stop it!' Rico said with an angry gesture. 'You come here to Cazulas. You seek help for your show, which I give to you freely. We make love—at least I did. Yes, I love you, Zoë,' he confirmed fiercely. 'But you just used me. You're no better than Beba!'

'Rico!' Through her shock, Zoë knew what he was saying was true. She reached out to him. 'Rico—don't go yet. Can't we talk?'

'Why shouldn't I go? The only reason I can think of for you wanting me to stay is that you need some more reassurance in bed. And frankly, Zoë, I'm not in the mood.'

The stool was kicked over as he snatched up his guitar, and then he went to the door. Halting with his hand on the heavy iron handle, he turned to her. 'You might as well have this.'

Zoë started towards him, but she was too late.

Putting an envelope on the table by the door, he walked out.

The castle was like a deserted shell. There was no life, no sound, nothing. Zoë's footsteps echoed on the stone-flagged floors as she completed her final check. Even the towering walls seemed to have grown cold and unfriendly. She was glad when she finally closed the heavy oak door behind her; an empty castle was a lonely place.

The removal van had taken the last of her things away, and the few bits and pieces she had found now could be loaded into the car. There was nothing for her to stay for. But before she left Cazulas for good there was one more stop she had to make.

Maria ushered her into the cottage. 'It's very good of you to see me,' Zoë said.

'Rico told me you were leaving.'

'Now I'm here, I don't know where to begin...'

'At the beginning?' Maria suggested gently. 'But first you must sit down. You look worn out.'

'No, no, I'm fine.' Rico's face flashed into her mind, and then the contents of the envelope he had left behind. She bit her lip. 'Truthfully, Maria, I'm not fine.'

'I can see that. Come and sit here with me at the fireside. You take this chair across from mine.'

The overhead fan was whirring. It was almost midday. The shutters were closed and it was hot in the small room. But the fireside was a symbol to Zoë—a symbol of Maria's happy, well-ordered life.

And as she talked things through with Maria it was as if Zoë saw everything clearly for the first time. She saw how she was pushing Rico away each time he got close, grabbing at excuses to justify her actions. She understood the bewilderment she had felt at discovering that having the most wonderful sex with him hadn't been enough to exorcise her demons, after all. She had to stop holding back before that could happen, but she was still terrified of risking herself in a relationship again—so terrified she hadn't even paused to consider how Rico might feel.

And now she was ashamed. She was particularly ashamed in front of Maria, who had given so much of herself so generously—to Rico, to his father, and to the village of Cazulas. If Maria hadn't prompted her so gently, encouraged her so warmly, Zoë knew she would never have had the confidence to pour her heart out as she did.

When she had finished, she gave Maria the envelope Rico had left at the castle.

Maria hesitated, holding it in her hands.

'Please read what's inside,' Zoë prompted.

Maria read the papers, and then put them carefully back into the envelope.

'My son must love you very much. Did you doubt him?'

'Before I met Rico I couldn't see beyond what had happened to me in the past.'

'And after you met him?'

Zoë turned away, unable to meet Maria's candid stare.

'Since he inherited his father's title Rico has been prey to fortune hunters and the press. You have a mutual enemy in the paparazzi, Zoë.'

'Yes, I can see that now.'

'Rico was furious when he returned from his travels to discover that his land agent had leased Castillo Cazulas to a television company. But then he fell in love with you—'

'And made me a gift of the castle.'

'Don't look so surprised. He wanted you to have a Spanish headquarters; the castle is perfect. It is far too big for a family home. Imagine what a film set it will make. Rico must have been on the point of asking you to marry him.'

'Marry him? No, you're wrong about that, Maria.'

'Why else would he have done this? The castle was your wedding present.'

'He would never marry me.' Zoë tried to reason it out. She wanted nothing more than to accept that what Maria had said was true, made sense—but her mind just wouldn't accept it. Deep down she still believed she wasn't good enough. 'I could never—' She stopped, remembering Maria's history.

'Be his mistress?' Maria finished for her. 'As I was to his father? No, don't look so embarrassed, Zoë. You haven't offended me. I made my choice, and now you must make yours. But I can assure you Rico isn't looking for a mistress. He saw how unhappy it made his father. Yes.' She put her hand up when Zoë started to interrupt. 'Rico's father always wanted to marry me. He insisted my fears about our differing backgrounds were unfounded. He was ahead of his time; I was not. I know Rico loves you, Zoë. He wants you with him. He must have known how you would feel about such a life-change. He wanted you to keep your independence, your company—even your own accommodation, if that was what would make you happy.'

'A castle?' Zoë said wryly.

Maria sighed. 'Rico never does things by halves—and, after what you have told me today about your past, I think he wanted to protect you from uncertainty, do everything he could to reassure you. I think he loves you very much.' Maria's soft brown eyes bathed Zoë's face in compassion. 'And now you think it is too late. That is why you have come to me. You think you need my help.'

As their gazes locked, Zoë realised she had never needed anyone's help as much as she needed Maria's. 'I don't know what I can do to put things right,' she admitted huskily, 'or if it's possible to put things right.'

'You are strong enough to know what is right. You just

can't see it yet. You don't need me or your television company to cling to. You're a survivor, like me, Zoë. You know what you have to do.'

Zoë found Rico walking barefoot at the water's edge in front of the beach house. His jeans were rolled up and a soft breeze was lifting his blue-black hair as he faced the wind with his hands shoved deep inside his pockets.

She didn't have to see his face to know how much he was hurting—how much she had hurt him. There could be no more hiding inside the stockade. No more hiding, full stop. Reaching out, putting her heart on the same line as his, was exactly what she wanted to do.

'Zoë?' Rico whirled round with surprise. 'I thought you would have left for the airport by now.'

'Rico.' Zoë's heart lurched when she saw the weariness in his eyes. 'Can we talk?'

'Why not?' Opening his arms, he gestured around. 'There are only seabirds to hear us.'

Digging into the back pocket of her jeans, she pulled out the envelope. 'You didn't expect me to walk away after you left this at the castle?'

He didn't answer. He just folded his arms and stared at her.

'I've come to give it back to you.'

'That's a pity.' He looked at the envelope and turned it over in his hands. 'I grew up believing it was my destiny to own Castillo Cazulas. But when I brought it back into the family again I discovered it was just a large, empty building.'

'That's exactly what I thought when I locked it up just now.'

'When you were there the whole place was transformed.' Holding her gaze, Rico shook his head and smiled a smile that didn't quite make it to his eyes. 'Your programme, your team—you brought it back to life, Zoë. It was exactly what the old place needed.'

'Chaos?'

This time they both smiled.

Straightening the envelope he had tightly clenched in his fist, Rico held it out. 'When Castillo Cazulas was first built a whole community thrived there, not just one family. I want the castle to live again through you. Take it, Zoë. Castillo Cazulas is nothing without you. I'll probably sell it.'

'You can't give me a castle,' Zoë said incredulously. 'Rico, that's ridiculous.'

'That's what I keep telling myself.' He shrugged as he thrust the envelope into her hands.

Zoë shook her head. The only sound was the wind, and the sea pounding on the shore at their feet. 'I couldn't be in Cazulas, knowing I might see you, bump into you.'

'I don't want Castillo Cazulas for the very same reason,' Rico admitted. 'I could never see the castle now without thinking of you.'

'I'm sorry—this was a mistake. I should never have come.'

Turning, Zoë began walking quickly back across the sand towards the road, where she had left the car.

'Zoë—'

Rico's voice wavered on the wind, and then sank beneath the noise of the surf. Was this what she really wanted? Zoë wondered, her steps faltering. A lifetime of wondering, *What if?* A lifetime of running away from the past? A life without Rico in it? Hadn't the time come to stop running—to face up to life—to face him?

They both turned at the same moment.

Zoë didn't know who took the first step. She only knew that she was running with the wind at her back, and then Rico tasted of salt and sunshine, and when his arms closed around her she knew it was the only reassurance she would ever need.

The lease for Castillo Cazulas lay forgotten on the sand, and then the breeze picked it up and carried it away out to sea.

'You can't leave Cazulas, Zoë,' Rico said, pulling away

from her at last. 'We need you here. I need you. The village needs you. You're good for all of us. We love you. I love you. Please tell me you'll stay.'

'How can you ask me that when I've been so selfish—when I've hurt you so badly?'

'You haven't been selfish,' Rico assured her. Bringing her hands to his lips, he kissed them passionately. 'You were knocked down to the ground, Zoë. It takes time to grow straight again, to grow tall. But I'll wait for you for ever, if that's what it takes.'

Zoë was touched, dazed—even shamed by Rico's declaration. He saw so much where she had been blind. But her eyes were wide open now. This proud, passionate man was every bit as vulnerable when it came to love as she was.

Reaching up, she traced his cheek with her hand. 'I love you with all my heart, Rico. You've shown me what love should be, and I'll never leave you.' And she never would, Zoë realised; with or without his ring.

'I'm not asking you to give up anything, as long as you promise to leave some space in your life for me.'

'You've got it,' Zoë assured him. 'But it's a rather big space, if that's all right with you?'

'That's just perfect.' He dragged her close. 'Now, who shall we have to cater for the wedding?'

'The wedding?' Zoë stared incredulously into Rico's face as he heaved a mock sigh.

'I suppose you should have the night off on your wedding day.'

'Rico, what are you saying?'

'I'm saying the caterers will have quite a lot to live up to—'

'Rico!'

'Did I forget something?'

'You know you did!'

'Will you marry me, Zoë?' he said, growing suddenly serious. And when she just stared at him he knelt down in the wet sand and reached for her hand.

'You'll ruin your jeans—'

'Then say yes quickly, or I'll have to take them off.'

'Then it will take me a very long time indeed to accept your proposal.' Kneeling in front of him, Zoë put her hands in his. 'Yes, I'll marry you, Rico. And I'll love and honour and cherish you for ever—'

'There's just one condition for the wedding,' he cut in, drawing her close.

'Oh?' Zoë murmured against his mouth. 'What's that?'

'No cameras, *mi amor.*'

EPILOGUE

CAZULAS had never seen a wedding like it, the village *tio* assured Zoë excitedly. And they both agreed that it must be true when the King of Spain and his beautiful Queen attended the marriage ceremony—along with all of Zoë's friends and what seemed like half of Spain.

The dapple-grey horses that drew her wedding carriage had bells and ribbons bound through their glossy manes, and everything she wore for the wedding had been bought in Paris, where she had enjoyed a 'pre-marriage honeymoon', as Rico had insisted on referring to their trip.

Events had moved swiftly after that late afternoon together on the beach. It was the way they had both wanted it.

Breakfast in Madrid, lunch in Paris: Zoë discovered such things were commonplace in the life of El Señor Alarico Cortes de Aragon and his wife-to-be. To put the seal on their new life together, Rico never mentioned the little notebook Zoë took everywhere with her to jot down ideas for her new television series.

'Everyone in Cazulas can see that El Señor Alarico Cortes of Aragon has met his match,' the *tio* exclaimed, reclaiming Zoë's attention. 'Rico is very much in love.' He tapped the side of his nose in the familiar gesture.

'And I get to take the photographs,' Maria exclaimed, snapping away furiously.

'Are you really happy, Zoë?' Rico asked her later, when they danced together.

'Yes, I'm utterly, completely and totally happy. And as for this—' She gazed around at the glittering throng of friends and family Rico had assembled to celebrate their wedding day. 'This is *duende* for me—how about you?'

Rico drew her a little closer. 'Every moment I'm with you, Zoë, is a whole lot better than that.'

0808/24/MB165

These billionaires are used to getting what they want...

...and they want you in their bed!

Billionaire Heroes: *Jet-Set Billionaires*

The Disobedient Bride by Helen Bianchin
His Wedding Ring of Revenge by Julia James
The Doctor's Fire Rescue by Lilian Darcy

Available 1st August 2008

Billionaire Heroes: *Mediterranean Playboys*

The Greek Tycoon's Convenient Mistress
by Lynne Graham
The Purchased Wife by Michelle Reid
The Spanish Billionaire's Mistress by Susan Stephens

Available 5th September 2008

www.millsandboon.co.uk

M&B